A Grimoire from Under The Gallows Tree

Table of Contents

Introduction

My name is Hayley, and I have been a practicing witch for 20 years. I am the owner and founder of Under the Gallows Tree, an online witchcraft shop based in Edinburgh, Scotland.

I want to thank you for purchasing "A Grimoire from Under The Gallows Tree." I hope it becomes a foundational resource for your practice moving forward.

For those unfamiliar with the term, a Grimoire should not be confused with a Book of Shadows. A Grimoire serves as a guide for practicing the craft, while a Book of Shadows is a personal collection of spells and rituals gathered throughout your journey.

This book is primarily a Grimoire, designed as a reference for those new to the craft or those like me who are seeking to keep key aspects of the craft close to hand without the need to sift through numerous other texts.

In the final chapter, you will find some of my own spells and rituals, which I use regularly, and blank pages to help you begin creating your own Book of Shadows.

If you have any questions about the book, witchcraft in general, or my shop, you can reach out to me via the website - www.underthegallowstree.com

Witches Rede

Abide the witches law ye must,

In perfect love and in perfect trust.

Eight words the Witches Rede fulfil,

An harm ye none do as ye will.

And ever mind the rule of three,

What ye send oot comes back tae thee.

Follow this with mind and heart,

And merry ye meet and merry ye part.

Alters & Other Basics

Altars

An altar is far more than a simple arrangement of objects. It is a sacred sanctuary, intentionally created to support your spiritual practices. This personal space serves as a focal point for meditation, spell work, chakra alignment, crystal grid creation, and any other magical endeavors that inspire and empower you. Your altar can take any form that feels authentic, an ornate end table adorned with meaningful artifacts, a bookshelf housing spiritual texts, or even a modest shoebox decorated with personal symbols.

At its core, an altar is a reflection of your inner self. It is a physical expression of your beliefs, intentions, and aspirations. While there are many traditional tools that may enhance your practice, the most essential element is your intuition. Choose items that resonate deeply with your energy and purpose, allowing your altar to grow and evolve with your spiritual journey.

Basic Altar Tools

Athame
The athame is a ritual knife, typically double-edged and often engraved with mystical symbols. It represents the element of Fire and is used in practices such as casting circles, directing energy, and symbolizing the divine masculine in sacred rites. Though it may appear formidable, the athame is not used for physical cutting. If it ever draws blood accidentally, it is believed necessary to ritually cleanse or retire it to restore energetic harmony. Many practitioners maintain a separate blade for practical tasks and reserve the athame solely for sacred work.

Bell
The bell introduces the vibrational power of sound into your rituals. Whether soft and delicate or deep and resonant, each bell has the ability to invoke spiritual energy, mark transitions in ritual, and cleanse the environment. Bells made of brass, ceramic, crystal, or silver offer unique tonal qualities. A high, clear tone is often used to call upon Faerie spirits or to shift energy, enhancing the sense of focus and presence.

Boline
The boline is a practical, magical knife used for working with physical materials. It may be used to harvest herbs, inscribe candles, cut cords, or perform other tasks involving direct interaction with the natural world. Traditionally featuring a white handle and a curved or straight blade, the boline reflects your connection with the craft and its physical elements. Unlike the athame, it is designed for functional use and brings a hands-on dimension to your practice.

Book of Shadows
This sacred record serves as a deeply personal journal of your magical journey. Unlike a grimoire, which is typically more formal and structured, the Book of Shadows captures your evolving experiences. Within its pages, you may record spells, rituals, dreams, reflections, invocations, and spiritual insights. Over time, it becomes a rich and meaningful chronicle that offers guidance, inspiration, and documentation of your growth.

Bowls
Bowls are versatile and essential tools on any altar. You might use one to hold salt for purification, another for water to represent emotion and intuition, and others for herbs, offerings, or crystals. By assigning each bowl a specific role, you bring greater organization and intention to your spiritual practice. Having a selection of dedicated bowls helps maintain clarity and flow during ritual work.

Besom
The besom, or ritual broom, is used not for ordinary cleaning but for spiritual purification. It serves to sweep away negative or stagnant energy and to prepare your space for ritual. Often used before casting a circle, the besom invites clarity and protection. It is a symbol of threshold crossing, purification, and sacred intention, making it a cherished tool in any magical practice.

Candles

Candles are essential focal points in magical practice, their flames symbolizing transformation, energy, and intention. These luminous orbs come in a variety of sizes and colors, each color representing different elements or purposes, such as blue for peace, red for passion, and green for abundance. Before rituals, practitioners often dress candles by anointing them with essential oils and rolling them in herbs. This process infuses the candles with additional layers of energy, enhancing their effectiveness during spellwork.

Cauldron

The cauldron is often seen as the heart of magical work, a metal vessel that symbolizes the alchemical transformation of energies. It can be used for burning candles, herbs, or incense, creating a potent blend of intention and smoke that fills the ritual space. When melting wax, it is advisable to place a layer of clean sand at the bottom of the cauldron to ensure safety and containment. Ideally, the cauldron should have a lid, or a separate lid should be available to safely extinguish any flames once the work is complete.

Censer and Incense

A censer is a portable container designed for burning incense. It may be carried around a ritual circle or placed on an altar as a focal point. Censers can be made from brass, polished wood, ceramic, or even seashells, with each material contributing its own aesthetic and energy to the ritual space. For safety, the censer should be partially filled with clean, fine sand to act as a heat buffer. This protects the surface it rests on and helps hold the incense securely in place.

Chalice

The chalice is a sacred vessel used to serve ceremonial beverages during rituals, such as Cakes and Wine at Esbats or other gatherings. It serves both a practical and symbolic role, representing abundance and the connection to the divine. Chalices may be made from materials such as pottery, silver, brass, crystal, or natural substances like wood. This vessel is a reminder of the sweetness of life and the importance of communal sharing in sacred rites.

Compass

A compass is an essential tool for witches, used to determine the cardinal directions of north, south, east, and west. This orientation is especially important when casting spells or conducting rituals in unfamiliar locations. Proper alignment ensures that magical workings are in harmony with the natural elements and directional energies that support them.

Cords

Cords are ceremonial tools used to create magic circles or perform binding spells. They may be made from cotton, silk, or plant fibers and can be infused with specific colors or energies to enhance their purpose. The use of cords serves to contain magical energy within a defined space and symbolizes the interconnection of the various elements and intentions involved in the spell.

Crystal Ball

A crystal ball is a smooth, spherical object, often clear and free of facets, although some may contain bubbles or natural inclusions. Clear spheres made from natural quartz are especially valued for their metaphysical properties, though high-quality lead crystal can also be effective. The crystal ball is primarily used for scrying, a practice in which one gazes into the sphere to receive visions or insights during divination.

Crystals

Crystals are prized for their unique energetic properties and are often selected based on personal affinity and the specific energies they bring to spells. Each crystal possesses its own vibrational frequency, making it valuable for both enhancing the power of spells and serving as a decorative element on the altar. Practitioners often develop personal connections with specific crystals through experience, discovering which stones resonate most powerfully with their intentions.

Element Representation

On an altar, the elements can be represented in a variety of ways, enriching the sacred space and honoring the natural world. Common representations include soil or stones for Earth, feathers or incense for Air, candles for Fire, and bowls or vessels of water for Water. These physical manifestations of the elements help ground the practitioner in their surroundings and create a harmonious balance of energies.

Essential Oils

Essential oils are potent substances frequently used in magical practices. They can be employed on their own, used to dress candles, or blended with incense for burning in a censer. Due to their strength, essential oils should never be ingested or applied directly to the skin without proper dilution in a carrier oil, such as almond or jojoba. With the notable exception of lavender, often added to ritual baths for its soothing fragrance, care and caution are essential, especially for pregnant women, as some oils can cause adverse reactions.

God or Goddess Statue

Statues representing gods and goddesses hold a sacred place on the altar and serve as powerful embodiments of the divine. While not traditionally considered tools, their presence fosters a reverent atmosphere, reminding practitioners of the spiritual forces at play. These representations often reflect personal beliefs and spirituality, transforming the altar into a living temple infused with divine energy and serving as focal points for meditation and prayer.

Herbs

Herbs are a fundamental component of magic and spell work, easily sourced from local shops, farmers' markets, or home gardens. Their uses are varied; they may be burned on charcoal, incorporated into incense, or used to anoint candles to instill specific intentions. Carried spells made from herbs, often wrapped in natural cloth and kept in a pocket, serve as constant reminders of the practitioner's magical intent and connection to nature.

Mortar and Pestle

The mortar and pestle are traditional tools used in the preparation of magical ingredients. The mortar is a bowl-like container, typically made from wood, ceramic, metal, or stone, with a smooth interior for grinding. The pestle is a blunt tool used to crush and mix ingredients. Together, they allow practitioners to create powders, pastes, and infusions essential for spells and potions, adding a tactile, hands-on element to magical work.

Offerings

Offerings are items placed on the altar as expressions of gratitude, reverence, or prayer to the Divine. These may be as simple as fresh flowers or as elaborate as personally significant objects. The selection of offerings is highly individual; anything considered beautiful or meaningful by the practitioner may be used. Through these offerings, practitioners open a channel for receiving blessings and divine guidance.

Pentacle

The pentacle is a symbolic disk inscribed with a five-pointed star enclosed within a protective circle. It can be crafted from various materials such as wood, clay, metal, or simply drawn on paper. In ritual practices, the pentacle serves as a powerful emblem representing the unity of the elements and spirit. It acts as a focal point for channeling magical energies and intentions.

Tarot Cards

Tarot cards are rich visual tools used for divination and intuitive insight. Practitioners are encouraged to select a deck that resonates personally, as a strong connection enhances the quality of readings. Over time, many accumulate multiple decks, each offering unique perspectives and deepening understanding of life's mysteries, personal growth, and spiritual development.

Spell Jars

Spell jars are versatile vessels filled with magical components such as herbs, oils, crystals, or moon water, chosen to support specific intentions or manifestations. After use, cleanse the jars with spring water and sea salt to remove residual energies and prepare them for future work. They can be placed on altars or carried as charms, acting as potent, focused containers of intention.

Wand

The wand is a key tool in witchcraft, traditionally measuring the length from the forearm to the fingertips, approximately 12 to 16 inches. Commonly crafted from woods like oak, willow, hazel, apple, or elder, each believed to carry distinct energetic properties, the wand is a deeply personal item selected for its resonance with the practitioner. It is used to direct magical energy, cast spells, call or release circles, and may even substitute for an athame, strengthening the practitioner's link to the magical current.

By thoughtfully selecting and arranging these items on your altar, you create a dynamic, spiritually charged environment. This sacred space reflects your personal beliefs and intentions while enhancing the effectiveness and depth of your magical practice. Each element plays a vital role in your energetic work, transforming your altar into a sanctuary for growth, transformation, and divine connection.

Charging Altar Tools

Charging your altar tools is a fundamental practice that boosts their power and aligns them with your energy. It is recommended to charge tools when you first acquire them, after using them in a ritual or spell, or anytime they feel energetically depleted.

Here are several effective methods for charging your tools:

Visualization

Find a quiet, undisturbed space where you can focus. Hold the tool close to your heart and take several deep, calming breaths. Visualize your energy as a radiant light or flowing current merging with the tool. See this energy infusing it with clarity, strength, and purposeful intention. Remain in this state for several minutes, strengthening the bond between you and the tool.

Sound

Sound is a powerful method for energizing altar tools. Use instruments such as a singing bowl, tuning forks, or your own voice through chanting or mantras. As you produce these sounds, concentrate on your intention to charge the item. Sit in a meditative posture, allowing the vibrations to fill your space and saturate the tool. This auditory resonance amplifies the tool's energetic frequency.

Crystals

Crystals are natural amplifiers of energy and can be used effectively to charge your altar tools. Choose a high-energy crystal such as selenite or amethyst. Before using the crystal, ensure it has been properly cleansed, whether by salt, water, or sound, and charged with positive energy. Place the tool next to, on, or over the charged crystal, and visualize the crystal's energy filling the tool. You can leave them together for several hours or overnight, allowing the crystal's energy to fully imbue the tool.

Elements

Harnessing the elements can significantly influence your altar tools, as each element provides a unique form of energy.

For earth energy, bury your tool in clean soil or dirt while setting the intention to ground and stabilize its power. Leave it buried for at least one night, allowing the earth to connect with the tool and lend its fortitude.

To charge with air, create or find smoke from natural herbs or incense. Pass the tool carefully through the smoke, allowing the airy essence to cleanse it and fill it with uplifting vibrations.

To invoke fire energy, pass your tool through a candle flame with safety in mind. Focus on the flame's dynamic and transformative energy, imbuing the tool with passion and vigor.

For water energy, bring water to a boil while focusing on your intentions. Once it has cooled, anoint the tool with the infused water, visualizing the flow of energy revitalizing it.

Herbs & Tinctures
 Herbs carry significant energetic qualities and can be used to charge your tools. Create herbal smoke by burning dried herbs such as sage, cedar, or rosemary. As you pass your tool through the smoke, concentrate on the specific qualities of the herb and the energy you wish to imbue into the tool. Alternatively, you can anoint the tool with essential oils or tinctures that resonate with your intentions, further setting the energy before using it in rituals.

Sunlight & Moonlight
 Expose your altar tools to the natural energy of sunlight or moonlight to recharge them. For sunlight, place the tool outside during the day, ideally at sunrise or noon when the light is strongest, and imagine it soaking up the vibrant rays. For moonlight, leave the tool outdoors overnight, especially during a full moon, allowing it to absorb the gentle yet potent lunar energy. This method connects your tools to the cycles of nature and enhances their natural abilities.

Once you select the method that resonates most with you, approach the process with dedication and mindfulness. Ground yourself by standing or sitting firmly, maintaining focus on your intention as you work with your tool. Trust your intuition to guide you when the tool has reached a state of fullness and charge, knowing that your energy and intent have been successfully transferred.

By incorporating these techniques into your practice, you can ensure your altar tools are vibrant and ready to assist you in your spiritual work.

<u>The Clair Senses</u>

The Clair senses refer to a collection of unique abilities that enable individuals to perceive aspects of the world that lie beyond the reach of our traditional five senses—sight, hearing, touch, taste, and smell. These abilities, often collectively called the "clairs," consist of eight distinct forms: clairvoyance, clairaudience, clairsentience, claircognizance, clairgustance, clairscent, claircognizance, and clairtangency. Each Clair offers a different way to tap into and interpret subtle energies and vibrations around us, allowing for a richer experience of reality. Let's explore each of these intriguing psychic gifts in more depth.

Clairvoyance –

Clairvoyance, derived from the French term meaning "clear seeing," is the ability to perceive images or visions that are typically invisible to the naked eye. This psychic gift is often associated with the third eye chakra, which is thought to serve as a portal to the unseen spiritual realm. Individuals who possess clairvoyance may experience sudden flashes of colours, vivid imagery, symbols, or even short video clips that convey messages or insights. These visions often come through in a manner reminiscent of daydreaming or during guided meditations. Clairvoyants may also receive insights regarding future events, feelings, or circumstances, making this ability both fascinating and profoundly impactful.

Clairsentience –

Clairsentience translates to "clear feeling" and refers to the ability to perceive and interpret emotional energies. Those who have refined this ability can deeply empathize with others, sensing their feelings, pain, thoughts, and intentions even when expressed non-verbally. It's not uncommon for clairsentients to experience overwhelming emotional waves that seem to come out of nowhere, leading them to perceive feelings as if they were their own. This intense emotional connection can help clairsentients offer support to others but can also pose challenges, especially if they struggle to distinguish their emotions from those they are sensing from others.

Clairaudience –

Clairaudience, meaning "clear hearing," is the ability to hear sound, voices, and messages from beyond our typical auditory perception. Unlike ordinary hearing, clairaudience allows individuals to listen to a soft, inner voice that conveys information and guidance, often in a calm and reassuring manner. This voice can manifest as whispers or gentle thoughts that arise in the mind, providing clarity or insight about a situation. However, when a person's mind is overly stimulated or chaotic, distinguishing this intuitive voice from everyday thoughts can become challenging.

Clairgustance –

Clairgustance is the Clair sense associated with taste, enabling individuals to experience emotions or energies through their taste buds. People with this ability can taste the essence of different feelings; for example, experiencing a sense of sadness might evoke a bitter or sour taste in the mouth, while moments of happiness could manifest as sweet or delightful flavours. This intuitive taste can be triggered spontaneously and does not require physical interaction with food or drink, making it a unique way to navigate and understand emotional energies.

Clairscent –

Clairscent, or "clear scent," involves the intuitive ability to detect fragrances, scents, or odours that may carry profound meanings. This sense allows individuals to connect with unseen energies, often facilitating insights into the truth or falsehood of a situation. Those who possess this ability often describe themselves as having a heightened perception of authenticity, able to detect lies or deceit mere moments before they occur. This intuitive olfactory sense lends itself to a deeper understanding of people and environments.

Claircognizance –

Claircognizance is the gift of "clear knowing," which enables individuals to acquire information that transcends reasoning or conscious thought. Unlike gut feelings or intuitive instincts, claircognizance is characterized by sudden and profound insights that "download" into the mind without prior learning or experience. This ability allows individuals to receive knowledge about events, spiritual concepts, or practical solutions that can significantly benefit themselves and others. Moments of claircognizance often arise unexpectedly and can inspire creativity and problem-solving.

Clairtangency –

Also known as psychometry, clairtangency is the psychic ability associated with touch. This gift allows practitioners to garner information about people, objects, or places through physical contact. When someone with this ability touches another person or a physical item, they can intuitively extract energetic information, feelings, or memories linked to that entity. What makes clairtangency particularly remarkable is its ability to activate multiple psychic senses simultaneously, creating a comprehensive understanding of the energetic signals being received.

Clairempathy –

Clairempathy represents a heightened sensitivity to emotional and energetic vibrations, allowing individuals to feel the joys, sorrows, and physical sensations of people, animals, and even environments. Empaths can become strongly aware of residual energies—such as emotions connected to a specific location or object—sometimes feeling these sensations so intensely that it feels as if they were experiencing them firsthand. Because of this overwhelming sensation, many empaths find it challenging to navigate crowded or emotionally charged spaces and often seek solace in nature or tranquil environments.

Every person possesses some level of psychic abilities, often interacting with these clairs, whether consciously or unconsciously, in daily life. Tuning into our intuition and recognizing these subtle forms of perception can significantly enrich our decision-making processes and enhance our understanding of life's intricacies. It empowers individuals to navigate relationships, make informed choices, and explore the complexities of existence with greater clarity and insight.

<u>**Witches' Time**</u>

Understanding the Power of the Hours

Each hour of the day carries distinct magical properties that can enhance rituals and spell work. The ancient belief in the significance of time reflects how each fleeting moment can be harnessed for specific intentions. For example, the period from 3 AM to 4 AM is often referred to as the witching hour. During this mystical time, the barriers between our world and the spirit realm weaken, making it an optimal moment for paranormal encounters, such as ghostly visitations. This hour is particularly favourable for divination practices like tarot card readings and rune stone interpretations.

The Magical Qualities of Each Hour:

1 AM –

 This marks the beginning of a new day and is ideal for banishing shadows from your life. Use this hour to cleanse your spirit and strengthen your resolve against negativity. Focus on grounding techniques to solidify your energy.

2 AM –

A time for purification, 2 AM is potent for breaking free from toxic relationships. Whether they are friendships or romantic involvements, use this hour to perform rituals aimed at cutting cords and freeing yourself from unhealthy bonds.

3 AM –

Known for fostering determination, this hour can help you confront personal hurdles that are hindering your progress. Engage in practices that inspire resilience and a warrior mindset as you pursue your goals.

4 AM –

This hour is all about luck and victory. Perform rituals that invite good fortune and success into your life, whether in personal endeavours or professional pursuits.

5 AM –

At this hour, psychic abilities are heightened. Engage in meditative practices or exercises that promote psychic growth, such as intuitive journaling or connecting with spiritual guides.

6 AM –

Focused on tenacity and perseverance, this hour is perfect for tackling projects you've been putting off. Use affirmations or visualization techniques to strengthen your commitment to seeing things through.

7 AM –

Associated with hope and clarity, this hour encourages improved insight and fresh perspectives. Consider meditation or reflecting on the day ahead, inviting positive energy into your thoughts.

8 AM –

This time is conducive to personal change, particularly regarding the conscious mind. Embrace practices that promote self-awareness, intention setting, and mental clarity as you start your day.

9 AM –

Use this hour to lend a helping hand to others. Engage in acts of kindness or support, grounding yourself in the energy of altruism and community.

10 AM –

This hour focuses on personal convictions and resolutions. Dedicate time to self-improvement work, reinforcing your inner beliefs and goals for growth.

11 AM –

Transformation is at the forefront during this hour. Focus on learning new skills, whether through formal education, creative endeavours, or personal exploration.

Noon –

A powerful time for manifestation, the energy at noon amplifies spells for attracting love, success, financial stability, and prosperity into your life.

1 PM –

Concentrate on your self-image and personal security during this hour. Engage in practices that address anxiety and bolster self-esteem, reinforcing your sense of worth.

2 PM –

This hour encourages deepening relationships. Perform rituals or meditative practices aimed at fostering love, understanding, and open communication in your interactions.

3 PM –

Focus on chakra work, balancing the energies of mind, body, and spirit. Engage in practices that harmonize your internal systems, promoting overall well-being.

4 PM –

The energy of this hour brings harmony among the elements and emphasizes organization. Plan your evening effectively, ensuring you stick to your objectives.

5 PM –

Communicate with your spiritual guides during this hour. Seek insight and clarity about your path while honing your self-awareness.

6 PM –

Safety and protection are the primary themes. This hour is perfect for performing protective rituals and reflecting on the completion of daily tasks or goals.

7 PM –

An hour of diversity and healing, focusing on promoting care and concern for others. Engage in activities that nurture compassion and understanding from different perspectives.

8 PM –

This hour is about embracing leadership qualities. Encourage assertiveness and take command of your decisions, guiding others when necessary.

9 PM –

Delve into the universal knowledge and truth. Reflect on your experiences from the day and consider their broader implications for your spiritual journey.

10 PM –

Improve clarity of thought during this hour. Use it for rational decision-making, mental organization, and introspection to prepare for the day ahead.

11 PM –

This hour emphasizes coping with drastic changes positively. Turn your focus inward to release fears and embrace new beginnings constructively.

Midnight –

A powerful pivot point, midnight signifies change energy. It is an ideal time for initiating transformation and welcoming new possibilities into your life.

Both sunrise and sunset carry their unique energies.

Sunrise –

This time is filled with potential, perfect for new beginnings. Rituals aimed at welcoming new opportunities, love, friendships, careers, and healing are particularly potent. Embrace the light and vitality that a new day brings.

Sunset –

As day transitions to night, sunset serves as a powerful moment for release. Utilize this time for banishing negative energies, perform protection rituals, and setting intentions for letting go of what no longer serves your highest good.

With a keen understanding of these time-sensitive energies, you can enhance your magical practice, aligning your intentions with the natural rhythms of the universe.

Days of the Week

Each day of the week is imbued with its own unique magical properties and correspondences, influencing our emotions, actions, and decisions. Understanding these attributes can guide our practices and intentions throughout the week. Below is a detailed overview of each day:

Monday –

Associated with the colours blue and white, the element of water, the Moon, moonstone crystal, and the star sign Cancer.

Monday is associated with emotions and intuition. It is an ideal day for dream work and exploring clairvoyance, making it perfect for connecting with the divine feminine and addressing issues related to femininity.

Tuesday –

Associated with the colours red and orange, the element of fire, the planet Mars, carnelian crystal, and the star sign Scorpio.

This day embodies aggressive energy and courage, making it suitable for taking bold actions, starting new projects, or addressing challenges in marriage. Harness the power of passion and dominance on this day.

Wednesday –

Associated with the colours silver and blue, the element of air, the planet Mercury, clear quartz and malachite crystals, and the star signs Gemini and Virgo.

Midweek is focused on communication, creativity, and intellectual pursuits. It's an excellent day for writing, brainstorming, and engaging in artistic endeavours, allowing for the expression of ideas and thoughts.

Thursday –

Associated with the colours purple and Indigo, the element of fire, the planet Jupiter, aventurine and moss agate crystals, and the star signs Sagittarius and Pisces.

Thursday is a day of expansion and growth, encouraging the exploration of new opportunities and legal matters. It's an auspicious time for financial undertakings and manifesting abundance.

Friday –

Associated with the colours pink and red, the elements of air and water, the planet Venus, rose quartz and jade crystals, and the star signs Libra and Taurus.

Friday vibrates with love, beauty, and relationships. It's a wonderful day for nurturing friendships, enhancing romantic bonds, and engaging in self-care practices that promote emotional well-being and harmony.

Saturday –

Associated with the colours black and grey, the element of earth, the planet Saturn, onyx and obsidian crystals, and the star sign Capricorn.

This day is associated with grounding energies and introspection. It's favourable for banishing negativity, protection rituals, and addressing issues of responsibility and discipline. Use this time for self-reflection and retribution if needed.

Sunday –

Associated with the colours yellow and gold, the element of fire, the Sun, citrine and amber crystals, and the star sign Leo.

Sunday shines with healing energy and spiritual growth. It's an excellent day for self-improvement, engaging in physical activities that boost power and strength, and focusing on male-related issues while connecting with higher consciousness.

Months of the Year

As we journey through the calendar year, it's fascinating to recognize that each month carries its own unique magical significance, providing us with opportunities tailored to specific themes and energies.

January –

New Beginnings

January symbolizes fresh starts and rejuvenation. It's an ideal month for working on the Root Chakra, which is associated with our physical needs, stability, and foundational aspects of life. This time is particularly potent for fertility and reproductive magic, making it a favourable period for those seeking to manifest new life or engage in practices that nurture physical well-being. Harness energies of renewal to set intentions for the coming year.

February –

Clarity and Ambition

February encourages focus and clarity, making it an excellent time for spells that promote ambition, balance, and divination. Energy is aligned with the Crown Chakra, enhancing connection to spiritual insights and higher consciousness. This month encourages self-reflection and sharpens intuition, making it a wonderful time to gain a deeper understanding of personal matters or to pursue guidance on upcoming challenges.

March –

Resolution and Protection

As winter begins to melt away, March invites us to address unresolved issues, letting go of anger and old grievances. Protection spells, as well as darker forms of magic aimed at retribution, find strong footing during this time. The Throat Chakra is emphasized, encouraging honest communication and self-expression. This month is ideal for spells targeting self-love, career advancement, or any personal aims you wish to vocalize and manifest.

April –

Transformation

April is a powerful time for transforming dreams into tangible goals. It's an opportunity to take your passions and manifest them into reality through the right intentions and actions. Spells that assist in navigating difficult relationships or situations are particularly effective, as this month encourages growth and adaptability. Embrace the changing energy of this month to foster change and clear your path for what is to come.

May –

Wisdom and Growth

As spring reaches its peak, May shines with potential for personal growth and the acquisition of new skills. This month emphasizes the Heart Chakra, encouraging emotional healing and the banishment of negative habits. Spells that unite logic and emotion are potent now, ideal for improving self-esteem and enhancing relationships. It is an excellent time for introspection and seeking illumination on your personal journey.

June –

Fairy Magic and Transformation

With the arrival of summer, June brings an infusion of fairy magic, fostering communication, movement, and transformation in every aspect of life. This month encourages spells designed to either increase or decrease various influences in your life. The focus on the Solar Plexus Chakra promotes confidence, willpower, and personal strength, making it an ideal time to unleash your potential and embrace new beginnings.

July –

Leadership and Endurance

July ushers in a strong energy for manifesting leadership qualities and decisiveness. It's ideal for setting long-term goals and organizing your plans for success. This month supports perseverance and determination, fuelling your ambitions and helping you to stay on track. Utilize this time to solidify your plans and bolster your resolve in pursuits that require sustained effort.

August –

Harvesting Rewards

As summer begins to wane, August is a time to reap the rewards of the magical work you've put in throughout the year. This month is perfect for spells that encourage assertiveness and empowerment, as well as for cleansing your space to prepare for the challenges of winter. It's a good period to release unwanted emotions or habits, creating a fresh atmosphere filled with positive energy.

September –

Embracing Feminine Energy

September signifies the return of feminine energy, acting as a powerful time for spells that attract blessings into your life. This month's energy supports fertility, love, and protection spells, making it an auspicious time for women-oriented magic. Focusing on the Third Eye Chakra enhances intuition, providing clarity and insight into decisions that will benefit you personally and spiritually.

October –

Ancestors and Legacy

In October, the veil between worlds thins, making it a potent time for ancestor or spirit magic. Engage with ancestral wisdom and open channels for communication with those who have transitioned. This month is also powerful for spells related to ambition, justice, and navigating complexities of social and political issues. Embrace this energy to seek guidance and balance in your endeavours.

November –

Release and Freedom

November invites you to break free from burdens that hold you back. It's a time for spells focused on release, protection, and individuality. This month's energies bolster your efforts to emancipate yourself from any limitations or obstacles, encouraging liberation and personal authenticity. Reflect on what you can let go of to create space for new growth.

December –

Enlightenment in Darkness

As the year draws to a close, December is a reflective time to illuminate the darker aspects of your life, offering opportunities for resolution and self-improvement. This month encourages spells that shed light on your experiences and help foster growth as you prepare for the year ahead. Embrace the energies of renewal, allowing yourself to transition gracefully into a new beginning filled with hope and purpose.

Each month offers a unique energy to work with, enriching our magical practices and enhancing personal growth as we honour the cycles of the year.

Witches Alphabet

The Theban Script, also referred to as the Runes of Honorius, is a unique cipher derived from the Latin alphabet. It was first introduced to the world in 1510 by its creator, Honorius Thebes, and has since captivated those interested in cryptography, secrecy, and the occult.

In the 1960s, the Theban Script found a new purpose when it was embraced by witches and practitioners of various occult traditions. It was adopted as a secret alphabet, allowing these individuals to inscribe their thoughts, rituals, and magical workings in Grimoires and Books of Shadows without fear of prying eyes. This use of the script afforded them a level of privacy and protection, ensuring that their most sacred knowledge remained confidential.

Furthermore, the Theban Script served as a means of clandestine communication among witches. Those familiar with the script could exchange messages without outsiders deciphering their intentions. This ability to write in code was particularly valuable when discussing sensitive information or planning gatherings.

Additionally, the script played a crucial role in the creation of sigils—symbols crafted for specific magical purposes that could be placed in public spaces. By using the Theban Script, witches could inscribe their intentions covertly, allowing them to manifest their desires while maintaining discretion about their true objectives. Through these practices, the Theban Script became an integral tool in the modern witchcraft movement, symbolizing both secrecy and empowerment within the realm of magic.

A	B	C	D	E	F
G	H	I / J	K	L	M
N	O	P	Q	R	S
T	U / V / W	X	Y	Z	End of sentence

<u>**Casting & Closing a Circle**</u>

Casting a protective circle is a fundamental practice in many spiritual traditions, serving as a sacred space that safeguards your energy, intentions, and spells from external influences. This guide will walk you through the process of casting and closing a circle, ensuring a focused and safe environment for your rituals.

Before you cast your circle, it is essential to prepare your area to enhance the energy of your practice. Begin by cleansing the space, allowing a fresh and positive atmosphere to flow. Here are a few effective methods:

Smudging –

Use dried sage or a similar herb to smoke cleanse your area. As you move the smoke around, visualize negative energies being cleared away.

Sweeping –

Take a broom and gently sweep the area, symbolically sweeping away unwanted energies.

Burning Incense –

Lighting incense can set a calming mood and engage the senses. Choose scents that resonate with your intentions.

Visual and Auditory Aids –

Sprinkling water around the space or playing soft music can help manifest your intention of dispelling negativity.

Once your area is cleansed, it's time to invite the elements into your circle for protection and support. Each element should be represented by an object placed in its corresponding cardinal direction. Here are some suggestions:

Earth

Use herbs, salt, or soil to represent this grounding element, placing it in the North.

Air

A feather or incense can symbolize air, positioned in the East to evoke clarity and communication.

Fire

A candle, lit with intention, serves as the representation of fire, placed in the South to inspire transformation.

Water

A bowl of water can represent this element, located in the West, to embody emotions and intuition.

As you arrange each item, take a moment to connect with the element. Use the following invocations for each direction:

North (Earth)

"Hail to the Guardians of the Watchtower of the North, Spirits of Earth. Protect this circle and those within. Hear me."

East (Air)

"Hail to the Guardians of the Watchtower of the East, Spirits of Air. Protect this circle and those within. Hear me."

South (Fire)

"Hail to the Guardians of the Watchtower of the South, Spirits of Fire. Protect this circle and those within. Hear me."

West (Water)

"Hail to the Guardians of the Watchtower of the West, Spirits of Water. Protect this circle and those within. Hear me."

With the elements called upon and your offerings in place, it is time to cast your circle. Stand in the centre with your fingers pointing towards the ground, grounding your energy. Walk slowly around your offerings while envisioning a vibrant, radiant light surrounding you. This light serves as a protective barrier that encompasses your sacred space and the elements.

As you make your circuit, concentrate on the energy and visualize it growing stronger with each step. When you feel fully connected to the circle, proceed with your spell or ritual, ensuring you remain within the circle's protective boundaries.

Upon completing your spell or ritual, it is essential to close the circle properly to avoid inviting in negative energies. Begin this process by acknowledging and thanking the elements for their assistance.

Starting with North, release them in the reverse order of their calling:

North (Earth)

"Hail to the Guardians of the Watchtower of the North, Spirits of Earth. I thank you for protecting this circle and those within. You are free to leave or welcome to stay. Hear me."

West (Water)

"Hail to the Guardians of the Watchtower of the West, Spirits of Water. I thank you for protecting this circle and those within. You are free to leave or welcome to stay. Hear me."

South (Fire)

"Hail to the Guardians of the Watchtower of the South, Spirits of Fire. I thank you for protecting this circle and those within. You are free to leave or welcome to stay. Hear me."

East (Air)

"Hail to the Guardians of the Watchtower of the East, Spirits of Air. I thank you for protecting this circle and those within. You are free to leave or welcome to stay. Hear me."

After expressing gratitude to each element, stand once more with your fingers pointing towards the ground. Walk counterclockwise around the circle, envisioning the vibrant light that once surrounded you gradually fading.

As you visualize this energy dissipating, reinforce your intention that the circle is now closed. Once you feel the energy has fully evaporated, your sacred space is complete. You have successfully cast and closed your circle, ensuring that it served its purpose without any unwanted interference.

<u>**Crafting a Spell**</u>

Learning to craft your own spells can be a rewarding endeavour for numerous reasons. Not only does it empower you to assist friends and family during challenging times, but it also allows for customizing spells that don't seem to work as intended or addressing very specific needs. Crafting your own spells can enhance your magical practice, deepen your understanding of complex magical principles, and, ultimately, amplify the strength of your spell by infusing it with your personal energy and intent.

Six Essential Steps for Crafting a Spell:

1. Decide Your Purpose/Pick Your Intention

Begin by thoroughly defining the purpose of your spell. Write down your intention with as much detail as you can. Consider what you hope to achieve or what you wish to resolve. Are you seeking love, financial stability, protection, or perhaps a boost in confidence? Clearly articulating your intention will guide the entire spell-making process and clarify your focus.

2. Time Your Spell

Timing is crucial in spell work as different hours, days, months, and moon phases can influence the potency of your spell. For instance:

Moon Phases - A waxing moon is ideal for attracting and growth-related spells, while a waning moon is better suited for releasing and banishing spells.

Days of the Week - Each day holds unique energies (e.g., Monday for intuition, Friday for love). Align your spell's timing with these energies for enhanced efficacy.

3. Pick Your Ingredients

Choosing the right ingredients and tools can significantly impact the outcome of your spell. A variety of components can be utilized, including:

Candles - Different colours correspond to various intentions (e.g., green for abundance, red for passion).

Herbs - Each herb has distinct properties; for instance, basil attracts wealth, while lavender promotes peace.

Crystals - Examples include citrine for prosperity and black tourmaline for protection.

Incense and Oils - Scent plays a powerful role in magic, with particular fragrances enhancing specific intentions.

Salts and Spices - Often used for purification and protection, these can add another layer to your spell.

Select ingredients that resonate with your intention and feel right to you.

4. To Speak or Not To Speak

Consider whether you will verbalize your spell. Many traditional practitioners believed that the use of rhyming phrases or chants added strength and focus to spells. However, the energy and intention behind your words are what ultimately matter. If words do not resonate with you, it's perfectly acceptable to perform a spell without them. Ultimately, trust your intuition.

5. Write It Down

Document each step in the spell-crafting process, from your intention and chosen timing to the selected ingredients and any wording you intend to use. Having everything recorded allows you to replicate successful spells or adjust them if necessary. Additionally, it's important to note the outcomes of your spells. Over time, this will enrich your understanding of your magical practice and help you identify what works best for you.

6. Work Your Spell

Create the sacred space where your spell will take place, often referred to as casting a Circle. This helps to contain energy and focus your intention. Various methods can be employed to cast your spell, such as:

Witch's Bottles or Bags - Carry the spell ingredients with you.

Candle Magic - Use candles to represent your intention, focusing your energy while they burn.

Herb and Tincture Preparations - Creating potions or tinctures can add physical representation to your spell work.

Visualization - Envision the desired outcome as if it has already happened, channeling your energy towards this vision.

Sigils - Draw symbols that represent your intention and incorporate them into your spell.

Choose the methods that resonate most with you and align with your intention.

The most common types of spells are:

Fortune Spells –

Often referred to as money spells, these typically involve using a form of currency along with corresponding herbs and spices to attract financial abundance. When you spend this charmed money, it sends your intention into the universe, activating the spell.

Luck Spells –

These spells are designed to increase your chances of achieving specific goals, such as landing a job or securing a new home. While you can craft a general good luck spell, the more specific you are about your intention, the more effective the spell tends to be.

Sweetening Spells –

These are gentle love spells intended to draw someone to you or enhance relationships without enforcing love. Often using sweet ingredients like honey, these spells help to foster friendships or improve relationships.

Protection Spells –

Ranging from simple charms to complex workings, protection spells aim to safeguard you against negative energies. These can be created through witch bottles, amulets, crystals, or specific herbs that offer protective properties.

Freezing Spells –

Ideal for halting unwanted actions from others, freezing spells take a behavior that bothers you and stop it in its tracks. This can be a useful way to shield yourself from negativity.

Binding Spells –

These strong spells focus on controlling the actions of another person who may wish you harm. Similar to freezing spells, binding spells are intended for more severe situations where another's actions pose a significant threat to your well-being.

Warding Spells –

Milder than banishing spells, warding spells help redirect negative energies, spirits, or people away from you. While they don't eliminate these influences entirely, they create a protective barrier you can maintain using crystals, herbs, salt, visualization, or guardians.

Banishing Spells –

Unlike other protection spells, banishing spells actively remove negative energies, spirits, or individuals from your life. This form of defensive magic requires careful consideration and should be approached with respect, as it has the potential for profound impact. Techniques may include using candle magic, sigils, herbs & tinctures, or elemental magic.

Smudging

Smudging is a traditional practice that involves lighting various natural materials such as incense, herbs, or spices, allowing the smoke to purify an area or item of any negative, harmful, stale, or unwanted energies it may have accumulated. This ancient ritual is highly versatile and can be performed at any time, making it an effective way to restore balance and harmony to your surroundings.

Here are some compelling reasons to consider incorporating smudging into your routine:

Removal of Negative Energy - Smudging is particularly effective for dispersing lingering negativity from spaces or objects.

Welcoming New Beginnings - Whether you're moving into a new home, welcoming a new baby, or introducing a pet, smudging can help set a positive tone.

Seasonal Transitions - As the seasons change, smudging can help to clear out the old energies and make way for new ones.

Before Rituals or Spells - It's beneficial to create a purified space prior to spiritual practices to enhance their effectiveness.

Enhancing Meditation - Smudging creates a serene environment conducive to deeper reflection and connection.

Social Gatherings - Performing smudging before or after gatherings can help to cleanse the space of any residual energies from the interactions that took place.

There is a wide variety of herbs and spices that can be used for smudging, each carrying its own unique properties and intentions. For those interested in exploring this practice further, this Grimoire features an extensive directory of herbs, incense, and oils, providing guidance on creating your own smudge blends or selecting the right ones to purchase.

Once you've chosen your desired smudge stick, light it carefully, allowing the flame to catch. Use a feather or your hand to fan the flame and direct the aromatic smoke where it's needed. As you do this, concentrate on the characteristics of the herb you are using, visualizing the smoke as a purifying force, effectively cleansing your space, body, or the intended object of any negative, harmful, or stagnant energy. After you finish the smudging process, remember to extinguish the flame safely using a fireproof dish or container.

Water Properties

Water, depending on its source, carries unique energies and properties that can enhance spiritual practices and rituals. Each type of water is imbued with specific qualities based on its environment, offering a wide range of benefits when used in spells and rituals. The eight main types of water and their corresponding properties are:

Dew Water –

Collected from leaves or grass in the morning, this water is associated with beauty, calmness, fertility, glamour, and love. It embodies a fresh, nurturing energy ideal for attracting positive vibes.

Moon Water –

Charged under the moonlight, this water is excellent for enhancing beauty, cleansing spaces, and heightening intuition. It holds the mysteries of the night, making it perfect for spiritual work that requires insight.

Rain Water –

Gathered during a rainstorm, this water is potent for invoking change, cleansing, growth, and protection. It symbolizes renewal and can be used to facilitate personal transformation.

River Water –

This type of water, flowing and ever-changing, is powerful for processes of letting go, moving on, and transformation. Its continual motion embodies the notion of change and release.

Sea Water –

Infused with the essence of the ocean, seawater is ideal for banishing negativity, cleansing, healing, and protection. Its salty nature adds a deep layer of purification and emotional release.

Snow Water –

Collected from melted snow, this water is often used for balance, divination, freezing moments in time, and transformation. Its stillness offers clarity and focus.

Storm Water –

Harvested during thunderstorms, this water is powerful for infusing spells with charging energy, confidence, courage, and strength. The intensity of a storm can amplify the intentions behind your work.

Sun Water –

Created by harnessing sunlight, sun water promotes happiness, positivity, strength, and vitality. The warmth and brightness of the sun imbue this water with uplifting qualities, making it perfect for enhancing energy and joy.

By understanding and utilizing the properties of different types of water, you can significantly enhance the effectiveness of your spells and rituals, aligning with the natural energies around you.

Astrology

<u>**The Four Elements & The Zodiac Signs**</u>

The four fundamental elements—Earth, Air, Fire, and Water—serve as a framework for categorizing the twelve zodiac signs, each imbued with unique characteristics and attributes. These elements are not just mere classifications; they represent the vital forces that influence the personalities, behaviours, and relationships of those born under each sign. By understanding these elemental associations, individuals can gain insights into their own tendencies and how they connect with others, as well as with the natural world around them.

Earth Signs:

As the most grounded and stable element, Earth embodies practicality and reliability, characteristics that are exquisitely showcased in the signs of Taurus, Virgo, and Capricorn. Earth signs are often seen as the backbone of stability; they approach life with a methodical mindset, valuing what is tangible and real. These individuals are dependable and possess a strong sense of responsibility, often going out of their way to support family and friends. They thrive on logic and reason, making them excellent problem solvers. Earth signs also have an appreciation for the finer things in life, often seeking to create a serene and beautiful environment. Their persistence and dedication make them great achievers in both personal and professional realms.

Signs - Taurus, Virgo, Capricorn

Air Signs:

Air signs are known for their intellectual approach to life, showcasing a more fluid and adaptable nature. Represented by Gemini, Libra, and Aquarius, these signs are the social butterflies of the zodiac, thriving on communication and connection with others. Air signs are naturally curious, drawn to new ideas, and constantly seeking knowledge. They are often seen as the bridge between people, possessing a unique ability to engage with a diverse array of individuals. Their sociability is complemented by a strong sense of idealism, particularly in Libra, which values harmony and balance. Air signs can appear detached due to their analytical nature, but they are deeply invested in the relationships they cultivate, constantly seeking to understand and innovate.

Signs - Gemini, Libra, Aquarius

Fire Signs:

Representing passion and vitality, the Fire element is embodied by Aries, Leo, and Sagittarius. These signs are characterized by their exuberance and zest for life, often leading the way through their adventurous spirit. Fire signs are creative and spontaneous, regularly embracing new experiences and unafraid of taking risks. Their courage allows them to move beyond the conventional, often resulting in groundbreaking ideas and actions. However, this intensity can also translate into impatience and impulsiveness. Despite their fiery temperament, these individuals often have a strong sense of loyalty toward those they care about, and they inspire others to harness their own passions and aspirations.

Signs -Aries, Leo, Sagittarius

Water Signs:

Water is the element that captures deep emotions and intuition, represented by Cancer, Scorpio, and Pisces. These signs are often seen as the emotional cores of the zodiac, deeply attuned to the feelings of others. They embody the fluidity of water, adapting to various emotional landscapes and often forming profound connections with those around them. Water signs are nurturing and empathetic, with an innate ability to understand and share in the joys and sorrows of others. Their intuition guides them in relationships and decision-making, often leading them to be insightful and wise. While they can be profoundly reflective, Water signs may also experience intense emotions, resulting in a complex inner world that requires balance.

Signs - Cancer, Scorpio, Pisces

The Zodiac Signs

Aries (21st March – 20th April)

Element: Fire

Quality: Cardinal

Colour: Red

Ruling Planet: Mars

Symbol: The Ram

Aries is seen as the trailblazer of the zodiac, standing out for its bold and pioneering nature. With a youthful enthusiasm for life, Aries individuals thrive on adventure and new experiences, reflecting a courageous spirit that is eager to explore the uncharted. Their assertiveness and straightforwardness make them natural leaders, often taking the initiative in various settings. While their passionate and energetic approach can lead to quick outbursts of anger, they also have infectious laughter that helps them to move past conflicts quickly. Aries individuals are defined by their ambition and independence, consistently seeking to carve out their path in life.

Taurus (21st April – 20th May)

Element: Earth

Quality: Fixed

Colours: Red & Orange

Ruling Planet: Venus

Symbol: The Bull

Taurus individuals are synonymous with determination and loyalty, embodying a deep appreciation for security and stability. They have a strong affinity for the pleasures and beauty of life, often indulging in sensory experiences. Their practical approach allows them to navigate life with a steady hand, making them adept at managing finances and resources. This steadfast nature is complemented by their romantic side, as Taurus individuals seek meaningful and lasting connections. Known for their hard work and perseverance, they invest fully in their commitments, resulting in fulfilling, long-term relationships that resonate with harmony and love.

Gemini (21st May – 21st June)

Element: Air

Quality: Mutable

Colour: Orange

Ruling Planet: Mercury

Symbol: The Twins

Geminis are known for their quick wit, boundless curiosity, and eagerness to explore the world around them. Their inquisitive nature drives them to seek knowledge about a variety of subjects, making them natural learners. With a sharp intellect, they are adept at communicating their thoughts and ideas, often engaging in lively discussions and debates. The duality symbolized by their zodiac's representation as twins reflects their complex personalities; they may display one side more openly while keeping another aspect of themselves concealed. This ability to adapt to various social situations and connect with diverse groups of people adds to their charm. Geminis often rely on rational thought processes rather than solely on emotions, allowing them to navigate challenges with a sense of flexibility and resilience.

Cancer (22nd June – 22nd July)

Element: Water

Quality: Cardinal

Colour: Orange & Yellow

Ruling Planet: Moon

Symbol: The Crab

Cancers are profoundly sensitive and deeply emotional individuals who invest wholeheartedly in their beliefs and relationships. Their nurturing disposition drives them to care for others, and they particularly value family and home life. This is essential for their sense of stability; they often seek to create safe and comforting environments. However, akin to the crab, they possess a tough exterior that can guard their softer emotions, making it difficult for others to penetrate their protective shell. Cancers are known for their fluctuating moods, often swayed by their surroundings and the energies of those close to them. While they may experience significant emotional depth, this sensitivity can also lead to feelings of vulnerability or moodiness, compelling them to retreat and recharge in solitude.

Leo (23rd July – 22nd August)

Element: Fire

Quality: Fixed

Colour: Yellow

Ruling Planet: Sun

Symbol: The Lion

Leos are characterized by their creative flair, infectious enthusiasm, and a vibrant display of drama in their lives. Their natural confidence and charisma enable them to shine brightly in any situation, often positioning them as leaders or centre stage. This magnetic personality draws others in, and they revel in the recognition and admiration of those around them. While their zest for life can occasionally tip into pride or arrogance, the underlying nature of Leos is rooted in loyalty and generosity. They have enormous hearts and are often devoted partners, friends, and family members. Driven by their artistic nature, they express their inner fire through various forms of creativity, continuously inspiring others and seeking to share their artistic endeavours with the world.

Virgo (23rd August – 22nd September)

Element: Earth

Quality: Mutable

Colour: Yellow & Green

Ruling Planet: Mercury

Symbol: The Maiden

Virgos are known for their practicality, diligence, and keen analytical skills. They have a natural talent for dissecting complex situations and identifying the minutiae that others may overlook. Their organizational abilities make them exceptional planners and problem solvers, as they thrive on efficiency and consistency. Yet, their drive for perfection can sometimes morph into critical tendencies, particularly when outcomes do not align with their expectations. This inclination toward perfectionism can become an obsession, potentially leading to frustration. Despite this, Virgos' dedication and intellect equip them to transform chaos into order. At their core, they are kind-hearted, grounded individuals who are more than willing to lend a hand to loved ones in need, often investing their time and energy into supporting those who matter most to them.

Libra (23rd September – 22nd October)

Element: Air

Quality: Cardinal

Colour: Green

Ruling Planet: Venus

Symbol: The Scales

Libras are inherently charming, sociable, and diplomatic, driven by a profound appreciation for peace and harmony. They strive to cultivate balance in all aspects of their lives, including their relationships. Aesthetically inclined, they often surround themselves with beauty and luxury, viewing their environment as a reflection of their inner ideals. As quintessential romantics, they are drawn to partnerships and easily plunge into relationships with those they admire, sometimes leading them to become overly reliant on their connections. Their exceptional communication skills empower them to negotiate and navigate social dynamics effectively. However, their deep sensitivity can sometimes lead to indecision, as they go to great lengths to avoid conflict and maintain equilibrium. This thoughtful approach to relationships underscores their desire for fairness and harmony in their interactions with others.

Scorpio (23rd October – 21st November)

Element: Water

Quality: Fixed

Colour: Green & Blue

Ruling Planet: Pluto

Symbol: The Scorpion

Scorpios are known for their intense and passionate nature, embodying the "all or nothing" attitude in both their personal endeavours and relationships. Driven by a powerful inner fire, these individuals possess a remarkable ability to captivate those around them, skilfully employing their sharp minds and magnetic auras to take charge in various situations. Emotions run deep within Scorpios; they experience feelings to the fullest, often immersing themselves in the highs and lows of their emotional spectrum. Their craving for intimacy and psychological depth shapes their interactions, leading them to see the world as a strategic game in which they aim to conquer their goals and desires. This enchanting quality often cloaks their true selves in layers of secrecy and subtlety. Scorpios can be intensely sexual and are known for their complexity, often holding their cards close to their chest. While they are unwavering in their pursuits, their tenacity can be misinterpreted as stubbornness. Beneath their tough exterior lies a profound desire for transformation and rebirth, propelling them to actively seek personal growth, regardless of whether it leads to an uplifting or challenging outcome.

Sagittarius (22nd November – 21st December)

Element: Fire

Quality: Mutable

Colour: Blue

Ruling Planet: Jupiter

Symbol: The Archer

Sagittarians embody an adventurous spirit marked by spontaneity and relentless optimism. Deeply committed to the pursuit of freedom, they have an insatiable desire for exploration and expansion, constantly seeking new horizons in both thought and experience. This makes them natural wanderers, driven to encounter fresh perspectives, diverse relationships, and life lessons that reveal more about themselves and the broader world they inhabit. Despite their eagerness for discovery, Sagittarians may struggle with commitment and focus, often feeling restless or caged when presented with routine or obligations. Their cheerful, buoyant energy often draws good fortune, making them feel as though the universe conspires to aid them on their journey. This quest for adventure keeps their lives vibrant and full of potential memories yet to be made.

Capricorn (22nd December – 19th January)

Element: Earth

Quality: Cardinal

Colour: Deep Blue

Ruling Planet: Saturn

Symbol: The Goat

Capricorns exude ambition and resilience, characterized by their desire to create a life built on a solid foundation. Their practical approach often leads them to be hardworking individuals, fiercely focused on attaining career success, financial stability, and respect within their personal and professional spheres. Beyond their careers, they equally cherish meaningful long-term relationships and domestic harmony, seeing these as integral components of their life achievements. While Capricorns are disciplined and determined, their focused nature can sometimes manifest as aloofness, prompting them to prioritize practicality over emotional engagement. They possess an inherent sense of responsibility, which allows them to confront challenges with a steady demeanour. Yet, beneath their serious façade lies a delightful sense of humour, which they use to forge connections and relate to others more easily.

Aquarius (20th January – 18th February)

Element: Air

Quality: Fixed

Colour: Indigo

Ruling Planet: Uranus

Symbol: The Water Carrier

Aquarians are the thinkers and visionaries of the zodiac, characterized by their intellectual pursuits and deep contemplation. With an innate desire to understand the intricacies of society and the universe, they embrace knowledge and constantly seek to expand their perspectives. Open to new ideas, Aquarians will delve into various concepts but remain steadfast in their beliefs once they establish a strong opinion. This unyielding nature can bestow upon them a sense of brilliance as they often explore complex facets of life that others might shy away from. However, it can also lead to moments of stubbornness, where they become resistant to differing viewpoints. Highly social and often seen as unique or eccentric, Aquarians showcase their creative spirit and innovative thinking, distinguishing themselves from the conventional mould.

Pisces (19th February – 20th March)

Element: Water

Quality: Mutable

Colour: Violet

Ruling Planet: Neptune

Symbol: The Fish

Those born under the sign of Pisces are often recognized for their imaginative and intuitive qualities, reminiscent of wise old souls. With a strong connection to the spiritual and mystical realms, they tend to be attracted to romantic, artistic, or transformative experiences that allow for self-exploration and growth. Pisceans are exceptionally compassionate and empathetic, habitually placing the needs of others above their own, which endears them to many. This deep sensitivity can amplify their social lives as they navigate relationships with a unique flair, drawing diverse individuals toward them. However, due to their heightened ability to absorb the emotions and energies of those around them, they may sometimes become overwhelmed or too impressionable. When the weight of external influences becomes too much to bear, Pisceans often embark on new journeys, unafraid to reinvent themselves and embrace the cycles of life anew.

The Planets and Their Influence

The planets embody various facets of life, influencing our identity, emotions, and motivations in distinct ways. Each celestial body serves as a unique archetype that guides both our inner lives and the broader aspects of society.

The Sun –

Keywords: Consciousness, individuality, self-expression, leadership, confidence, creativity, masculinity

Transit Duration: The Sun spends approximately one month in each zodiac sign.

Personal Representation: The Sun is the essence of your ego, representing your fundamental personality traits and vitality. It shines a light on how you perceive and express yourself in the world, relating to your core identity.

Collective Impact: On a larger scale, the Sun influences global energy levels, casting a collective focus on certain issues and themes as it travels through the zodiac.

The Moon –

Keywords: Habits, instincts, behaviours, the unconscious, memories, femininity, domesticity, intuition

Transit Duration: The Moon transits through each sign roughly every 2 to 3 days, making its influence felt quickly and frequently.

Personal Representation: The Moon delves into your inner world, revealing your emotional landscape, subconscious motives, and habitual responses. It is a reflection of your feelings and memories, often linked to domestic life and nurturing instincts.

Collective Impact: On a societal level, the Moon captures the general mood of humanity, affecting collective emotional trends and shifts that align with its cycles.

Mercury –

Keywords: Communication, intelligence, technology, information, ideas, business, education, legalities

Transit Duration: Mercury stays in a zodiac sign for about 3 to 4 weeks.

Personal Representation: As the planet of thought and communication, Mercury signifies how you process information, express your ideas, and interact with others. It governs your mental agility and style of communication.

Collective Impact: Mercury reflects the collective mental patterns, shaping how societies exchange ideas, conduct business, and engage in education and politics. Its influence can also affect technological advances and media narratives.

Venus –

Keywords: Love, attraction, profit, harmony, relationships, art, pleasure

Transit Duration: Venus spends approximately 4 to 5 weeks in each sign.

Personal Representation: Venus embodies your aesthetic preferences and love language, dictating how you perceive beauty, connect in relationships, and experience pleasure.

Collective Impact: On a larger scale, Venus contributes to the collective romantic energy and sense of connection within societies, influencing cultural expressions through art and relationship dynamics.

Mars –

Keywords: Passion, courage, sex, desire, aggression, drive, competition, conflict

Transit Duration: Mars typically transits through each sign in about 6 to 7 weeks.

Personal Representation: Mars highlights your determination, sexual drive, and competitive spirit, pushing you toward action and personal assertion.

Collective Impact: As Mars influences collective focus and aggression, its movements can mirror societal conflicts and the collective will to achieve desired outcomes.

Jupiter –

Keywords: Luck, optimism, hope, vision, growth, wisdom, influence, prosperity

Transit Duration: Jupiter stays in a zodiac sign for approximately 12 to 13 months.

Personal Representation: Jupiter signifies areas of your life where you can experience growth and good fortune, as well as where you seek knowledge and wisdom.

Collective Impact: In society, Jupiter embodies collective hope and the aspiration for prosperity, guiding the zeitgeist towards optimism and expanded horizons.

Saturn –

Keywords: Karma, strength, perseverance, discipline, restriction, law, authority, life lessons, obstacles, tradition

Transit Duration Saturn moves through the zodiac roughly every 2 to 3 years.

Personal Representation: Saturn teaches responsibility and discipline, marking areas of your life where you may face challenges and learn life lessons.

Collective Impact: Saturn's influence affects global structures, governmental authority, and the collective understanding of karma and tradition.

Uranus –

Keywords: Change, freedom, rebellion, individuality, chaos, progressive ideas, humanitarianism, invention, astrology

Transit Duration: Uranus transits each sign for about 7 years.

Personal Representation: Uranus encourages you to express your uniqueness and embrace change, representing your drive for freedom and innovative ideas.

Collective Impact: Societally, Uranus signifies progress and humanitarian efforts, often heralding technological revolutions and shifts in social movements.

Neptune –

Keywords: Spirituality, fantasy, dreams, art, mysticism, illusion, deception, escapism

Transit Duration: Neptune typically moves through each sign in about 10 to 12 years.

Personal Representation: Neptune taps into your imagination and spirituality, shaping your dreams and artistic inclinations.

Collective Impact: Globally, Neptune guides artistic trends, influences spiritual beliefs, and highlights societal illusions or deceptions.

Pluto –

Keywords: Transformation, destruction, death, evolution, domination, power, regeneration, the subconscious

Transit Duration Pluto takes around 12 to 15 years to transit through a sign.

Personal Representation: Pluto represents the areas where you transform and experience profound changes, touching on the deepest aspects of your psyche.

Collective Impact: On a larger scale, Pluto governs global power dynamics, institutional changes, and the societal evolution surrounding issues of control and rebirth.

As with the Sun, all planets journey through each zodiac sign sequentially. Understanding the interplay between a planet and a sign enriches the interpretation of astrological influences, offering insights into personal and collective experiences.

Planetary Aspects

In astrology, each planet is believed to possess its own distinct personality, and these characteristics are influenced by their relationships with each other in the celestial sphere. The angles formed between the planets, known as aspects, can reveal a range of dynamics—neutral, harmonious, or tense. In the context of your birth chart, these aspects serve as a cosmic map, indicating various facets of your life where you may experience prosperity or face challenges.

Understanding the aspects within your birth chart can significantly illuminate the areas in which you may effortlessly find success or abundance. They help to identify not only where luck appears to favour you but also highlight the more complex experiences you may encounter. This level of awareness can empower you to take proactive steps toward aligning with your unique astrological blueprint. Ultimately, it fosters not just self-acceptance but opens avenues for personal healing and thriving in life.

Favourable Aspects

Favourable aspects draw attention to the positive, supportive energies emanating from the interacting planets. These aspects signify realms in your life where your endeavours are likely to flourish with minimal resistance. It's common for people to overlook these advantageous connections, sometimes leading to complacency. Nonetheless, it's crucial to maintain diligence in these areas to truly harness the potential blessings they offer. The key favourable aspects include:

Conjunction –

This aspect occurs when two planets are aligned within a degree range of approximately 8 degrees. Conjunctions usually indicate areas where your efforts may yield particularly fruitful outcomes as the energies of the two planets combine to enhance each other's influence.

Trine –

Formed when planets are roughly 120 degrees apart, with a flexibility of 8 degrees on either side, the trine is often heralded as the most auspicious aspect. The interaction between the planets in a trine fosters an effortless exchange of energies, typically manifesting as your greatest strength. This aspect can signal times when life seems to flow smoothly and achievements come with ease.

Sextile –

This aspect manifests when two planets are approximately 60 degrees apart, again allowing for an 8-degree margin. The sextile is considered an "easy" aspect, where opportunities may arise naturally, requiring little effort on your part. It's a favourable configuration that generally encourages progress and growth.

Semi-sextile –

Occurring when planets are about 30 degrees apart, this aspect also comes with a leeway of 8 degrees. While considered a more minor connection, the semi-sextile indicates areas where you are likely to shine. However, it's essential not to underestimate its potential, as it can provide opportunities for self-expression and talent development.

Unfavourable Aspects

Conversely, unfavourable aspects highlight the negative or challenging characteristics of the planetary relationship. These aspects often serve as catalysts for action; they motivate individuals to confront and overcome the difficulties presented by these cosmic tensions. The notable unfavourable aspects are:

Opposition –

This occurs when two planets are roughly 180 degrees apart, with an allowance of 8 degrees. An opposition represents a significant challenge, often manifesting in conflicts or obstacles that require considerable effort to navigate. This dynamic can bring about feelings of tension or struggle, demanding active engagement to work through the issues at hand.

Square –

Formed when two planets are positioned about 90 degrees apart, again with a leeway of 8 degrees, the square is notorious for creating friction within your life. This aspect tends to work against your best interests, often resulting in internal or external conflicts. Overcoming the negativity that arises from a square requires dedication and hard work, as it typically signals areas where you may need to exert substantial effort to find resolution or growth.

By understanding these aspects in your birth chart, you can better navigate the complexities of your life, recognizing where you have natural advantages and where your challenges lie. This knowledge equips you to make more informed choices and to fully engage with your unique astrological journey.

The Houses in Astrology

Astrology is structured around twelve houses, each symbolizing distinct areas of human experience and life. These houses provide a framework through which the traits of the planets and zodiac signs can manifest in our daily lives. While it may seem that the twelve houses align seamlessly with the twelve zodiac signs, they operate under different principles. The zodiac signs follow the apparent yearly journey of the Sun across the sky, while the houses reflect the Earth's rotation over a twenty-four-hour cycle. This distinction is crucial for a comprehensive understanding of astrological interpretation.

In a natal chart, planets and signs express their characteristics most vividly in the context of the houses they occupy. It is common for various houses in a chart to remain unoccupied by planets. Although these empty houses still hold significance and can be interpreted, they often play a less pivotal role in shaping the individual's life compared to those houses that contain one or more planetary influences.

1st House: Identity and Self

The first house is fundamentally about identity and the self—a cornerstone of astrological analysis. Alongside the Sun and Moon, the Ascendant (or Rising Sign) found at the cusp of the first house serves as a key component in understanding an individual's horoscope. The sign occupying this house provides insight into a person's core personality traits, instinctual responses, and how they choose to present themselves to the world around them. The planet that rules the Ascendant sign carries particular weight in interpretation, influencing the individual's disposition and behaviour significantly.

2nd House: Money and Possessions

The second house delves into material aspects of life, focusing on finances, possessions, and one's relationship with the physical world. It reveals how we manage our resources, our values regarding material wealth, and even our relationship with our own bodies. Insights gleaned from this house can inform us about our acquisitive instincts, spending habits, and overall attitudes toward ownership and wealth accumulation.

3rd House: Communication

In the third house, we explore communication styles and the social interactions that colour our everyday experiences. This house encompasses relationships with siblings, neighbours, and the environments that influence our daily lives. It sheds light on how we express ourselves verbally; the thought processes that guide our interactions, and how we forge connections within our immediate social circles. The dynamics of these relationships can greatly affect our learning capacities and communication effectiveness.

4th House: Home and Family

The fourth house represents the roots of our being—our family origins, home environment, and the emotional foundation laid during childhood. It encodes our feelings toward family dynamics, particularly our relationship with our parents, especially the father figure. This house unearths the influences of upbringing and domestic environments, shaping our attitudes towards home life, stability, and emotional security.

5th House: Pleasure and Creativity

Fostering self-expression, the fifth house is the domain of pleasure, romance, and artistic endeavors. It captures our approach to love affairs, creativity, hobbies, and interactions with children. This house highlights our innate desire for enjoyment and playfulness, revealing how we embrace life's pleasurable moments and the ways we engage in leisure activities that spark joy and foster self-discovery.

6th House: Work and Routine

The sixth house focuses on the practicalities of daily life, emphasizing work, health, and routines. It provides insights into our professional environment, job responsibilities, and how we manage day-to-day tasks. This house also reflects our attitudes toward health, personal hygiene, and responsibilities towards subordinates, offering a glimpse into our work ethics, productivity habits, and the potential for health-related issues that may arise over time.

7th House: Relating

The seventh house, linked to partnerships and relationships, provides a lens through which we assess our connections with others. It reveals how we choose partners, the qualities we look for in relationships, and the dynamics of our close associations. Often, we find ourselves drawn to individuals whose astrological profiles resonate strongly with the traits associated with the sign present in our seventh house, leading to involuntary attractions grounded in deeper astrological alignments.

8th House: Loss and Common Property

The eighth house addresses themes of shared resources, transformation, and dealing with loss. It examines how we navigate communal goods, financial ties, and issues surrounding material loss, such as debts or taxes. Additionally, this house is traditionally associated with deeper metaphysical concepts, including death, rebirth, and the unknown. In this context, understanding death—and the emotional and spiritual processing of loss—can yield profound insights into how we relate to both tangible and intangible aspects of life, ultimately reflecting the inevitable transitions we all face.

9th House – Philosophies and Far Countries

The ninth house is often seen as a gateway to our spiritual inclinations, core life philosophies, and overarching worldviews. Within this house, we explore our beliefs and ideals, and we may find that these are significantly shaped by our experiences and travels to distant lands. Journeys—both physical and metaphorical—can lead to profound shifts in perspective, nurturing a deeper understanding of cultural differences and universal truths. As we cultivate the attitudes and beliefs found within this house, we may notice their strong influence on our approach to the tenth house, which deals with our public life and career aspirations.

10th House – Occupation and Calling

The tenth household's tremendous significance as it outlines our professional choices and sense of purpose in life. It is not merely a reflection of our career but also a glimpse into how we wish to contribute to society and what legacy we desire to leave behind. The energies of the tenth house influence our personal development and sense of identity over the course of our lives. Historically, this house has been associated with the image of the mother and the nature of our relationship with her, suggesting that maternal influences may shape our ambitions and professional endeavours. Understanding this house can reveal how our familial roots and upbringing inform our career paths and public persona.

11th House – Friends and Acquaintances

The eleventh house provides insight into our connections with friends, mentors, benefactors, and those within our social circles who influence our lives positively. It reflects not only how we perceive our relationships but also how we function as friends, supporters, and learners in return. This house encompasses our social networks, our sense of belonging within a community, and our aspirations tied to collective goals and humanitarian issues. By examining the dynamics of the eleventh house, we can better understand our role in society and our capacity to connect with like-minded individuals who share our values and vision for the future.

12th House – Beyond the Personal

The twelfth house delves into the more profound and often elusive aspects of existence, where the individual self begins to merge with the larger universe. It symbolizes the realms where our personal identities might fade into something greater, encompassing experiences related to sacrifice, solitude, and spiritual exploration. Traditional astrology associates this house with places of confinement or retreat, such as hospitals, prisons, and psychiatric facilities, as well as spiritual havens like monasteries. The

Twelfth House encourages us to reflect on the ways we can transcend the ego and connect with a collective consciousness, emphasizing themes of compassion, surrender, and the inner workings of our psyche.

The transition from one astrological house to another may not always present a stark difference, as it does with the passage from one zodiac sign to another. Planets positioned near the end of a house may exhibit characteristics of the next house, leading to a blending of influences that requires careful interpretation.

The Horizon – Ascendant and Descendant

The axes of ascendant and descendant play a crucial role in our horoscopic framework by illustrating the duality of the self and its external relationships. This axis divides the horoscope into an 'upper' (dayside) and 'lower' (night-side) half, reflecting the local horizon at the time of one's birth. The point where the eastern horizon meets the ecliptic is known as the ascendant, marking the cusp of the first house—this is often regarded as the surface layer of an individual's personality and outward expression. In stark contrast, the descendant sits at the cusp of the seventh house, providing insights into how we relate to others in partnerships and significant relationships. Planets near the ascendant at birth are said to be rising or about to rise, suggesting a burgeoning presence, while those close to the descendant indicate a setting, pointing to connections that may have deeper implications.

The Meridian – A Vertical Division

The meridian serves as another important axis for house division, partitioning the horoscope into eastern (left side of the chart) and western (right side of the chart) halves. At the zenith of this axis, where it intersects the ecliptic, lies the Medium Coeli (MC) or midheaven, representing our aspirations, professional goals, and public image. Conversely, the Imum Coeli (IC) is located below the horizon, symbolizing our roots, home life, and internal emotional landscape. Planets positioned near the MC are at their highest elevation in the sky during birth, often reflecting ambitions and societal roles, while those at or near the IC suggest a foundation that grounds us in our personal lives and emotional well-being. Understanding the interplay of these points can illuminate the relationship between our inner self and outward aspirations.

By interpreting the houses in this intricately interconnected way, we can gain nuanced insights into the multiple dimensions of life that influence personal growth and relational dynamics.

Decans

In astrology, each zodiac sign covers a span of 30 degrees on the circular zodiac wheel. These signs can be further divided into three 10-degree segments called decans. Each decan offers a unique perspective on the traits associated with its corresponding zodiac sign, influenced by different ruling planets.

Aries:

- Decan 1 (0-9 degrees): Governed by Mars, the planet of action and drive, this decan embodies qualities such as being outspoken, aggressive, and impulsive. Individuals born under this decan are often recognized for their ambitious nature and passionate approach to life. Their natural leadership abilities stand out, driving them to take charge in various situations.

- Decan 2 (10–19 degrees): Under the influence of the Sun, this decan is characterized by attributes like sensuality and fluidity. Those born during this period are typically bold and confident, with an innate sense of optimism. Their restless spirit often propels them to seek out new experiences and challenges.

- Decan 3 (20-29 degrees): Ruled by Jupiter, the planet associated with expansion and luck, this decan produces individuals who are independent and freedom-loving. They often exhibit a strong desire for knowledge, embracing their role as lifelong learners. However, they can also be perceived as bossy, reflecting their assertive character.

Taurus:

- Decan 1 (0-9 degrees): Venus rules this decan, imbuing it with a love for beauty and aesthetics. Those born here tend to be sociable and charming, though they may lean towards materialism. Their outspoken nature often draws others to them, enhancing their social interactions.

- Decan 2 (10–19 degrees): Mercury's influence in this decan fosters a perfectionistic and detail-oriented mindset. Individuals often excel at communication and enjoy collaborating in group settings, making them excellent team players.

- Decan 3 (20-29 degrees): This decan is ruled by Saturn, whose attributes encourage practicality and determination. Those born in this segment are typically reliable and loyal, taking relationships seriously and demonstrating dedication to their loved ones.

Gemini:

- Decan 1 (0-9 degrees): With Mercury as the ruling planet, this decan brings out traits such as quick thinking and sociability. Individuals are often chatty and flexible, though they might sometimes appear scatterbrained due to their wide range of interests.

- Decan 2 (10–19 degrees): Influenced by Venus, this decan produces expressive and attention-seeking individuals. Their knowledge and opinions are often shared openly, reflecting their generous spirit. They are also driven by goals and eager to achieve what they set out to do.

- Decan 3 (20-29 degrees): Uranus rules this decan, encouraging an adventurous and optimistic outlook. Individuals are often seen as out-of-the-box thinkers with a humanitarian bent, making them conversational and engaging in social settings.

Cancer:

- Decan 1 (0-9 degrees): Ruled by the Moon, the first decan of Cancer is marked by emotional sensitivity and intuition. These individuals are adept at making decisions based on their feelings and often avoid conflict, preferring to nurture those around them.

- Decan 2 (10–19 degrees): This decan, ruled by Pluto, introduces practicality tempered with a hint of stubbornness. Those influenced by this decan are deep thinkers and often sentimental, thriving in caretaker roles where they can provide support and comfort.

- Decan 3 (20-29 degrees): Under Neptune's influence, this decan fosters creativity and imagination. These individuals are often daydreamers loyal in their relationships, but they may also be prone to forgetfulness.

Leo:

- Decan 1 (0-9 degrees): Linked to the Sun, individuals born in this decan are bright and playful, exuding charm and dignity. They possess a certain pridefulness and can be a bit egotistical, seeking recognition and admiration.

- Decan 2 (10–19 degrees): This decan is ruled by Jupiter, promoting a love for freedom and a rebellious streak. Leos born under this influence often have a romantic nature and a positive outlook, though they may appear scattered at times.

- Decan 3 (20-29 degrees): With Mars as the ruling planet, this decan highlights qualities such as daring and passion. Individuals here tend to be impulsive and stubborn, but they are also deeply kind and generous in spirit.

Virgo:

- Decan 1 (0-9 degrees): Governed by Mercury, this decan produces detail-oriented individuals who are practical and ambitious. They often have a strong drive for self-improvement, continually seeking ways to better themselves.

- Decan 2 (10–19 degrees): This decan is influenced by Saturn, leading to focused and determined personalities. While they may sometimes seem stand-offish, they tend to plan meticulously and can display a people-pleasing side, especially when seeking approval.

- Decan 3 (20-29 degrees): Ruled by Venus, this decan offers warmth and creativity. Individuals born in this segment are artistic and generous, though they may also exhibit shyness and timidity in social situations.

Libra:

- Decan 1 (0-9 degrees): Governed by the planet Venus, individuals born under this decan possess a deep appreciation for luxury and beauty. They often find themselves enchanted by love, showing a genuine affinity for romantic relationships.

- Decan 2 (10-19 degrees): Those born in this segment are influenced by Uranus, endowing them with a strong urge to challenge societal norms and push against the status quo. Their originality and unique perspectives set them apart as determined thinkers who thrive on innovation.

- Decan 3 (20-29 degrees): Under the influence of Mercury, these Librans are often seen as social butterflies, effortlessly navigating social situations and charming those around them. They possess a natural sense of fairness and balance, making them excellent mediators in conflicts.

Scorpio:

- Decan 1 (0-9 degrees): Pluto rules this decan, imbuing Scorpios born during this period with a profound sense of loyalty and dependability. They are often extremely committed to those they hold dear, making their relationships deeply meaningful.

- Decan 2 (10–19 degrees): Governed by Neptune, these Scorpios often embody a selfless demeanour, frequently putting the needs of others before their own. They can be dreamers, caught up in their fantasies, which sometimes makes them seem impatient and moody.

- Decan 3 (20-29 degrees): This segment is ruled by the Moon, lending these Scorpios a heightened intuition and sensitivity to the feelings around them. They are often popular and well-liked due to their dynamic personalities.

Sagittarius:

- Decan 1 (0-9 degrees): Under the expansive influence of Jupiter, these Sagittarians exhibit a sunny disposition characterized by optimism and enthusiasm for adventure. They value their independence and often resist commitment, embracing a lucky streak that seems to follow them.

- Decan 2 (10–19 degrees): Ruled by Mars, these individuals combine discipline and reliability into their adventurous nature. While they can be controlling, particularly in their pursuits, they also exude humour and are fiercely loyal friends.

- Decan 3 (20-29 degrees): Those born in this final decan, under the influence of the Sun, exude a charismatic charm that draws others to them. They are hopeless romantics, always seeking the thrill of new experiences and the excitement of meeting new people.

Capricorn:

- Decan 1 (0-9 degrees): Dominated by Saturn, these Capricorns embody bravery and distinction. They carry an air of glamour while simultaneously being grounded, though they may come off as a bit old-fashioned.

- Decan 2 (10–19 degrees): Blessed by Venus, these individuals are characterized by their friendliness and agreeable nature. They radiate energy and enthusiasm in social settings, coupled with a tender-hearted approach to relationships.

- Decan 3 (20-29 degrees): Ruled by Mercury, these Capricorns are known for their inquisitive minds and thoughtfulness. They maintain an air of mystery, drawing people in with their poised demeanour.

Aquarius:

- Decan 1 (0-9 degrees): Under the radical influence of Uranus, individuals born during this decan are known for their defiance and unwavering individuality. They thrive on innovation and originality, often expressing their eccentricities in unique and witty ways, which sets them apart from conventional standards.

- Decan 2 (10–19 degrees): Governed by Mercury, these Aquarians are sociable and chatty, frequently engaging with a diverse range of people. Their versatility helps them navigate various social situations, though they may sometimes feel restless or dual-sided in their pursuits, constantly seeking new experiences and connections.

- Decan 3 (20-29 degrees): Under the loving influence of Venus, these individuals embody a romantic and affectionate nature. They seek autonomy in their relationships, valuing their independence while also making sound judgments based on their experiences. Their lively spirit shines through, making them magnetic in both personal and social realms.

Pisces:

- Decan 1 (0-9 degrees): Ruled by Neptune, those born under this decan are inherently kind and courteous, often exhibiting creativity and imagination in their endeavours. Their friendly nature draws people in, and they tend to prioritize their relationships, showcasing a deep devotion to loved ones.

- Decan 2 (10–19 degrees): Influenced by the Moon, these Pisceans often possess an independent spirit, though it may come across as unique or even a bit spacey. They are genuine in their interactions and carry a graceful demeanour, often preferring solitude to recharge and reflect on their thoughts and emotions.

- Decan 3 (20-29 degrees): This decan is influenced by Pluto, endowing these Pisceans with persistence and a deep sense of empathy. They are known to be good listeners, often able to pick up on the emotions of those around them.

Auras & Chakras

<u>**Aura.**</u>

Understanding Auras

Auras are intricate layers of energy emanating from individuals, closely linked to their chakras. Each layer of the aura reflects various aspects of a person's being, including their physical health, emotional state, and spiritual well-being. These layers are dynamic, expanding and contracting in response to the individual's vibrations and emotional condition. For instance, someone who is feeling positive and vibrant may project a larger, more vibrant aura, while stress or negativity can lead to a more subdued or constricted energy field.

Aura Encounters

Many people have intuitively sensed auras at various points in their lives, often without realizing it. This ability is particularly pronounced in young children. When children draw others, they frequently use colours that do not correspond to the typical human skin tones. This phenomenon occurs because children are often more attuned to the energy surrounding individuals, allowing them to perceive the emotional or spiritual qualities represented by different colours in a person's aura. However, as they grow and receive feedback like "humans aren't purple," their natural psychic abilities may dull, and they often lose this innate sensitivity. Reawakening the ability to sense auras may require conscious practice and a willingness to reconnect with those early perceptions.

Learning to Sense Auras

To begin your journey in interpreting auras, cultivate an awareness of your emotional reactions when you are close to others. This practice is referred to as clairsentience. Find a quiet space, take a deep breath, and focus on your exhalation while tuning into your five senses and intuitive feelings. Ask yourself reflective questions: Are you feeling a sense of anxiety? Do you experience sudden anger? Or do you feel drawn towards this person? Strive to avoid overthinking past interactions and, instead, concentrate on the colour that resonates with your impression of their overall demeanour. With time and practice, your ability to sense auras will develop and strengthen.

Palm Chakra Stimulating Exercise

Here's a practical exercise to stimulate your palm chakras, enhancing your ability to feel energy:

1. Rub your hands together vigorously for about 30 seconds to generate heat and energy.

2. Pull your hands apart about 2 inches, maintaining awareness of the energy between them.

3. Repeat the rubbing motion and pull your hands apart again, preserving that 2-inch distance.

4. On the third attempt, reduce the distance to 1 inch and close your eyes.

Pay close attention to any sensations you feel emanating from your palms. You might experience tingling, warmth, or a magnetic pull – these sensations can help you connect with and recognize the energy flow.

How to See Auras

Seeing auras can initially appear challenging, but it is a skill that can be mastered with practice. The key technique involves relaxing your gaze, allowing your eyes to drift out of focus. While it seems counterintuitive, achieving a soft visual state requires effort and consistency. This technique not only aids in aura visualization but is also beneficial if you wish to explore other divination methods, such as scrying or crystal ball gazing.

Training the Eye

1. Choose an appropriate setting: Select a room with soft, dim lighting that isn't too bright or completely dark.

2. Use a plain backdrop: Position yourself in front of a solid white or light-coloured wall, avoiding any distracting patterns or colours.

3. Extend your hand: Hold your hand at arm's length against the background, spreading your fingers apart.

4. Adjust your focus: Look at your hand, but do not concentrate on the fingers. Instead, direct your attention to the space between them. After a minute or two, you may start to notice a subtle haze surrounding your fingers.

5. Avoid focusing: If you find yourself zooming in on the haze, gently redirect your attention— starting over may be necessary. With continued practice, the haze may eventually morph into distinct colours, revealing your aura.

How to Practice on Another Person

Once you feel confident in perceiving an aura around your own hand, it's time to practice on someone else. This part can be particularly enjoyable. Choose a volunteer, or if none is available, you can always practice in front of a mirror. It's crucial to maintain consistent conditions: low light and a plain background are essential for clear perception.

1. Prepare your subject: Have your volunteer stand against a plain, preferably white wall, to ensure a clear background.

2. Focus your attention: Look just above one of their shoulders at a fixed point on the wall, staying near but not directly on the shoulder. This technique helps maintain a relaxed gaze while you perceive the aura.

3. Practice regularly: With enough repetition, you'll enhance your ability to quickly read auras, often within 20-30 seconds. Additionally, consider practicing with animals or pets—observing their auras, especially when they are calm or sleeping, can provide insight and enhance your skill.

Through consistent practice and a willingness to explore this intuitive connection, you will become adept at sensing and seeing auras, unlocking a deeper understanding of the energies surrounding yourself and others.

Why Auras Need to Be Cleansed

Developing the ability to see and sense auras is a profound journey, and an essential part of this process is understanding when your aura requires cleansing. An aura is closely tied to the alignment of your chakras; when these energy centres become unbalanced or misaligned, it can lead to a variety of negative experiences. Individuals often report feeling "off," experiencing a sense of general negativity, and some even indicate that they've felt physically ill when their auras are clouded or dirty. Regular cleansing of the aura not only helps to restore physical harmony but also aids in bringing your body, mind, and spirit into alignment. This state of alignment is crucial for any divination practices you may engage in, whether that involves reading auras, tarot, crystals, or other spiritual methods.

How Often Do You Need to Align Your Chakras?

After practicing the visualization technique for chakra cleansing—note that it may take several attempts to achieve the desired effect—you should experience a marked sense of relaxation and alignment. This newfound calmness is beneficial not just for your day-to-day life but also enhances your divination techniques and other spiritual practices. When your chakras are properly aligned, energy can flow freely through your system, attracting positivity and harmony into your life.

Just as one cannot expect the body to remain clean forever after a single bath or shower, the same applies to your chakras and aura. They require consistent care and attention. As a basic guideline, it is advisable to practice this cleansing technique a few times a month. Ideally, once a week would be perfect, and performing the cleansing even more frequently can yield tremendous benefits.

Visualization Technique to Cleanse Your Aura

1. Focus on Your Root Chakra: Begin by centring your attention on your root chakra, which is located at the base of your spine. This chakra serves as your grounding mechanism and is associated with the colour red.

2. Visualize Red Light: Imagine a vibrant red light radiating from your root chakra, anchoring you firmly to the Earth. Picture this light extending down into the ground, creating a strong connection with the energy of the Earth.

3. Envision a Golden Shower of Light: Next, envision a brilliant golden shower of beams of light cascading down from the sun, penetrating your body and aura. Allow yourself to feel this golden light envelop you for at least two minutes, imagining it nurturing and invigorating your entire being.

4. Picture a Protective Violet Light: Finally, visualize a violet light enveloping you from the soles of your feet to the crown of your head, acting as a protective blanket. See this violet light healing any gaps or holes in your aura and trust that it is actively restoring your energy field to its optimal state.

The 7 Layers of Auras:

1. Ethric Layer

Traits: Vibrates closely to the body.

Information: Reflects physical health and vitality.

Colour: Displays shades of blue.

Reach: Extends approximately 1.25 to 2 inches from the body.

Reading: Attuning to this layer helps in sensing pain or pleasure.

2. Emotional Layer

Traits: Becomes muddied in the presence of negative emotions.

Information: Represents emotions and feelings.

Colour: Exhibits a bright combination of rainbow colours.

Reach: Spans 1 to 3 inches from the physical body.

Reading: Issues in this layer can negatively impact the first three layers of the aura.

3. Mental Layer

Traits: Connected to the solar plexus chakra, influencing mental clarity.

Information: Encodes ideas, thoughts, and mental processes.

Colour: Characterized by bright yellow hues.

Reach: Extends from 3 to 8 inches.

Reading: Misalignment in colour may indicate potential mental issues.

4. Astral Layer

Traits: Linked to the heart chakra, serving as a bridge to the spiritual plane.

Information: Facilitates the connection between physical and astral experiences.

Colour: Displays vibrant rainbow colours.

Reach: Covers 8 to 12 inches from the body.

Reading: A healthy spiritual state is indicated by vibrant colours; muted colours may signal issues.

5. Ethric Template

Traits: Connected to the throat chakra, functioning as the blueprint of the physical body.

Information: Creates a template for physical existence.

Colour: Appears like a photographic negative.

Reach: Extends 1 to 2 feet.

Reading: Creates areas of negative space that may affect one's energy.

6. Celestial Layer

Traits: Associated with unconditional love and harmony.

Information: Functions as a gateway to the spirit realm.

Colour: Exhibits shimmering pastel shades.

Reach: Expands from 24 to 36 inches away from the body.

Reading: Communication with the spirit realm occurs within this layer.

7. Ketheric (Spiritual) Template

Traits: This layer surrounds all other layers of the aura.

Information: Stores the universal experiences of the soul.

Colour: Features various shades of gold.

Reach: Extends up to 3 feet outward.

Reading: Vibrates at the highest frequency, reflecting the entirety of the events that the soul has traversed.

By understanding these layers and regularly cleansing your aura, you can greatly enhance your spiritual practices and overall well-being.

Aura Colour Meanings

Auras are energy fields that surround all living beings, reflecting their emotional and spiritual states. The colours within an aura can indicate various aspects of a person's personality, mental state, and health. Below is a detailed breakdown of the common colours found in auras, categorized by their positive and negative aspects:

Red:

- Positive Light: Represents deep love, dynamic energy, immense power, unwavering strength, passionate feelings, and robust health. Red is often associated with vitality and courage, inspiring motivation and action.

- Negative Light: Can indicate feelings of anger, potential danger, or a warning sign. It may reflect a volatile temperament or aggressive tendencies when overly present.

Blue:

- Positive Light: Symbolizes tranquillity, a sense of security, deep loyalty, trustworthiness, and intelligence. Blue is calming and encourages clear communication and self-expression.

- Negative Light: May signify coldness, fear, or an overly masculine aura. It can also indicate emotional detachment or isolation.

Brown:

- Positive Light: Reflects friendliness, a strong connection to nature, a grounding presence, and conservative values. Brown is often associated with stability and reliability.

- Negative Light: Can indicate dogmatism, suggesting a rigid mindset that may resist new ideas or perspectives.

Green:

- Positive Light: Represents growth, prosperity, success, fertility, and freshness. Green is the colour of nature and renewal, often symbolizing balance and harmony.

- Negative Light: Indicates jealousy, envy, or feelings of guilt. An excessive presence of green may suggest overattachment to material wealth or competition.

Pink:

- Positive Light: Signifies happiness, femininity, compassion, sweetness, and a playful spirit. Pink embodies warmth and nurturing qualities.

- Negative Light: May convey weakness or immaturity, reflecting a longing for validation or insecurity in relationships.

Purple:

- Positive Light: Symbolizes royalty, ambition, luxury, spirituality, and nobility. Purple is associated with higher consciousness and creativity.

- Negative Light: Can indicate mystery or moodiness, suggesting emotional ups and downs or indecisiveness.

Yellow:

- Positive Light: Represents brightness, energy, sunshine, creativity, intellect, and happiness. Yellow encourages optimism and mental clarity.

- Negative Light: May reflect instability or irresponsibility, indicating a tendency towards overenthusiasm without follow-through.

Orange:

- Positive Light: Symbolizes courage, confidence, friendliness, and success. Orange is vibrant and invigorating, encouraging social interaction and enthusiasm.

- Negative Light: Might reflect ignorance or sluggishness, indicating a lack of motivation or awareness.

Turquoise:

- Positive Light: Associated with spiritual healing, protection, and sophistication. Turquoise encourages emotional balance and communication.

- Negative Light: May signify envy, jealousy, or aggression when not well integrated within the aura.

Silver:

- Positive Light: Represents glamour, grace, and sleekness. Silver is connected to intuition and adaptability.

Negative Light: Can indicate feelings of worry, anxiety, or grouchiness, reflecting uncertainty or emotional struggles.

Gold**:**

- Positive Light: Symbolizes wealth, prosperity, and intrinsic value. Gold is seen as a positive force, promoting abundance and success.

- Negative Light: May convey egotism, self-centeredness, or problems related to finances, reflecting an unhealthy attachment to material possessions.

White**:**

- Positive Light: Represents innocence, purity, goodness, and a clean slate. White encapsulates clarity and freshness.

- Negative Light: May suggest dullness, boredom, or a lack of enthusiasm, indicating a need for more engagement and vitality.

Black**:**

- Positive Light: Symbolizes dramatic flair, elegance, formality, and class. Black can convey sophistication and depth.

- Negative Light: Might represent themes of death, evil, or mystery. An overwhelming presence of blacks may suggest unresolved fears or negativity.

Aura Focus Trainer

To enhance your awareness of auras, this practice circle assists in focusing your energy. Begin by concentrating on the centre of the image. Allow your eyes to relax while picturing the spirals in front of you. Visualize two spirals merging into three, and then observe as they condense into one. Maintain your focus on this singular spiral for as long as possible to deepen your connection to your own aura.

Auras and chakras are interconnected systems that play significant roles in our overall well-being. The chakras are energy centres in the body that correspond to various emotional and physical states of health. If either your chakras or aura falls into imbalance, it may lead to a myriad of health issues, affecting you both physically and emotionally. Recognizing blockages or holes within these energy fields is essential for healing. By fostering awareness of your aura and chakras, you can explore and implement practices to restore balance, ultimately promoting better health and emotional stability.

Chakras

The term "chakra" is derived from the Sanskrit word meaning "wheel" or "disk." In the context of human energy systems, it refers to the seven primary energy centres located throughout the body, each of which plays a vital role in maintaining our overall health and well-being. These chakras are aligned along the spine, beginning at the crown of the head and extending to the base of the spine, creating a pathway for energy flow.

Each of the seven chakras is associated with specific physical, emotional, and spiritual functions, making them integral to various aspects of our health. The chakras are:

Root Chakra

The Root Chakra, also known as Muladhara, is situated at the base of the spine and serves as the foundational energy centre of the body. This chakra is essential for establishing a sense of security, stability, and grounding in reality. When it is balanced and well-aligned, individuals may experience profound feelings of calmness and a strong connection to their physical existence. Confidence and courage blossom, empowering one to venture into new experiences and face challenges with ease. The Root Chakra is believed to govern vital physiological systems, including the adrenal glands, kidneys, spine, and the entire nervous system, which collectively support survival. Furthermore, it enhances qualities such as vitality, patience, stability, and material success, making it particularly crucial while pursuing significant life goals. The colour associated with the Root Chakra is a vibrant red, and it can be represented by the gemstone Red Jasper, known for its grounding properties.

Sacral Chakra

Located between the pubic bone and the navel, the Sacral Chakra, or Svadhisthana, is a vital centre for creative and sexual energy. This chakra influences one's artistic pursuits, imaginative capacities, and ability to embrace change in various aspects of life. A well-balanced Sacral Chakra fosters not only physical vitality and strength but also ignites creativity, passion, and endurance. It opens pathways to new ideas and enhances sexual vitality, making it a crucial element in both artistic expression and intimate relationships. The colour associated with the Sacral Chakra is a warm orange, and it can be represented by Carnelian, a stone that enhances creativity and emotion.

Solar Plexus Chakra

The Solar Plexus Chakra, or Manipura, is positioned between the navel and the base of the rib cage. It is often referred to as the "personal power" chakra and is crucial for self-esteem, autonomy, and determination. When this chakra is functioning optimally, individuals experience a clear sense of direction and understand what is necessary for success. This clarity fosters independence and the belief that personal goals are within reach. The Solar Plexus Chakra is believed to shape one's identity and personality, enhancing qualities like humour, confidence, authority, and warmth. Its associated colour is bright yellow, and it can be represented by Citrine, a stone known for its uplifting and empowering properties.

Heart Chakra

The Heart Chakra, or Anahata, is located in the center of the chest and is intricately linked to love, compassion, and emotional balance. This energy center serves as a bridge between the mind, body, and spirit, promoting empathy and emotional openness. A balanced Heart Chakra allows individuals to engage fully with their emotions while maintaining cognitive awareness, leading to deep inner peace. It governs crucial physiological functions, including the thymus gland, heart health, blood pressure, circulation, and overall immune function. This chakra embodies our emotional center and is vital for qualities such as understanding, sharing, and forgiveness. The Heart Chakra is associated with the colours green or pink and can be represented by stones like Aventurine or Rose Quartz, both known for their properties of love and healing.

Throat Chakra

Situated in the throat area, the Throat Chakra, or Vishuddha, governs self-expression and communication. It plays a crucial role in how authentically individuals convey their thoughts and feelings to the world, influencing emotional honesty and ownership of personal needs. When aligned effectively, the Throat Chakra enables clear and honest expression, allowing one to articulate thoughts and emotions appropriately. This chakra also serves as a vital link between the self and the surrounding environment, emphasizing the importance of sound and communication. The associated colour is a soft light blue, and it can be represented by Calcite, a stone known for promoting clarity in communication.

Third Eye Chakra

The Third Eye Chakra, or Ajna, is located just above the eyebrows in the center of the forehead and is a powerful source of intuition and insight. This chakra encourages a deeper alignment with the Universe, enhancing one's ability to perceive the bigger picture of life. When the Third Eye Chakra is open, individuals are attuned to intuitive messages and signs, trusting their gut feelings while actively pursuing their life goals. This openness can lead to successful manifestation experiences and a greater understanding of one's purpose. The Third Eye Chakra is believed to influence the pituitary gland, which regulates other glands within the endocrine system, as well as sensory organs such as the nose and ears. It promotes vision, intuition, psychic abilities, and self-knowledge. The associated colour is deep blue, represented by Sodalite, known for enhancing intuition and insight.

Crown Chakra

The Crown Chakra, or Sahasrara, is situated at the top of the head and represents the pinnacle of spiritual connectivity. Often referred to as the "thousand-petaled lotus," this chakra serves as the gateway to higher consciousness and spiritual insight. A well-balanced Crown Chakra fosters a profound sense of joy and beauty in the world, creating a life filled with purpose and richness. Although working with the Crown Chakra can be subtle and complex, its alignment is essential for creating a fulfilling existence. This chakra governs the pineal gland and is associated with positive thought patterns, inspiration, and boundless imagination. The colour linked to the Crown Chakra is a deep purple, often represented by Amethyst, a stone that aids in spiritual growth and enlightenment.

Imbalances or blockages in any of these chakras can lead to physical ailments, emotional distress, and psychological challenges. For instance, a blocked heart chakra may manifest as difficulty in forming connections with others, while an unbalanced root chakra could lead to feelings of insecurity or anxiety.

To promote healing and maintain optimal health, various meditation techniques specifically designed for chakra alignment are often utilized. These practices aim to open the chakras, allowing energy to flow freely through each center.

When beginning the process of balancing and aligning your chakras, it's essential to start with the base chakra, also known as the root chakra, located at the base of your spine. This chakra serves as your foundation and connects you to the earth. Gradually make your way up through each of the seven chakras, culminating at the crown chakra, which is located at the top of your head and represents your connection to higher consciousness.

To enhance your practice, consider placing an anchor stone between your feet at the end of the alignment process. This can help ground your energy and stabilize your connection to the earth. A highly recommended grounding stone is Hematite, known for its ability to absorb negative energy and promote a sense of calm and stability.

If you don't have the specific crystals that correspond to each chakra, clear quartz is an excellent alternative. Often referred to as the universal crystal, clear quartz contains all the colours of the light spectrum, making it a powerful tool for amplifying energy and intention. It can effectively assist in balancing and harmonizing your chakras while providing clarity and focus during your meditative practice.

Tuning into the sensations and locations of your chakras can enhance your ability to recognize areas of blockages. As you become more attuned to your body's energy, you can develop insights into any issues that may be arising. This heightened awareness allows you to address emotional wounds or past traumas, facilitating a deeper healing process.

Ultimately, maintaining clear and aligned chakras is essential for achieving holistic health. By nurturing these energy centers, you pave the way for a balanced life filled with vitality, peace, and harmony. Through consistent practice and self-awareness, the journey toward chakra healing can lead to profound transformations in both body and mind.

Candle Magic

The Basics of Candle Magic

Candle magic is an ancient practice that involves channeling unseen energies from the universe into tangible thought forms, with the goal of bringing about change in the physical realm. This mystical art combines various elements: fire, air, water, and earth, along with a careful selection of colours, oils, and herbs, all harmoniously working together to create effective spells. Among these elements, fire holds a particularly significant role as it serves as the transformative force essential for manifesting the desires and changes one wishes to see after performing a spell.

At its core, candle magic is about casting spells. Understanding the different meanings associated with candle colours is crucial, as it helps the practitioner choose the appropriate colour that aligns with the desired intention. For instance, a red candle could be employed to enhance romantic passions in a love spell, while a yellow candle might be more suitable for attracting new job opportunities. The unique properties of fire not only facilitate transformation but also amplify and release the energy bound within coloured candles as they burn.

To practice candle magic effectively, it is vital to articulate your intentions clearly and with sincerity. Select a candle colour that resonates with your desired outcome and vocalize your wish aloud. Enhancing your ritual with herbs, oils, or gemstones can create a more balanced and harmonious atmosphere, but it is essential to thoroughly understand the meanings associated with different candle colours to optimize your spellcasting experience.

When considering directional associations with colours, the following correlations should guide your selection:

- North corresponds to Brown.

- East corresponds to Yellow.

- South corresponds to Red.

- West corresponds to Blue.

Furthermore, for elemental associations, the colours align as follows:

- Earth is represented by Green.

- Air is represented by Yellow.

- Fire is represented by Red.

- Water is represented by Blue.

- Spirit is represented by White.

Different candles serve distinct purposes in magical practices. For example, any candle used for spell work should be brand new, completely unworn, and designed to burn for a short period. Here are some suggestions for suitable candle types:

-   Chime Candles: These are ideal for spell work as they are small, coloured, and burn evenly, making them perfect for focused rituals.

-   Tea Light Candles: Small, white, and encased in their own tins, tea lights are excellent for setting intentions due to their simplicity and ease of use.

-   Pillar Candles: If your ritual requires a longer burn time, consider using tall pillar candles in glass jars that can be relit multiple times, allowing for extended rituals.

-   Beeswax Candles: While they may come at a higher price point, beeswax candles are believed to enhance certain earth and air-based spells, providing a natural, powerful option.

Now, let's delve into the specific meanings behind various candle colours and their magical uses:

Colour	Quality	Magical Use
Red	Passion, Courage, Strength & Intense Emotions	Love, Energy, Health & Willpower
Orange	Energy, Attraction, Vitality & Stimulation	Adaptability To Sudden Change, Power & Encouragement
Yellow	Intellect, Inspiration, Imagination & Knowledge	Communication, Confidence, Divination & Study
Green	Abundance, Growth, Wealth, Renewal & Balance	Prosperity, Employment, Fertility, Health & Good Luck
Blue	Peace, Truth, Wisdom, Patience & Protection	Healing, Understanding, Psychic Ability, Home & Harmony
Indigo	Emotion, Fluidity, Insight & Expressiveness	Meditation, Clarity of Purpose & Self Mastery
Violet	Spirituality, Wisdom, Devotion, Peace & Idealism	Divination, Nurturing Quality Enhancement, & Balancing Senses
White	Innocence, Peace, Purity & Illumination	Cleansing, Clarity, Spiritual Growth & Establishing Order
Black	Dignity, Force, Stability & Protection	Banishing, Releasing Negative Energy & Transformation
Silver	Wisdom, Psychic Ability, Intelligence & Memory	Spiritual & Psychic Development, Meditation & Warding Negativity
Gold	Inner Strength, Self Realization & Intuition	Success, Health, Ambition, Finances, Good Fortune & Divination

Brown	Endurance, Solidarity, Grounding & Strength	Balance, Concentration, Material Gain, Companion Animals & Home
Grey	Stability, Contemplation, Neutrality & Reserve	Complex Decisions, Binding Negative Influences & Reaching Compromise
Pink	Affection, Friendship, Companionship & Spiritual Healing	Romance, Spiritual Awakening, Partnership & Children's Magic

By understanding the foundational principles of candle magic and the significance of candle colours, you can harness this potent practice to manifest your intentions and enhance your personal growth journey.

Preparing_a_Candle_for_Your_Spell

Preparing a candle properly is crucial for ensuring that your spell is conducted with intention and purity. Begin by selecting a candle that has never been used for any other purpose, as this will help to ensure that the energy associated with the candle is fresh and aligned with your intention.

Step 1 - Cleansing the Candle

To cleanse the candle, there are several effective methods you can choose from depending on your preference and the tools you have on hand, such as:

- Purifying Smoke: Pass the candle through the smoke of burning sage, sweetgrass, or other purifying herbs. As you do this, focus on the smoke enveloping the candle and visualize it removing any negative or lingering energies.

- Earth Element: Bury the candle in salt or dirt for a specified period, allowing the earth to absorb any residual energies. Salt is particularly known for its cleansing properties, so consider using it for its vibrational benefits.

- Moonlight: If you have time, place the candle outside or near a window to bathe in the light of the moon, especially during the full moon, to charge it with lunar energy. This natural cleansing method is ideal for those who connect deeply with lunar cycles.

- Visualization: Should you prefer a more meditative approach, hold the candle in your hands and visualize a white light surrounding it. Imagine this light purifying the candle and filling it with your intentions.

Step 2 - Modifying the Candle

Once cleansed, evaluate if you wish to modify the candle to further enhance its capabilities. This could involve carving symbols or sigils that resonate with your desired outcome writing specific words, initials, or phrases directly onto the candle. Use a sharp object like a knife or a pen; ensure your markings are clear and intentional, as they add an extra layer of energy to your spell.

Step 3 - Anointing the Candle

Anointing the candle with oil is a vital step, as oils carry their own vibrational properties and can enhance the energy of your spell. Choose an oil that aligns with your intention. Options could include:

- Jojoba oil

- Olive oil

- Essential oils (like lavender for peace or cinnamon for attraction)

- Specially prepared oils you may have

Application of Oil:

- For spells that attract positivity, success, or abundance towards you, rub the oil starting from the bottom of the candle and moving upwards toward the wick. For tea light or jar candles, apply the oil in a clockwise direction.

- For spells that aim to release negativity or send energy away, rub the oil from the top of the candle down toward the base, thereby drawing energy away from you. Similarly, for tea light or jar candles, anoint the oil counterclockwise.

Step 4 - Adding Herbs and Spices

If your spell calls for specific herbs or spices, this is the appropriate time to incorporate them. You can either dab them onto the candle directly or roll the candle in a mix of herbs. Don't worry if some herbs fall off; as long as they have made contact with the candle, their energy is present.

Step 5 - Safety Precautions

With your candle now prepared, remember to always burn it on a fire-safe surface, such as a heat-resistant plate or holder. Ensure the area is well-ventilated to avoid inhaling excessive smoke. Never leave a burning candle unattended, as safety is paramount during any spell work.

By following these steps with care and intention, you will create a candle imbued with your energy, ready to assist you in manifesting your desires.

Candle Flame Meanings

Once you have completed the preparations for your spell and successfully cast your circle, you can begin the transformative practice of candle magic. The behaviour of the candle's flame serves as a powerful indicator of how your spell is progressing and the energy surrounding it. Here's a detailed interpretation of various candle flame types:

Clean Burn

A candle that burns quickly and evenly is often seen as a positive omen. In this scenario, the absence of smoke, dripping, movement, or noise suggests that your spell is on track, indicating a smooth and uncomplicated manifestation of your intentions. This steady and uneventful burning usually means that the energies align well with your desired outcome, leading to results that should manifest as you expect.

Strong Flame –

When you observe a tall, bright flame dancing higher than usual, take this as a sign of robust energy behind your spell work. A strong flame not only symbolizes a potent charge but also suggests that the universe is in harmony with your desires. This intensity often predicts rapid and favourable results, so stay focused and allow the energy to flourish.

Small & Steady Flame –

A small but consistently steady flame conveys that while there is less energy fuelling your spell, it does not mean you should lose hope. This stability implies that a positive outcome is still within reach, albeit perhaps on a delayed timeline. Patience and persistence are key here—maintain your focus on your intention and continue to visualize your goal, even as you wait for the results to unfold.

Puny Flame –

If you notice a weak and flickering flame that appears small and feeble, this can be a cause for concern. This lack of vigour often suggests that something is amiss; it might indicate an unfavourable timing for your spell or that your desired outcome may not be in alignment with your highest good. Should the flame start faltering or even become smothered by wax, it can signal that your request is unlikely to be granted at this moment. Take time to reevaluate your intentions and consider adjustments.

Dancing Flame –

A flame that dances erratically or moves wildly often represents high energy levels but also signifies chaos. A large, vibrant flame suggests success is within reach, while a smaller flame may indicate that you're facing strong opposing forces or obstacles that could be hindering your progress. If you find the flame is leaping about, remain adaptable and open to change while continuing to direct your energy toward your goals.

Flickering Flame –

A candle that dims and brightens repeatedly—like a switch being flipped—can hint at the presence of spiritual entities or energies surrounding your ritual. If you're engaged in devotional work targeting higher spirit guides, deities, or angels, this flickering can be an encouraging sign of their acknowledgment and support. Use the trance-like state induced by the flickering flame to gaze into the fire and glean additional insight into your situation.

Popping Flame –

A candle that emits popping or sputtering sounds is indicative of interference from external forces or can signal communication with spirits. This uneven burn pattern suggests that there may be obstacles working against your intended outcome, which requires you to concentrate even more intently. Additionally, any hissing, sputtering, or whistling can be interpreted as messages from spirits or ancestors, urging you to be receptive and attentive to their guidance.

Candle Will Not Extinguish –

When a candle defiantly remains lit despite your efforts to extinguish it, it often signifies that there are unresolved matters linked to your spell work. This stubborn flame may indicate that you have overlooked an important step in your ritual or missed a vital message. Consider this a gentle nudge from a guiding spirit, urging you to revisit your intentions and the work you have done thus far. Take a moment to reflect on what you might have forgotten or bypassed and embrace the opportunity to delve deeper into your spiritual practice.

Candle Will Not Light –

If you find that your candle refuses to catch fire, it could signal that the outcome of your spell is not aligned with your highest good or that the results have already been predetermined by unseen forces. This can be a moment for introspection; take the time to reevaluate your desires and intentions. Focus your energy inward, and consider employing a divination technique, such as tarot or runes, to uncover any blockages hindering your manifestation. Engaging in meditation or a spiritual cleansing can also help reset your focus and clear any negative energy before attempting to relight the candle.

Candle Goes Out –

When a flame unexpectedly snuffs out, it typically signifies that the energetic work is complete or that a more potent opposing force has intervened to halt your progress. This moment calls for grounding; acknowledge the end of your ritual by opening the circle and returning to a state of balance. Often, this extinguishing of the flame indicates that your spell is unlikely to manifest or that the objective you were pursuing has already been achieved, whether consciously or unconsciously.

Lots Of Smoke –

A candle that produces a significant amount of smoke is neither inherently good nor bad; rather, it suggests that the air element is strongly present in your magical workings. Air symbolizes observation, communication, and intellect. If you notice an unusual or excessive amount of smoke, take the time to analyse the situation further. Pay attention to the colour, shape, timing, and movement of the smoke, as these elements can provide insights into the energy surrounding your spell. This heightened awareness will help you interpret the messages being conveyed.

White Smoke –

A puff of white smoke emitted from the candle is a signal of benevolent forces at play, often indicating the presence of protective spirits and blessings. If you experience a sudden release of white smoke at a crucial moment in your ritual, consider it a powerful affirmation that your wish is aligned to be fulfilled. This ethereal presence enhances the positive energy of your spell and suggests that good fortune is on its way.

Black Smoke –

If the candle produces thick, dark clouds of smoke, it serves as a cautionary signal, often indicative of negative energy, conflict, or unforeseen bad luck. This phenomenon usually points to the existence of opposing forces actively working against your spell. In response to this unsettling sign, it's wise to engage in a reflective meditation or a cleansing ritual to dispel the negativity before attempting your magic again. Purging any lingering bad energy will create a more favourable environment for your intentions.

Candle Smoke Moves Towards You –

Smoke that moves towards you can be a highly encouraging omen, symbolizing that you are on the right path to attracting your desires. This is especially favourable for spells aimed at drawing love, wealth, or healing into your life, as it suggests that your intentions are being met with success and will manifest quickly. However, if the spell you are working on involves negative intentions, this can warn you that you may become entangled in the consequences of your actions.

Candle Smoke Moves Away from You –

When the smoke from your candle floats away, it often indicates an outward dispersal of energy, which is generally a less favourable sign. This direction suggests that something vital may be slipping from your grasp or drifting away from your influence. However, if your spell aims to heal, influence, or manipulate others positively, this movement can still represent a successful outcome. Observing the speed, direction, and patterns of the smoke can provide additional clues regarding the effectiveness of your spell.

Blue Flame –

A blue flame is a noteworthy phenomenon, often recognized as a sign of spiritual presence and protection. This unique colour is associated with angelic energies and fairy fire, indicating that spiritual beings are attentive to your ritual and the energies at play. If you notice your candle flame shifting to a blue or bluish-white hue, consider this a sign that divine entities are supporting your magical endeavours. While red or yellow flames still hold power, a blue flame particularly emphasizes a connection to the spiritual realm and reinforces the validity of your intentions.

Candle Crater –

When a candle burns down and forms a crater in the center, particularly common with pillar or container candles, it indicates potential issues with your spell. A crater suggests that your will may not be strong enough to cast an effective spell at this moment, or there might be external energies or blockages that are hindering your spell from reaching its intended target. This is not an ideal sign and may require you to reassess your focus and intention before attempting spell work again.

Quick Burn –

A candle that burns too fast often creates a hole in the side, causing wax to melt away rapidly. This behaviour typically indicates a passionate, accelerated spell process. When witnessing this phenomenon, take time to examine the remaining wax remnants thoughtfully. Look for shapes or figures that may provide insights or messages relevant to your intention. The quick burn might reflect intense energy moving through the spell, but it is essential to stay grounded to harness that energy appropriately.

No Wax Drips –

A candle that burns cleanly without dripping wax suggests a well-executed spell. This result denotes that your intentions are aligned and that the spell is likely to manifest as you planned. The absence of drips indicates clarity and focus on your magical work, suggesting a smooth path forward in achieving your desired outcome.

Candle Is Dripping Wax –

When a candle is dripping wax, it signifies an imbalance either within your emotional or mental state. Drips on the left side of the candle may indicate psychic or emotional disturbances that could hinder your success. Conversely, drips on the right side suggest that your thoughts or beliefs may be working against your intentions. This state of imbalance indicates that the outcome may be incomplete, urging you to address any underlying issues before continuing with your spell work.

Candle Debris & Crud –

Finding debris or unwanted residue in the wax after burning reveals underlying complications. This debris signifies unintended consequences resulting from your spell, indicating specific challenges that may arise once the spell is completed. It could manifest as guilt, heartache, or minor inconveniences. While these issues are not dire, they require attention and may necessitate additional work to restore balance after the spell's conclusion. Be prepared to navigate through these aftereffects as you move forward.

Candle Soot –

The presence of black soot on the jar or container of the candle can be a concerning sign of negative energy or interference during the spell. If soot appears primarily at the top of the jar, it suggests that this negative energy has been overcome but should still not be overlooked. If the soot covers the entire surface of the jar, it signals that your spell may not be fully effective and may need to be repeated to achieve the desired result. Pay attention to this residue, as it can reveal important insights about the energy surrounding your spellcasting efforts.

By paying close attention to these flame behaviours, you can gain deeper insight into the dynamics of your spellcasting and the energies at play, guiding your actions and intentions more effectively.

Crystals

Charging & Cleansing Crystals

The enchanting power of crystals is widely recognized in various spiritual practices, including among witches and healers. Each crystal possesses unique properties and energy frequencies, making them valuable allies in spells, healing, and meditation work. Before utilizing a crystal, it is crucial to cleanse and charge it to remove any lingering negative energies and to maximize its potential effectiveness.

When to Charge or Cleanse Your Crystals:

- -Weak or Unbalanced Energy: If a crystal feels depleted or lackluster, it's time for a cleansing session.

- Negative Events: If the crystal was involved in a negative situation, it should be cleansed to release those energies.

- Post-Ritual Use: After being used in a ritual or spell, a crystal retains energies that may need to be cleared.

- Connection Difficulties: If you're struggling to connect with a crystal, refreshing its energy can help reestablish your bond.

- New Crystals: Newly acquired crystals should always be cleansed and charged to clear any residual energies from prior handling.

- Long Periods of Inactivity: Crystals not used for an extended time can absorb stagnant energy, necessitating a cleanse.

Methods to Cleanse and Charge Your Crystals:

- Sunlight/Moonlight: Place the crystal outside or on a windowsill to absorb the rejuvenating light of the sun or moon. Be mindful; some crystals can fade in direct sunlight.

- Water: Running water or a water bath can effectively cleanse crystals. For stronger purification, add salt to the water. However, ensure your crystal is not water-sensitive before attempting this method.

- Candle Flames/Incense: Passing a crystal through the flame of a candle or the smoke of burning incense can clear negative energies. It's often helpful to meditate on the crystal while doing this.

- Earth: Bury the crystal in the earth for 24 hours to connect it back to nature and allow it to absorb grounding energies.

- Selenite: This crystal is unique; it does not require cleansing itself and can be used to cleanse other crystals due to its high vibrational frequency and purifying properties.

Understanding Crystal Shapes

The shape of a crystal can significantly influence how it is utilized in your practice, with each shape holding specific meanings and purposes.

Tumbled Stones:

These are the most commonly found crystals. Their smooth, rounded surfaces allow them to radiate energy gently from all directions. They are perfect for carrying in your pocket or incorporating into crystal grids due to their versatility.

Crystal Pyramids:

Crystals shaped like pyramids are excellent for anchoring and directing energetic flow. They are particularly helpful for setting intentions, working with the chakras, and for placement in the home to enhance energy balance.

Crystal Spheres (or Balls):

Used typically for scrying and divination purposes, spheres radiate energy uniformly in all directions. Their shape can also help slow down harmful or imbalanced energies.

Heart-Shaped Crystals:

As their name suggests, these stones are ideal for working with the heart chakra and love-related practices. They assist in attracting new love and healing emotional scars.

Crystal Points:

These are designed to focus energy from their termination point. They amplify energy and intentions, making them excellent tools for altar work or directing energy during rituals.

Raw Crystals:

Uncut and in their natural state, raw crystals often possess a potent, raw energy that can be overwhelming. Approach these with intention, as their unpredictable energies can be powerful.

Double Terminated Crystals:

Crystals with points on both ends are particularly effective for energy work, healing practices, astral projection, dream work, and meditation, as they can move energy through both ends.

Cluster Crystals:

These formations are beneficial for charging other crystals and enhancing the harmony of the surrounding space. They amplify the energy of stones displayed nearby.

Crystal Eggs:

Symbolizing new beginnings and transformation, egg-shaped crystals are ideal for meditation and serve as centers for protection spells or crystal grids.

Crystal Infused Water

Crystal-infused water, also known as gem water, is created by letting water absorb the vibrational frequency of a selected crystal. This infused water is often charged under moonlight or sunlight and is believed to offer various health benefits. There are multiple applications for crystal-infused water, including applying a few drops to pulse points, using drops under the tongue, adding to bathwater, or enhancing your drinking water.

To make your own crystal-infused water, you will need:

- A small bowl

- A cleansed crystal of your choice (be mindful of the crystal's properties when selecting)

- Purified water

- A dark glass or spray bottle for storage

- Labels for organization

Steps:

1. Choose Your Light Source:

   Depending on whether you choose to use sun or moonlight, appropriate charging times differ—sunlight infusions typically need at least 3 hours, while moonlight charges are ideal during a new or full moon.

2. Charge the Crystal:

   Place the crystal in the bowl and completely cover it with the mineral or spring water. Position the bowl where it can absorb sunlight or moonlight for the designated time—until sunrise for moonlight or for three hours for sunlight.

3. Bottling the Water:

   Once charged, decant the infused water into your chosen dark glass bottle. If desired, you can place the actual crystal used in the jar to enhance potency.

4. Label Your Infusion:

   Clearly label your water, noting its intention, the date it was created, the specific crystal used, and whether it was charged in moonlight or sunlight. This practice not only helps keep your creations organized but also allows for reflection on the specific energies and intentions tied to each infusion.

By taking the time to cleanse, charge, and understand your crystals, you'll be able to harness their full potential in your spiritual and healing practices.

Crystal Directory

Agate –

Agate is a stone of strength and courage; it tones and strengthens the mind & body, grounding and stabilising emotions and physical energy. Agate helps with the acceptance of oneself and the ability to see the truth. Its healing and cleansing qualities eliminate negative energy, soothing and calming the mind, body & spirit. Agate occurs naturally in many colours but is also often dyed in brilliant, bright colours.

Healing: Tones and strengthens the body, heals emotional tension-related diseases, stimulates the digestive system, and heals skin disorders.

Chakras: Third Eye & Crown

Amethyst –

Amethyst is a stone of intuition, spirituality, calming, and contentment. It bestows stability, strength, and inner peace. It is a great stone for meditation and enhancing your intuition and psychic abilities with its calming and peaceful energy. Amethyst provides clarity and enhances conscious perception and understanding. Do not Cleanse/Charge with sunlight.

Healing: Assists in calming the mind, reduces insomnia and allows restful sleep, reduces stress, eases headaches, helps with hormone production, strengthens the immune system, cleanses organs and the respiratory system, and reduces bruising and swelling. Assists in the function of the pineal and pituitary glands.

Chakras: Third Eye & Crown

Ametrine –

Ametrine is the combination of both Amethyst and Citrine, which creates a stone of optimism. Its high energy balances out stress, tension, and emotional blockages to help harmonise and heal the body, creating a feeling of well-being. Ametrine connects the physical realm with the higher consciousness, facilitating protection during physic experiences. It can also aid meditation, allowing greater focus.

Healing: A powerful cleanser, useful in treating and getting to the bottom of long-standing illnesses, helps with depression, fatigue, headaches, and stress-related illnesses.

Chakras: Solar Plexus, Third Eye & Crown

Amazonite –

Amazonite is known for its harmonising energies. It is a stone of balance, hope, and communication, aiding in both inner and outer harmony. It encourages you to speak your truth with compassion and clarity, fostering healthy relationships and open dialogue. It connects you to your heart's desires and promotes a sense of peace and emotional well-being, allowing you to flow with the rhythm of life like a gentle river.

Healing: Amazonite is believed to assist in alleviating stress and anxiety, helping to calm the mind and soothe the spirit. It is also associated with enhancing communication and self-expression, making it a valuable tool for effective and heartfelt communication.

Chakras: Heart & Throat

Angelite –

Angelite is the stone of great awareness. It helps with clear, compassionate, and truthful communication, allowing you to speak your truth. Angelite promotes feelings of compassion, understanding & acceptance, allowing you to find peace in the matter at hand. It also helps facilitate contact with the angelic realm while helping you maintain contact with everyday reality. Do not Cleanse/Charge with water.

Healing: Supports bone density & health, helping with arthritis and fractures.

Chakras: Throat

Apophyllite –

Apophyllite is a stone of truth. It creates a conscious connection between the physical and spiritual realms, allowing you to access the Akashic Records and past life experiences. It helps you recognise and act upon the truth in all situations. Apophyllite is mentally and spiritually calming and grounding. It can be used to open the third eye and bring light and energy into the heart.

Healing: Helps release suppressed emotions, is used in Reiki healing, allows for deep relaxation, helps overcome anxiety, worry, and fear, and aids in treating respiratory problems like asthma.

Chakras: Heart and Third Eye

Aragonite –

Aragonite is a stone of patience, acceptance, and the ability to take on more responsibility; it strengthens reliability and practicality. Aragonite is an earth healer and grounding stone attuned to Gaia. It transforms empathic stress and clears blockages, deepening your connection to the earth.

Healing: Warms the extremities and aids with nerve and muscle spasms and twitches; it helps heal the bones and discs.

Chakras: Base & Earth Chakra

Aquamarine –

Aquamarine purifies the body and enhances clarity of mind with its gentle and compassionate energy. It helps bring closure to unresolved situations. It is especially good for sensitive people, promoting self-courage and elevating fears and phobias. Aquamarine is an excellent stone for meditation, calming, and balancing the physical, emotional, and mental aspects.

Healing: Calms the nerves and reduces fluid retention; is good for sore throats. It strengthens the kidneys, liver, spleen, and the pituitary & thyroid glands.

Chakras: All (aligning), especially the Throat

Blue Lace Agate –

Blue Lace Agate gently opens and expands the consciousness, stimulating intuitive and spiritual insight and encouraging creativity and confident expression. It aids communication and purification, promotes harmony with others, calms the mind, soothes emotions, and reduces stress. Blue Lace Agate gives us patience, peace, wisdom, kindness, and honesty. It enhances a positive attitude, aligns one's center, and encourages listening and understanding. Blue Lace Agate is nurturing and supporting, bringing a deep inner peace.

Healing: A powerful healing stone, particularly for the throat, good for fluid retention and blockages of the nervous system, releases neck and shoulder tension, lowers fevers, and treats arthritic and bone conditions.

Chakras: Throat & Heart

Blue Quartz –

Blue Quartz purifies the mental, emotional, and physical bodies. It helps calm the mind, allows expression of the individual's will, and assists in reaching out to others. It stimulates intuitive insight and enhances communication and creative expression.

Healing: Reduces stress and negative thoughts, heals the throat, and purifies the blood.

Chakra: Throat & Third Eye

Clear Calcite –

Calcite is a strong stone used to help amplify and cleanse the energy around you. It will ground you and bring joy and light-heartedness into your life. It helps to balance emotions, boosts memory, calms the mind, alleviates stress, enhances trust in oneself, and strengthens the ability to overcome setbacks by connecting emotions with the intellect. Calcite helps overcome laziness, increasing and stimulating your energy. It is a spiritual stone that is linked to the higher consciousness, aiding spiritual development. Do not Cleanse/Charge with Water.

Healing: Strengthens the teeth, bones, and joints; helps the organs to eliminate toxins; aids skin conditions blood clotting; heals tissue; opens and clears the eyes; fortifies the immune system; elevates fear and reduces stress.

Chakra: All Chakras

Calcite (Golden) –

Golden Calcite is a stone of joy and light-heartedness. Golden Calcite is excellent for meditation and attuning your mind to the higher planes, and it induces a deeper sense of relaxation. Do not Cleanse/Charge with water.

Healing: Enhances digestion and metabolism, strengthens the teeth, bones, and joints, helps the organs eliminate toxins, and heals connective tissue and skin.

Chakra: Sacral, Solar Plexus & Crown

Carnelian –

Carnelian enhances and vitalises the physical, emotional, and mental bodies. Its warm, inviting, and joyous energy attunes to the inner self, helping to open the heart. It helps restore vitality and increase one's motivation to get up and go. It is great for stimulating creativity. Carnelian is full of life force and gives us courage and vigour to make the right life choices. It helps anchor you in the present reality, aiding concentration and willpower, allowing you to trust yourself and your perceptions.

Healing: Improves the quality of the blood and stimulates the metabolism, circulation, and blood flow. Aids tissue regeneration, helping the kidneys, lungs, liver, gall bladder, and pancreas. Helps to overcome abuse.

Chakras: Sacral, Solar Plexus & Heart

Celestite –

Celestite has a gentle, positive, and uplifting energy, bringing harmonious balance and alignment into your life, revealing the truth, and helping to resolve conflict. Its gentle, open energy enhances feelings of inner peace, opening up your heart and allowing you to see things that reason can never know. Celestite is an ideal crystal to place in your bedroom or healing room as an environment cleanser and a source of soft, positive energy. It helps you to access the angelic realm and urges you towards spiritual development and enlightenment.

Healing: Dissolves pain and helps with the elimination of toxins from the body, releasing chronic tension and reducing hardening in bones, tissue, and organs. It aids in helping with disorders of the eyes and ears and can help with fainting.

Chakras: Throat & Crown

Chevron Amethyst –

Chevron Amethyst is a unique blend of Amethyst and White Quartz, creating a crystal that harmonises the energies of both. It is renowned for its ability to balance the physical, mental, and spiritual aspects of your life. This crystal stimulates spiritual growth and enhances your connection with higher realms, making it a valuable tool for those on a spiritual journey. Chevron Amethyst is a potent ally for those seeking balance, clarity, and spiritual enlightenment. Its energy can help you align your thoughts and actions with your higher self, leading to a more harmonious and spiritually awakened life.

Healing: Chevron Amethyst is thought to aid in overcoming addictive behaviours and finding inner peace. It also supports mental clarity and can be used for meditation to deepen your insights and intuitions.

Chakras: Third Eye & Crown

Citrine –

Citrine is an energising stone that provides happiness, courage, hope, and warmth. It is said to hold the energy of the sun, enhancing our self-esteem, self-expression, and creativity. Citrine is a powerful cleansing and revitalising stone that invigorates and awakens the mind, body, and soul. It attracts abundance and prosperity into our lives. Do not Cleanse/Charge with sunlight.

Healing: Helps the digestive organs and the heart, reduces infection, aids tissue regeneration circulation, and detoxifies the physical, emotional & mental bodies. It is also helpful for menstrual and menopausal symptoms, balancing hormones, and alleviating fatigue.

Chakras: Solar Plexus & Crown

Clear Quartz –

Clear Quartz is known as a powerful and universal healing stone. It works on all areas of the mind and body, awakening, amplifying, and transmitting energy, and clarifying thought processes. It is an excellent stone for meditation, directing energies with more intensity. It connects to the higher self, removes negativity, and allows access to your spirit guides. Clear Quartz provides clarity in thinking and awareness. Improving your memory and providing clarity of mind.

Healing: Clear Quartz is known as the Master Healer, a powerful healing stone that can be used across the whole body on its own or to amplify the energy of other crystals. It stimulates and balances the energy of the whole body, boosting the immune system. It is also excellent for soothing and healing burns, balancing emotions, and activating the pineal and pituitary glands.

Chakras: All Chakra

Desert Rose –

The Desert Rose symbolises all things that are possible, they are said to be carved by the spirits of the American Indians. They enhance love and teamwork; they tell you to go for your dreams without restraint and help to dissolve self-imposed restrictions and programs holding you back. Desert Roses can be used to strengthen affirmation of purpose in your life.

Healing: Aligns the spinal column and promotes flexibility, aids teeth and bones, soothes the nerves, and helps with conditions like epilepsy.

Chakra: Crown

Epidote –

This is a stone that can encourage recovery and regeneration after a severe illness. Epidote helps to lift the emotions and also helps to dissolve sadness, sorrow, self-pity, and grief.

Fire Agate –

Fire Agate is the stone of courage, protection, and strength, enhancing vigour and positive thinking. It has a deep connection to the earth bringing safety and security with its calming energy. Fire Agate promotes initiative, commitment, and understanding. It helps alleviate fears and reflect harm away. It helps to eliminate cravings, addictions, and destructive desires.

Healing: Helps overcome addiction, aids in problems of the stomach and intestines as well as chronic inflammation, and circulatory and nervous disorders, helps with night vision.

Chakra: Sacral & Solar Plexus

Fluorite –

Fluorite promotes focus, intuition, and understanding. It helps to bring chaos into order, promoting stability, free-thinking, and clear unbiased reasoning. Fluorite is excellent for the advancement of the mind, aiding in meditation and inter-dimensional communication. It is a highly protective stone, especially on a psychic level and from outside influences. Fluorite draws away negative energy and stress, cleansing and purifying the body. Do not Cleanse/Charge with sunlight.

Healing: Strengthens teeth and bones, aiding the spine and arthritic conditions, protects against common illnesses such as colds and flu, treats highly infectious diseases, and helps with emotional trauma.

Chakras: Third Eye.

Green Aventurine –

Aventurine promotes a positive, easy-going attitude towards life, balances male and female energies, and brings joy, happiness, and emotional tranquillity. It aligns one's centers, and purifies the physical, mental, and emotional bodies, promoting health and wellbeing. Aventurine promotes compassion and empathy, calming our anger. It stimulates our minds, creativity, motivation, and independence. It protects us against electromagnetic energy and environmental pollution. It is also a stone of prosperity. Do not Cleanse/Charge with sunlight.

Healing: Stimulates healing of the muscles and bones, relieves headaches and migraines, helps blood pressure and cholesterol, aids in releasing fear, anxiety, and stress, aids in sleep disorders, and helps protect against heart conditions and inflammation.

Chakras: Heart

Green Jade –

Jade is a powerful emotional balancer, nurturing and bringing peace and purity into your life, removing negative thoughts and energy. It radiates the divine, promoting unconditional love, serenity, clarity of mind, courage, and wisdom. Jade is believed to be a stone of luck, prosperity, and friendship. It can enhance your dreams, allowing you to awaken hidden knowledge and become who you really are. It is a protective stone that keeps you from harm.

Healing: Strengthens the heart, kidneys, and immune system, it cleanses and filters toxins from the organs and blood, heals stitches, assists fertility and childbirth, helps relieve menstrual and menopausal symptoms, and promotes longevity.

Chakras: Heart

Golden Healer Quartz –

Golden Healer Quartz is characterised by its translucent, golden/yellow hues. This crystal is highly regarded for its ability to facilitate deep healing on multiple levels, the physical, emotional, and spiritual. Often associated with divine wisdom and universal consciousness, it can be a valuable tool for spiritual growth and transformation. Golden Healer Quartz radiates a powerful energy that can help you release old patterns and blockages, allowing you to embrace your full potential.

Healing: Golden Healer Quartz is believed to support physical healing by amplifying the body's natural healing processes. It is also thought to assist in emotional healing, promoting self-acceptance, and enhancing spiritual growth and awareness.

Chakras: All Chakras, primarily Solar Plexus and Crown

Hematite –

Hematite is a grounding and protective stone that energises and vitalises the physical body. It promotes optimism, determination, courage, self-esteem, and willpower, helping you to magnetise what you truly want and to strive for improvement. Hematite harmonises the mind, body, and spirit, helping to dissolve negativity.

Healing: Aids circulatory problems, increases iron in the blood and the flow of oxygen through the body, stimulates the glands, activates the spleen, liver, and gall bladder, increases resistance to stress, and eases leg cramps.

Chakras: Base

Himalayan Green Quartz –

Himalayan Green Quartz is a stunning crystal found in the high elevations of the Himalayan mountains. It is known for its translucent green colour and its connection to the energies of the Earth and higher realms. This crystal combines the purifying properties of Clear Quartz with the heart-healing energies of green minerals, creating a harmonious blend of energies. Himalayan Green Quartz encourages you to open your heart to love and spiritual growth. It helps you release emotional wounds and past traumas while connecting you to the healing energies of nature and the higher self. This crystal invites you to find inner peace, balance, and a deeper sense of connection with the Earth and the divine.

Healing: Himalayan Green Quartz is believed to purify and cleanse the heart chakra, promoting emotional healing, love, and compassion. It can also assist in physical healing by supporting the immune system and detoxifying the body.

Chakras: Heart and Crown

Jasper –

Jasper represents the earth and is a grounding stone that promotes stability and balance in life. It balances the vibrations and emotional energies of the body and is very nurturing. It helps to bring balance between assertiveness and sensitivity, bringing tranquillity and wholeness into your life, sustaining and supporting you in times of stress.

Healing: Supports the circulatory and digestive systems and the sexual organs.

Chakras: Base, Sacral & Solar Plexus

Labradorite –

Labradorite is a highly mystical and protective stone, it works on all areas of the mind and body increasing energy and clarifying thought processes. It is known as the bringer of light and is excellent for meditation, directing energies with more intensity allowing you to connect to your high self and seek out your spiritual purpose. Helps clear and protect your aura. Labradorite stimulates intuition, raising consciousness and connecting to the universal energy. It is a stone of transformation, reflection, and showing true intentions. Do not Cleanse/Charge with water.

Healing: Balances hormones, lowers blood pressure, and helps with disorders of the eyes and brain. Helps treat colds.

Chakras: Heart, Third Eye & Crown

Lapis Lazuli –

Lapis Lazuli is a mesmerising blue gemstone that has been cherished for centuries for its deep colour and spiritual significance. It is often associated with wisdom, truth, and inner vision. Lapis Lazuli is a stone of deep insight and self-awareness, inviting you to explore the depths of your consciousness and connect with your higher self. Lapis Lazuli's energy empowers you to speak your truth with clarity and authenticity. It enhances your intuition and mental clarity, making it an excellent tool for meditation and spiritual growth. This crystal encourages you to seek inner wisdom, release limiting beliefs, and align with your true purpose, ultimately leading to greater self-awareness and a deeper connection with universal truths.

Healing: Lapis Lazuli is believed to support physical healing by alleviating pain and inflammation. It is also thought to promote emotional healing by encouraging self-expression, self-acceptance, and emotional balance.

Chakras: Heart, Third Eye & Crown

Lemurian Seeded Crystal –

Lemurian Seeded crystals are said to have been used in the ancient culture of Lemuria, holding ancient knowledge and wisdom from the past and bringing it into the present to awaken our spirit. Lemurians hold a blessing of unconditional love as the earth enters into a new vibration, they show us how to move beyond boundaries and learn about ourselves from the past, reawakening the spirit and giving us self-belief so that we can reach our full potential. They are excellent healers, used for balancing and clearing the chakras.

Healing: Assist in removing the diseased or worn out, opening new energy channels in the subtle and physical bodies.

Chakras: All Chakras

Moonstone –

Moonstone is highly aligned to the female energy of the universe and the energy of the moon and its cycles. It is known as the stone of new beginnings and with its new beginnings it brings insight and intuition. Moonstone is uplifting and calming, it enhances psychic ability and calms reactions, aiding in self-analysis.

Healing: Moonstone is a powerful calmer of emotions, helping to balance the emotions and to relieve anxiety and stress. It is also particularly helpful with female problems, digestion, elimination, and reproductive organs.

Chakras: Sacral & Heart

Moss Agate –

Agate is a stone of strength and courage; it tones and strengthens the mind & body, grounding and stabilizing emotions and physical energy. Agate helps with the acceptance of oneself and to see the truth. Its healing and cleansing qualities eliminate negative energy, soothing and calming the mind, body & spirit. With its deep earthy energy, Moss Agate is strongly connected to nature and Mother Earth.

Healing: Tones and strengthens the body, heals emotional tension-related diseases, stimulates the digestive system, and heals skin disorders.

Chakras: Heart

Nuummite –

Nuummite is known as the Sorcerer's Stone, drawing upon the fiery energies of the Earth's core offering us the gift of inner power, facilitating our journey deep into the psyche, and enhancing clairvoyance. It is a stone of personal magic enhancing one's good luck and can be used as a powerful mediation stone. Nuummite is also a very strong protective stone, warding off negative energies. It reinforces the courage needed to be healed and whole. It aids in releasing energies trapped in the subconscious connected to fear, trauma, and guilt.

Healing: Helps with stress and anxiety, and channels healing energy for oneself and for others. It also helps with degenerative diseases.

Chakras: All Chakra

Peridot –

Peridot is a stone of compassion. It has a friendly energy and is excellent for healing. It assists in rebirth and renewal of all kinds. Peridot also brings abundance and prosperity. It enhances the healing and harmony of relationships of all kinds, but particularly marriage.

Healing: Peridot can lessen stress, especially in relationships, anger, and jealousy, and heal ulcers and digestive problems. It has been said to make a shield of protection around the body of the wearer.

Chakras: Heart

Petrified Wood –

Petrified Wood promotes inner harmony helping you to see the good and positive side of life. It helps relieve worries and provides a sense of well-being, composure, and calm allowing you to accept and external influences and use them to meet your own goals in life.

Healing: Helps with the circulatory system aiding with arthritis, rheumatism, and blood clots, strengthens the back, muscle tissue, and alignment of the skeletal system, calms the nerves and helps appetite.

Chakras: Base, Sacral &Solar Plexus

Pyrite –

Pyrite is known as a stone of protection; it wards off negative energy and physical danger as well as stimulating the intellect. Pyrite helps to nourish the mind and body, promoting good health. It enhances the emotional body strengthening the will and helps create a positive outlook on life.

Healing: Relieves anxiety and frustration. Aids digestion and improves circulation and oxygenation of the blood, enhances brain function.

Chakras: Base, Solar Plexus & Heart

Rainbow Obsidian –

Rainbow Obsidian is a captivating variety of Obsidian known for its distinctive sheen and iridescent rainbow colours that shimmer across its dark surface when polished. This crystal is often associated with protection, emotional healing, and the integration of light and shadow aspects of the self. Rainbow Obsidian's energy is gentle yet profound, aiding in the release of emotional wounds and providing a shield against negativity. This crystal encourages inner harmony and balance, allowing you to move forward with greater emotional clarity and a renewed sense of protection and self-awareness.

Healing: Rainbow Obsidian is believed to support emotional healing by assisting in the release of past traumas and negative emotions. It can also promote physical healing by alleviating tension and stress-related ailments.

Chakras: Root & Sacral

Red Aventurine –

Red Aventurine enhances creativity and the ability to see possibilities, bringing prosperity and lessening negativity. It also enhances the perceptive abilities of the senses. Do not Cleanse/Charge with sunlight.

Healing: Red Aventurine enhances blood flow and circulation helping to heal nerves and the reproductive system and can help fight disease.

Chakras: Sacral & Base

Red Jasper –

Red Jasper represents the earth and is a grounding stone that promotes stability and balance in life. It warms and enlivens the will and enhances courageous and dynamic energy that sustains and supports in times of stress. Red Jasper brings feelings of peace and tranquillity, gently stimulating your energy, helping you to face your problems, taking away your worries, and calming your emotions. Its grounding energy brings a sense of fulfillment and wholeness.

Healing: Stimulates blood flow, the circulatory and digestive systems, as well as the sexual organs of the body.

Chakras: Base

Red Phantom Quartz –

Red Phantom Quartz is a powerful Earth healer like all other phantom crystals. They stimulate the earth to repair itself by recalling what it was like before the damage was done, allowing for healing to be total and complete. It is also good for enhancing creativity and providing inspiration, stimulating intuition and intellect.

Healing: Red Phantom Quartz is a powerful earth healer providing a strong grounding connection to the earth through the lower chakras.

Chakras: Heart

Red Quartz –

Red Quartz, also known as Fire Quartz, is a variety of Quartz crystal that derives its red colour from inclusions of iron oxide or hematite. This crystal is associated with passion, vitality, and heightened energy. Red Quartz's energy is fiery and invigorating, making it a valuable tool for boosting motivation and enhancing life force. Red Quartz inspires you to take action and pursue your goals with determination and enthusiasm. It stimulates creativity and passion, making it an excellent choice for those seeking to reignite their zest for life. This crystal reminds you of the importance of staying grounded and connected to the present moment while channeling your energy toward achieving your dreams and desires.

Healing: Red Quartz is believed to support physical healing by increasing vitality, stamina, and circulation. It can also aid in emotional healing by boosting your courage and self-confidence.

Chakras: Root & Sacral

Rhodonite –

Rhodonite is the stone of emotional balance, stimulating and promoting the energy of self-love and acceptance. It activates and opens the heart allowing you to see both sides of a situation. It helps provide emotional support in times of destructive self-loathing behaviour, promoting feelings of love and forgiveness often helping heal old wounds.

Healing: Rhodonite helps heal emotional shock and pain and strengthens the heart. It is also used to aid in fertility issues and diseases that cause inflammation.

Chakras: Heart

Rose Quartz –

Rose Quartz promotes unconditional love, forgiveness, peace, and compassion. It creates harmony in relationships and teaches us about the true essence of love. It purifies and opens up the heart allowing us to express our emotions. It reduces stress and tension, allowing us to express love, sensitivity, and compassion towards ourselves and others. Rose Quartz brings deep inner healing, enhancing self-love, self-trust, self-worth, and self-confidence. It can be used to attract love into your life and maintain happy loving relationships. Do not Cleanse/Charge with sunlight.

Healing: Aids in the healing and strengthening of the heart and circulatory system. It promotes the healing of respiratory problems, releasing impurities from the body. It is also used to increase fertility.

Chakras: Heart

Selenite –

Selenite enhances clarity of the mind and concentration, expanding one's awareness of the self and of one's surroundings and having a positive effect on the brain. It soothes the nerves and enhances willpower.

Septartian –

Septartian is a grey clay called bentonite clay made up of yellow calcite and red/brown aragonite formations. It enhances communication abilities. A very good healing stone for yourself or others. Uplifting, it helps you to understand yourself spiritually.

Shungite –

Shungite is a hard black, amorphous, coal-like material composed of more than 98% carbon. Regarded as a "wonder stone" It transforms and absorbs negative energies and aids in psychic protection.

Healing: Clears negative energies and dysfunctional patterns

Chakras: All

Shiva Lingam –

Shiva Lingams are only found in India and are said to represent the Hindu God Shiva. They serve to activate the movement of the sacred energy, which is slumbering in all of us, raising and controlling the kundalini. A symbol of sexuality, they unify the male and female world into a harmonious balance.

Healing: Stimulates the electrical flow of the body's systems and subtle meridians, useful for infertility, and menstrual cramps.

Chakras: Base & Sacral

Smokey Quartz –

Smokey Quartz dissipates blocked energy & negativity, providing a mildly sedative effect, and helping you to relax. It is an excellent stone for meditation as it assists in grounding, centering, and enhancing awareness, dream recollection, and channeling abilities. Do not Cleanse/Charge with sunlight.

Healing: Smokey Quartz can be used to help alleviate depression and clear blocked negative energy on all levels.

Chakras: Base

Sodalite –

Sodalite is the stone of self-truth and insight. It stimulates your intuition and observation abilities allowing you to uncover the truth, whilst making it possible to remain true to yourself and stand up for what you believe in. Sodalite brings emotional balance and can be helpful in times of stress or panic. It helps to release the fears that hold us back from being who we truly are, promoting self-trust and self-acceptance.

Healing: Sodalite helps balance the metabolism and cleanses the lymphatic system, reducing inflammation and boosting immunity. It can also help clear electromagnetic energy and pollution.

Chakras: Throat & Third Eye

Spirit Quartz –

Spirit Quartz is also known as Fairy Quartz or Cactus Quartz and has a highly spiritual and magical energy. Its uplifting, high-vibration energy makes it excellent for meditation and psychic awareness, enhancing harmony and peace. Within its magical energy, Spirit Quartz carries with it the gift of universal love and rebirth, opening, aligning, and purifying the entire chakra system, perfectly balancing the male and female energies.

Healing: Facilitates multi-dimensional spiritual healing, it is also a good stone for overcoming grief or death.

Chakras: All Chakras, through opening the Crown.

Tibetan Quartz –

Tibetan Quartz are found in the Himalayas of Tibet, one of the most sacred places on earth, they are regarded as being amongst the most powerful stones of spiritual protection ever found. Carrying or wearing one of these crystals creates a bubble of light around the body allowing only positive energy to penetrate your aura. Tibetan Quartz purifies and cleanses negative influences its energy can activate and balance the chakras and meridian system.

Healing: Helps to heal the nervous system and the brain, it removes negative energy patterns and bathes the body in light for spiritual growth and repair, it also protects against negative electromagnetic energies.

Chakras: All Chakras

Tiger Eye –

Tiger Eye brings confidence, strength, courage, protection, and good luck. It sharpens the senses, promotes intuition, and helps one to be practical, centered, and grounded. It enhances personal power, and allows clarity, good judgment, clear perception, and insight, aiding in good decision-making. Tiger Eye can be used to stimulate wealth and maintain it.

Healing: Balances emotions, reduces headaches and aids the digestive organs, spleen, pancreas, and colon. Helps the reproductive system, relieves asthma attacks, and enhances night vision.

Chakra: Sacral & Solar Plexus

Tiger Iron –

Tiger Iron is a blend of Hematite, Red Jasper, and Tiger Eye. It enhances creativity, dreams, and ideas and brings balance into your life, helping to overcome difficulties. It is a good stone for manifesting safety in times of trouble. A very grounding stone, Tiger Iron brings vitality and life force into the body.

Healing: Enhances physical energy overcoming exhaustion, helps with circulation problems, promotes blood production, increasing red /white blood cell count. Strengthens immune function and the nervous system.

Chakra: Base, Sacral & Solar Plexus

Tourmaline (Black) –

Black Tourmaline (Schrol) is a very supportive stone that protects us from external influences, dispersing stress, tension, and negative energy. It grounds and anchors light energy within the physical body, promoting inner wisdom, mastery, individuality, stability, courage, and patience being peace to the heart and mind. Black Tourmaline also protects against the negative effects of electromagnetic radiation and inharmonious energies.

Healing: Aids sleep, strengthens the immune system, and provides pain relief. It helps with the adrenal glands, kidneys, spinal column, colon & legs.

Chakras: Base

Tourmalated Quartz –

Tourmalated Quartz encourages a large amount of light to encircle your body, and this will heal you on many levels. The combination of clear quartz with its strong vibration enhances the energy of the black tourmaline, giving Tourmalated quartz a strong spiritual grounding energy as well as being a potent psychic protection stone.

Healing: Encourages a large amount of light to encircle your body's healing on many levels.

Chakras: Base

Turquoise –

Turquoise is a captivating gemstone admired for its brilliant blue/green colour, which has made it a symbol of protection and spiritual significance across cultures for centuries. This stone embodies the energies of sky and water, representing a connection between heaven and Earth. Turquoise promotes harmony, communication, and the alignment of mind, body, and spirit. Turquoise encourages clear and honest communication, making it an excellent aid for public speaking and self-expression. It also facilitates a deeper connection with one's intuition and spiritual awareness, guiding you on a path of self-discovery and higher consciousness. As a protective stone, it serves as a guardian, keeping you safe on your journey toward spiritual enlightenment. Do not Cleanse/Charge with

Healing: Turquoise is believed to provide physical and emotional healing, particularly in addressing respiratory issues, promoting detoxification, and enhancing overall well-being. It is also considered a stone of emotional balance and protection against negative energies.

Chakras: Throat and Third Eye

Zebra Marble –

Zebra Marble aids transformation and self-liberation helping you to overcome inner discontentment and unhappiness in life by opening up new perspectives and bringing creative solutions to your problems.

Healing: Eases allergies and fortifies the kidneys, spleen, intestines, muscle tissue, and the skin.

Chakra: Solar Plexus

Divination

Divination is a prominent and diverse practice within the realm of witchcraft, revered for its ability to offer insights into the future, address any pressing questions, or seek wisdom from the Universe, Spirits, Gods, Goddesses, or even Spirit Animals through various supernatural techniques. While it might initially seem daunting, when you delve deeper, divination fundamentally revolves around harnessing your intuition to navigate the complexities of life and uncover answers.

There is a vast array of divination methods available, and it's not necessary to limit yourself to widely known practices like Runes, Tarot, or Tasseography. Instead, explore the techniques that resonate with you personally. Here are several intriguing forms of divination to consider -

Abacomancy:

This ancient method involves using dust, salt, or sand, combined with an animal's movements over the medium. Originating in Africa, practitioners interpret the patterns or disturbances caused by the animal as messages or guidance from the divine.

Aeromancy:

Utilizing the elements of the weather, this practice interprets phenomena such as thunder, lightning, wind, and rain. By observing these natural occurrences, diviners can discern messages or predictions related to their queries.

Apantomancy:

This form of divination relies on chance encounters with animals or objects, interpreting these as symbols or signs that the universe is providing guidance. For instance, witnessing a specific bird can hold significance in your current life situation.

Arithmancy:

This method is rooted in numerology, where numbers are assigned spiritual meanings. Practitioners analyse the significance of numbers in their lives, such as calculating life paths or personal years to reveal insights about character and destiny.

Astrology:

Dating back to at least 2000 BC, astrology examines the movements and positions of celestial bodies— planets and stars—to forecast events or understand personality traits. It has a rich history across various cultures, including Mayan, Indian, Chinese, and the roots of Western astrology in Mesopotamia.

Augury:

This ancient practice involves observing the behaviour and movements of birds. It can be broken down into two approaches: one revolves around tracking the flight patterns of birds, while the other interprets ground activities by offering food in letter shapes, observing the direction in which birds disperse, akin to an ancient form of the Ouija board.

Automatic Writing:

In this practice, a person uses a pen and paper, clearing their mind to allow messages from the universe, deities, or spirits to flow through them. The act of writing becomes a channel for communication, often producing unexpected insights.

Belomancy:

This method entails using arrows, historically noted in cultures such as those from Tibet, Greece, and Arabia, as recorded in biblical texts. There are two forms: one involves asking a question before randomly pulling arrows from a specially prepared bag, while the other requires shooting arrows into the air and interpreting their landing patterns.

Bibliomancy:

A simple yet profound technique, bibliomancy uses books—often sacred texts. Practitioners pose a question and then randomly open the book, selecting a passage that resonates as guidance or insight.

Bone Reading (Osteomancy):

An ancient African technique where different parts of animal bones are assigned specific meanings based on regional traditions. The patterns and placements of the bones offer insights into questions posed by the practitioner.

Brontomancy:

This divination method interprets the sounds of thunder as approval or messages from higher powers. The intensity and frequency of thunder can serve as indicators of forthcoming events.

Capnomancy:

Also known as smoke divination, this practice observes the shapes formed by smoke from candles, fires, or incense. The figures created by the smoke are similarly to cloud-gazing, providing insight into the questions at hand.

Casting:

This involves using charms or small objects that have been assigned meanings. Practitioners ask their questions, toss the charms onto a divination board, or randomly select them from a bag. Common items can include thimbles, wine corks, keys, nuts, seeds, crystals, or rocks bearing symbols.

Ceromancy:

In this method, melted wax is dripped into water to create shapes that are then interpreted. The formed shapes and patterns hold significance and can guide the practitioner's decisions.

Chirognomy:

This form of palmistry focuses on analysing the shape of a person's hands, fingers, and overall hand features to gain insights into their personality traits and character.

Chiromancy:

Unlike chirognomy, chiromancy examines the lines and markings on a person's palms to predict their future. Each line is interpreted to reveal various aspects of life, from love to career.

Cledonism:

This method involves listening for occurrences or statements heard at significant moments, interpreting them as messages or signs from the universe or deities.

Conchomancy:

Using seashells, this fortune-telling technique may involve casting shells or interpreting sounds by holding them to the ear. The shapes and sounds can lead to revelations about future events.

Crystal Ball Reading:

In this mesmerizing practice, a practitioner gazes into a true quartz crystal ball, often clearing their mind to divine shapes or visions that manifest within the crystal. The imagery and feelings inspired by the ball can provide deep insights and guidance.

Dice Divination:

This method of divination utilizes dice, which can be standard six-sided dice or specially designed fortune-telling dice that often feature unique symbols or meanings. To perform this form of divination, participants will typically ask a specific question before rolling two or more dice. The results are interpreted based on the numbers that appear: if all the rolled numbers are odd, the answer to the question is "no." Conversely, if all numbers are even, the answer is "yes." If the outcome is a mix of odd and even numbers, it signifies uncertainty or ambiguity regarding the question posed.

Domino Divination:

This unique form of divination relies on the numbers displayed on domino tiles to derive insights or foresee future events. To conduct this practice, two domino tiles are drawn randomly. Each pair of numbers on the tiles holds specific meanings: for instance, drawing two blank tiles may be interpreted as a sign of great misfortune, while drawing two sixes might indicate future happiness, success, and flourishing family life. The interpretation of the numbers can vary based on personal or cultural significance as well.

Dowsing:

Dowsing encompasses two primary techniques. The first typically involves the use of forked branches or dowsing rods to locate natural resources like water or oil underground. The second method employs a pendulum made of crystal, glass, or metal, which is used to answer questions. The pendulum's movements are then analysed: swaying to one side or making circular motions may signify "yes" or "no," while stillness may indicate uncertainty. Dowsers must develop skills in interpreting these movements for effective results.

Favomancy:

Favomancy is a form of divination based on the interpretation of the way beans or peas fall and land when scattered. This method has ancient origins in the Middle East. Practitioners observe the positions and arrangements of the beans to gain insights or answers related to their inquiries. The meaning ascribed to each position may vary, often influenced by cultural traditions or personal beliefs.

Gypsy Fortune Cards:

This divination practice is a type of cartomancy similar to tarot readings but uses a unique set of cards known as Gypsy Fortune Cards. Each card features images of everyday objects and symbols, each assigned specific meanings. When a card is drawn, the image and its interpretation provide insights or guidance regarding the question at hand.

I Ching:

Also known as the Book of Changes, I Ching is a venerable Chinese divination system where individuals pose questions and subsequently toss coins multiple times. The results from these coin tosses form hexagrams, which are then looked up in the I Ching text. Each hexagram corresponds to various interpretations that illustrate the dynamics of the situation and offer wisdom or guidance.

Lenormand Cards:

This divination style involves a set of 36 cards featuring straightforward images such as objects, animals, and symbols. Lenormand cards are distinct from tarot due to their simpler imagery, facilitating quicker learning and interpretation. When drawn in spreads or single pulls, each card's position and relationship to others further enrich the insight provided.

Libanomancy:

Libanomancy is a fascinating method of divination that focuses on interpreting the movement of incense smoke. Observers analyse how the smoke swirls or takes shape, as well as the ashes that fall after burning, for signs and messages. This method is often used in rituals for spiritual connection or seeking guidance from higher powers.

Lithomancy:

In this form of divination, practitioners use stones, crystals, or rocks, which may be drawn randomly from a bag, tossed, or arranged in a spread. Each stone typically carries distinct meanings, and their arrangement or interaction provides insights into the questions being asked or predictions about the future.

Mirror Scrying:

A reflective divination practice that is similar to cartomancy, mirror scrying involves using a reflective surface to gain insights. Practitioners may observe reflections or shapes on the surface, interpreting these visions as messages or guidance. This can also extend to the use of water or crystal balls in the scrying process.

Necromancy:

Often surrounded by mystery and misconceptions, necromancy involves divination through the spirits of the deceased. This practice typically includes elaborate rituals designed to summon spirits to convey messages or answers to questions. Necromancy can be a deeply spiritual and personal experience, as practitioners seek to connect with those who have passed on.

Nephomancy:

This method involves interpreting the shapes and patterns seen in clouds as significant signs or messages. Practitioners of nephomancy might observe cloud formations to derive meanings — for example, recognizing the shape of a turtle might suggest the need to slow down or consider broader perspectives in life.

Oracle Cards:

While primarily focused on offering guidance, oracle cards serve as a form of cartomancy. Each deck is unique, often depicting a variety of imagery and themes, which can be used for divination through spreads or single pulls. Oracle cards are versatile tools for self-reflection and insight, allowing individuals to explore their feelings and situations.

Ouija:

Originally designed in the 1890s for divination, the Ouija board consists of a flat board with letters, numbers, and symbols. Users place a planchette on the board and lightly touch it, allowing it to move to spell out messages. Although often depicted in popular culture as a means of summoning malevolent spirits, many find that Ouija boards can be effective tools for communicating with higher energies, spirits, or the universe.

Rune Stones:

This ancient method involves using stones inscribed with runic symbols to seek answers or guidance. Practitioners can utilize a variety of techniques—such as random draws, spreads, or tossing—to interpret the arrangement of rune stones. Each symbol carries a unique meaning, and together they form a narrative reflective of the inquirer's situation.

Tarot:

As one of the most widely recognized forms of cartomancy, tarot consists of a deck divided into the Major and Minor Arcana, along with four suits. The cards encompass a rich tapestry of symbolism and meanings, allowing for complex interpretations when used in various spreads or drawn randomly. Many seek tarot readings for personal insight, guidance, or to explore their paths in life.

Tasseography:

This intriguing method involves reading tea leaves left at the bottom of a teacup after drinking. Practitioners interpret the shapes, patterns, and formations of the leaves to extract meanings and insights regarding the querent's life or future. The method requires both intuition and skill in symbol recognition, with each shape potentially signifying different messages.

Exploring these diverse methods of divination can open up new avenues for personal understanding and spiritual connection. Choose the ones that resonate deeply with you and embrace the journey of discovering your unique intuitive path.

Charm Casting

Charm Casting is a practice that embodies both power and simplicity, making it accessible to anyone interested in divination or personal insights. Unlike other forms of divination that may have extensive rulebooks or complex rituals, Charm Casting is marked by its open-ended nature, allowing for a personalized approach.

To begin your journey into Charm Casting, start by gathering a variety of items that resonate with you on a personal level. These items can include beads, buttons, coins, jewellery charms, shells, stones, or any trinkets that attract your attention. The key is to select items that evoke a sense of connection or have significance in your life.

As you collect these charms, it's crucial to ensure a balance between the positive and negative interpretations associated with them. This duality will enhance the objectivity of your readings, allowing for a more nuanced understanding of the messages that may arise. By incorporating items that can represent both beneficial and challenging aspects, you create a well-rounded toolkit for your divination practice.

Once you have amassed your collection of charms, the next step is to assign meanings to each item. This process is deeply personal; take the time to reflect on what each charm signifies to you. For example, a charm shaped like a heart might symbolize love and connection, while a stone that's rough might represent life's challenges or obstacles. Here's an overview of some jewellery charms I have collected and the meanings I have assigned to them:

Charm	Meaning
Acorn	Growth
Anchor	Stuck In Place
Angel	Good News
Apple	Learning
Arrow	Purpose
Axe	Destruction
Bag	Letting Go of Baggage
Balloons	Getting Carried Away
Bat	Misunderstandings
Bee	Working With Others
Believe	Believe In Yourself
Book	Knowledge / Research
Brain	Think Things Through
Brave	Be Brave
Broom	Clear Out / Clean Up
Butterfly	Significant Change
Camera	Memories / Reflection
Cat	Independence
Candles	Shed Light
Circle	Completeness

Clock	Patience / Timing
Cloud	Clouded Judgement
Coffin	Ending
Cog	Movement / Progress
Compass	Direction
Cross	Sacrifice
Crown	Take The Lead
Diamond	Clarity
Dice	Take a Chance
Dollar	Money
Dragonfly	New Beginning
Elephant	Strength
Eye	Be Observant / Pay Attention
Fairy	Unlock Your Magic
Fawn	Gentle / Timid
Fearless	Be Fearless
Feather	Guidance / Look Deeper
Feet	Stay Grounded
Flamingo	Learn To Stand on Your Own Two Feet
Fleur De Lys	The Past
Flower	Appreciate What You Have
Fox	Cunning / Deception
Ghost	Holding On to The Past
Grace	Be The Better Person
Grapes	Abundance
Grim Reaper	Time Is Running Out
Guitar	Harmony
Hand	Out Of Reach / Within Reach
Hand Of Fatima	Protection
Heart	Compassion
Horseshoe	Good Luck
House	Seek Shelter
Infinity Symbol	Endless Possibilities
Key	Unlocking Potential
Knife	Arguments / Fights
Leaf	Nourish
Lips	Watch What You Say
Love	Love
Mask	Lies /Hiding the Truth
Miracle	Miracle
Moon	Female / Feminine / Woman
Owl	Wisdom Is Needed
Padlock	Secrets / Something Hidden
Poison Bottle	Temptation

Scissors	Cut Ties
Seahorse	Change Your Perspective
Sewing Machine	Get Creative / Inspiration
Shell	Gratitude
Ship	Adventure
Ships Wheel	Success
Shoe	Walk Tall
Skeleton	Fragility Of the Situation
Skull & Cross Bones	Warning
Snail	Slow Down
Snake	Betrayal
Square	Think Outside the Box
Spider	Hard Work
Squirrel	Be Prepared
Star	Hope
Starfish	Healing / Regeneration
Sun	Male / Masculine / Man
Tennis Rackets	Get Moving
Treble Clef	Sing Your Own Song
Triangle	Something Unexpected Will Happen
Tree	Re-Connect
Trust	Trust
Turtle	Go The Distance
Umbrella	A Storm Is Coming
Unicorn	Imagination
Warrior	Time To Fight
Webb	A Trap
Wine Glass	Time To Relax
Wing	Blessings

When casting your charms, it is highly advisable to do so on a flat, enclosed surface to ensure that none of your charms are lost during the process. An organized casting area can greatly enhance your experience and help maintain focus.

To create your own casting mat, tray, or table, consider incorporating elements that hold personal significance or that align with your intentions. You might want to design your surface to reflect various aspects of life, such as the months of the year, which can help you connect your readings to specific periods and energies. Alternatively, you could segment your space to represent different stages, like past, present, and future, allowing for a clearer understanding of the influences at play.

Furthermore, another useful approach is to create sections that highlight your current situation, the challenges you face, and the potential outcomes. This structure can guide your interpretation and provide a comprehensive overview of your circumstances.

For instance, a Life Wheel Casting Mat can be an excellent tool. It may include segments that correspond to various areas of life—such as relationships, career, health, and personal growth—making it easier to analyse how different aspects interact and affect one another. By thoughtfully designing your casting space, you can create a more meaningful and insightful experience.

An example would be:

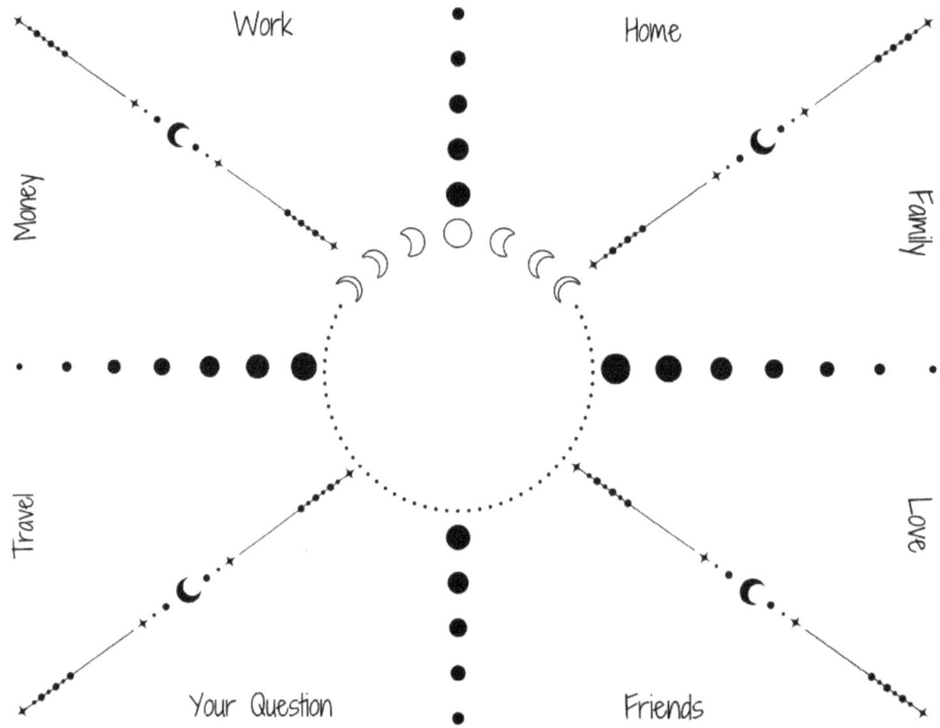

The central circle in the above casting mat symbolizes the essence of the questioner, representing their inner self and personal journey. It serves as a focal point for introspection and understanding.

As you engage with the charms, it's important to refrain from focusing on them visually during the selection process. Allow your intuition to guide you, rather than consciously directing where you wish to place them on the mat. This approach encourages a more genuine and spontaneous connection with the energies at play, enhancing the overall experience.

<u>**Numerology**</u>

Numerology is an ancient system rooted in the belief that numbers hold specific meanings and energies that can provide insight into the world and our individual experiences within it. This mystical practice has origins that trace back to ancient civilizations, including the Egyptians and Babylonians, and has been extensively utilized across cultures spanning from China and Japan to Greece and Rome for thousands of years.

At the core of numerology lies the idea that each person has a unique set of numerological numbers that influence various aspects of their lives, including personal life paths, career choices, and romantic relationships. By understanding these numbers and the energies they represent, individuals can make informed decisions that align with their true potential and lead to a more fulfilling life.

Numbers are not only foundational to the structure of the universe; they can also be observed in the natural world in various forms. The mathematical constant pi, for instance, appears in everything from the circular shapes of celestial bodies to the spiral structure of DNA and the winding paths of rivers. Numbers possess their own inherent energies that can significantly impact our lives.

A deep understanding of numerology allows individuals to explore various dimensions of their existence, such as:

- Personality Traits: Discovering how different numbers reflect core attributes and characteristics.

- Life Obstacles and Struggles: Identifying challenges one might face based on their numerological profile.

- Romantic Partners: Determining compatibility with potential partners and understanding who may be beneficial or detrimental to one's happiness.

- Career Guidance: Uncovering the careers that align best with one's natural talents and inclinations.

- Innate Talents: Recognizing unique gifts and abilities linked to specific numbers.

- Hopes and Fears: Gaining insight into what drives an individual and what anxieties they may need to confront.

Calculating the Life Path Number

Similar to astrology, one of the most significant elements in numerology is the date of birth. This date, expressed in the format DD/MM/YYYY, provides crucial insights into a person's character and life journey. The life path number is derived from this information and serves as a foundational number that shapes an individual's life experiences, personality, and purpose.

Numerology Number Chart

In numerology, each letter of the alphabet is assigned a corresponding numerical value between 1 and 9. This system is vital for calculating different important numbers in a person's numerological profile, such as the Soul Number, Karmic Number, and Destiny Number. Below is a reference chart for translating letters into their numerical assignments:

1	2	3	4	5	6	7	8	9
A	B	C	D	E	F	G	H	I
J	K	L	M	N	O	P	Q	R
S	T	U	V	W	X	Y	Z	

Using this chart, individuals can tap into the vibrational essence of each letter corresponding to their names, allowing for deeper insights into their soul's essence and life's purpose.

How to Calculate Your Four Major Numerology Numbers

In the field of numerology, there are four primary numbers that provide insights into various aspects of your life and personality. Each of these numbers is derived from either your birth date or the letters in your name, creating a unique numerology chart that reflects your individuality. Below, we delve into the calculations and meanings of each number in detail.

1. Life Path Number

The Life Path Number is arguably the most significant component of your personal numerology chart. It offers profound insights into your personality, the accomplishments you are likely to achieve, the challenges you may face, and the opportunities that will arise for you throughout your life. Understanding your Life Path Number can guide you on your journey toward happiness and fulfillment.

Calculation:

To find your Life Path Number, sum each digit in your birth date. Continue to add the resulting digits together until you arrive at a single-digit number (1 through 9) or one of the master numbers, 11 or 22.

Example: For a birth date of 31/10/1972:

- Break it down: 3 + 1 + 1 + 0 + 1 + 9 + 7 + 2

- Calculate: 3 + 1 + 1 + 0 + 1 + 9 + 7 + 2 = 24

- Reduce to a single digit: 2 + 4 = 6

2. Soul Number

The Soul Number, also known as the Spiritual Number, reveals your inner self and highlights your spiritual essence. It sheds light on your true motivations, desires, and the deep-seated feelings that drive your actions and decisions.

Calculation:

To calculate your Soul Number, focus on the vowels in your full name. Assign each vowel a single-digit value based on its position in the alphabet (A=1, E=5, I=9, O=6, U=3). Sum the values of all vowels and continue reducing until you achieve a single-digit number, or one of the master numbers, 11 or 22.

Example: For the name Jane Doe:

- Vowel breakdown: A (1) + E (5) + A (1) + O (6) + E (5)

- Calculate: 1 + 5 + 1 + 6 + 5 = 18

- Reduce: 1 + 8 = 9

3. Karmic Number

Your Karmic Number delves into your hopes, fears, and aspirations. It serves as a mirror, reflecting the underlying factors influencing your life experiences and emotional landscape. Understanding your Karmic Number can open your eyes to the patterns that govern your behaviour and emotional responses.

Calculation:

To determine your Karmic Number, focus on the consonants in your full name. Assign each consonant a single-digit value based on its position in the alphabet (B=2, C=3, D=4, etc.). Sum the values of all consonants and reduce them to a single digit, or the numbers 11 or 22.

Example: For the name Jane Doe:

- Consonant breakdown: J (1) + N (5) + D (4)

- Calculate: 1 + 5 + 4 = 10

- Reduce: 1 + 0 = 1

4. Destiny Number

The Destiny Number serves as a guiding force in reaching your life's goals. It encapsulates the traits, characteristics, and potential you possess, influencing your path and purpose. By understanding your Destiny Number, you can align your actions with your innate attributes to fulfill your life's mission.

Calculation:

To calculate your Destiny Number, add the values of all the letters in your full name, using the same position-in-the-alphabet values (A=1, B=2, C=3, etc.). Sum these values and reduce until you arrive at a single digit, or one of the master numbers, 11 or 22.

Example: For the name Jane Doe:

- Letter breakdown: J (1) + A (1) + N (5) + E (5) + D (4) + O (6) + E (5)

- Calculate: 1 + 1 + 5 + 5 + 4 + 6 + 5 = 27

- Reduce: 2 + 7 = 9

By exploring and calculating these four major numerology numbers, you can gain valuable insights into your life's journey, helping you understand not only who you are but also where you're heading.

Number Meanings

1

Individuals possessing number 1 traits are often natural leaders, embodying a robust masculine energy. This characteristic isn't limited to men; both genders can exhibit the qualities associated with this dynamic number. In the professional realm, number 1s frequently find themselves in positions of authority such as CEOs, managers, entrepreneurs, or inventors. They are characterized by their remarkable drive, creativity, and independence, allowing them to thrive in various fields of their choice. However, alongside these admirable traits, number 1s might sometimes exhibit overly demanding or critical behaviours toward others. Beneath their confident exterior, they may grapple with self-doubt and insecurity.

Character Traits Include:

- Strong: They possess resilience and inner strength, although at times can be forceful in their approach.

- Creative: Innovation and original thinking come naturally to them.

- Impassioned: They approach their pursuits with enthusiasm and fervour.

- Independent: They prefer to carve their own paths and make decisions autonomously.

- Prefer action and practical solutions: They value practicality over abstract theories.

- Perfectionists: They have high standards for themselves and for those around them.

- Visionaries: They often see the bigger picture and have the ability to strategize effectively.

- Popular: Their charisma often makes them well-liked in social settings.

- Honest: They value truthfulness and integrity in their interactions.

- Fair: They strive for justice and equity in their dealings with others.

2

The essence of number 2 is imbued with feminine energy, which manifests in traits of diplomacy and emotional atonement. Individuals with this number often excel in influential roles such as diplomats, negotiators, mediators, teachers, caregivers, counsellors, or therapists. Their exceptional listening skills and communication abilities allow them to connect deeply with others and navigate complex interpersonal dynamics. However, a potential downside of their sensitivity is that it can lead to emotional overwhelm and dramatic consequences in times of stress.

Character Traits Include:

- Influential: They have a natural ability to sway opinions and inspire others.

- Intuitive: They possess a keen sense of intuition regarding others' feelings and needs.

- Social: They thrive in social environments and can easily engage with a variety of individuals.

- Poised: Their calm demeanour under pressure makes them excellent mediators.

- Charismatic: They often exude an infectious charm that attracts others.

- Trustworthy: Their integrity and reliability make them confidants and good friends.

- Deep Thinkers: They enjoy exploring profound subjects and complex ideas.

- Humorous: A great sense of humour helps them connect with others and diffuse tension.

- Artistic: They often express their sensitivity and creativity through artistic endeavours.

3

People characterized by number 3 are uniquely positioned between the assertive traits of number 1 and the empathetic qualities of number 2, making them vibrant and lively individuals. They tend to be extremely extroverted, embracing life with openness and curiosity. Frequently, they are the center of social gatherings, bringing joy and excitement to the atmosphere. Those with number 3 traits have an innate optimism, often recognizing the silver lining in various predicaments. They flourish in flexible work environments that allow them to express their creativity and spontaneity; however, they must continually work on self-discipline to overcome their lack of structure.

Character Traits Include:

- Optimistic: They maintain a positive outlook even in challenging circumstances.

- Excellent communication: Their ability to express themselves clearly helps them connect with others effectively.

- Fun-loving: They prioritize enjoyment and playfulness in life.

- Charming: Their natural charm makes them endearing to others.

- Attractive: They often draw attention and admiration effortlessly.

- Extroverted: They gain energy from social interactions and often seek them out.

- Talkative: They enjoy engaging in conversations and sharing thoughts with others.

4

Individuals embodying number 4 are characterized by a concrete view of the world, often seeing things in stark black-and-white terms. This binary perception drives them to adhere to rules and standards, leading them to excel in structured environments. They typically thrive in fields related to the sciences, law, or military service, where their disciplined approach is highly valued. While their firm viewpoint can seem rigid, it is balanced by their dependability and reliability. Their primary struggle lies in their difficulty to unwind and embrace spontaneity, which can limit their enjoyment of life.

Character Traits Include:

- Disciplined: They possess the self-control necessary to follow through on commitments.

- Systematic: Their methodical nature allows them to structure tasks effectively.

- Organized: They thrive on order and are adept at managing details.

- Dependable: Others can count on them to fulfill their promises and responsibilities.

- Attentive to detail: They notice subtleties that others might overlook, enhancing their performance.

- Strong: They possess both physical and mental strength, often facing challenges head-on.

- Loyal: Their loyalty to friends and family is unwavering and steadfast.

5

Number 5 individuals embody a free-spirited essence, marked by their non-judgmental, social, and friendly nature. They thrive in environments that allow personal interaction and connection, making them well-suited for careers in hospitality, sales, and real estate, where their engaging personality shines. Their adventurous spirit fuels a love for exploration and new experiences, rendering them vibrant conversationalists. However, their free-spirited nature sometimes leads to perceptions of being flaky or unreliable, especially if they struggle to commit to plans.

Character Traits Include:

- Free-spirited: They prioritize independence and personal freedom in their lives.

- Loving: Their warmth and affection enhance their relationships.

- Fun to be around: Their lively spirit makes them delightful companions.

- Non-judgmental: They accept others without passing judgment, fostering inclusivity.

- Adventurous: They are drawn to experiences that expand their horizons and challenge their perspectives.

- Filled with wanderlust: Their desire to explore new cultures and places fuels their adventurous endeavours.

- Defender of the underdog: They often advocate for those who are vulnerable or marginalized.

- Often restless: They may find it challenging to settle into routines, constantly seeking new stimuli.

6

Individuals represented by number 6 are often regarded as some of the most compassionate and nurturing among us. Their joy comes from genuinely helping others, making them ideal candidates for professions such as teaching, counselling, therapy, medicine, nursing, or even being caring stay-at-home parents. While their commitment to aiding others brings immense fulfilment, the emotional burden of feeling they have failed to assist someone can profoundly impact their mental health and self-esteem.

Character Traits Include:

- Compassionate: They deeply empathize with others' struggles and pain.

- Kind: Their innate kindness manifests in their interactions.

- Nurturing: They take pleasure in fostering and supporting those around them.

- Peaceful: They strive to create harmonious environments and resolve conflicts.

- Helpful: They often go out of their way to lend a hand to those in need.

- Supportive: They provide encouragement and strength, especially during tough times.

- Great for Advice: Their life experiences and insights make them reliable advisors for friends and family.

7

Number 7 individuals are often recognized as deep thinkers with introverted tendencies. They display a certain detachment from societal expectations, often caring little for what others think of them. This introspective nature drives them toward careers in the sciences or academia, where they can delve into solo research and exploration. While they may struggle with forming friendships, they are fiercely loyal and devoted to those who earn their trust.

Character Traits Include:

- Deep thinking: They enjoy contemplating profound concepts and analysing details.

- Quiet: Their reserved demeanour may be misinterpreted as aloofness.

- Introverted: They recharge in solitude and typically prefer one-on-one interactions.

- Idiosyncratic: They embrace their unique perspectives and eccentricities.

- Intuitive: They possess a strong ability to perceive underlying truths.

- Analytical: Their critical thinking skills enable them to dissect problems effectively.

- Problem solvers: They thrive on tackling challenges with innovative solutions.

- Fair: They value equity and justice, often advocating for balanced outcomes.

- Sensitive: They possess an acute awareness of others' emotions, which can make them empathetic.

8

Individuals associated with the number 8 are characterized by an unyielding drive for success. This determination equips them with the potential for significant accomplishments, as they are willing to put in the effort necessary to achieve their goals. While their intense focus may lead them to be perceived as workaholics or excessively blunt, they find fulfillment in not only material success—such as wealth, nice clothing, and possessions—but also in maintaining a balanced and satisfying family life.

Character Traits Include:

- Strong: Their resilience allows them to overcome obstacles with determination.

- Reliable: They are dependable, showcasing a steadfast commitment to their responsibilities.

- Hard Working: They dedicate themselves tirelessly to their pursuits and ambitions.

- Intuitive: They possess a strong gut instinct, allowing them to make decisions confidently.

- Organized: Their systematic approach ensures efficiency in their efforts.

- Focused: They maintain a clear sense of direction, often setting high goals for themselves.

9

Individuals identified with the number 9 are often seen as champions of justice, driven by a compelling desire to rectify wrongs and promote fairness. Whether they are championing causes related to global warming or advocating for individuals who have experienced injustice, their innate sense of what is right fuels their activism. These individuals possess a profound spiritual nature, which imbues all of their efforts with passion and purpose. In the pursuit of justice, number 9s thrive in roles related to activism and humanitarian work, frequently engaging in pro-bono initiatives or volunteering their time and skills to worthy causes. They may also find fulfillment in independent work, where they can express their values and ideals. Although their strong convictions about right and wrong can occasionally create barriers in their relationships—making them appear somewhat difficult to approach—they are incredibly loving and devoted at their core.

Character Traits include:

- Fighting Injustice: Consistently advocating for the oppressed and marginalized members of society.

- Spiritual: Possessing a deep connection to spiritual beliefs and a quest for deeper meaning.

- Compassionate: Demonstrating genuine empathy and care towards others.

- Nurturing: Providing emotional support and encouragement to family and friends.

- Helpful: Always willing to lend a hand or provide assistance when others are in need.

- Loyal: Demonstrating steadfast commitment in relationships and friendships.

- Creative: Often expressing themselves through various forms of artistic or creative endeavours.

11

The number 11 is regarded as a master number in numerology, carrying an inherent spiritual significance that is often present only in specific individuals' numerological charts. Those aligned with the number 11 are seen as exceptionally unique, drawing upon the potent energies of both numbers 1 and 2, but with an enhanced intensity that can create both incredible strengths and significant challenges. People who resonate with the number 11 often exhibit profound insights, but such depth of thought can lead to introversion, as they may prefer solitude and reflection over engaging in superficial social interactions. Their spiritual awareness fuels a desire for quieter environments, steering them away from petty dramas that can be draining. Professionally, they flourish in creative fields, where they can express their imaginative insights, as monotony and repetitive tasks are the antithesis of their vibrant spirits.

Character Traits include:

- Spiritual: Deeply connected to spiritual practices and beliefs.

- Inspiring: Able to uplift and motivate those around them through their actions and words.

- Introverted: Preferring solitary pursuits and deep contemplation over social gatherings.

- Empathic: Possessing a heightened sensitivity to the emotions of others.

- Sometimes Anxious: Their depth of thought can sometimes lead to feelings of anxiety or overwhelm.

- Fascinating to Those Around Them: Their unique viewpoints and insights captivate others.

- Free-thinkers: Challenging conventional ideas and encouraging forward-thinking.

- Often Psychic: Displaying intuitive abilities or a strong sense of insight.

22

In numerology, the number 22 is highly esteemed as a master number, recognized for embodying the traits of practicality and pragmatism. Individuals who carry the essence of the number 22 are often on a profound journey of self-discovery, guided by a deeper sense of mission to uplift humanity. Those associated with the number 22 possess a remarkable ability to radiate joy, bringing an uplifting energy to their surroundings. They exhibit a strong connection to their higher self, which directs them towards endeavours that foster well-being and positivity in others. Although they are grounded and selfless, their desire to support others can sometimes lead to a neglect of self-care, which may result in feelings of insecurity or periods of frustration that could manifest as bossiness.

Character Traits include:

- Visionary: Possessing a keen ability to see the bigger picture and inspire others.

- Wise: Drawing from a deep well of experience and understanding to guide others.

- Spiritual: Frequently engaged in spiritual practices and seeking deeper truths.

- Inspiring: Able to motivate and uplift those around them.

- Peaceful: Maintaining calm and serenity even in challenging circumstances.

- Selfless: Prioritizing the needs of others and providing support without expectation of reward.

- Often called "Old Souls": Believed to have a deep, innate wisdom that transcends time.

- Loving and Caring About Humanity: Demonstrating a genuine concern for the welfare of others.

- Humble: Often downplaying their achievements and putting the needs of others first.

- Psychic: May possess intuitive abilities and heightened awareness of their surroundings.

33

The number 33 is regarded as the Master Teacher in numerology, representing the pinnacle of spiritual evolution and guidance. Known for their substantial influence, individuals who resonate with the 33 embody qualities from both the 11 and 22, elevating their potential even further. When fully realized, those embodying the number 33 do not pursue personal ambition for their benefit, but instead dedicate their impressive abilities and energies to the spiritual upliftment of humanity. They are characterized by a sincere devotion to the greater good, often leading and teaching through example rather than authority.

Character Traits include:

- Spiritual: Deeply committed to their spiritual practices and beliefs.

- Don't Focus on the Negativity: Choosing instead to embody positivity and hope.

- Optimistic: Maintaining a hopeful outlook that inspires others around them.

- Highly Talented in the Arts: Frequently demonstrating exceptional artistic abilities.

- Versatile: Able to adapt their skills in various creative and professional pursuits.

- Good Fortune: Often blessed with opportunities that align with their paths and passions.

<u>**Pendulums**</u>

A pendulum is an apparatus consisting of a weighted object, often referred to as the bob, which is affixed to a flexible string or chain. The length of this string or chain allows for a range of motion, permitting the bob to swing back and forth in a rhythmic motion. This simple yet effective device has applications in various fields, including physics for demonstrating principles of motion, as well as in divination or spiritual practices for gaining insights or guidance.

Programming a Pendulum

To obtain clear and consistent answers from your pendulum, it can be beneficial to program it to communicate specific responses. Before you begin, it is essential to allow your pendulum to demonstrate how it communicates, as each pendulum may have its own tendencies.

Steps to Program Your Pendulum:

1. Select Your Setup: Hold your pendulum just above a flat, stable surface or a designated circle where it can swing freely without obstruction.

2. Establish Motion: Swing the pendulum in the direction that you wish it to signify. For example, you might first decide that swinging left indicates "no" and swinging right indicates "yes."

3. Assign Responses: Verbally communicate what each motion means by saying, "This is yes," "This is no," or associating each movement with any other desired answer. Be clear and decisive in your instructions.

4. Repeat and Confirm: For reliability, repeat this process for every possible answer you want the pendulum to recognize. Consistency is key in programming your pendulum effectively.

5. Conduct a Test: Before using the pendulum for significant questions, test its responses by asking questions for which you already know the answers. This will help you gauge its accuracy and establish trust in the communication.

Bonding with Your Pendulum

While it is not strictly necessary to cultivate a profound relationship with your pendulum for it to function, many users find that building a connection enhances the accuracy of the readings.

Here are several methods to strengthen your bond with your pendulum:

- Carry It with You: Keep your pendulum in your pocket or purse so that it can become attuned to your energy throughout the day.

- Sleep With It: Place your pendulum under your pillow or beside your bed to connect with it during your subconscious state.

- Daily Use: Incorporate the pendulum into your routine; whether for divination purposes or simply as a meditative practice, frequent use fosters familiarity.

- Wear It: If your pendulum takes the form of jewellery, such as a necklace, wearing it allows for an ongoing connection and interaction with your energy.

- Keep with Personal Items: Store your pendulum in a special place alongside other cherished belongings, such as a jewellery box, to create a sense of reverence and attachment.

Once you find a pendulum that resonates with you, nurture it with care and attention. This mutually respectful interaction can yield more profound insights and benefits.

Using a Pendulum Board

If you find yourself uncertain about interpreting your pendulum's movements, especially with more intricate or complex inquiries, utilizing a pendulum board can significantly enhance the experience. These boards come in various designs and layouts, tailored to assist in clarifying responses. You also have the creative option to craft your own board that aligns with your energy and intentions.

In addition, if you do not have access to a board, you can simply position your pendulum over your hand or any flat surface to facilitate the same process.

When seeking a pendulum, trust your instincts; certain pendulums will naturally stand out, fitting comfortably within your grip and feeling right in your energy. Exploration and intuition are crucial in this selection. Additionally, consider crafting your own pendulum from objects that hold personal significance, such as old necklaces, or by attaching a weighted item to a length of string or chain. The possibilities are limitless, allowing for a uniquely personal experience in your practice.

<u>**Scrying**</u>

Scrying is an ancient practice of divination that involves gazing into a transparent or reflective medium to perceive visions, sensations, or signs. These insights can then be interpreted to provide answers or guidance on specific questions or situations. This mystical art has been utilized across various cultures and eras to connect with the subconscious and the spiritual realm.

The practice of scrying can be performed using a variety of tools, each offering a different experience:

1. Crystal Balls: Often made of glass or quartz, crystal balls are the classic tool for scrying. Their smooth surface can create a sense of depth, allowing the practitioner to enter a meditative state more easily.

2. Mirrors: Black mirrors, or obsidian mirrors, are particularly favoured as they can absorb light and create a deep, reflective surface that enhances the clarity of visions.

3. Bowls of Water: Water is often used in its still state, providing a natural medium that reflects light and imagery. It can also represent the unconscious mind, making it a powerful tool for scrying.

4. Flames: Gazing into a candle flame or a fire can evoke different sensations and insights, as the shifting flames may reveal images or messages.

In addition to these traditional tools, new methods have gained popularity in recent times:

- Wax: Observing melted wax can reveal shapes and images that can be interpreted in a divinatory context.

- Clouds: Watching the formations and movements of clouds can inspire intuitive revelations.

- Glass: Various transparent or translucent glass objects can be used to create reflections and refractions that facilitate scrying.

- Crystals: Specific crystals are believed to enhance intuition and psychic abilities when gazed upon.

Creating the Ideal Environment for Scrying -

For scrying to be effective, it is essential to cultivate a conducive environment. Here are some recommendations:

- Cleanliness: A tidy space helps clear the mind and promotes a sense of purity and focus.

- Comfort: Choose a comfortable seating arrangement or floor setting where you can relax fully.

- Privacy: Ensure you are in a location free from distractions and interruptions. This will help maintain your concentration.

- Ambiance: Dim lighting or the use of candles can enhance the atmosphere, creating an intimate setting for scrying.

Steps for Scrying:

1. Prepare Your Environment: Set the stage by incorporating elements that facilitate relaxation and concentration. Consider lighting incense, using aromatic herbs, or ringing a singing bowl to create a calming soundscape.

2. Ground Yourself: Before starting, take a moment to ground yourself. Engage in meditation or gentle yoga to connect with your body and the present moment, ensuring that your mind is clear.

3. Select Your Scrying Tool: Choose a scrying tool that resonates with you. This could be a crystal ball, a mirror, a bowl of water, or any other medium you feel drawn to.

4. Raise Your Energy: To increase your focus, rub your hands together briskly, generating warmth and energy. Place your hands on either side of the scrying tool without making contact, allowing the energy to flow into the tool while keeping your eyes closed and visualizing this transfer.

5. Focus on Your Question: When you feel ready, gently touch the scrying tool with both hands. Concentrate on a specific question or intention, allowing it to permeate your thoughts.

6. Open Your Eyes: Take a slow, calming breath and open your eyes. Locate a fixed point on your scrying tool that seems to draw you in. Allow your gaze to rest lightly upon it.

7. Observe Sensations and Visions: As you concentrate, remain aware of any sensations, visions, colours, or scents that arise in your mind's eye. Trust your intuition as you interpret these impressions, allowing them to guide you toward understanding your question or situation.

Through practice and patience, scrying can become a powerful tool for insight and reflection, helping to unlock the mysteries within and guide you on your path.

The Elements

Witches have long drawn upon the four fundamental elements—Earth, Air, Fire, and Water—to enhance their magical practices. Each of these elements possesses its own distinct properties, energies, and influences, which can also be connected to individuals through their zodiac signs, enriching the spiritual experience for practitioners.

Earth

Earth, as the very foundation of our existence, provides not only our habitat but also the resources necessary for sustenance, material creation, and daily life. It embodies the most grounding energy among the four elements, characterized by its stability and weight—qualities that offer a sense of calm and reassurance. Although Earth often appears static in our everyday experiences, it is teeming with life; the slow growth of towering trees, the subtle movements of wildlife, and the steady presence of humanity itself all exemplify the dynamic nature of this element. The essence of Earth resonates with qualities such as permanence, patience, endurance, and resilience.

When one feels drained or unsteady, it may be an indication of a disconnection from the grounding energies of Earth. To re-establish this connection, various practices can be undertaken:

- Wear Earth Tones: Incorporating colours such as deep greens and rich browns into your wardrobe can help channel the energy of the earth.

- Nature Immersion: Spend meaningful time in nature, particularly in areas rich with flora, fauna, rocks, and soil, fostering a deeper bond with the natural world.

- Grounding Rituals: Lie down beneath a large tree, allowing your body to connect with the ground. Visualize yourself drawing energy from the Earth, stabilizing and rejuvenating your spirit.

- Indoor Plants: If getting outside isn't feasible, engage with houseplants by touching the dirt and leaves, fostering a tactile connection with the earth element.

Earth Correspondences:

- Colours: Green and Brown, reflecting the lushness of plant life and the rich, nurturing soil.

- Crystals: Amethyst, Emerald, Onyx, and Quartz—each possessing unique properties that harness Earth's grounding energy and promote stability.

- Direction: North, representing the stillness and strength of Earth.

- Plants: Cedar, Patchouli, and Sage—plants that symbolize protection, purification, and longevity.

- Tarot: The Pentacles suit, is associated with material aspects of life and earthly manifestations.

- Time: Midnight, a moment of introspection and potential, when the subconscious may communicate more freely.

- Season: Winter, a time associated with reflection, rest, and the nurturing qualities of Earth.

- Zodiac Signs: Taurus, Virgo, and Capricorn—each reflecting the practicality, steadfastness, and reliable nature of Earth.

Individuals embodying an Earth personality type—often determined by their zodiac sign—are typically grounded and pragmatic. They are seen as sensible, with a strong focus on tangible, evidence-based realities. This practical mindset allows them to build long-term, stable relationships, making them reliable partners and loyal friends, characterized by honesty and kindness.

However, those with strong Earth traits may face challenges, particularly when it comes to openness. Their preference for structure and order can sometimes lead to resistance against new experiences and ideas, potentially closing them off to opportunities for growth and enrichment. Balancing their natural inclination toward practicality with a willingness to embrace change can lead to profound personal development and a broader perspective on life.

Air

Unlike the solid, visible element of Earth that surrounds us, Air is an invisible force that plays a crucial role in our daily lives. Although we cannot see it, we experience Air through various sensations: the sound of the wind howling past, the gentle caress of a breeze on our skin, or the refreshing chill that fills our lungs. Our interaction with Air is constant and vital; it is a fundamental element for sustaining life as we rely on it to breathe. Interestingly, we often overlook Air until we find ourselves deprived of it, reminding us of its essential nature.

Air symbolizes the essence of imagination and inspiration. It embodies qualities associated with travel, mental clarity, communication, knowledge, and the free flow of ideas. When moments arise where you feel the need to get clarity or seek wisdom, this indicates a call to reconnect with the powerful element of Air. There are numerous ways to cultivate this connection:

- Wear Air Colours: Incorporate shades of yellow and gold into your wardrobe to embrace this element's energy.

- Practice Controlled Breathing: Focus on your breath, allowing for deep, calming inhalations and gentle exhalations to clear your mind.

- Meditate in a Breeze: Find a quiet spot outdoors where you can sit comfortably and let the air wash over you while you reflect.

- Lay on the Ground on a Clear Day: Observe how the air moves the clouds across the sky, creating a sense of tranquillity.

Air Correspondences:

- Colours: Yellow & Gold

- Crystals: Amber, Citrine & Topaz

- Direction: East

- Plants: Clover, Lavender & Lemongrass

- Tarot: Swords

- Time: Dawn

- Season: Spring

- Zodiac Signs: Libra, Aquarius & Gemini

Individuals with Air personalities often exhibit a unique blend of emotional detachment and open-mindedness. They are adept at recognizing patterns and possibilities that others might overlook, enabling them to sidestep common pitfalls in life. Socially, they tend to radiate energy, contributing to conversations with new ideas and expanding upon the thoughts of others. However, because of their craving for movement and exploration, they may frequently travel yet yearn to return to their familiar surroundings.

A common challenge for those with Air personalities is maintaining a balance between their high energy and the need to ground themselves. While they may have lofty thoughts and aspirations, they must remember to keep their feet on the ground—a delicate combination that can be difficult to manage.

Fire

Among the classical elements, Fire tends to draw the most attention due to its striking presence and dynamic nature. Its wonders can captivate anyone, but it commands respect as one of the most hazardous elements. Fire relies on the consumption of another material to exist, setting it apart from the other elements. This characteristic makes Fire perpetually transformative and infinitely fascinating.

Often regarded as the element of illumination, Fire is intrinsically linked to the sun and brings light to the shadows. It embodies passion, strength, initiative, courage, willpower, creativity, and vibrancy. Fire is not merely a passive element; it is the embodiment of action and animation.

When you sense a need for strength or courage in your life, this is a clear signal to reconnect with the invigorating energy of Fire. Here are some ways to tap into this element's essence:

- Wear Fire Colours: Integrate bold hues like red and orange into your attire as a means of channelling Fire's passion and energy.

- Gaze at Flames: Allow yourself to be entranced by the flickering beauty of a candle or a bonfire, letting the flames inspire your thoughts.

- Soak in Sunlight: Spend time outdoors basking in the warmth of the sun, allowing its rays to energize and uplift you.

- Meditative Flame Gazing: Focus your attention on the flicker of a candle flame, observing how it shifts and twists, perhaps seeing images manifest within its dance.

Fire Correspondences:

- Colours: Red & Orange

- Crystals: Fire Opal, Garnet & Ruby

- Direction: South

- Plants: Allspice, Basil, Cinnamon, Garlic & Juniper

- Tarot: Wands

- Time: Noon

- Season: Summer

- Zodiac Signs: Aries, Leo & Sagittarius

People with Fire personality types often possess a magnetic presence, exuding an energy that naturally draws attention. They tend to be vibrant, easily excitable, and full of enthusiasm, traits that make them dynamic leaders. Their courage and willingness to seize opportunities often inspire others, lighting a spark of joy and positivity in social situations simply by their presence.

However, this intensity can sometimes come with challenges. Fire personalities might struggle with impulsiveness, occasionally overshadowing others in conversation due to their vibrant energy. Their passionate nature can lead to quick tempers, requiring them to learn how to temper their fiery disposition and find moments of calm amidst the fervour of their spirit. Finding the right balance is key for these spirited individuals to thrive both personally and in their interactions with others.

Water

Water, an essential and dynamic element, possesses the remarkable ability to move fluidly and change its form. It is not only a vital component of the Earth's landscapes, filling vast oceans and forming towering glaciers that remain largely untouched by human exploration, but it also plays a crucial role in the human body, constituting a significant portion of our physical makeup. Water is an extraordinary element, ranging from the gentlest droplet of rain to the immense power of a tsunami. It can exist in a tranquil state or in relentless motion, a testament to its versatility.

One of the defining characteristics of water is its ability to exist in three distinct states of matter: liquid, solid (ice), and gas (vapor). Regardless of its state, water takes on the shape of whatever vessel contains it, symbolizing adaptability and resilience. Known for its cleansing and purifying properties, water flows effortlessly, often choosing the path of least resistance. Furthermore, it is deeply intertwined with the mystical forces of the moon and ocean tides, suggesting a profound connection to our intuitive faculties.

When you sense a need to enhance your intuition or seek emotional healing, it may be a sign to reconnect with the element of water. There are numerous ways to foster this connection:

- Wear Water Colours: Incorporate shades of blue, aqua, and turquoise into your wardrobe to resonate with water's essence.

- Natural Swimming: Engage in swimming or floating in natural bodies of water, such as lakes, rivers, or oceans, to immerse yourself in water's healing energies.

- Mindful Walks: Take leisurely walks along riverbanks or beaches, paying close attention to the soothing sounds of water flowing or crashing, allowing this auditory experience to ground and center you.

- Scrying: Utilize a bowl of water for scrying, a form of divination where you gaze into the reflective surface to tap into your intuition and gain insight.

Water Correspondences:

- Colours: Blue, Aqua, & Turquoise

- Crystals: Aquamarine, Blue Topaz, & Lapis Lazuli

- Direction: West

- Plants: Aloe, Apple, Chamomile, & Jasmine

- Tarot Suit: Cups

- Time of Day: Twilight

- Season: Autumn

- Zodiac Signs: Cancer, Scorpio, & Pisces

Individuals with a "water personality" typically exhibit a natural affinity for psychic abilities, often surpassing those of the other elements. These individuals are often acutely sensitive to the emotions and energies of those around them, making them empathetic healers with a deep understanding of the human psyche. They tend to gravitate towards artistic expressions and cultivate rich and fulfilling relationships, remaining fully engaged in their connections with others. However, this sensitivity can also lead to challenges; many with a water personality may experience recurring bouts of depression. They might find themselves caught in a cycle of seeking answers to unresolved questions or attempting to assist individuals who are not open to their help, which can be emotionally exhausting.

The Fifth Element: Spirit

The fifth element, spirit, encompasses an intangible and invisible force that binds the other four elements together—earth, air, fire, and water. It represents the essence of all things, existing beyond the physical realm and transcending specific correspondences. While the elemental forces contribute to our physical reality, spirit acts as the underlying energy, fundamental for establishing connection and balance among them.

In any ritualistic practice, such as invoking a deity or performing a spell, it is a spirit that is summoned, as it resonates within each living being, whether or not we are conscious of its presence. Spirit is unique; it has no defined gender, season, direction, or energy and is instead aligned with the entirety of the wheel of the year and all magical tools. The colour that embodies the spirit element is white, representing purity and the integration of all elements.

Spirit manifests as the foundational energy behind the vibrancy of a crystal, symbolizing the symbiotic relationship between a plant and its surrounding environment, both visible and invisible. By attuning to the spirit, individuals may gain clarity and focus on their intentions, harnessing this energy to manifest changes in the material world. Understanding and engaging with the spirit element is vital for achieving true harmony and balance in one's life and magical practice.

<u>Herbs, Incense & Oils</u>

Herbs, incense, and oils play a pivotal role in the toolkit of a witch. Whether you're using herbs for spell work, cooking, or spiritual practices, there are numerous ways to incorporate these elements into your daily life.

Herbs

When it comes to herbs, their versatility shines in various applications. They can be utilized to create tinctures that serve to cleanse your ritual items, purifying them before use. Additionally, selecting a herb that aligns with the intention of your spell and incorporating it into a spell jar can amplify its effects, enhancing the overall power and focus of your magical work.

In the realm of cooking, herbs can elevate your meals not only in flavour but also energetically. Adding fresh or dried herbs to your culinary creations or herbal teas can help raise your vibrations, uplift your mood, and promote a sense of well-being. Moreover, you can incorporate herbs into your crystal grids, effectively setting intentions and manifesting your desires by allowing the combined energies to intermingle.

The ideal time to harvest herbs is in the morning after the dew has dried. This ensures the plants retain their essential oils, which are most potent when the sun is not yet scorching. To dry herbs effectively, gather them into bundles of about a dozen, secure them with twine or string, and hang them upside down. Choose a location that is airy, dark, and dry; this method typically takes about three weeks. You'll know your herbs are ready when their leaves crumble easily when pinched. Alternatively, for a quicker process, you can use an oven: spread the herbs on a sheet pan and set the temperature to the lowest setting. Keep a close watch, as this method can lead to burning if not monitored carefully.

For short-term storage, fresh herbs can last several days. Wrap them in a paper towel, place them in a plastic bag, and store them in the refrigerator or place the stems in a glass of water, similar to cut flowers. Dried herbs, on the other hand, can be stored in glass jars, resealable baggies, or plastic containers, where they have a shelf life of up to three years. If you want to further preserve the longevity of your herbs, consider freeze-drying them.

Incense

Incense can be simply defined as any plant matter that is burned to release its aromatic or spiritual properties. While many people are familiar with stick or cone incense, raw plant materials such as Palo Santo chips and sweetgrass also fall under this category. These ingredients are cherished not just for their fragrances, which can enhance meditation or create a calming environment, but also for their potential to purify spaces and elevate spiritual practices.

Oils

Essential oils are aromatic compounds extracted from plants through distillation, capturing their fragrant qualities. These oils are exceptionally potent and should ideally be used with care. Pure essential oils and undiluted fragrance oils can have profound effects, but their application on the skin or ingestion can lead to significant health issues if not handled correctly. Always take the time to research and understand the properties of each essential oil and how to use them safely, especially if you plan to incorporate them into your rituals or well-being practices.

By understanding and utilizing these elements thoughtfully, you can enhance your spiritual practices, elevate your energy, and connect more deeply with the natural world around you.

Acacia – Protection, psychic and spiritual enhancement, money, platonic love, and friendship. Use to anoint candles & censers and to consecrate chests or boxes that hold ritual tools. Use in incense to promote a meditative state.

Also Called: Gum Arabic, Arabic Gum

Aconite – Use aconite as a magical wash for ritual tools & space. Wear as an amulet for protection from vampires and werewolves.

Also Called: Wolfsbane, Monkshood

Note: Poisonous, do not consume.

Acorn – Good luck, protection, wisdom, and personal power. A dried acorn is an excellent natural amulet for keeping a youthful appearance.

Adam & Eve Root – Principally used by lovers; one lover carries the Eve Root & the other lover carries the Adam Root. This keeps your lover true to you & discourages rivals. Carry both roots in a small bag at all times for attraction, to bring love to you, or for a marriage proposal.

Adder's Tongue – Stops gossip and slander, and promotes healing. Sacred to serpent goddesses. Used in divination, healing magic, lunar magic, and dream magic.

Also Called: Dogtooth Violet

African Violet – Spirituality, protection, and healing. Wear in an amulet for protection. Keep in the home to increase spirituality. Frequently burned as incense during the spring Equinox sabbat.

Agar Agar – Promote joy and success, and attract opportunities and blessings to the household. Mix with Fast Luck powder and rub on your hands before playing bingo or other games of chance.

Agrimony – Overcoming fear & inner blockages; dispelling negative emotions. Also used for reversing spells. Sew into a dream pillow with Mugwort for best results. Use as a wash or oil to increase the effectiveness of all forms of healing rituals. Wards off evil entities and poison.

Ague – Protection, hex breaking. Used in amulets to protect against evil. Mix with incense and burn to break a hex that has been placed on you.

Also Called: Ague Root, Ague Weed

Alder – Associated with divination, music, poetry, wind magic, weather magic, teaching, and decision-making. Also used in rituals of death & dying to provide protection for the deceased.

Alfalfa – Money, prosperity, anti-hunger. Put a small jar in the cupboard or pantry to ward off poverty and hunger. Burn in a cauldron and use the ashes in amulets for protection from hunger and poverty.

Also Called: Lucerne, Buffalo Herb, Purple Medic

Alkanet – Purification, prosperity. Protects from snakebites and helps ease fear of snakes. Burned as an incense to replace negativity with positive influence.

Also Called: Anchusa, Dyer's Bugloss, Orchanet, Spanish Bugloss

Allspice – Money, luck, healing, obtaining treasure. Provides added determination and energy to any spells and charms. Burn crushed allspice to attract luck and money. Use in herbal baths for healing.

Also Called: Jamaica Pepper

Almond – Wisdom, money, fruitfulness, and prosperity. Invokes the healing energy of the deities. Provides magical help for overcoming dependencies & addiction. Associated with Candlemas and Beltane. Carry, wear, or use as incense to attract abundance.

Also Called: Greek Nuts, Shakad

Aloe – Protection and luck. Place on the grave of a loved one to promote peaceful energy. Thought to relieve loneliness and assist with success. Hang in the home to attract luck and protection for those who live there. Grow in the home to provide protection from household accidents. Burn on the night of a full moon to bring a new lover by the new moon.

Also Called: Burn Plant, Medicine Plant

Althea Root – Burn or place in a sachet to bring protection, calm an angry person, and aid psychic powers. Keep on the altar or burn on candles to attract good spirits.

Alyssum – Protection and moderating anger, protection.

Amaranth – Healing, summoning spirits, healing broken hearts, protection from bullets, and invisibility.

Amber – Protection from harm, outside influences, and psychic attacks. Mental clarity & focus. Transforming negative energy into positive energy.

Ambergris – Enhancing dreams and psychic ventures, attracting men.

Anemone – Healing and Protection

Angelica Root – A very powerful protection herb - protects against negative energy and attracts positive energy; creates a barrier against negative energy. Use in healing & exorcism incenses, scatter for purification, protection, and uncrossing. Add to incense to promote healing or to the bath to remove curses, hexes, or spells. Also thought to promote temperance. Sprinkle ground herb in the shoes to prevent tiredness and weakness. Sprinkle around the outside perimeter of the home for protection and exorcism. Burn to bring a lost love back to you.

Also Called: Masterwort, Archangel, Garden Angel, Angelica Root

Anise – Used to help ward off the evil eye, find happiness, and stimulate psychic ability. Fill a sleep pillow with anise seed to prevent disturbing dreams. Use to invoke Mercury and Apollo. Great for aromatherapy. Use in purification baths with bay leaves. A sprig of Anise hung on the bedpost will restore lost youth. Use in protection and meditation incense.

Also Called: Aniseed, Anneys, Anise Seed

Apple – Love, Garden Magic, Immortality, Friendship, Healing. Place seven apple seeds in a bag with Orris Root to attract sexual love. Use in rituals to give honour to gods and goddesses of fertility. Considered the food of the dead, which is why Samhain is called the 'Feast of Apples'. Symbolizes the soul and is burned at Samhain in honour of those who will be reborn in the spring. When doing a house blessing, cut an apple in half - eat half and put the other half outside of the home as an offering.

Also Called: Fruit of the Underworld, Fruit of the Gods, Silver Brough, Silver Branch, Tree of Love

Apricot – Love. Add leaves and flowers to love sachets or carry apricot pits to attract love.

Arabic Gum – Protection, psychic and spiritual enhancement, money, platonic love, and friendship. Use to anoint candles & censers and to consecrate chests or boxes that hold ritual tools. Use in incense to promote a meditative state.

Also Called: Acacia, Gum Arabic

Arnica Flowers – Increases psychic powers.

Arrow Root – Purification and healing; can be used as a substitute for graveyard dust.

Ash – Sea spells/magic/rituals, image magic, invincibility, protection from drowning, general protection, and luck. Burning an ash log at Yule brings prosperity. The leaf of this plant is used for travel safety. Place one tablespoon of ash leaves in a bowl of water in the bedroom overnight, then toss out in the morning -- doing this daily is said to prevent illness.

Asofoetida – Protection and banishing negativity. Burned to force someone to leave you alone. Be forewarned that this herb is powerful but has an awful smell when burned.

Also Called: Devil's Dung, Food of the Gods

Asparagus – Male Sex Magic

Aspen – Eloquence, clairvoyance, healing, and anti-theft. Plant in your garden for protection against thieves.

Aster – Love

Also Called: China Aster, Michaelmas Daisy, Starwort

Astragalus Root – Protection and energy

Avocado – Love, lust, and beauty. Also used for sex magic.

Also Called: Ahuacotl, Alligator Pear, Persea

Azalea – Happiness, gaiety, and light spirits, first love.

Note: Poisonous, do not consume.

Bachelor Buttons – Love

Also Called: Devil's Flower, Red Campion

Bakuli Pods – Difficult to find magic itcms also uscd in sachcts and potpourri.

Balm of Gilead Tears – Love, manifestations, protection, healing, de-stressing, and assisting in healing from the loss of a loved one. Use in love sachets; carry for healing, protection, and mending a broken heart. Use to dress candles for any form of magical healing. Burn to attract spirits.

Also Called: Poplar Buds, Balsam Poplar, Balm of Gilead, Mecca, Mecca Balsam, Balessan, Bechan

Balmony – A plant in the figwort family that is ground and used for hexing. Steadfastness, patience, and perseverance. Associated with the tortoise or turtle.

Also Called: Hummingbird Tree, Bitter Herb, Snake Head, Turtle Head, Turtle Bloom

Balsam Fir – Strength and breaking up negativity; Insight, progress against goals, and bringing about change. Balsam fir needles can be burned on charcoal as incense and also make a great ingredient in sachet bags, dream pillows, and potpourri mixes.

Bamboo – Hex breaking, wishes, luck, and protection. Carve a wish into bamboo and bury it in a secluded area to make your wish come true. Carry a piece of bamboo for good luck.

Banana – Fertility, potency, and prosperity

Banyan – Happiness, Luck

Barberry – Cleansing, sorcery, atonement, freeing oneself from the power or control of another.

Also Called: Witches Sweets

Barley – Love, healing, and protection. Harvests. Scatter on the ground to keep evil at bay. Tie barley straw around a rock and throw it into a river or lake while visualizing any pain you have to make the pain go away.

Basil – Love, exorcism, wealth, sympathy, and protection. Dispels confusion, fears & weakness. Drives off hostile spirits. Associated with Candlemas. Carry to move forward in a positive manner despite perilous danger. Strewn on floors to provide protection from evil. Sprinkle an infusion of basil outside of the building where you hope to be employed for luck in a job interview (be careful not to be seen!) or in your business to attract money and success. Wear or carry to aid in attracting money and prosperity.

Also Called: Common Basil, Sweet Basil, St. Joseph's Wort, Tulsi, Tulasi, Krishnamul, Kala Tulasi, Witches' Herb, Alabahaca, American Dittany

Bat's Head Root – Use in spell work, rituals, gris gris bags, etc. to obtain wishes.

Bay Laurel – Purification, house and business blessing, and clearing confusion. Attracts romance. Keep potted plants to protect your home from lightning. Place in a dream pillow for sound sleep and to induce prophetic dreams.

Also Called: Bay, Sweet Laurel, Sweet Bay, True Laurel, Lorbeer, Noble Laurel, Baie, Daphne

Bay Leaf – Protection, good fortune, success, purification, strength, healing, and psychic powers. Write wishes on the leaves and then burn the leaves to make the wishes come true. Place under the pillow (or use in dream pillow) to induce prophetic dreams. Place in the corner of each room in the house to protect all that dwell there. Carry bay leaf to protect yourself against black magic.

Bayberry – Good fortune, luck, healing, and stress relief. Burn a white candle sprinkled with bayberry bark for good fortune and money.

Also Called: American Vegetable Tallow Tree, Myrtle, Wax Myrtle, Candleberry, Candleberry Myrtle, Tallow Shrub, American Vegetable Wax, Vegetable Tallow, Waxberry, Pepperidge Bush, Berbery

Bedstraw (Fragrant) – Love and lust.

Bee Pollen – Friendship, attraction, love, strength, happiness, and overcoming depression.

Beech – Wishes, happiness, and divination. Improves literary skills. Place a leaf of beech between the covers of the Book of Shadows to increase inspiration.

Beeswax – Traditionally used for making candles, decorative seals, natural polish, protective finish, and use as a base for herbal salves.

Beet – Love. Beet juice can be used as ink for love magic or as a substitute for blood in spells and rituals.

Belladonna – Healing & forgetting past loves. Provides protection when placed in a secret place in the home. Place on a ritual altar to honour the deities and add energy to rituals.

Also Called: Banewort, Deadly Nightshade, Sorcerer's Berry, Witch's Berry, Death's Herb, Devil's Cherries, Divale, Dwale, Dwaleberry, Dwayberry, Fair Lady, Great Morel, Naughty Man's Cherries

Note: Deadly poison, do not ingest.

Benzoin – Purification, prosperity, soothing tension, dispelling anger, diminishing irritability, relieving stress & anxiety, and overcoming depression. Promotes generosity and concentration. Good to burn while using the Tarot or for success in intellectual matters. Smoulder for purification. An incense of benzoin, cinnamon, and basil is said to attract customers to your place of business.

Also Called: Snowbells, Storax, Gum Benzoin, Siam Benzoin, Siamese Benzoin, Benzoin Gum, Ben, Benjamen

Bergamot – Money, prosperity, protection from evil and illness, improving memory, stopping interference, and promoting restful sleep. Carry in a sachet while gambling to draw luck and money. Very powerful for attracting success. Burn at any ritual to increase its power.

Also Called: Orange Mint

Betel Nut – Protection and banishing

Bilberry Bark – Used for protection.

Also Called: Whortleberry, Black Whortles, Whinberry, Huckleberry, Bleaberry, Blueberry, Airelle

Bindweed – Used for curses/hexing

Birch – Protection, exorcism, and purification. A birch planted close to the home is said to protect against lightning, infertility, and the evil eye.

Also Called: White Birch, Canoe Birch, Paper Birch, Tree of Life, Lady of the Woods

Bird's Eye Chilis – From the Solanaceae (nightshade) family used for cursing, heating up spells, and crafting Hoodoo powders like hot foot powder and goofer dust.

Bistort – Fertility, divination, clairvoyance, psychic powers. Carry in a sachet for fertility and conception. Add to any herbal mixture to boost divination. Burn with frankincense during divination or to enhance psychic powers. Carry in a yellow flannel bag to attract wealth & good fortune. Sprinkle an infusion of bistort around the home to drive out poltergeists.

Also Called: Bistort Root, Dragonwort

Black Cohosh – Love, courage, protection, and potency. Use in love sachets or in the bath to prevent impotence. Carry in a pocket or amulet for courage and/or strength. Sprinkle around a room to drive away evil. Add an infusion of the herb to bath water to ensure a long and happy life. Burn as a love incense. Put in a purple flannel bag for protection from accidents and sudden death and to keep others from doing you wrong.

Also Called: Black Snake Root, Bugbane, Squawroot, Bugwort, Rattleroot, Rattleweed, Rattlesnake Root, Richweed

Black Haw – Protection, gambling, luck, power, and employment. Carry in the pocket while seeking employment, if you are having problems at work, or if you are asking for a raise.

Also Called: Devil's Shoestring, Stagbush, American Sloe

Black Pepper – Banishing negativity, exorcism, and protection from evil.

Black Walnut – Access to divine energy, bringing the blessing of the Gods, wishes.

Blackberry – Healing, protection, and money. Sacred to Brighid. Leaves and berries are said to attract wealth and healing.

Blackthorn Thorns – Thorns are traditionally used for cursing and protection. The thorns of the Blackthorn tree have long been used in witchcraft for pricking wax or cloth poppets to curse an intended victim.

Bladderwrack – Protection, sea spells, wind spells, money, psychic powers, and attracting customers. Wear in a charm for protection during travel, especially when traveling by water.

Also Called: Kelp, Seawrack, Kelpware, Black-tang, Cutweed, Sea Oak, Sea Spirit

Blessed Thistle – Purification, protection against negativity and evil, hex breaking. Carry for strength and protection. Place a bowl of blessed thistle in a room to renew the vitality and strengthen the spirit of its occupants. Men who carry thistles become better lovers.

Also Called: Holy Thistle, Saint Benedict Thistle, Spotted Thistle, Cardin

Bloodroot – Love, protection, and purification. Steep in red wine for a full cycle of the moon to use as a "blood offering" for spells that call for this - DO NOT DRINK THE WINE. Place in windows and doorways to keep curses and evil spirits out. A favourite root for use in voodoo to defeat hexes and spells aimed against you.

Also Called: Red Root, Red Indian Paint, Tetterwort, Blood Root, Indian Paint, Pauson, Red Paint Root, Red Puccoon, Sanguinariat

Blowball – Love and wishes. Carry in a red bag to grant wishes. Blow to the four directions when searching for love.

Blue Cohosh – Empowerment, purification, money drawing, love breaking, and driving away evil.

Blue Violet – Love, inspiration, good fortune, and protection from all evil. Carried for protection and to encourage fortune and changed luck. Mixed with lavender to attract lust and love. Worn to calm tempers and bring sleep.

Also Called: Sweet Scented Violet

Bluebell – Luck, truth and friendship. Incorporate into rituals of death & dying to comfort those left behind and ease their sorrow.

Also Called: Jacinth, Culverkeys, Auld Man's Bell, Ring o' Bells, Wood Bells

Blueberry – Protection. Though not recommended, blueberry is said to cause confusion & strife when tossed in the doorway or path of an enemy.

Boneset – Protection, exorcism, and warding off evil spirits. Sprinkle an infusion of boneset around the home to rid it of evil and negativity. To curse an enemy, burn as incense with a black candle inscribed with the name of the enemy (not recommended - remember karma).

Also Called: Feverwort, Agueweed, Crosswort, Eupatorium, Indian Sage, Sweating Plant, Teasel, Thoroughwort, Vegetable Antimony

Borage – Courage and psychic powers. Float the flowers in a ritual bath to raise one's spirits. Carry or burn as an incense to increase courage and strength of character. Sprinkle an infusion of Borage around the house to ward off evil.

Also Called: Bee Bread, Starflower, Herb of Gladness, Bugloss, Burrage, Cool Tankard

Brazil Nut – Good luck in love affairs.

Brewer's Yeast – Used in facial mask potions.

Brimstone – Dispels or prevents a hex on you; destroys an enemy's power over you. Burn at midnight near your back door to ward off evil.

Also Called: Sulphur Powder

Broom Tops – Purification, wind spells, divination, and protection. Sprinkle an infusion of broom tops around the home to clear away all evil.

Also Called: Irish Broom, Scotch Broom, Besom, Broom

Buchu – Divination, wind spells, psychic powers, and prophetic dreams. Add buchu leaves to the bath to enable yourself to foretell the future.

Also Called: Bucco, Agathosma Betulina, Bookoo, Bucku, Buku, and Bucco

Buckeye – Divination, good luck, and attracting money & wealth. Carried whole anointed with money oil and/or wrapped in a dollar bill for constant increase in money flow. A popular Hoodoo charm for gamblers. Carry it in your pocket for protection against arthritis.

Also Called: Horse Chestnut

Buckthorn – Sorceries, elf magic, and driving away enchantments. Used as a luck generator in legal matters and for winning in court. Place the branches of a Buckthorn near doors or windows to drive away evil and bad vibrations. To make a wish, stand in an open area facing east and concentrate on your wish; turn to your left until you are facing east again, continually sprinkling buckthorn bark powder (or an infusion made with buckthorn bark) as you turn.

Also Called: Arrowwood, Black Dogwood, Black Alder Dogwood, Black Alder Tree, Persian Berries

Buckwheat – Money, protection, and fasting. Use in charms and spells to obtain treasure, riches, and wealth.

Burdock – Used for cleansing magic when feeling highly negative about oneself or others. Use in protection incense and spells. Rinse with a decoction of burdock to remove negative feelings about yourself or others.

Also Called: Bardana, Burr Seed, Clotbur, Cocklebur, Hardock, Hareburr, Hurrburr, Turkey Burrseed, Fox's Clote, Happy Major, Lappa, Love Leaves, Personata, Beggar's Buttons

Burnet – Used for protection, consecration of ritual tools, and counter magic; also used to magically treat depression and despondency.

Also Called: Italian Pimpernel, Salad Burnet, Greater Burnet

Butcher's Broom –		Wind spells, divination, protection, psychic powers.

Butterbur – Used for love divination and raising one's spirits by increasing a sense of hope and faith.

Also Called: Bog Rhubarb, Butterdock, Umbrella Plant, Lagwort, Sweet Coltsfoot

Cabbage – Fertility, profit, good luck, lunar magic, money magic.

Cactus – Chastity, banishing, and protection. Bury with other banishing symbols for protection. Grow in the home or garden to prevent unwanted intrusions. Place in all directions of the home (north, south, east, and west) for full protection.

Calamint – Soothes sorrows and helps in recovery from emotional pain. Increase joy and restore a bright outlook on life.

Also Called: Basil Thyme, Mountain Balm, Mountain Mint

Calamus – Luck, money, healing, and protection. Place in corners of the kitchen to prevent hunger & poverty. Use to strengthen and bind spells.

Also Called: Calamus Root, Bach, Vacha

Note: Use with caution, can be poisonous.

Calendula Flowers – Protection, legal matters, and psychic/spiritual powers. Pick at noon for comfort and strength. Place garlands of calendula at doors to prevent evil from entering. Scatter under the bed for protection and to make dreams come true. Carry to help justice favour you in court. Touch the flowers with bare feet to better understand birds.

Also Called: Marigold, Summer's Bride, Bride of the Sun, Sun's Gold, Ruddes, Ruddles

Camellia – Riches

Camphor – Dreams, psychic awareness, and divination; Adds strength to any mixture; used for purification and to increase personal influence & persuasiveness. Burn on incense or use camphor oil for ritual cleaning when moving into a new home or setting up a new altar. Add to water when scrying.

Also Called: Laurel Camphor, Gum Camphor

Caper – Potency, lust, and love

Caraway – Health, love, protection, mental powers, memory, passion, and anti-theft. Prevents lover from straying when used in love spells & potions. Ideal for consecrating ritual tools. Carry to improve memory or use in dream pillows to help you to remember your dreams. Sew caraway seed into a small white bag with white thread and hide it under the mattress of a child's crib or bed to keep the child free of illness.

Cardamom – Lust, love, and fidelity.

Carnation – Protection, strength, healing, enhancing magical powers, and achieving balance. Burn to enhance creativity. Use in bath spells.

Also Called: Gilliflower, Jove's Flower, Nelka, Scaffold Flower, Sops-in-Wine, Gillies

Carob – Health and protection

Carrot – Lust, fertility

Cascara Sagrada – Legal matters, money spells, and protection against hexes. Sprinkle an infusion of the herb around the home the night before court proceedings to help in winning a court case. Wear as an amulet for protection against evil and hexes. Wear or keep in a bowl on your altar or reading table to help you concentrate.

Also Called: Cascara Sagada, Sacred Bark, Purshiana Bark, Persian Bark, Chittem Bark, Bearberry

Cashew – Money

Catnip – Sacred to Bast; should be used in any ritual involving cats or cat deities. Use with rose petals in love sachets. Use in sachets and spells designed to enhance beauty or happiness. Provides protection while sleeping. Mix with Dragon's Blood to rid oneself of a behavioural problem or bad habit. Burn dried leaves for love magic. Grow near the home or hang over the door to attract good spirits and luck.

Also Called: Cat's Play, Catmint, Nip, Nepeta, Field Balm, Catswort, Catnep

Cat's Claw – Vision quests, shamanic journeys, and money drawing.

Also Called: Una de Gato

Cat-tail – Lust

Cayenne – Dealing with separations or divorce; Cleansing & purification; Repels negativity; Speeds up the effect of any mixture to which it is added.

Cedar – Confidence, strength, power, money, protection, healing and purification. Used in the consecration of magic wands. Carry a small piece of cedar in your wallet or near money to attract wealth. Hang in the home to protect against lightning. Use in sachets to promote calmness.

Cedar Berries – Uses include anti-theft and repelling snakes.

Also Called: Juniper Berries

Celandine – Cures depression, brings victory and joy, and assists in legal matters. Serves as a protective ward when worn. Carry to increase self-confidence when facing adversaries. Use in ritual work when you feel trapped in undue negativity. Note: Deadly poison, use with caution.

Also Called: Devil's Milk

Celery – Mental powers, psychic powers, lust, fertility, and male potency.

Celery Seed – Mental and psychic powers, concentration. Burn with Orris root to increase psychic powers. Use in sleep pillow to induce sleep. Chew celery seed to aid in concentration.

Centaury – Counter magic herb; snake removing. Adds power to any magical workings. Used to repel anger and hurtful energy.

Also Called: Bitter Herb, Lesser Centaury, Feverwort

Chamomile – Love, healing, and reducing stress. Add to a sachet or spell to increase the chances of its success. Sprinkle an infusion of chamomile around the house to remove hexes, curses, and spells. Burn or add to prosperity bags to increase money. Burn as incense for de-stressing, meditation, and restful sleep.

Wash hands in an infusion of chamomile for luck before gambling or playing cards. Use in bath magic to attract love. Keep a packet of the herb with lottery tickets for luck.

Also Called: Whig Plant, Scented Mayweed, Camomyle, Ground Apple, Manzanilla (Spanish), Maythen, Earth Apple, Camomile

Cherry – Love, divination, gaiety, and happiness.

Cherry Bark – Lust, direction, frugality, favor, invisibility, and magical potency. Burn as an incense while performing divination to enhance the results, or while performing love spells to find a partner. Use to revitalize the Magical energy needed to finish an old project.

Also Called: Virginia Prune Bark

Chervil – Brings a sense of the higher self, placing you in touch with your divine, immortal spirit. Helps in making contact with a deceased loved one.

Also Called: French Parsley, Anise Chervil, British Myrrh, Sweet Cicely, Sweet Fern

Chestnut – Love

Chia – Protection and health

Chickweed – Fertility and love. Carry or use to attract a lover or maintain your current relationship. Useful for lunar and animal magic, especially the healing of birds.

Also Called: Starweed, Satin Flower, Starwort, Winterweed, Stitchwort, Tongue Grass, Adder's Mouth, Indian Chickweed, Passerina

Chicory – Frigidity, Favors, removing obstacles, and invisibility. Promotes a positive outlook and improves a sense of humour. Place fresh flowers on the altar or burn them as an incense. Anoint your body with chicory juice or an infusion of chicory to obtain Favors from others. Burn as incense with a black skull candle to place a hex on an enemy (not recommended).

Also Called: Blue-Sailors, Coffeeweed, Succory

Chili Pepper – Fidelity, love, and hex breaking. Scatter powder around the house to break hexes and spells against you. Use in love charms & spells.

Also Called: Bird Pepper, Pod Pepper, Cayenne

China Berry – Luck

Chives – Protection and weight loss

Chrysanthemum – Protection. Grow in the garden to ward off evil spirits.

Also Called: Mum

Cilantro – Protection of gardeners; brings peace to the home and helps to attune one with their soul.

Cinnamon – Spirituality, success, healing, protection, power, love, luck, strength, and prosperity. Burn as incense or use it in a sachet to raise spiritual and protective vibrations, draw money, and stimulate psychic powers. A popular herb for use in charms to draw money & prosperity. Wear in an amulet to bring passion.

Also Called: Sweet Wood

Cinquefoil – An all-purpose magical herb. The five points of the leaf represent love, money, health, power, and wisdom. Stimulates memory, eloquence, and self-confidence. Carry, burn, or wear to possess these traits. Used for business & house blessing. Use in spells to bring protection to a friend or loved one taking a journey. Burn as an incense during divination to bring dreams of one's intended mate. Frequently associated with ritual work involving romance. Wash hands and forehead with an infusion of this herb nine times to wash away hexes and evil spells against you. Fill an empty eggshell and keep it in the home for powerful protection from evil forces. Wrap in red flannel and hang over the bed to ward off dark spirits of the night.

Also Called: Five Finger Grass, Synkefoyle, Witches Weed, Five Leaf, Tormentilla, Sunkfield, Bloodroot, Moor Grass, Goosegrass, Goose Tansy, Crampweed, Silverweed, Silver Weed, Sunkfield

Citronella – Draws friends to the home, and customers to the business. Promotes eloquence, persuasiveness, and prosperity. Protects and cleanses the aura. Encourages self-expression and creativity (great for writers & actors!) and brings clarity to the mind. Repels insects and deodorizes.

Clove – Exorcism, love, money, and protection

Clover – Fidelity, protection, money, love, and success. Strong association with the Earth, useful in consecrating both pentacles and ritual tools made of copper. Carry as an amulet or use in sachets for luck, attracting money, fidelity, maintaining mental acuity, and/or protection. When grown outside, is thought to keep snakes away from property. Sprinkle around the home to remove negative spirits.

Also Called: Trefoil, Cleaver Grass, Marl Grass, Cowgrass, Three Leaved Grass, Honeystalks, Shamrock, Trifoil

Clover (Red) – Put in baths to aid in financial arrangements. Also used in potions for lust. Used in sachets or incense for money, love, fidelity, success and luck. Protects and blesses domestic animals. Used in the consecration of ritual tools made of copper.

Also Called: Trefoil, Cleaver Grass, Marl Grass, Cowgrass, Three Leaved Grass, Honeystalks, Shamrock, Trifoil

Cloves – Magical uses include protection, banishing hostile/negative forces, and gaining what is sought. Cloves are burned to stop gossip as well as to purify & raise the spiritual vibrations of an area. Use to bring a sense of kinship to a social gathering. Wear for protection and mental clarity. Said to protect babies in their cribs if strung together and hung over the crib (being sure that the strand can't fall into the crib, of course!). Burn to attract riches, drive away hostile forces, and stop any gossip about you. Carry to attract the opposite sex or bring comfort during bereavement. Cleanses the aura.

Also Called: Ding Xiang

Club Moss – Protection and power. Use in bath magic for purification. Burn as incense as an offering to the deities and to open channels of communication with them. Use in amulets and charms for power and protection.

Also Called: Wolf's Claw

Coconut – Chastity, protection, and purification

Coffee – Helps to dispel nightmares and negative thoughts and to overcome internal blockages. Provides peace of mind and grounding.

Coltsfoot – Wealth, prosperity, and love. Use in love sachets. Sacred to Brighid. Use in spells for peace and tranquillity.

Also Called: Coughwort, Hallfoot, Horsehoof, Foalswort, Fieldhove, Donnhove

Columbine – Love and courage. Grow in the garden to attract fairies. Use in spells and charms to increase courage in stressful situations.

Also Called: Granny's Bonnet, Culverwort

Comfrey – Magical uses include money, safety during travel, and any Saturnian purpose. Use for workings involving stability, endurance, and matters relating to real estate or property. Put some in your luggage to help prevent loss or theft. Wear for travel safety and protection. Use the root in money spells and incense.

Also Called: Knitbone, Knit Bone, Ass Ear, Blackwort, Bruisewort, Knitback, Miracle Herb, Boneset, Gum Plant, Slippery Root, Wallwort

Copal Resin – Love, purification. Add to love and purification incense. Use a piece of copal to represent the heart in poppets.

Coriander – Love, health, immortality, and protection. Tie fresh coriander with a ribbon and hang it in the home to bring peace & protection. Add to love charms and spells to bring romance or use in ritual work to ease the pain of a broken love affair. Promotes peace among those who are unable to get along. Throw the seeds in lieu of rice during Handfasting and other rituals of union. Use the seeds in love sachets and spells. Add powdered seeds to wine for an effective lust potion. Wear or carry the seeds to ward off disease and migraines.

Also Called: Cilantro, Chinese Parsley, Yee Sai

Corn – Protection, divination, good luck

Cornflower – Sprinkle over the area where you and your mate argue the most to alleviate discord and strife. A patron herb of herbalists. Use the blue petals to make homemade ink for a Book of Shadows. Use in rituals to give honour to the Mother of all nature.

Also Called: Bachelor Button, Hurtsickle, Bluet, Blue Cap, Bluebottle, Blue Corn Flower

Cotton – Fishing magic, rain, protection, luck, and healing. Burn to attract rain. Cloth made of cotton is the best for magical use. Place cotton in a sugar bowl to draw luck.

Cowslip – Treasure finding, youth, concentration, focus, and house & business blessing. Use in ritual work involving Goddesses associated with love. Carry to increase attractiveness and increase romantic appeal, providing the energy to attract a partner.

Also Called: False Primrose, Keyflower, Fairy Cup, Paigle, Key of Heaven

Coxcomb – Protection

Cramp Bark – Used for protection and female energy.

Also Called: Guelder Rose Parts

Crowfoot – Love. Use in rituals & ceremonies associated with marriage and Handfasting, engagements, and rituals involving commitments and sacred binding vows.

Also Called: Buttercup, Gold Cup, Grenouillette, Meadow Buttercup

Cubeb Berries – Love, lust, and adding fire to spells. Use in sachets for love & sex.

Also Called: Tailed Pepper

Cucumber – Chastity, fertility, and healing

Culvers Root – Purification

Also Called: Black Root, Bowman's Root, Brinton Root, Culver's Physic, Physic Root

Cumin – Fidelity, protection, and exorcism. The seed is said to prevent the theft of any object which contains it. Burn with frankincense for protection. Scatter on the floor alone or with salt to drive out evil. Use in love spells to promote fidelity. Steep in wine to make love potions.

Curry – Protection. Burn curry powder to keep evil forces away.

Cyclamen – Fertility, happiness, lust, and protection. Reinforces romance between consensual partners and increases the potential of a relationship carrying into the next incarnation.

Also Called: Groundbread, Sowbread, Ivy-Leafed, Swine Bread

Cypress – Associated with death and mourning; stimulates healing and helps overcome the pain of loss. Calmness and tranquillity. Hang in the home for protection. Burn crushed cypress wood to aid in understanding grief and death or to aid in divination. Wear or carry at funerals to ease the mind and minimize grief. Useful at any time of crisis.

Also Called: Tree of Death

Daffodil – Love, luck, and fertility. Used to keep negative energy away from the home or altar. Place fresh daffodils in the home to increase fertility. Wear near the heart to bring good luck.

Also Called: Narcissus, Lent Lily, Jonquil, Goose Leek, Lentlilly

Daisy – Love, luck, and innocence. Associated with babies and newborn infants. Incorporate into baby blessings & Wiccaning or bring protective Magic into a baby's sleeping area. Wear or carry to draw love.

Also Called: Bairnwort, Bruisewort, Eyes, Field Daisy, Maudlinwort, Moon Daisy

Damiana – Lust, sex magic, and attracting love. Useful for any love or sex spells. Used by solitary practitioners to open the chakras and increase psychic abilities. It is said that this herb should be stored in a container with a quartz crystal. Highly useful in tantra magic, astral travel, deep meditation, and spirit quests. Note: Internal use of this herb can be toxic to the liver.

Also Called: Love Leaf, Mexican Damiana

Dandelion Leaf – Summoning spirits, healing, purification, and defeating negativity. Bury in the northwest corner of the yard to bring favourable winds. Use sachets and charms to make wishes come true.

Also Called: Blowball, Cankerwort, Lion's Tooth, Priest's Crown, Puffball, Swine Snout, White Endive, Wild Endive, Piss-a-Bed

Dandelion Root – Magical uses include divination, wishes, and calling spirits. Use in dream pillows & sachets for sleep protection. Bury on the northwest side of the house to draw good luck.

Also Called: Blowball, Cankerwort, Lion's Tooth, Priest's Crown, Puffball, Swine Snout, White Endive, Wild Endive, Piss-a-Bed

Deer's Tongue – Wear, carry, or sprinkle on your bed to attract men and aid in increasing psychic powers.

Devil Bone Root – Cut into small pieces and carry in a red flannel bag to ward off arthritis.

Devil's Bit – Exorcism, love, protection, and lust

Devil's Bone Root – Sexual attractiveness, warding off negative energies

Devil's Claw – Protection and dispelling unwanted company.

Devil's Shoestring – Protection, luck, attracting a new raise or job, giving control over the opposite sex, and invisibility. Carry in the pocket while seeking employment, if you are having problems at work, or if you are asking for a raise.

Also Called: Black Haw, Stagbush, American Sloe

Dill – Money, protection, luck, and lust. Used in love & protection charms. Effective at keeping away dark forces, useful for a house blessing. Keeps the mind cognizant of the line between superstition and the realities of magic. Place seeds in muslin and hang them in the shower to attract women. Use dill seeds in money spells. The scent of dill is said to stimulate lust. Add grains of dill seed to a bath before going on a date to make yourself irresistible.

Also Called: Aneto, Aneton, Dill Weed, Dill Seed, Dilly, Garden Dill

Dogwood – Wishes, protection, and good health. Used in meetings in which attendees must maintain confidence in the topics of discussion. Used to guard diaries, journals, and Books of Shadows. Seal letters with dogwood oil to keep the contents for the intended eyes only. Use powdered bark or flowers as an incense.

Also Called: Boxwood, Squawbush, Budwood, Flowering Cornel, Green Osier

Dragon's Blood – Protection, energy, and purification. Burn as an incense to increase the potency of a spell. Has strong banishing powers against negative influences and bad habits. A pinch under the mattress is believed to prevent impotency. Used as a form of magical ink. Carry or sprinkle around the home or place of business to drive away negativity. Carry or wear it for good luck.

Also Called: Blood, Blume, Calamus Draco, Dragon's Blood Palm

Dulse – Lust, harmony in the home, sea rituals, and pacifying sea winds. Throw into the ocean or lake to have the sea spirits send peace your way. Likewise, throw from a high place to have the wind spirits send peace. Leave in the home to induce harmony.

Ebony – Protection, power. Use in protection amulets.

Also Called: Obeah Wood

Echinacea – Adds powerful strength to charms, sachets, and herb mixes. Useful for money-drawing magic. Dried flowers can be burned as incense. Use on the altar as an offering to the spirits.

Also Called: Purple Coneflower, Coneflower, Black Sampson, Rudbeckia

Elder – Sleep, releasing enchantments, protection against negativity, wisdom, house blessing, and business blessing. Elder flowers are useful in dream pillows. Wear to provide protection against evil, negativity, attackers, and the temptation to commit adultery. Used in rites of death & dying to protect the loved one during transport to the Otherworld.

Also Called: Sweet Elder, Tree of Doom, Pipe Tree, Witch's Tree, Old Lady, Devil's Eye

Note: Elder leaves, bark, roots, and raw berries are poisonous. Use with caution.

Elecampane – Magically used for banishing and to dispel angry or violent vibrations. Associated with elves. Use in a sachet to attract love or in incense to purify initiates. Strong association with the Elven world and Tarot. Useful for baby blessings. Hide a sachet of elecampane or sprinkle it around doorways to keep out bad vibrations. Ground together with vervain and mistletoe for a powerful love powder.

Also Called: Yellow Starwort, Elfdock, Elfwort, Horse-elder, Horseheal, Scabwort, Elecampagne, Velvet Dock

Elm – Love, protection from lightning. Strong correspondence with the Elven world. To stop slander, bury elm bark in a box with a piece of paper containing the name of the person who is speaking adversely about you.

Also Called: Elven, European Elm, English Elm

Endive – Love spells, sex magic

Epsom Salt – Common ingredient in ritual baths and bath salt recipes.

Eucalyptus – Attracts healing vibrations, great for protection and healing sachets. Use to purify any space. Use dried leaves to stuff healing poppets, pillows, or sachets. Arrange a ring of dried leaves around a blue candle and burn the candle for healing vibrations. Carry in a sachet or amulet to help reconcile difficulties in a relationship, for protection, and/or to maintain health.

Also Called: Blue Gum, Curly Mallee, River Red Gum, Mottlecah, Maiden's Gum, Fever Tree, Stringy Bark Tree

Evening Primrose – Magical uses include love and attracting faeries. Use in ritual baths to increase inner beauty & desirability.

Also Called: Fever Plant, Field Primrose, King's Cure-all, Night Willow-herb, Scabish, Scurvish, Tree Primrose, Primrose

Eyebright – Carry this herb to increase psychic ability, improve memory, encourage rationality, and increase positive outlook. Carry to bring a humorous and bright outlook when life seems dark and negative.

Also Called: Eye Bright, Euphrasia, Casse-lunette

False Unicorn Root – Magical uses include lusty spells and protection for mother and baby.

Also Called: False Unicorn, Starwort, Helonias Root

Fennel Seed – Imparts strength, vitality, and sexual virility; prevents curses, possession, and negative problems. Use in spells for protection, healing, and purification. Provides help and strength when facing danger or dire times. Fennel is thought to increase the length of one's incarnation. Hang in windows and doors to ward off evil.

Also Called: Large Fennel, Sweet Fennel, Wild Fennel, Finocchio, Carosella, Florence Fennel, Fennel Seed

Fenugreek – Used for money drawing and fertility magic. Use in floor washes to bring money to the home. Place in a jar and add a few seeds every day to increase money flow to the household.

Also Called: Greek Hay, Foenugreek, Fenigreek, Fenugreek Seed

Fern – Mental clarity, cleansing, purification, and dispelling negativity. Keep in the room where studying is done to help concentration. Burn a sprig of fern before an exam. Use in sachets and amulets for powerful auric protection.

Feverfew – Protection against accidents and cold/flu. Use in charms or sachets for love magic or spiritual healing. Keep flowers in a suitcase or car when traveling.

Also Called: Featherfew, Rainfarn, Wild Quinine, Featherfoil, Prairie Dock, Missouri Snakeroot, Flirtwort, Parthenium, Febrifuge

Fig – Divination, fertility, and love. Place a branch in front of the door before traveling to ensure a safe return. Write a question on a fig leaf -- if the leaf dries slowly, the answer is yes, otherwise the answer is no.

Also Called: Common Fig

Figwort – Magical balms, house & business blessing, protection for the home. Wear around the neck for health and protection against the evil eye.

Flax Seed – Used for money spells and healing rituals. Mix seeds with red pepper and keep them in a box in the home to protect it. Put in a sachet to protect against hostile magic. Place some in the shoe or in pocket, wallet, purse, or altar jar with a few coins to ward off poverty. Sprinkle an infusion made with flax seed around the area before divination to get a more accurate reading of someone's future. Burn for divinatory powers.

Also Called: Linseed

Fleabane – Exorcism, protection, chastity.

Foxglove – Protection of home & garden, vision, and immortality. Used to commune with those of the Underworld.

Also Called: Fairy Caps, Deadman's Bells, Fairy's Glove, Fox Claws, Fairy Thimbles, Witch's Bells, Folk's Glove, Witches Glove

Note: Poisonous, use with caution.

Frangipani – Promoting openness in those around you; attracting love, trust, and admiration.

Frankincense Resin – Successful ventures, cleansing, purification. Burn for protective work, consecration, and meditation. Used as an offering at Beltane, Lammas, and Yule. Enhances the power of topaz. Use in rituals and magic associated with self-will, self-control, or the ego. Represents the ability of the divine to move into manifestation. Add to charm bags and sachets to bring success. Mix with Cumin and burn as incense for powerful protection.

Also Called: Frankincense Tears, Olibanum

Fumitory – Associated with the underworld. Excellent for use at Samhain. Infusion is useful as a wash for consecrating ritual tools. Use in purification rituals or when moving into a new residence.

Make an infusion, then sprinkle the infusion around the house and rub it on the bottom of your shoes to bring quick financial gain.

Also Called: Earth Smoke

Galangal Root – Magical uses include winning in court, doubling money, hex breaking, and sex magic. Burn as incense to remove evil spells and break curses. Carry for protection, to improve psychic abilities, and to bring good health. Carry to court to make the judge or jury feel favourably inclined toward you. Wrap money around the root and it will multiply threefold. Burn vigilantly for 14 days before a court case, saving the ashes and bringing them to court in a green flannel bag for luck.

Also Called: Lo John, Low John, Lo John the Conqueror, Lesser Galangal, Galanga, Colic Root, Gargaut, Catarrh Root, India Root, China Root

Gardenia – Promoting peace/repelling strife, protection from outside influences. Carry or wear to attract love or friendship. Burn with other healing herbs to bring peace and comfort to one who is ailing. Use dried flowers in healing incenses and mixtures. Scatter around a room to bring peaceful vibrations.

Garlic – Magical uses include healing, protection, exorcism, repulsion of vampires, and purification of spaces and objects. Used to invoke Hecate. Guards against negative magic, spirits, and the envy of others. Hang in the home to bring togetherness to the family or keep your willpower strong. Said to ward off bad weather when worn or carried during outside activities. Believed to absorb diseases -- rub fresh, peeled garlic against ailing body parts then throw the garlic into running water.

Also Called: Stinkweed

Gentian – Add an infusion to the bath for power and strength.

Geranium – Overcoming negative thoughts & attitudes, lifting spirits, promoting protection & happiness. Repels insects. Balances mind and body.

Ginger – Draws adventure and new experiences. Promotes sensuality, sexuality, personal confidence, prosperity, and success. Adds to the strength and speed of any mixture of which it is a part. Place in an amulet, mojo, or medicine bag to promote good health & protection. Use in herbal mixtures for the consecration of athames to strengthen and energize the ritual blade. A ginger root in the form of a human is a very powerful magical token.

Also Called: African Ginger

Ginkgo Biloba – Aphrodisiac, associated with fertility. Carry or use in amulets and charms as a healing herb. Useful in ritual healing. The dried nuts represent male fertility. Useful in all creative work. Immerse in water, then remove and keep in the bedroom to gain grace, love, and beauty.

Also Called: Maidenhair Tree, Living Fossil, Gingko

Ginseng – Magical uses include love, beauty, protection, healing, and lust. Carry to draw love, health, money, and sexual potency. Carve a wish into a whole root and throw it into the water to make the wish come true.

Also Called: Sang, Wonder of the World Root

Goldenrod – Money, divination

Also Called: Aaron's Rod, Woundwort, Sweet Goldenrod, Solidago, Ver d'Or

Goldenseal – Healing rituals, money spells, success. Beneficial in business dealings and matters of finance. Work into any charm or spell to increase its power.

Also Called: Yellow Root, Orange Root, Yellow Puccoon, Ground Raspberry, Eye Balm, Eye Root, Indian Paint, Yellow Paint, Golden Root, Wild Turmeric, Indian Turmeric, Jaundice Root, Yellow Eye, Wamera

Goosegrass – Wisdom, tenacity, luck in love, and pleasant dreams.

Gorse is Associated with love, protection, romance, and weddings. Used to further the romance of a consensual relationship. Protects against negativity and dark magic.

Also Called: Whin, Prickly Broom, Furze

Gotu Kola – Burn prior to (but not during) meditation.

Grape – Fertility, money, mental powers, and garden magic.

Grape Seed – Used for garden magic and fertility.

Grapefruit – Cleansing and purification.

Gravel Root – Used to increase the chances of getting a job. Aids one during times of distress. Useful as an altar offering, especially during love magic. Burn or strew about the house to relieve disharmony in the home or remove tensions. An infusion of the herb rubbed on an erect member is said to improve the male potency.

Also Called: Meadow Sweet, Bride of the Meadow, Bridewort, Little Queen, Gravelweed, Joe-Pye Weed, Purple Boneset, Kidney Root, Trumpet Weed, Trumpet Vine, and Meadowsweet.

Guinea Peppers – Hexing and cursing

Gum Arabic – Protection, psychic and spiritual enhancement, money, platonic love, and friendship. Use to anoint candles & censers and to consecrate chests or boxes that hold ritual tools. Use in incense to promote a meditative state.

Also Called: Acacia, Arabic Gum

Hawthorn – Magical uses include chastity, fertility, fairy magic, fishing magic, and rebirth. Also used for success in matters related to career, work, and employment. Place around the bedroom or carry to enforce or maintain chastity or celibacy. Sacred to the fairy. Used to decorate maypoles. Used in weddings and handfasting to increase fertility. Wear while fishing to ensure a good catch. Wear or carry to promote happiness and protect against lightning. Keep in a house to repel ghosts and evil spirits. An infusion of the herb used to wash floors will remove negative vibrations.

Also Called: Hawthorne, Haw, May Bush, May Tree, Mayblossom, Mayflower, Quickset, Thorn-apple Tree, Whitethorn, Bread and Cheese Tree, Quick, Gazels, Ladies' Meat

Hay – Pregnancy and fertility.

Heal All – Uses include all-purpose healing and successful gambling.

Heather – Protection, luck, and immortality. Dip in water and sprinkle it around in a circle to bring rain. Carry in sachets or charms to protect against rape and other violent crimes. Hang or use in-home decorations to promote peace. Burn with fern to bring rain.

Also Called: Ling, Scotch Heather

Heliotrope – Cheerfulness, gaiety, prosperity, and protection. Use in rituals of Drawing Down the Sun or in magical workings requiring strengthening of the solar aspects of the self. Place under the pillow to induce prophetic dreams. It is said that if you sleep with fresh heliotrope under your pillow, you will dream of the person who has stolen from your home.

Also Called: Turnsole, Cherry Pie

Hemlock – Use to paralyze a situation. Used for discord, cursing, and sadness.

Note: Highly poisonous, do not consume.

Henbane – Dried leaves are used in the consecration of ceremonial vessels. Used in love sachets and charms to gain the love of the person desired. Thrown into the water to bring rain.

Also Called: Hogs Bean, Devil's Eye, Henbells, Sukran

Henna – Attracts love if worn close to the heart. Wear to ward off the evil eye and provide protection from illnesses. Also great for temporary tattooing and hair colouring.

Hibiscus – Attracting love and lust, divination, and dreams. Carry in a sachet or burn as incense to attract love.

Also Called: Kharkady

Hickory – Legal matters, love, lust, and protection

High John – An "all-purpose" herb, the uses of High John include strength, confidence, conquering any situation, obtaining success, winning at gambling, luck, money, love, health, and protection. Useful in all ritual work pertaining to prosperity. Wash hands in an infusion of the herb before playing games of chance.

Also Called: High John the Conqueror, John the Conqueror, Jalap Root

Holly – Marriage, dream magic, luck, and love. Planted around the outside of the home for protection. Used as a decoration at Yule. When carried by men, is thought to heighten masculinity.

Also Called: Tinne, Bat's Wings, Hulm, Hulver Bush, Holm Chaste

Hollyhock – Increase success in the material world, increase the flow of money, or acquire new possessions. Grown near the home to help the success of the family flourish.

Honey – For attraction and solar magic.

Honeysuckle – Draws money, success, and quick abundance; Aids persuasiveness and confidence, sharpens intuition. Ring green candles with honeysuckle flowers or use honeysuckle in charms & sachets to attract money. Crush the flowers and rub them into the forehead to enhance psychic powers.

Also Called: Woodbine, Jin Yin Hua, Dutch Honeysuckle, Goat's Leaf

Hops – Relaxing and sleep producing; a fantastic herb for dream pillows. Believed to increase the restfulness & serenity of sleep. Also used for healing rituals, sachets, and incense.

Also Called: Beer Flower, Hop Flower

Horehound – Sacred to Horus. Protective; helps with mental clarity during ritual; stimulates creativity/inspiration; balances personal energies. Excellent for use in home blessings. Place near doorways to keep trouble away.

Also Called: White Horehound, Hoarhound, Marrubium, Bugleweed

Horseshoe Chestnut – Magical uses include money and healing.

Also Called: Buckeye

Hyacinth – Promotes peace of mind and peaceful sleep. Attracts love, luck, and good fortune. Named for Hiakinthos, the Greek God of homosexual love, this is the patron herb for gay men. Guards against nightmares when used as an oil, burned as incense, or included in dream pillows. Carry in an amulet or sachet to ease grief or the pain of childbirth.

Hydrangea – Hex-breaking, love drawing, bringing back a lover, fidelity, and binding.

Hyssop – The most widely used purification herb in magic. Lightens vibrations and promotes spiritual opening; used for cleansing and purification. Said to protect property against burglars and trespassers. Used to consecrate magical tools or items made of tin. The best herb for physical cleansing and washing of temple, ritual tools, or oneself (bath magic). Add to baths & sachets, infuse and sprinkle on objects/people for cleansing, or hang in the home to purge it of evil & negativity.

Also Called: Yssop, Ysopo

Indigo Weed – Protection

Also Called: Baptisia

Iris – Attracts wisdom, courage, and faith. Use fresh iris flowers to purify an area. Represents a belief in happy reincarnation. Symbolizes faith, wisdom, and valour. Useful for consecrating ritual wands. Used in rituals designed for baby blessings.

Irish Moss – An excellent luck herb. Carry or place under rugs to increase luck and ensure a steady flow of money; carry on trips for protection & safety; use to stuff luck or money poppets. Add to luck oil to increase its strength. An excellent gambler's herb. Sprinkle an infusion of the herb around a business to bring in customers.

Iron Weed – Carry in a purple flannel bag for control over others, including boss and co-workers (not recommended - remember the Witches Rede).

Ivy – Protection, healing, fertility, and love. Hang an ivy plant in front of the home to repel negative influence and discourage unwanted guests. Mix in a sachet with Holly as a wedding gift to provide protection to the newly married couple. Place ground ivy around the base of a yellow candle on a Tuesday, then burn the candle to discover who (if anyone) is working negative magic against you.

Jamaican Ginger – Gambling luck

Jasmine – Uses include snakebite and divination; good for charging quartz crystals. Use in sachets and spells to draw spiritual love and attract a soul mate. Carry or burn the flowers to draw wealth and money. Use in dream pillows to induce sleep or burn in the bedroom to bring prophetic dreams. Helps to promote new, innovative ideas.

Also Called: Pikake, Ysmyn, Jessamin, Moonlight on the Grove

Jezebel Root – Used for spells and castings for money and achievement. Used in the famous Jezebel curse, but can also be used in other curses as well as hexes.

Job's Tears – Luck in finding employment, wishes, and blessings. Used in counts of 3 or 7 in charm and mojo bags to attract luck, wishes, and money. Carrying three will assist in finding a good job. Count out seven seeds while concentrating on a wish, then carry the seeds with you at all times for seven days -- the wish should come true by the end of the week.

Juniper – Banishes all things injurious to good health; attracts good, healthy energies and love. Juniper berries can be carried by males to increase potency. Use a string of juniper berries to attract love. Burn for magical protection. Place a sprig of juniper near the door to a home or with valuables to help safeguard against theft (but keep locking the doors, too!). Use juniper oil in magical workings to increase money and prosperity.

Also Called: Juniper Berries, Ginepro, Enebro, Wachholder

Kava Kava – Uses include aphrodisiac; potent sacramental drink; potions; induces visions; astral work; and travel protection. Carry for success and job promotion.

Also Called: Ava, Ava Pepper, Intoxicating Pepper

Knotweed – Binding spells, health, and cursing. To get rid of one's enemy, stuff it into a black cloth or voodoo doll and sew it up, then bury the doll. It is also used with balmony herbs in curses.

Kola Nut – Peace, removing depression, and calming

Lady Slipper – Used for protection against hexes, curses, and the evil eye.

Lady's Mantle – Aphrodisiac, transmutation. Use in love potions or to increase the power of any magical workings.

Also Called: Nine Hooks, Dewcup, Lion's Foot, Bear's Foot, Stellaria

Larch – Protection and anti-theft

Larkspur – Health and protection

Laurel – Love and protection. Worn by brides to guarantee a long and happy marriage.

Lavender – uses include love, protection, healing, sleep, purification, and peace. Promotes healing from depression. Great in sleep pillows and bath spells. Believed to preserve chastity when mixed with rosemary. Burn the flowers to induce sleep and rest, then scatter the ashes around the home to bring peace and harmony. Use in love spells and sachets, especially those to attract men.

Also Called: Spike, Nardus, Elf Leaf, Nard

Leek – Love, protection, exorcism, and strengthening existing love.

Lemon – Cleansing, spiritual opening, purification, and removal of blockages. Add lemon peel to love sachets and mixtures. Soak the peel in water and use the mixture as a wash for magical objects to remove unwanted negativity, especially for objects received second-hand. Use an infusion of lemon to induce lust.

Also Called: Citronnier, Neemoo, Leemoo, Limone, Limoun

Lemon Balm – Love, success, healing, and psychic/spiritual development. Use in love charms & spells to attract a partner. Use in healing spells & rituals for those suffering from mental or nervous disorders.

Also Called: Melissa, Sweet Balm, Balm Mint, Bee Balm, Blue Balm, Cure-all, Dropsy Plant, Garden Balm, Sweet Balm

Lemon Grass – Psychic cleansing and opening, lust potions.

Lemon Verbena – Worn to increase attractiveness or to bed to prevent dreams. Added to other herbal mixtures and charms to increase their effectiveness. Used in purification baths. Carried in an amulet to attract the opposite sex.

Lettuce – Divination, lunar magic, sleep, protection, love spells, and male sex magic.

Liquorice – Love, lust, and fidelity. Carry to attract a lover.

Also Called: Liquorice Root, Yashtimadhu, Mithilakdi, Mulathi, Liquorice, Sweet Root, Lacris, Lacrisse, Lycorys, Reglisse

Lilac – Wisdom, memory, good luck and spiritual aid.

Also Called: Common Lilac

Lily – Fertility, renewal, rebirth, marriage, happiness, and prosperity.

Also Called: Easter Lily, Tiger Lily

Lily of the Valley – Soothing, calming, draws peace and tranquillity and repels negativity. Assists in empowering happiness and mental powers. Use in magical workings to stop harassment. Married couples should plant Lily of the Valley in their first garden to promote the longevity of the marriage.

Also Called: Jacob's Ladder, Male Lily, Our Lady's Tears, Ladder-to-Heaven, May Lily, Constancy

Lime – Purification and protection, promoting calmness and tranquillity, and strengthening love.

Linden Flowers – Used in love spells/mixtures and protection spells & incense. Mix equal parts Linden and Lavender flowers and place them in a sachet under your pillowcase to relieve insomnia. Keep Linden on a table to release the energies needed to keep the spirit alive and healthy.

Also Called: Lime Blossoms, Linden Flowers, Tilia

Little John – Place in holy water to bring good luck in everything you attempt.

Lo John – Money, success, and luck

Lobelia – Used for attracting love and preventing storms.

Also Called: Pukeweed, Indian Tobacco, Bladderpod, Wild Tobacco, Emetic Herb, Emetic Weed, Asthma Weed, Rag Root, Vomit Wort

Lotus – Love, protection, psychic opening, and spiritual growth. Sacred to Egyptian gods, Indian gods, Hermes, Oshun, and Osiris.

Lotus Root – Carry to keep thoughts pleasant and clear. Mark one side 'Yes' and the other 'No', then toss the root into the air as you make a wish to find out if the wish will come true.

Lovage – Prophetic dreams, energy, and purification. Use in bath spells for psychic cleansing. Use in sachets, amulets, or bath magic to enhance attractiveness and make yourself more love-inspiring. Add an infusion of lovage to the bath immediately prior to attending court to help bring victory.

Lucky Hand Root – Magical uses include bringing good luck, protecting the owner from all harm, travel safety, and gaining employment. Great for use in mojo & charm bags. Carry for general success and to obtain & maintain employment.

Also Called: Orchid Root

Lungwort – Air magic, offering to the Gods of air, blessing while traveling by air

Mace – Promotes concentration, focus, and self-discipline; great for study and meditation. Used in reuniting rituals.

Also Called: Macis, Muscadier

Magnolia Flowers – Magical uses include health, beauty, love, loyalty, peace, calming anxieties, marital harmony, and overcoming addictions & obsessive behaviour.

Magnolia Bark – Magical uses include fidelity, love, and hair growth.

Also Called: Cucumber Tree, Blue Magnolia, Swamp Sassafras, Magnolia Tripetata

Maidenhair Fern – Brings beauty and love into your life.

Mandrake – Magical uses include protection, prosperity, fertility, and exorcising evil. Carry to attract love. Wear to preserve health.

Also Called: Mandragora, Satan's Apple, Manroot, Circeium, Gallows, Herb of Circe, Mandragor, Raccoon Berry, Ladykins, Womandrake, Sorcerer's Root, Wild Lemon

Maple – Love, money, wealth, longevity, and good luck

Maple Syrup – Longevity, money, and love

Marigold – Attracts respect and admiration, and provides good luck in court and other legal matters. Great for bath spells -- add an infusion of marigold to the bath for 5 days to find "Mr. Right". Add to sachets, amulets, and incense to attract new love or add life to your current relationship. Place above the bed or in dream pillows for prophetic dreams. Scatter under the bed for protection while sleeping.

Also Called: Bride of the Sun, Ruddes, Marygold

Marjoram – Cleansing, purification, and dispelling negativity. Place under pillow to bring revealing dreams. Place in the corners of the home for protection. Use in love spells or place in food to strengthen love. Carry for protection or place in money mixtures and sachets to draw wealth. Put a pinch in the corner of each room in the house each month to attract a husband. Use an infusion in the bath for 7 days to aid in resolving sadness or grief.

Also Called: Joy of the Mountain, Mountain Mint

Marshmallow Root – Protection and psychic powers. Burn as an incense for protection and psychic stimulation. Place on the altar during ritual to draw in good spirits.

Also Called: Althea, Sweet Weed, Mallards, Guimauve, Mortification Plant, Schloss Tea, Wymote

May Flowers – Attract adventure and chaos to your life

Meadowsweet – Used to increase the chances of getting a job. Aids one during times of distress. Useful as an altar offering, especially during love magic. Burn or strew about the house to relieve disharmony in the home or remove tensions. Carry to gain popularity and friendship.

Also Called: Gravel Root, Bride of the Meadow, Bridewort, Little Queen, Gravelweed, Joe-Pye Weed, Purple Boneset, Kidney Root, Trumpet Weed, Trumpet Vine, Meadowsweet

Mesquite – Healing. Use in healing incense and mixtures. Use to fuel ritual fires or burn as an incense for cleansing & purification. Use an infusion of mesquite in the bath for purification.

Milk Thistle – Magical uses include strength, perseverance, wisdom, and aid in decision-making.

Mimosa – Protection, purification, love, dream magic. Use in sleep pillows to draw prophetic dreams. Use in bath magic to break hexes and prevent future problems. Scatter around an area for purification.

Mint – Promotes energy, communication, and vitality. Draws customers to a business. Use dried leaves to stuff a green poppet for healing. Place it in a wallet or purse or rub on money to bring wealth and prosperity. Use on the altar to draw good spirits to assist in your magic. Place in the home for protection.

Also Called: Garden Mint

Mistletoe – Used for fertility, creativity, prevention of illness/misfortune, and protection from negative spells & magic. Hang in the home for protection from lightning & fire. Wear in an amulet to repel negativity & ill will and protect against unwanted advances. Carry for luck in hunting. Use to draw in customers, money, and business. Use in ritual baths or prayer bowls for healing.

Also Called: Birdlime, Devil's Fuge, Golden Bough, Holy Wood, Mistletoe, Druid's Bough, Witch's Broom, Thunderbesom, Wood of the Cross

Note: Poisonous, use with caution.

Monkshood – Magical uses include invisibility and protection from evil. Use only the flowers in magic, as the roots give off fumes when drying. Excellent for redirecting predators who come after you. Note:

Also Called: Aconite, Garden Wolf's Bane, Helmet Flower, Friar's Cap, Soldier's Cap, Wolfbane

Note: Poisonous, use with caution and do not consume.

Morning Glory – Used for binding, banishing, and promoting attraction to someone or something. Wrap the vine around a poppet nine times to banish someone. Remember - the use of negative magic is not recommended.

Also Called: Devil's Guts

Note: Poisonous, use with caution.

Motherwort – Magical uses include bolstering ego, building confidence, success, and countermagic. Keep in a jar by family pictures to keep the family safe.

Also Called: Lion's Tail, Lion's Ear, Throwwort, Roman Motherwort

Mugwort – Carried to increase lust & fertility, prevent backache, and cure disease & madness. Place around divination and scrying tools to increase their power or near the bed to enable astral travel. Use in sleep pillow or place it in a sachet under your pillowcase to bring about prophetic dreams. Use an infusion of mugwort to clean crystal balls and magic mirrors.

Also Called: Artemisia, Felon Herb, St. John's Plant, Naughty Man, Oild Man, Sailor's Tobacco

Mullein – Protection from nightmares & sorcery, courage, cursing, and invoking spirits. Place beneath a pillow or use in dream pillow to guard against nightmares. Carry to instill courage and help attract love from the opposite sex. Use in place of graveyard dust in spells. Wear to keep wild animals at bay in unfamiliar areas. Burn to banish bad influences and bring an immediate halt to bad habits.

Also Called: Flannel Flower, Shepherd's Club, Hare's Beard, Pig Taper, Cow's Lungwort, Aarons Rod, Velvet Plant, Verbascum Flowers, Woolen Blanket Herb, Bullock's Lungwort, Hag's Tapers

Musk – Encourages self-esteem and desirability. Can assist in transmuting sexual love into spiritual connection. Stimulates the root chakra.

Mustard Seed – Courage, faith, and endurance. Frequently used in voodoo charms. Carry a few grains in a small bag to guard against injury. Sprinkle red mustard seed around the house to ward off burglars. Use yellow mustard seed in an amulet to bring faith followed by success -- this is one of the oldest known good luck amulets.

Also Called: Yellow Mustard, White Mustard

Myrrh – Spiritual opening, meditation, and healing. This herb has high psychic vibrations that will enhance any magical working. Burn as a potent incense to bring peace and for consecration, and blessing of talismans, charms, and magical tools. Increases the power of any incense of which it is a part. Usually burned with Frankincense.

Also Called: Molmol, Mirra, Didthin, Bowl

Myrtle – Love, fertility, youth, peace, and money. Carry myrtle leaves to attract love, burn as incense to bring beauty. Wear myrtle while preparing love spells/mixes to increase their intent. Wear or carry to attract true friendship. Use in sachets to ensure a peaceful and loving atmosphere.

Also Called: Bayberry Tree

Narcissus – Calms vibrations and promotes harmony, tranquillity, and peace of mind.

Also Called: Asphodel, Daffy Down Lily, Fleur de Coucou, Goose Leek, Lent Lily, Porillon

Neroli – Joy, happiness, confidence, and overcoming emotional blockages. Soothes, relaxes, and uplifts the spirit. Instils confidence and courage when carried or worn.

Nettle – Magical uses include dispelling darkness & fear, strengthening the will, and aiding in the ability to handle emergencies. Sprinkle in the home to drive off evil & negativity. Carry in a sachet or use with a poppet to turn back a spell on the one who cast it. Sprinkle on self to remove petty jealousies, gossip, envy, and uncomfortable situations.

Also Called: Nettle Leaves, Common Nettle, Stinging Nettle, Beggar's Lice

Nutmeg – Magical uses include attracting money/prosperity, bringing luck, protection, and breaking hexes. Include in money magic and sachets. Carry as a good luck charm and/or to increase the intellect. Sprinkle nutmeg powder on green candles for prosperity.

Also Called: Myristica

Oak – The most sacred of all trees, its wood is often used in the making of magical tools. Burn the leaves for purification. Use in fertility amulets. Hang a sprig in the home to ward off negativity and strengthen family unity. Carry for wisdom and strength, for luck, to preserve youthfulness, and/or to increase attractiveness.

Also Called: Duir, Jove's Nuts

Oak Moss – Magical uses include luck, money, protection, and strength.

Oatmeal – To invoke or worship Brighid.

Oatstraw – Keep a small amount in your wallet or purse to draw in money and prosperity.

Olive – Fidelity, marriage, peace, money. Assures fidelity in love and is used to attract a marriage partner. Inspires fruitfulness and security in love, family, and business.

Olive Leaf – Magical uses include peace, potency, fertility, healing, protection, and lust.

Onion – Prosperity, stability, endurance, and protection. Burn onion flowers to banish bad habits and negative influences. Cut onions in half and place them in the corners of a room to absorb illness, then bury or burn the onion halves in the morning. Sacred to the moon.

Orange – Attracts abundance and happiness through love and marriage. Concentrate on a yes/no question while eating an orange, then count the seeds -- an even number of seeds means the answer is no, and an odd number of seeds means yes. Use the leaves and flowers in love rituals to bring on a marriage proposal. Add an infusion of orange to the bath to increase attractiveness and beauty.

Orange Bergamot – Money drawing. Put leaves in a wallet or purse to attract money. Rub fresh leaves on money before it is spent to ensure its return.

Also Called: Bergamot, Orange Mint

Orange Blossoms – Attracts prosperity and stability; brings harmony, peace, emotional openness, and love. Use in herbal baths for attractiveness.

Orange Peel – Magical uses include love, divination, luck, money, and house & business blessing. Add to love sachets to help someone make up their mind. Use in sachets & amulets to bring luck to business negotiations.

Orchid – Concentration, strengthening memory, focus, and willpower.

Oregano – Joy, strength, vitality, and added energy

Orris Root – Promotes popularity, persuasiveness, and personal success. Aids communication and helps to open dialogs. Used to draw (or hold) love and romance. Add to the bath for personal protection.

Also Called: Florentine Iris, Queen Elizabeth Root

Orris Root Powder – Used to bring love, romance, companionship, and a loving mate. Called 'Love Drawing Powder' in voodoo/hoodoo. Add to sachets and sprinkle on sheets and around the house to draw or hold love. Place a pinch in the corners of the room to open a new love. Use in bath magic to attract the opposite sex.

Also Called: Love Drawing Powder, Florentine Iris, Queen Elizabeth Root

Osha Root – Protection against evil spirits

Palm – Fertility, focus, potency, and divination

Palo Santo – Cleansing and banishing negative energy. If you feel you have been cursed, rub this herb on your body and then bathe.

Pansy – Love, divination related to love & relationships, rain magic

Papaya – Hang twigs of papaya wood over a door to keep out evil. Eat papaya with a loved one to intensify your love. Mix papaya leaves with mandrake and burn or use in the bath to reverse hexes and jinxes.

Paprika – Use to add energy to any spell or mixture. Throw in someone's yard to cause them problems.

Also Called: African Pepper, Bird Pepper, Chili Pepper, Goat's Pod, Grains of Paradise, Red Pepper, Sweet Pepper, Tabasco Pepper, Zanzibar Pepper, Capsicum

Papyrus – Protection

Parsley – Calms and protects the home; Draws prosperity, financial increase, and luck. Restores a sense of well-being. Use in spells to increase strength & vitality after surgery or illness. Use in amulets or other magical workings to help yourself out of a rut. Eat to provoke lust and promote fertility. Place on plates of food to guard against contamination. Useful for bath magic to purify and end misfortune. Mix with jasmine and carry in your shoe to make you more attractive to the opposite sex.

Parsnip – Male sex magic

Passion Flower – Magical uses include attracting friendship and prosperity and heightening libido. Carried to bring great popularity & attract new friends. Placed in the house to calm trouble & arguments and bring peace. Used as a wash to diminish disagreements & stress. Placed beneath a pillow to promote sleep. Bathe in an infusion of passion flower for 5 days to attract the opposite sex.

Also Called: Passion Vine, Granadilla, Maracoc, Maypops, Purple Passion Flower, Granadilla

Patchouli – Used in spells, sachets, baths, and mixtures for money & love. Put in the wallet or purse to draw money. Place in a charm or use in incense for fertility. Helps to ground you and bring your consciousness back to the physical level. Burn to bring business growth.

Also Called: Patchouly, Pucha Pot

Pau d'Arco – Magical use is for the ritual healing of severe diseases.

Also Called: Lapacho, Taheebo, Pau Darco

Peach – Fertility, love, and wisdom. Eating peaches induces love. Wear a peach pit to keep away evil. Carry peach wood for longevity. Use peach pits or dried fruit in amulets and sachets for fertility and love.

Pear – Lust and love Eating pears induces love. Use dried fruit in amulets and sachets for love and lust.

Pearl Moss – Sprinkle across the doorway of a home to allow only good spirits to enter.

Peas – Money and love

Peat Moss – Protection

Pecan – Associated with employment, success, job security, and career matters. To ensure that you do not lose your job, shell a small amount of pecans. While eating them, slowly visualize yourself working and enjoying your job. Take the shells to work and place them where they won't be found or removed.

Pennyroyal – Magical uses include peace and tranquillity. Carried to avoid seasickness or for physical strength & endurance. Worn to bring success to business. Use it to rid the home of negative thoughts against you. Carry when dealing with negative vibrations of any kind. Place on a candle before or during uncomfortable meetings.

Also Called: Tickweed, Squaw Mint, Stinking Balm, Thickweed, Mosquito Plant, Squaw Balm, Lurk in the Ditch, Run by the Ground

Peony – Protection from hexes and jinxes. Good luck, good fortune, prosperity, and business success. Hang in the home or car for protection. Used to attract faeries. Use in rituals to cure or reduce lunacy. Warning: While the flowers & petals have the positive qualities listed, the seed is called 'Jumby Bean' and is known for promoting dissension and strife.

Pepper (Black) – Courage, banishing negative vibrations. Burn to rid home or office of bad vibrations. Carry to ward off petty jealousy against you or aid in providing courage to face difficult situations.

Also Called: Piper

Peppermint – Use to increase the vibrations of a space or in spells and incense for healing & purification. Place in a sleep pillow to ensure peaceful sleep and bring about prophetic dreams. Use to anoint furnishings and household objects. Burn in a new home to clear out sickness and negative energy. Use in magical workings to provide the push needed to bring change to one's life. Carry with other herbs to boost love & abundance wishes.

Also Called: Brandy Mint, Lammint

Periwinkle – Love within marriage, mental powers, and money. Carry to obtain grace, attract money, and protect against snakes and poison. Use in magical workings to restore lost memory. Burn with love incense before having sex with your husband or wife.

Also Called: Sorcerer's Violet

Note: Can be poisonous, use it with caution.

Persimmon – Changing sex, healing, and luck

Petitgrain – Protection

Pikaki – Draws comfort, prosperity success, and well-being

Pimento – Love

Pimpernel – Protection and health

Pine – Promotes clean breaks, new beginnings, prosperity, success, strength, grounding, and growth; Also used for cleansing, purification, and repelling negativity. Great for house and business blessing.

Pineapple – Luck, money, and chastity. Add an infusion of pineapple to the bath to attract luck.

Pink Root – Healing

Also Called: Indian Pink, Maryland Pink, Wormgrass, Wormroot, Starbloom

Pink Rose Buds – Divine, emotional, and thinking love; start with these to build a long-lasting relationship.

Pistachio – Breaking love spells

Plantain – Protection from evil spirits and snake bites, removing weariness, healing headaches; house & business blessing. Place a pinch of dried leaves in the flame of a candle or throw them into an East wind for healing. Hang plantain leaves in the car for protection from evil and jealousy.

Pleurisy Root – Healing

Also Called: Butterfly Weed, Wind Root, Canada Root, Silkweed, Orange Swallow Wort, Tuber Root, White Root, Flux Root, Asclepias

Plum – Healing, peace, and love

Plumeria – Promotes persuasiveness, eloquence, and success in dealing with people; Attracts the notice of others.

Also Called: Graveyard Flowers, Melta, Temple Tree

Poke Root – Magical uses include finding lost objects and breaking hexes and curses. Carry to increase courage. Add an infusion of poke root to bath water to break hexes.

Also Called: Phytolacca, Shang Lu

Pomegranate – Divination, wishes, wealth and fertility

Poppy – Fertility, prosperity, love, and abundance.

Also Called: Opium Poppy, Mawseed

Poppy Seeds – Pleasure, heightened awareness, love, luck, invisibility. A popular ingredient in food magic. Sleep on a pillow stuffed with poppy seeds to bring relief from insomnia.

Also Called: Opium Poppy, Mawseed

Potato – Image magic, money, luck, and healing

Prickly Ash Bark – Magical uses include safe travel, fertility, removing spells, and breaking hexes.

Also Called: Toothache Tree, Yellow Wood, Suterberry

Primrose – Promotes the disclosure of secrets, resolution of mysteries, and revelation of truth; Breaks down dishonesty and secrecy. Put an infusion in a child's bath water or the dried herb in their pillows to get them to behave.

Also Called: English Cowslip, Butter Rose, Password

Pumpkin – Lunar magic

Pumpkin Seed – Health

Quassia – Love. Mix with a snippet of hair from yourself and your lover (with his/her permission, of course!) with quassia chips, burn, and keep the ashes in a small bottle to preserve the love.

Quince – Love, happiness, luck, and protection from evil. Carry quince seeds in a red flannel bag to protect against physical attacks and harm. Use quince seeds in charms and spells pertaining to love, protection, and happiness.

Radish – Protection and lust

Ragwort – Courage. Used in charms to ward off evil spirits. Associated with faeries.

Also Called: Fairie's Horse, Faerie's Horse, Fairy Horse, Faery Horse

Raspberry Leaf – Used for healing, protection, and love. Raspberry leaves are carried (NOT EATEN) by pregnant women to reduce the pain involved in pregnancy & childbirth. Bathe in an infusion of raspberry to keep your current love relationship alive.

Red Willow Bark – Magical uses include meditation and clearing. A fabulous incense wood with a sweet and dry aroma.

Rhubarb – Fidelity and protection

Rice – Rain, fertility, money, and protection. Use in money spells and fertility charms.

Rose – Magical uses include divine love, close friendships, domestic peace/happiness, and lasting relationships. Great for use in incense, potpourri, or bath magic. Place around sprains and dark bruises to help them heal faster.

Rose Geranium – Averts negativity, especially in the form of gossip or false accusations.

Rose Hips – Used in healing spells and mixtures, brings good luck, calls in good spirits.

Rosemary – Carried and used in healing poppets for good health, used in love/lust spells, worn to improve memory, used in dream pillows to prevent nightmares, burned as incense for purification and removing negativity. Wear or carry while reading or completing tasks to improve memory of the material and aid clear thinking (great for students!). Use an infusion of rosemary to wash your hands before any healing magic. Use in bath magic for purification. Associated with faeries.

Also Called: Elf Leaf, Sea Dew, Polar Plant, Guardrobe, Compass Weed, Dew of the Sea, Mary's Cloak, Stella Maria, Star of the Sea, Incensier

Rowan – Protection, magical power, success, anti-haunting. Use leaves and berries in amulets for healing and promoting psychic powers. Also good for use in luck spells and mixtures. Rowan wood is often used to make wands and divining rods.

Also Called: Mountain Ash, Delight of the Eye, Quickbane, Ran Tree, Rowanberry, Thor's Helper, Witch Bark, Wicken Tree, Wild Ash, Witchwood

Rue – Magical uses include healing, health, mental powers, freedom, and protection against the evil eye. Use as an Asperger to cast salt water for purification of the circle or removing negativity from the home. Hang the dried herb indoors to help yourself see and understand your mistakes. Burn to banish negativity or bad habits. Add to incense and poppets to prevent illness or speed recovery. Add to baths to break hexes and curses that may have been placed against you.

Note - Rue should not be handled by women who are pregnant.

Also Called: Herb-of-Grace, Herb of Grace, Herbygrass, Garden Rue, Mother of Herbs, Rewe, Goat's Rue

Rye – Love, fidelity, and self-control

Safflower – Mix with jinx incense to cause destruction to an enemy. Rub on the inside of the knees to attract exciting sexual encounters.

Saffron – Aphrodisiac, love, healing, happiness, wind raising, lust and strength. Burn, wear, or carry for healing and strengthening psychic awareness. Commonly used in love magic, healing spells, and to control the weather. Wash hands with water and saffron or keep saffron sachets in your home to bring happiness.

Also Called: Kum Kuma, Zaffran, Kesar, Autumn Crocus, Spanish Saffron, Dyer's Saffron, Thistle Saffron, Bastard Saffron, American Saffron, Parrot's Corn

Sage – Used for self-purification and dealing with grief and loss. Carried to improve mental ability and bring wisdom. Used in healing sachets & incense. Promotes spiritual, mental, emotional & physical health and longevity. Removes negative energy. Place near a personal object of a person who is ailing when performing healing spells or rituals. Write a wish on a sage leaf and place it under your pillow for 3 nights - if you dream of your wish, it will come true; if not, bury the leaf in the ground so that no bad will come to you.

Also Called: Garden Sage, White Sage, Red Sage, Sawge

Salt Petre – For women who do not want their partners to have outside relationships. Stops sexual tension.

Also Called: Salt Peter, Petre Salt, Saltpetre, Saltpeter

Sandalwood – Scatter sandalwood powder around the home to clear it of negativity. Burn during protection, healing, and exorcism spells. Use the wood for healing wands. Write your wish on a chip of sandalwood and burn it in the censer or cauldron while visualizing your wish to make it come true. Helps in healing by aligning the chakras for better energy flow. Good for meditation, healing, and manifestation. Facilitates concentration.

Also Called: Sandal, Santal, White Saunders, White Sandalwood, Red Sandalwood, Yellow Sandalwood

Sanicle – Used for safety in travel.

Also Called: Sancile, American Sanicle, Black Snakeroot, Wood Sanicle, Pool Root, Butterwort, Alum Root

Sarsaparilla – Sexual vitality, health, love, and money. Mix with sandalwood and cinnamon and sprinkle around home or business to draw money. Alleged to prolong life, hinder premature aging, excite passion, and improve virility when worn or carried.

Also Called: Black Creeper, Sariva, Kalisar, Dudhilata, Sugandhi, Red Sarsaparilla, Tu Fu Ling, Dwipautra

Sassafras – Magical uses include health, money, and overcoming addictions. Placed in a wallet or purse to attract money and make the money you have to go farther. Used as a prosperity incense. Added to sachets for healing.

Also Called: Ague Tree, Cinnamon Wood, Saxifrax, Saloip

Savoury – Sensuality, sexuality, and passion; great for sex magic!

Saw Palmetto Berries – Magical uses include healing protection, exorcism, passion, and spiritual openings.

Also Called: Dwarf Palm Tree, Cabbage Palm, Sabal, Sabal Serrulata

Skullcap – Worn by women to keep their husbands faithful. Used in sleep pillows for relaxation & peace. Used to bind oaths and consecrate vows & commitments (handfasting, initiations, etc.). Used in bath magic to clam the aura of tension and stress. Burned for relief from disharmony and disruptive situations. Place a pinch in a lover's shoes to keep them from being affected by the charms of others.

Also Called: Skullcap, Skullcap, Hoodwort, Quaker Bonnet, Helmet Flower, European Skullcap, Greater Skullcap, American Skullcap, Blue Skullcap, Blue Pimpernel, Hoodwart, Hooded Willow Herb, Side-Flowering Skullcap, Mad Dogweed, Mad Weed, Madweed, Helmet Flower, Hoodwort

Sea Salt – Uses include cleansing crystals, purification, grounding, protection magic, and ritual. Used on the altar to represent the Earth. Used with water for asperging, sea spells, consecration, and casting circles. Used with garlic and rosemary to banish evil.

Senna – Magical uses include all matters of lust and love. Enhances tact & diplomacy. Bathe with your mate in an infusion of senna to ensure faithfulness.

Also Called: Senna Pod, Rajavriksha, Fan Xia Ye, American Senna, Locust Plant, Wild Senna, Fan Xie Ye

Sesame – Money, lust, and passion

Shallots – Add an infusion of shallots to the bath for luck.

Shave Grass – Magical uses include snake charming & fertility. Place in the bedroom to increase fertility.

Also Called: Scouring Rush, Equisetum, Pewterwort, Corncob Plant, Bottle Brush, Horsetail, Dutch Raisins, Paddock Pipe

Sheep Sorrel – Carry to protect against heart disease. Place in sickrooms to aid in recuperation from illnesses and wounds.

Shepherd's Purse – Healing

Also Called: Mother's Heart, Shepard's Purse/Heart, Cocowort, Pickpocket, Toywort, Pick Purse, St. James' Weed, St. James' Wort, St. Anthony's Fire, Pepper Grass, Case Wort, Permacety

Skunk Cabbage – Legal matters

Slippery Elm – Magical uses include protection and halting gossip. Tie a knotted yellow thread around slippery elm and throw it into a fire to cease all gossip about you.

Also Called: Red Elm, Moose Elm, Sweet Elm, Indian Elm

Snapdragon – Protection, exorcism, and purification

Snowdrop – Passing of sorrow

Solomon's Seal Root – Magically used for protection and cleansing. Used in offertory incense. Used to bind magical workings and keep sacred oaths & promises forever binding. Carry in an amulet or sachet for all-purpose protection. Use in protection magic to exorcise spirits and ward off negative influences and demons. Keep on the altar to promote success in all rituals. Sprinkle an infusion of the root to drive away evil.

Also Called: Lady's Seals, St. Mary's Seal, Sigillum Sanctae Mariae, Scean de Solomon

Sow Thistle – Increases strength & stamina, repels witches, and provides invisibility from enemies.

Spanish Moss – Protection, opening blockages, and dispelling negativity

Spearmint – Healing, love and protection while sleeping. Burn for healing magic, especially of respiratory conditions. Carry for healing. Use in ritual baths for strength and vitality. Write a wish on paper and wrap it in spearmint leaves; place in a red cloth and sew with red thread, then keep in a safe and secret place - by the time the scent is gone, your wish should have come true.

Also Called: Garden Mint, Mackerel Mint, Our Lady's Mint, Green Mint, Spire Mint, Lamb Mint, Yerba Buena, Sage of Bethlehem, Fish Mint

Spiderwort – Love

Spikenard – Wear in a sachet around the neck to bring luck & ward off illness. It is said that wetting a picture of a loved one in an infusion of spikenard will keep them close to you.

Also Called: Spignet, Life of Man, Pettymorell, Old Man's Root, Indian Root, Bitter Root, Nard, Nardo

Squaw Vine – Magical uses include all matters of fertility & childbirth. Pregnant women can add an infusion of squaw vine to bath water once a week to protect the unborn child from jealousy.

Also Called: Squawvine

Squill Root – To draw money, place in a container with a dime, a quarter and a dollar and say a prayer for prosperity.

Stinging Nettle – Can be burned to drive out negativity or unwanted spirits. It can also be used in protection bags, our ground into a powder and used in spells to break curses.

St. John's Wort – Worn to prevent colds & fevers. Placed under pillow to induce prophetic, romantic dreams. Protects against all forms of black witchcraft. Place in a jar in a window or burn in a fireplace to protect from lightning, fire and evil spirits. Used for banishing, protection & blessing. Carry to strengthen courage and convictions or when confronting nasty situations. Burn to banish spirits and demons. Used in divination for the care of crystals.

Also Called: Saint John's Wort, Goat Weed, Herba John, Kalimath Weed, Tipton Weed

Note: Can be poisonous, use with caution.

Star Anise – Burned as incense to increase psychic awareness & abilities. Placed on the altar to increase the power generated. Carried to bring luck.

Also Called: Chinese Anise, Anise Star

Straw – Image magic and luck

Straw Flower – Luck, longevity, and protection. Use in magic to get the effects to last. The flower of Samhain, signifying the transition from one type of life to another.

Note: Poisonous, use with caution.

Strawberry – Attracts success, good fortune, and favourable circumstances. Served as a love food. Leaves are carried for luck. Pregnant women carry a packet of the leaves to ease the pain of pregnancy and childbirth.

Sugar – Love spells, sex magic

Sugar Cane – Love, lust, and sympathy

Sulphur Powder – Dispels or prevents a hex on you; destroys an enemy's power over you.
Also Called: Brimstone

Sumac – Used for curses, hexing, bringing bad luck. Hoodoo traditions mention Sumac as a sort of peacekeeper, bringing harmony and squashing conflicts, or even assisting those facing legal troubles with a lighter than expected sentencing.

Sunflower – Energy, protection, power, wisdom, and wishes.

Sweet Bugle – Crush and place under the mattress to attract love and marriage prospects.

Sweet Pea – Attracts friends and allies; Draws the loyalty and affection of others.

Sweet Potato – Image magic

Sweetgrass – Peace, unity, and calling spirits

Tamarind – Love

Tangerine – Promotes energy, strength, and vitality. Awakens joy and dissolves negativity.

Tansy – Health, invisibility, immortality, longevity; keeps evil out of the home. Place a small amount in the shoe or add an infusion of tansy to the bath to keep the law away.

Tarragon – Healing in abuse situations, compassion magic for others. Use for consecrating chalices.

Tea Leaves – Use in talismans for courage or strength. Use as a base for lust drinks. Burn leaves to ensure future riches.

Tea Tree – Eliminating confusion and increasing harmony

Thistle – Healing, protection. Use in sachet or amulet to aid in speedy recovery from surgery or illness. Hang in the home to ward off thieves and unwanted visitors.

Thyme – Attracts loyalty, affection, and the good opinion of others. Wear a sprig to ward off unbearable grief or provide strength and courage when needed. Burn or hang in the home for banishing, purification, and to attract good health for all occupants. Use in cleansing baths prior to working candle magic. Use in dream pillows to ward off nightmares and ensure restful sleep. Add a thyme infusion to the bath regularly to ensure a constant flow of money. Place in a jar and keep in the home or at work for good luck.

Also Called: Garden Thyme, Common Thyme

Toadflax – Protection and hex breaking

Toadstool – Rain magic

Tobacco – Promotes peace, confidence, and personal strength. Also used for banishing. Mix with salt and burn with a black candle to win a court case.

Tomato – Love spells

Tonka Bean – Magical uses include rituals and spells for love, wishes and courage. Worn to gain prosperity & courage. Carried to grant luck & protect from disease and/or to attract love. Promotes the accomplishment of goals. Keep on the altar when performing love magic to enhance intent. Carry in a red flannel bag to attract good fortune and financial success, especially when attending business negotiations or job interviews. A favourite hoodoo good luck charm to make wishes come true.

Also Called: Tonqua, Tonqua Bean, Tonquin Bean, Wish Beans, Coumaria Nut

Tormentil – To cause distress, harm and discord to a foe, sprinkle this on a picture of her or him and place in a box.

True Unicorn Root – Hex-breaking, uncrossing, and protection against evil & malevolent magic.

Tuberose – Sensuality, serenity, and calming nerves. Brings peace to the mind and heart, enhances the capacity for emotional depth. Add to sachets designed to increase psychic ability. Use in love magic to awaken erotic feelings and attract romance. Wear or carry to attract inspiration.

Also Called: Mistress of the Night

Turnip – Ending relationships

Uva Ursi – Magical uses include increasing intuitive and psychic powers. Great in sachets for this purpose. American Indians used Uva Ursi in religious ceremonies.

Also Called: Bearberry, Bear's Grape, Foxberry, Crowberry, Hog Cranberry, Kinnikinnick, Mealberry, Arberry, Mountain Box, Mountain Cranberry, Sandberry, Uva Ursa, Universe Vine

Note: Can be poisonous, use with caution.

Valerian – Dream magic, reconciliation, love, and harmony. Placed in sachets for love & protection and used in sleep pillows. It is said that having Valerian Root nearby will settle an argument between a couple. Used to purify sacred space. Used as a substitution for graveyard dirt/dust in spells. Use in protection baths. Burn for reconciliation in ailing relationships, but only with the permission of all parties involved in the relationship. Wear to calm the emotions.

Also Called: Valerian Root, All-Heal, Garden Heliotrope, Graveyard Dust, Phu, Setwell, Vandal Root

Vanilla Bean – Magical uses include love, lust, passion, and restoring lost energy. Carried to increase energy & strengthen mental abilities.

Venus Flytrap – Love and protection

Vertivert – Draws money and prosperity, love, and attraction; Overcomes obstacles, breaks hexes, and repels negativity. Place a small amount in cash registers to increase business. Burn to overcome evil spirits.

Also Called: Khus-khus

Vervain – Protection, purification, money, youth, peace, healing, and sleep. Bury in the yard or keep in the home to encourage wealth, protect from lightning & storms, and bring peace. Put under the pillow to prevent nightmares. Use as an incense to end unrequited love. Use in prosperity spells. Carry to prevent depression and/or bring creativity. Use in cleansing baths and rituals before working magic. Use in amulets, sachets, dream pillows, and baths for all-purpose protection of home sand people (especially children).

Also Called: Verveine, Verbena, Brittanica, Enchanter's Plant, Enchanter's Herb, Herba Sacra, Juno's Tears, Holy Wort, Lemon Verbena, Van-Van, Herb of Grace, Herb of the Cross, Pigeon's Grass, Pigeonwood, Simpler's Joy

Vetch – Fidelity

Vinegar – Banishing, binding, averting evil.

Violet – Calms the nerves, draws prophetic dreams and visions, stimulates creativity, and promotes peace & tranquillity. Violet leaf provides protection from all evil. Violet crowns are said to cure headaches and bring sleep. Carry or give to newly married couples or new baby & mother to bring luck to the bearer. Keep a spray of violets on the altar to enhance night magic. Wear the leaves in a green sachet to help heal wounds and prevent evil spirits from making the wounds worse.

Also Called: Sweet Violet, Blue Violet, Wild Violet

Walnut – Access to divine energy, bringing the blessing of the Gods, wishes

Watercress – For lunar magic and sex magic.

Wheat – Inducing fertility and conception, attracting money

White Sage – Use as an incense, for smudging or for purification.

White Willow Bark – Brings blessings of the moon into one's life and guards against negativity & evil forces. Used in healing spells.

Willow – Used for lunar magic, drawing or strengthening love, healing, and overcoming sadness. Willow is considered a sacred wishing tree. Wear a sprig of willow when facing the death of a loved one. Place on the altar for lunar magic and divination work. Keep a piece of willow in home or business to protect against evil.

Also Called: Osier, Pussy Willow, White Willow, Witches' Aspirin, Withy, Tree of Enchantment, Saille, Salicyn Willow, Saugh Tree

Wintergreen – Add an infusion to your children's bath to bring them good fortune and luck throughout their lives. Sprinkle an infusion of wintergreen around an area for purification.

Wisteria – Raises vibrations, promotes psychic opening, overcomes obstacles, and draws prosperity.

Witch Hazel – Magical uses include chastity and protection. Carry to ease grief over a lost love. Use in a sachet to reduce passions. Use in love spells and spells to ward off evil.

Also Called: Winter Bloom, Striped Alder, Spotted Alder, Hazelnut, Snapping Hazel and Tobacco Wood

Witches Burr – Adds great power to spells & rituals. Presence of witches burr is said to defeat any kind of evil force.

Witches Grass – Happiness, lust, love, and exorcism. Sprinkle around the home for seven consecutive days to overcome depression and dispense of petty spirits. Reverses hexes.

Also Called: Couch Grass, Rhizomes, Twitch Grass, Scotch Quelch, Quick Grass, Dog Grass

Wood Aloe – Protection, consecration, success, and prosperity.

Also Called: Lignaloes, Lignam Aloes

Wood Betony – Magical uses include purification, protection, and the expulsion of evil spirits, nightmares, and despair. Excellent for magical healing and protecting against dark fears of the emotions

& imagination. A good addition to dream pillows. Carry in an amulet to draw love and strengthen the body. Burn to banish disharmony in a relationship. Pass through the smoke of burning wood betony at Midsummer to purify the body of ills and evils. Burn with any uncrossing incense to defeat witchcraft.

Also Called: Betony, Bishopswort, Stachys Betonica, Lousewort

Woodruff – Victory, protection, and money. Place a pinch in your left shoe before a game and your team will be victorious.

Wormwood – Used to remove anger, stop war, inhibit violent acts, and for protection from the evil eye. Carry in vehicle to protect from accidents on dangerous roads. Use as incense for clairvoyance, to summon spirits, or to enhance divinatory abilities. Can be sprinkled in the path of an enemy to bring them strife and misfortune (not recommended, remember the law of threes).

Also Called: Absinthium, Green Ginger, Absinthe, Old Woman, Crown for a King

Note: Can be poisonous, use with caution.

Xanthan Gum – Incense bonding agent

Yarrow Flower – Uses include healing, handfasting & weddings, and divination. Draws love. Carry as a sachet or amulet to banish negativity, ward off fear, and promote courage, confidence, and psychic opening. Frequently used in marriage charms and love sachets. Said to keep a newly married couple happy for seven years by keeping their love alive and preventing upsetting influences from entering the relationship. Place in a yellow flannel bag with a piece of parchment on which you have written your fears, carry with you to overcome them.

Also Called: Bloodwort, Death Flower, Devil's Nettle, Lady's Mantle, Soldier's Woundwort, Thousandleaf, Millefoil, Carpenter's Weed, Knight's Milfoil, Sanguinary, Arrow Root, Thousand Seal

Yellow Dock – Fertility, healing and money. Sprinkle an infusion of yellow dock around a place of business to attract customers.

Also Called: Curled Dock, Curly Dock, Sour Dock, Narrow Dock, Garden Patience, Rumex

Yerba Mate – Fidelity, love and lust. Worn to attract the opposite sex. Spill an infusion of yerba mate on the ground to break off a relationship.

Also Called: Mate, Mate Leaf, Green Mate

Yerba Santa – Beauty, healing, psychic powers and protection. Carry or use in bath magic to obtain beauty from within and make your body more desirable. Wear around the neck to ward off illness and prevent wounds. Use the leaves in healing or protection incenses. Use in bath water if you feel your sickness has been caused by a hex.

Also Called: Consumptive's Weed, Gum Plant, Gum Bush, Bear's Weed, Bear Weed, Mountain Balm, Tar Weed, Tarweed, Holy Herb, Sacred Herb

Yew – Raising the dead, protection against evil, immortality, and breaking hexes. Also used for contacting spirits, but can also be used for curses.

Ylang Ylang – Increases sexual attraction and persuasiveness. Also used for peace, love, and faery magic. Promotes calm, peaceful relaxation and relieves anxiety and depression.

Yohimbe Bark – Love, lust, virility and fertility. Curing impotency. Cursing. Used in Pagan rituals of union.

Yucca – Transmutation, protection and purification. A cross of yucca fibre placed on the hearth protects the home from evil. Use an infusion of yucca to cleanse and purify the body before magic. Repeat this cleansing afterwards if performing spells to remove curses, hexes, or illness. Rub a slice of yucca root all over your body once a day for seven days to remove jinxes and hexes.

Also Called: Yucca Stalk, Yucca Root

Moon Magic

The powers of the Moon hold significant importance for witches and practitioners of various magical traditions. Many look to the phases of the Moon not only as a source of inspiration but also as a guiding force in their spiritual practices. Each phase of the Moon carries unique energies and influences that can aid in achieving balance, prosperity, success, and love in one's life. By casting spells and conducting rituals aligned with these lunar phases, individuals can organize their intentions and bring clarity and order to their magical workings.

Correspondences of the Moon

Day: The Moon is traditionally associated with Monday, a day that reflects its energy and influence.

Celebrations: Important celebrations linked to the lunar cycle include Imbolc—a festival marking the midpoint between winter and spring—Beltane, which celebrates fertility and the coming of summer, and Lammas, a harvest festival honouring abundance.

Element: The element associated with the Moon is Water, symbolizing intuition, emotion, and fluidity.

Colours: The Moon is connected to a variety of colours, including Silver—representing purity and clarity; Gray—symbolizing neutrality; White—denoting purity and new beginnings; along with Blue, Orange, and Green—each providing unique vibrations and energies to lunar workings.

Metal: Silver is the metal of the Moon, renowned for its reflective qualities and its association with intuition and the subconscious mind.

Energy: The Moon embodies Yin energy, representing receptivity, intuition, and a nurturing presence.

Numbers: The numbers of significance related to the Moon are 2, 3, 9, and 13, each reflecting different aspects of lunar energy and cycles.

Zodiac: Cancer is the zodiac sign closely associated with the Moon, embodying traits such as emotional depth, nurturing, and sensitivity.

Tarot: In tarot, the Moon is represented by cards such as The Chariot—denoting mastery and triumph; The High Priestess—symbolizing intuition and inner wisdom; and The Moon card itself, which reflects dreams, the subconscious, and illusions.

Runes: The runes linked to lunar energy include Is, which signifies ice and stillness, and Lagu, representing water and flow.

Chakra: The Sacral Chakra corresponds with the Moon, governing creativity, emotions, and the nurturing aspects of our nature.

Angel: The archangel Gabriel is associated with the Moon, known as a messenger who supports emotional insight and communication

Plants and Herbs: Various plants and herbs resonate with lunar energy, including Jasmine, known for its calming properties; Lemon Balm, which promotes tranquillity; Aloe, which aids in healing;

Sandalwood, favoured for its spiritual applications; and Grape, Palm, Olive, and Gardenia, each contributing their unique magical qualities. Other herbs like Bergamot promote joy; Rosemary is used for clarity; Nutmeg enhances prosperity; and Moonwort, Birch, Saffron, Lotus, Mesquite, Poppy, and Willow are all significant in lunar rituals, invoking their specific energies to amplify intentions.

Incorporating the Moon's correspondences into your practices can deepen your connection with its energy and enhance your magical endeavours. Embrace the rhythms of the lunar cycle, and let the Moon guide you toward your desires and goals.

New Moon

The New Moon marks a significant phase in the lunar cycle when the moon is not visible in the night sky. This time represents a powerful opportunity for setting intentions and initiating personal growth. It is considered an auspicious period for casting spells focused on new beginnings and cleansing rituals aimed at releasing the old and welcoming the new. The New Moon serves as a blank canvas for aspirations related to personal health, love, romance, and pursuing new job opportunities. You can harness the energy of the New Moon for your spells from the moment it begins and continue to do so for up to three and a half days afterward.

Correspondences of the New Moon:

- Colour: Black is associated with the New Moon, symbolizing the unknown and the potential that comes from darkness. This colour can help ground your intentions and provide a sense of security as you embark on new paths.

- Celebration: Samhain, often regarded as a time for reflection on the past year and preparing for the future, resonates well with the themes of the New Moon. It is an opportunity to honour those who have passed and to set intentions for the cycle ahead.

- Plants: Certain plants are traditionally linked to the New Moon.

    - Wormwood is known for its cleansing properties and ability to protect against negativity.

    - Locust represents resilience and the power of transformation.

    - Vervain is revered for its purifying qualities and is often used in spells for love and healing.

The New Moon is a favourable time for various types of spells and magical practices, particularly those focused on:

- Spiritual Cleansing: Use this phase to rid yourself of residual negative energy and emotional burdens.

- Purification Spells: These can help to clear your aura and environment, making space for positive energies to enter your life.

- Blessings: This is an ideal time to bless new ventures, relationships, or personal goals, infusing them with your intentions and hopes.

- True Love Spells: Focus on manifesting the kind of love you desire, whether it's self-love or a romantic partnership.

- Beauty Spells: Channel new energies into enhancing your self-esteem and physical presence, inviting a sense of beauty and confidence into your life.

New Moon Spell Idea:

Bath Magic

For a simple yet profound cleansing ritual, consider engaging in bath magic. Water and salt are potent symbols of purification and renewal. To begin, draw a warm bath and add bath salts or simple sea salt. As the salt dissolves, visualize it absorbing any residual negative energy within you.

Create a serene atmosphere by lighting soft, flickering candles around your bathing space, perhaps in black or white to align with the New Moon's energies. Dim the lights, play soft music, or enjoy the tranquillity of silence, allowing yourself to relax.

As you sink into the water, take a moment to focus on the feelings, experiences, or hurt from the past that you wish to release. With each breath, imagine these pains dissolving and being washed away, swirling down the drain as you prepare to rise anew. This spell doesn't need to be overly complicated; its effectiveness lies in your intention and the sincerity of your focus as you evoke a sense of renewal and fresh beginnings.

Waxing Moon

The Waxing Moon is a powerful phase for constructive magic and is ideally suited for a variety of spells aimed at attracting positive energies and opportunities in our lives. During this period, which occurs approximately seven to fourteen days after the New Moon, the moon visibly increases in size, symbolizing growth and development. This phase is characterized by the moon's illumination expanding from the right side as it approaches the Full Moon, making it an auspicious time for positive or white magic. The Waxing Moon is believed to manifest intentions and bring forth that which is desired, making it highly favourable for rituals aimed at personal enhancement.

Correspondences of the Waxing Moon:

- Celebration: Imbolc, a festival that marks the midpoint between winter and spring, symbolizing the return of light and fertility.

The Waxing Moon is an ideal time for a variety of spells, including:

- Love Spells: To attract new love or deepen existing romantic relationships.

- Returning a Lost Lover: Aimed at rekindling a past romance.

- Job and Career Spells: For those seeking advancement, new opportunities, or career shifts.

- Attraction Love Spells: To enhance charisma and magnetism.

- Protection Spells: For safeguarding oneself and loved ones from negativity.

- Fertility Spells: To promote conception, growth, and abundance.

- Friendship Spells: To forge and strengthen bonds with friends.

- Luck Spells: To invite fortunate circumstances into one's life.

- Money Spells: Aimed at attracting financial prosperity.

Waxing Moon Spell Idea:

One effective practice during the Waxing Moon is to write a detailed letter of intention. This letter should express your career desires, whether you wish to obtain a raise, change your job title, or make a complete transition to a different field. Writing has been shown to be beneficial in helping us process our emotions and clarify our goals. By articulating your desires, you create a powerful manifesting tool that can motivate you toward achieving your aspirations.

Waning Moon

The Waning Moon represents a period of release and shedding, occurring after the Full Moon has completed its brightness. It involves the moon gradually diminishing in visibility, symbolizing the importance of letting go and banishing negative energies. This phase takes place approximately three and a half to ten and a half days following the Full Moon, and it is an ideal time for spells and rituals intended to dispel negativity, illness, and harmful influences. The Waning Moon encourages us to rid ourselves of what no longer serves us, making it an essential time for cleansing and purification.

Correspondences of the Waning Moon:

- Celebration: Lammas, a harvest festival that marks the beginning of the harvest season, representing completion and relinquishing the old for new beginnings.

The Waning Moon is potent for a range of spells focused on:

- Banishing Spells: To remove obstacles and negative influences from your life.

- Breaking a Spell: To negate any harmful magic cast upon you.

- Weight Loss Spells: For those looking to shed unwanted pounds and promote healthy changes.

- Break-up Spells: To end toxic relationships and free oneself from unwanted ties.

- Banishing Negativity: To eliminate negative thoughts and emotions.

- Hex Removal: To counteract any curses or bad luck.

- Curse Removal: To relieve oneself from any longstanding effects of negative magic.

Waning Moon Spell Idea:

A simple yet effective spell during the Waning Moon involves writing down on a piece of paper your current worries or the aspects of your life that you wish to eliminate. This might pertain to a bad habit, a person who brings negativity, a specific situation, or even an overwhelming emotion. After writing this, light a white candle in a secure location, always observing candle safety practices to prevent any risk. Read aloud what you have written to imbue it with your intent. Once you are finished, leave the paper beside the candle as it burns. Reflect on your intentions while meditating, and when the candle extinguishes, take the paper and tear it into pieces. Dispose of the fragments along with the remnants of the candle, symbolically releasing those burdens from your life.

Dark Moon

The Dark Moon represents a powerful phase in the lunar cycle, typically occurring about ten and a half to fourteen days after the Full Moon. This period is designated for introspection, allowing individuals to confront and navigate their deepest emotions, including passions and angers that may have been suppressed. It's also an essential time for addressing conflicts and dealing with adversaries, making it an excellent phase for spells related to justice and resolution. The Dark Moon phase culminates just two to three days before the New Moon, when the moon is barely visible, which contributes to its mysterious and introspective nature.

Correspondences of the Dark Moon:

- Colour: Black – symbolizing protection, mystery, and the unknown.

- Celebration: Samhain – a time to honour ancestors and reflect on the cycle of life and death.

- Plants: Wormwood, Locust, Verbena – often used in various rituals for protection and guidance.

Dark Moon Spell Idea:

This spell is simple yet incredibly effective for creating a protective barrier around your home. Begin by finding a quiet space at the centre of your home. Take a moment to relax and ground yourself. Visualize your house in detail, imagining every room and corner as vividly as possible. As you do this, tap into the energy of Mother Earth. Envision a strong, white protective light emanating from the ground, rising up around the boundaries of your property. See this light growing and expanding, forming a formidable protective bubble that encapsulates your home.

Once you feel this shield is established, take the time to regularly reinforce it with your intention and the nurturing energy of Mother Earth. Just a few moments of quiet reflection can strengthen this shield, enhancing your home's protective qualities.

Full Moon

The Full Moon is often regarded as the pinnacle of the lunar cycle, emanating a bright and powerful energy that lasts for approximately seventeen and a half days before transitioning into the Waning Gibbous phase. This time is ideal for performing rituals that focus on protection, divination, and healing. Any matters requiring significant healing—whether physical, emotional, or spiritual—are best addressed during this phase. It's a prime time for spells related to love, dreams, financial abundance, and personal aspirations, as the moon's fullness magnifies the intention behind your actions.

Correspondences of the Full Moon:

- colours: Red and Green – red for passion and energy, green for growth and prosperity.

- Celebration: Beltane – a festival that celebrates fertility, love, and the blossoming of life.

- Metal: Silver – associated with intuition and the feminine.

- Plant: Sandalwood – known for its calming properties and use in purification rituals.

The Full Moon is a favourable time for various types of spells and magical practices, particularly those focused on:

- Healing Spells – focusing on health and wellness.

- Job and Career Spells – to attract opportunities and success.

- Psychic Spells – to enhance intuition and psychic abilities.

- Love Spells – inviting romantic energies into your life.

- Beauty Spells – for self-empowerment and confidence.

- Money Spells – to attract financial abundance.

- Friendship Spells – to strengthen existing relationships or attract new connections.

Full Moon Spell Idea:

During the Full Moon, the potency of magic is amplified, making it a fantastic opportunity for conducting any type of work, especially those related to psychic development. The energy is ripe for enhancing intuition, so trust your instincts during this time, even if your emotions feel heightened. One effective practice is to meditate under the light of the Full Moon. This simple act can bring clarity to a situation you may be facing. Find a quiet outdoor space or near a window where you can soak in the moonlight. Close your eyes, take deep breaths, and allow yourself to simply be present. As the moonlight envelops you, focus on a question or situation that needs resolution, welcoming the insights that arise during this meditative state.

<u>**The Full Moons**</u>

Throughout the year, there are typically 12 to 13 Full Moons, commonly referred to as esbats. Each month is usually marked by a full moon, and occasionally, there is an additional full moon within a single month. This rare occurrence is known as a "blue moon," which adds a special significance to its celebration.

Esbats, while traditionally celebrated within covens—groups of witches who come together for rituals—are equally meaningful for solitary practitioners. Each witch is encouraged to follow their personal inclinations when deciding whether to honour the full moon, the new moon, or any other phase that resonates with them.

Historically, the moon has served as humanity's earliest calendar, marking the passage of time through its illuminated phases. It is often viewed as a symbol of femininity, representing the goddess due to its cyclical nature. The moon's cycle lasts approximately 29 days, 12 hours, and 44 minutes, closely mirroring the average menstrual cycle of 28 to 30 days. This connection has deepened the association of the moon with the sacred feminine. The phases of the moon symbolize various aspects of the goddess— the waxing phase embodies the virgin aspect, the full moon signifies the nurturing fullness of the mother, and the waning phase represents the wisdom and reflection of the crone.

During esbats, two key rituals are often performed to tap into the energies of the full moon. The first is known as "drawing down the moon" or "invoking the goddess." This ritual involves calling upon lunar energies or the goddess's presence to infuse the ceremony with powerful spiritual significance. The second essential practice is the ceremony of cakes and ale, serving as a closing ritual where participants make offerings of bread or cookies, along with wine or ale, on an altar. This act is both a celebration of abundance and a way to show gratitude for the blessings received.

In contrast, esbats occurring during the new moon are referred to as dark moon esbats. They provide an opportunity to explore and honour the more obscure, often overlooked dimensions of magic. These gatherings focus on shadow work—delving into the subconscious to confront personal fears and hidden aspects of the self. Aimed at transformation and healing, dark moon esbats may also involve practices like journeying to the other world or engaging in hedge witchery, which emphasizes the connection between the practitioner and the natural world.

Overall, whether celebrated in a group or alone, the full moons and new moons offer significant periods for reflection, intention setting, and spiritual growth for those who embrace their cyclical wisdom.

January – Wolf Moon

The January full moon is known as the Wolf Moon, a name that reflects the howling of hungry wolves as they traverse the winter landscape, often lamenting the scarcity of food during this harsh season. This moon is also referred to by several other names, including the Moon After Yule, Old Moon, Ice Moon, and Frost Moon, each evoking the themes of reflection and endurance through winter's chill.

Correspondences:

- Element: Air, representing communication and intellect.

- Colours: Black, White, Silver, symbolizing clarity, balance, and protection.

- Gemstones: Hematite, known for its grounding properties and ability to promote stability.

- Herbs: Thistle (for resilience), Nuts and Seeds (representing potential and sustenance), Basil (for love and protection), and Marjoram (for joy and happiness).

- Goals: A time to thoughtfully review your intentions and focus on achieving your dreams.

- Actions: Encourage personal development and cultivate your inner self through meditation and reflection.

- Magic: Ideal for crafting protection sachets and charms, to safeguard against negative energies.

February – Snow Moon

February's full moon, known as the Snow Moon, derives its name from the heavy snowfall that often blankets the landscape during this month. It is sometimes referred to as the Hunger Moon and Storm Moon, signifying the challenges faced in winter.

Correspondences:

- Element: Fire, embodying passion and drive.

- Colours: Blue and Purple, representing spirituality and intuition.

- Gemstones: Rose Quartz (for love and compassion), Amethyst (for intuition and peace), and Jasper (for stability).

- Herbs: Hyssop (for purification), Sage (for wisdom), and Myrrh (for protection and clarity).

- Goals: Use this time to focus on your personal development and the goals you wish to pursue this year.

- Actions: Embrace accountability and take responsibility for past mistakes to facilitate growth.

- Magic: This moon is favourable for practices such as astral travel, expanding your spiritual horizons.

March – Worm Moon

In March, the full moon is known as the Worm Moon, named after the earthworms that begin to appear as the ground thaws. This moon is also referred to as Crow Moon, Crust Moon, Sap Moon, Sugar Moon, and Chaste Moon, each name reflecting different aspects of nature's renewal.

Correspondences:

- Element: Water, symbolizing emotion and intuition.

- Colours: Green (for growth), Yellow (for clarity), and Lavender (for tranquillity).

- Gemstones: Bloodstone (for rejuvenation) and Aquamarine (for calm and clarity).

- Herbs: Apple Blossom (for love), Betony (for protection), High John (for luck), and Thyme (for courage).

- Goals: A time to evaluate your financial aspirations and plan for future abundance.

- Actions: Focus on creating balance in your life by integrating various aspects of existence.

- Magic: Perfect for luck spells, charms, and amulets to attract good fortune.

April – Pink Moon

April brings the Pink Moon, named after the pink wildflowers that bloom around this time of year. This moon also carries various names such as Grass Moon, Fish Moon, Hare Moon, Egg Moon, Seed Moon, and Paschal Moon, all celebrating the vibrancy of spring.

Correspondences:

- Element: Air, highlighting communication and new ideas.

- Colours: Yellow (for cheerfulness), Red (for passion), and Blue (for tranquillity).

- Gemstones: Quartz (for clarity), Selenite (for cleansing), and Angelite (for peace).

- Herbs: Dandelion (for healing), Dill (for protection), Fennel (for strength), and Dogwood (for emotional balance).

- Goals: Use this time to focus on educational and knowledge-based goals, seeking to expand your mind.

- Actions: Shift from planning to action—take the steps necessary for progress.

- Magic: Ideal for visualization practices to manifest your intentions.

May – Flower Moon

May celebrates the Flower Moon, a time when the landscape bursts into bloom. Known also as the Bright Moon, Corn Planting Moon, and Milk Moon, this moon signifies fertility and abundance.

Correspondences:

- Element: Fire, representing vibrancy and passion.

- Colours: Red, Orange, and Yellow, symbolizing joy, warmth, and creativity.

- Gemstones: Amber (for grounding), Ruby (for vitality), and Garnet (for passion).

- Herbs: Cinnamon (for success) and Mint (for healing and protection).

- Goals: Take a moment to review your career goals and aspirations, seeking growth and fulfilment in your professional path.

- Actions: Embrace major life changes with confidence, making necessary adjustments to pursue your true passions.

- Magic: This month is particularly suited for candle magic, using the element of fire to enhance your intentions.

June – Strawberry Moon

June's full moon is called the Strawberry Moon, marking the peak season for strawberry harvesting. It is also known as Honey Moon, Hot Moon, Mead Moon, and Rose Moon, celebrating abundance and warmth.

Correspondences:

- Element: Earth, reflecting stability and nourishment.

- Colours: Gold, Yellow, and Orange, embodying the richness of summer.

- Gemstones: Topaz (for clarity) and Agate (for balance).

- Goals: Focus on evaluating your current goals and aspirations, ensuring you align with your true desires.

- Actions: Engage in home improvement projects and take steps to declutter and cleanse your space—both physically and energetically.

- Magic: Ideal for cleansing items, tools, and spells, facilitating renewed energy and clarity in your life.

July – Buck Moon

The Buck Moon is named to honour the majestic growth of new antlers that appear on bucks during this time of year, signalling the peak of summer. This full moon is also known by several other names, including the Blessing Moon, Thunder Moon, Wort Moon, and Hay Moon, each reflecting different cultural traditions and seasonal activities.

Correspondences:

- Element: Water

- colours: Shades of green, silver, and blue/grey that evoke the essence of tranquillity and renewal.

- Gemstones: Moonstone, White Agate, Opal, and Pearl, each carrying meanings of intuition and emotional growth.

- Herbs: Lemon Balm, Hyssop, Chamomile, and Mugwort, commonly used for their soothing properties and enhancements in meditation.

- Goals: This month invites reflection on recreational or vacation goals to reconnect with oneself.

- Actions: Emphasize finding time for personal reflection and rejuvenation.

- Magic: Focus on meditation practices that clear the mind and encourage inner peace.

August – Sturgeon Moon

The Sturgeon Moon derives its name from the plentiful sturgeon fish that are traditionally caught during this time, highlighting the cycle of nature and abundance. In some cultures, it is also referred to as the Green Corn Moon, Fruit Moon, and Grain Moon.

Correspondences:

- Element: Fire

- colours: Vibrant shades of red, yellow, and orange reflecting warmth and vitality.

- Gemstones: Tigers Eye, Carnelian, and Red Agate, known for their grounding and energizing properties.

- Herbs: Rosemary, Basil, Rue, and Catnip, each imbued with protective qualities and energy-enhancing benefits.

- Goals: Concentrate on physical health and wellness goals to rejuvenate the body.

- Actions: Contemplate what sacrifices can be made now for greater benefits in the future.

- Magic: Engage in familiar spell work to strengthen connections and harness oneself.

September – Corn Moon

The Corn Moon marks the onset of the corn harvesting season, reminding us of the importance of agriculture and sustenance. It is also known as the Barley Moon, Harvest Moon, and Singing Moon, reflecting the abundance of this period.

Correspondences:

- Element: Earth

- colours: Earthy tones of brown and green, representing grounding and stability.

- Gemstones: Citrine, Bloodstone, and Peridot, each known for promoting prosperity and growth.

- Herbs: Wheat, Witch Hazel, Valerian, and Flax Seed, utilized for their nourishing qualities.

- Goals: Direct focus onto home and family, setting intentions for stability and harmony.

- Actions: Set up a kitchen altar to honour the harvest and prepare for the coming winter months.

- Magic: Explore kitchen witchery and herbal magic to infuse your space and meals with intention.

October – Hunter's Moon

The Hunter's Moon is named to commemorate the hunting season that occurs before winter, symbolizing preparation and survival. It is also referred to as the Blood Moon or Leaf Moon.

Correspondences:

- Element: Air

- colours: Dark blue, black, and purple, conveying mystery and depth.

- Gemstones: Obsidian, Amethyst, and Tourmaline, known for their protective and introspective qualities.

- Herbs: Rose, Apple Blossom, and Mint, often used for their healing and invigorating attributes.

- Goals: Contemplate spiritual advancement and personal development as the seasons change.

- Actions: Learn from your ancestors and explore family history to deepen your spiritual roots.

- Magic: Engage in scrying and dream work to tap into intuition and the subconscious.

November – Beaver Moon

The Beaver Moon mirrors the industrious nature of beavers as they prepare for winter by building their dams, emphasizing resilience and preparation. It is also called the Dark Moon, Oak Moon, or Mourning Moon.

Correspondences:

- Element: Water

- colours: Subdued grey and blue shades, reminiscent of the calming depths of water.

- Gemstones: Lapis Lazuli, Turquoise, and Topaz, celebrated for their wisdom and communication properties.

- Herbs: Thistle, Fennel, Betony, and Pepper, often associated with protection and courage.

- Goals: Time for reflection on personal goals; consider what has been achieved and what requires adjustment.

- Actions: Let go of past grievances and focus on forward movement and growth.

- Magic: Utilize banishing and warding spells to clear negative energy and create a safe, positive space.

December – Cold Moon

The Cold Moon is named to evoke the deep chill of winter, a time of endurance and reflection. Other names for this moon include the Moon Before Yule and the Long Night Moon.

Correspondences:

- Element: Earth

- colours: Timeless white, red, and black, representing clarity, passion, and the shadows of winter.

- Gemstones: Obsidian, Ruby, and Serpentine, thought to provide protection and invigorate the spirit.

- Herbs: Ivy, Mistletoe, Holly, Berries, and Cinnamon, often associated with festive energy and warmth.

- Goals: Create new aspirations for the upcoming year, setting intentions for growth and achievement.

- Actions: Emphasize volunteer work and donating as a way to spread goodwill and share prosperity.

- Magic: Engage in gemstone and crystal magic to harness energies and manifest desires.

Any Month with a Second Full Moon – Blue Moon

A Blue Moon, occurring when there is a second full moon within a single month, is a rare phenomenon. This moon is sometimes referred to as the Wishing Moon, symbolizing hope and possibility.

Correspondences:

- Element: Spirit

- colours: Ethereal white, purple, and black, representing the connection between earth and the spiritual realm.

- Gemstones: Obsidian, Onyx, and Quartz, each known for their grounding and amplifying properties.

- Herbs: Ginger, Nutmeg, and Hyssop, used for their empowering and purifying effects.

- Goals: Take time to evaluate long-term dreams and plans set for 5, 10, or even 15 years into the future.

- Actions: Centre your attention on personal development and self-improvement.

-   Magic: Focus on initiations, welcoming new beginnings and transitions in your life journey.

Palmistry

APOLLO MOUNT
HEAD LINE
Heart line
life LINE
logic
VENUS
MOON
Bracelets

Palm reading, a fundamental practice within the realm of palmistry, provides fascinating insights into an individual's personality and character traits through the examination of the lines on their hands. The intricate markings etched on a person's palm are believed to reflect various aspects of their life, including emotional tendencies, intellectual capabilities, and even potential life challenges.

How to Read the Lines

1. Evaluate the Depth of Each Line:

The depth of each line in the palm serves as an indicator of its strength or weakness. A line that appears deep and pronounced signifies a robust, well-established trait or aspect of life, while a shallow line may suggest a more inconsistent or transient nature. For instance, a deeply etched head line may indicate a strong intellectual capacity and analytical mindset, whereas a faint or shallow head line might imply a more whimsical, less focused thought process.

2. Assess the Length of the Lines:

The length of a line can provide additional context regarding the extent to which its corresponding trait influences an individual's life. A long heart line, for example, may point toward a fulfilling and successful romantic life, characterized by deep affection and emotional engagement. Conversely, a short heart line might suggest limited romantic experiences or a more guarded approach to relationships.

3. Look for Breaks and Interruptions:

Breaks, interruptions, or unusual markings found along the lines can signify challenges or obstacles faced throughout one's life. Each break can represent a turning point or a hardship that has impacted the individual's journey, indicating areas where growth or re-evaluation has occurred.

In addition to the lines, the mounts and plains of the palm are strongly associated with astrological influences, as they correlate with the planets and zodiac signs. Observing these mounts can yield insights into a person's attributes:

- Even and Slightly Raised Mounts: This condition suggests well-rounded and balanced traits, indicating a person who possesses a healthy blend of qualities.

- Prominent Mounts: When mounts are very pronounced, this may indicate that specific traits are overly developed or exaggerated, potentially leading to imbalances in personality.

- Sunken or Underdeveloped Mounts: If certain mounts are barely perceptible or sunken, this may signify areas of weakness or underdeveloped traits, suggesting where the individual may struggle.

Beyond the main lines and mounts, certain notable marks—such as crosses, circles, or clusters of smaller lines—can have significant implications. Each of these marks is often assigned a specific meaning and can symbolize key experiences or influences in one's life. It's beneficial to take time to document these marks as their meanings can evolve, and they may change over time, reflecting shifts in personal development or circumstances.

The Lines in Palmistry

In palmistry, the four major lines serve as the focal points for interpreting a palm reading. These lines, which are essential for understanding an individual's personality and potential life paths, include the Heart Line, Head Line, Life Line, and Fate Line. Each line provides insight into different aspects of a person's emotional state, intellectual tendencies, life experiences, and life purpose. By examining the characteristics, shapes, and intersections of these lines, a palm reader can offer a comprehensive analysis of one's life journey and personal traits.

Heart Line:

The heart line, often referred to as the love line, is located above the head line. It begins at the edge of the palm beneath the little finger and extends across the palm to either end below the middle finger or forefinger, or at the juncture of the two. This line reveals crucial insights about an individual's emotional landscape, including their approach to love, the complexity of their feelings, and the smoothness of their relationships. The shape and depth of the heart line can reflect one's capacity for affection, openness in relationships, and overall emotional well-being.

Head Line:

The head line commences at the palm's edge between the thumb and forefinger and stretches horizontally across the palm, placed below the heart line and above the life line. This line is key in understanding a person's mental faculties, including their intellect, beliefs, creative abilities, and overall capacity for reasoning and memory. Variations in the head line can indicate different styles of thinking, problem-solving capabilities, and levels of self-control.

Life Line:

The life line curves around the base of the thumb, beginning near the edge of the palm between the thumb and forefinger and extending downwards. Contrary to popular belief, the life line does not dictate the length of one's life; rather, it reflects a person's physical vitality, life energy, and potential experiences of accidents or illnesses throughout their life. The general shape and extent of this line can provide clues about one's zest for life and overall health.

Fate Line:

Also known as the career line, the fate line runs vertically up the palm, typically originating from the base of the palm and leading towards the base of the middle finger. Its starting point can vary, and some individuals may not have a distinct fate line at all. This line primarily relates to a person's career trajectory, professional accomplishments, and shifts in fortune throughout their working life. The presence of breaks or changes along the fate line can indicate significant life transitions or pivotal moments in one's career.

There are several minor lines on the palm that can provide deep insights into an individual's talents, interests, strengths, and weaknesses. The interpretations of these lines can vary based on various factors such as the hand shape, additional markings, the mounts, and the proximity of other lines that may connect or intersect with them. It's not uncommon for these minor lines to be barely visible or entirely absent in some cases. However, when they do manifest on the palm, they offer valuable information for the palm reader. The significant minor lines include:

Marriage Line:

The Marriage Line, often referred to as the Relationship Line or Affection Line, is situated just below the base of the little finger and above the Heart Line. This line primarily reflects the state of an individual's marriage life and romantic relationships, as well as the timing of significant love events. Additionally, it reveals the person's attitude towards love and partnership, suggesting whether their relationships are typical, harmonious, or troubled.

Sun Line:

Also known as the Apollo Line, the Sun Line typically originates from the Mount of Moon and ascends towards the Mount of Sun. This line is a key indicator of an individual's potential capabilities and talents, along with their popularity, which can pave the way for success in various endeavours. It is frequently called the Line of Success because it may enhance the influence of the Fate Line, indicating a person's path to achievement and recognition.

Children Line:

The Children Lines are vertical lines found below the base of the little finger and just above the Marriage Line. They serve as indicators of the number of children a person is likely to have and provide insights into their life statuses. Deeply etched lines typically signify the presence of male children, while shorter, narrower, and shallower lines may suggest the likelihood of female children, thus offering a glimpse into the family dynamics a person might experience.

Money Line:

Located beneath the ring and little fingers, the Money Lines are vertical lines that signify financial acumen and potential wealth. If these lines are numerous, deeply carved, and straight, they suggest that the individual possesses intelligence and skill in investment, indicating the potential for substantial wealth. However, it is important to note that the Money Line alone does not determine financial success, as various other signs and lines in the palm collectively inform one's financial destiny.

Health Line:

The Health Line does not have a fixed starting point and can originate from various places, most commonly from the base of the little finger and stretching across the palm towards the base of the thumb. In some instances, it may begin beneath the Heart Line and end independently without touching the Life Line. In Chinese palmistry, this line is referred to as the Unhealthy Line. The presence of the Health Line usually suggests the individual's overall health status. A straight Health Line that does not touch the Life Line generally indicates robust health, while other configurations may indicate differing health conditions.

Travel Line:

Travel Lines are identifiable upward or horizontal lines emerging from the edge of the palm, often found near the bottom section of the Life Line. These lines signify potential opportunities for travel, living abroad, or emigration for purposes such as study, work, or marriage. The position and nature of these lines can provide clarity on whether the travels are temporary or may lead to a permanent relocation.

Bracelet Line:

The Bracelet Lines, also known as Rascette Lines or Wrist Lines, are located where the palm meets the wrist. Typically, most individuals have three prominent Bracelet Lines, although few possess three complete and distinct lines without irregularities or accompanying markings. The condition and clarity of these lines can reflect the person's overall material well-being and life conditions.

Line of Mars:

The Line of Mars is often found running almost parallel to the Life Line, potentially stretching from the initial point of the Life Line to the wrist. When positioned very close to the Life Line, it is termed the Support Life Line, indicating protective influences in one's life. In contrast, a Line of Mars that is situated further away indicates a Family Influence Line, reflecting the impact of familial relationships on the individual's life path.

Through careful examination of these minor lines and their characteristics, palm readers can gain a fuller picture of a person's life journey, relationships, and potential futures.

In addition to the major and minor lines found on the palm, there are several lesser-known lines located at the base of the fingers that can provide insights into an individual's luck and personality traits. These lines are not present on every person's hand; one notable example is the Girdle of Venus. Certain lines are interpreted as negative indicators, such as the Ring of Saturn, while others, like the Ring of Solomon, are seen as desirable traits. Each of these lines serves as a tool for understanding various aspects of a person's character.

Ring of Solomon:

Also known as the Ring of Jupiter, this line is situated at the base of the index finger, specifically on the Mount of Jupiter. It can manifest as either a straight line or a semi-circular arc. Individuals who possess this line are often seen as intelligent, intuitive, and mysterious. There is a strong affinity for exploring various fields of science, particularly those tied to mystery and the unknown. Those with the Ring of Solomon tend to have a deep curiosity and a desire to uncover hidden truths.

Ring of Saturn:

This line is located on the Mount of Saturn, surrounding the base of the middle finger in the form of a short semi-circle. Typically, people who have the Ring of Saturn may struggle with enjoying life fully. They can be prone to a negative outlook, often harbouring biases against others, and may experience persistent feelings of gloom. In severe cases, individuals with this line may even become susceptible to harmful thoughts, including those related to suicide.

Girdle of Venus:

Positioned above the Heart Line, the Girdle of Venus is characterized by an arched line that encompasses both the middle and ring fingers. It is often viewed as a complementary line to the Heart Line and is commonly found on more delicate, softer palms. Those with a Girdle of Venus exhibit a strong appreciation for beauty and often possess significant artistic talent and creativity. They may also demonstrate precocious development, leading to experiences of puppy love at a young age.

Ring of Mercury:

This rare line starts between the ring and little fingers, curving towards the edge of the palm. Individuals with the Ring of Mercury may exhibit a proclivity for bold sexual behaviours and encounter challenges in maintaining loyalty within relationships. People with this line often prioritize their personal pleasures, sometimes disregarding the needs and feelings of their partners.

Ring of Apollo:

Beginning between the ring and middle fingers, the Ring of Apollo bends towards the ring and little fingers. It is indicative of potential obstacles and frustration that might hinder an individual's natural responses and optimistic nature. Those with this ring may find it challenging to appreciate beauty fully and may experience a repression of their creative impulses.

Note - While the planetary mounts are a primary focus in palmistry, one should not overlook the significance of zodiac signs. Wearing rings on fingers corresponding to astrological signs can serve as a form of portable magic, enhancing one's personal energies.

Mount of Jupiter:

Found at the base of the forefinger, above the Mount of Inner Mars, it symbolizes attributes such as willpower, authority, ambition, and self-respect. A well-developed Mount of Jupiter suggests strong leadership qualities.

Mount of Saturn:

Located at the base of the middle finger, this mount relates to integrity and one's perspective on various matters. A pronounced Mount of Saturn may indicate a deep sense of responsibility and a strong moral compass.

Mount of Apollo:

The base of the ring finger houses the Mount of Apollo, which is primarily associated with emotion, aesthetic interests, wealth, and the appreciation of beauty. A well-defined Mount of Apollo can signify a rich emotional life and a keen sense of artistry.

Mount of Mercury:

Found at the base of the little finger, above the Mount of Outer Mars, it represents wisdom and cognitive ability. A prominent Mount of Mercury often indicates good communication skills and an analytical mind.

Mount of Moon:

This mount is situated below the Mount of Outer Mars, lying at the base of the palm on the little finger side. It is connected to imagination, intuition, and the mysteries of life. A robust Mount of Moon can suggest strong intuitive abilities and a vivid imagination.

Mount of Venus:

Located at the base of the thumb, this mount is nestled below the Mount of Inner Mars and is encompassed by the life line. It is intrinsically linked to love, health, and affection. A well-developed Mount of Venus often signifies a warm, loving nature and strong health.

Mount of Mars:

Found in the centre of the palm, nestled between the Mounts of Inner Mars and Outer Mars, the Mount of Mars reveals insights about courage and adventure. A wide, flat Mount of Mars is viewed favourably, while a low mount in conjunction with other low mounts may suggest challenges in these areas.

- Mount of Inner Mars: Positioned on the palm side between the Mounts of Jupiter and Venus, it represents qualities such as courage and a zest for adventure.

- Mount of Outer Mars: Located on the palm side between the Mounts of Mercury and Moon, it symbolizes self-control and endurance.

By examining these lines and mounts, one can gain deeper insights into their character, potential challenges, and strengths.

In summary, palm reading can offer a rich tapestry of insights into a person's character, relationships, and life experiences. By carefully analysing the lines, mounts, and special marks on the palm, one can embark on a journey of self-discovery and deeper understanding.

<u>Rune Stones</u>

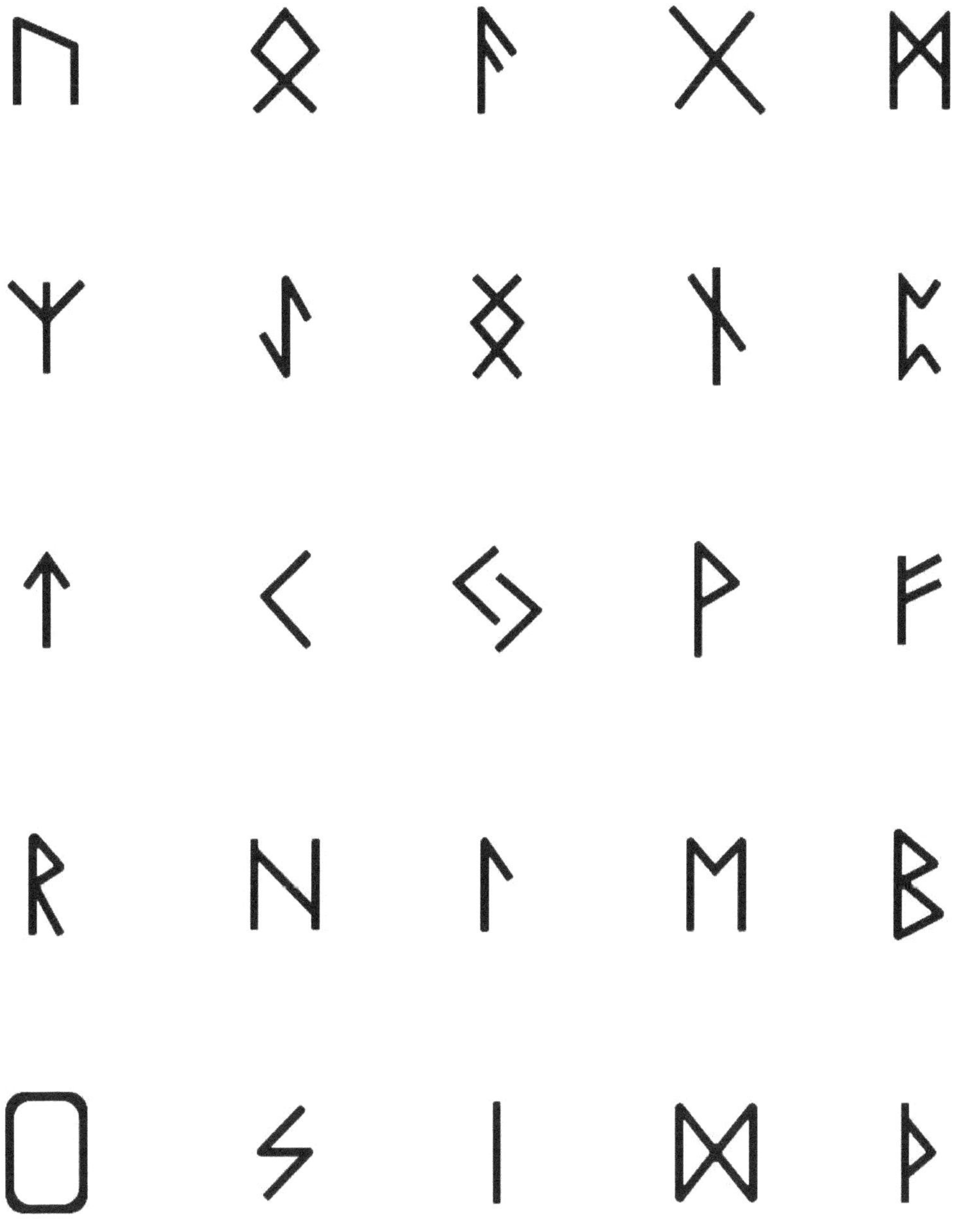

Runes, a collection of 24 ancient alphabetic symbols, have been utilized for centuries as a form of divination, offering insights into the past, present, and potential futures. These symbols are rich in history and mystique, each embodying specific meanings and energies. Runes can be crafted from various materials such as wood, glass, or precious stones, making them not only functional tools for divination but also beautiful objects of art. Traditionally, these runes are kept securely in a pouch or box, safeguarding their energies and ensuring they remain accessible for consultation in moments of need.

In addition to being used for casting and divination, runes can also be inscribed or drawn on paper or other objects. This practice allows individuals to carry the symbols with them or display them in their homes, creating an environment conducive to manifesting positive energies aligned with their goals and intentions. The intention behind keeping runes nearby is to harness their unique powers, inviting prosperity, protection, and clarity into one's life.

Runes are categorized into three distinct Aetts (families), each representing different themes and aspects of existence:

Freyr's Aett –

Freyr's Aett encompasses eight runes: Fehu, Uruz, Thurisaz, Ansuz, Raidho, Kenaz, Gebo, and Wunjo. These symbols are fundamentally connected to the necessities of basic existence on Earth. They speak to the human experience, highlighting our interactions with one another as well as with the divine. Each rune in this Aett plays a significant role in promoting a fulfilling life. For instance, Fehu emphasizes wealth and abundance, while Gebo symbolizes gifts and partnership. In navigating the complexities of life, these runes remind us of the importance of relationships and the balance between giving and receiving.

Hagal's Aett –

Hagal's Aett includes the runes Hagalaz, Nauthiz, Isa, Jera, Eihwaz, Perthro, Elhaz, and Sowilo. This Aett addresses the multifaceted nature of life's unavoidable experiences. The runes within this group provide guidance through disruption, change, and periods of stalled progress, offering solace during challenging times. For example, Hagalaz represents transformation through adversity, while Sowilo embodies the triumph of light over darkness. By engaging with Hagal's Aett, one is reminded that hardships are temporary, and unexpected luck may arise even amidst chaos, instilling resilience and hope in the journey of life.

Tyr's Aett –

Tyr's Aett consists of the runes Tiwaz, Berkana, Ehwaz, Mannaz, Laguz, Ingwaz, Dagaz, and Othala. These symbols delve into the intricate interplay between the visible and invisible realms, connecting to ancient deities, natural forces, and the essence of humanity. Each rune carries a profound significance; for instance, Tiwaz symbolizes justice and honour, while Berkana represents growth and new beginnings. This Aett encourages exploration of one's spiritual path and the understanding of unseen influences in life, guiding individuals in their quest for harmony with the universe.

By recognizing the unique contributions of each Aett and their associated runes, one can cultivate a deeper appreciation for the rich tapestry of human experience, drawing on ancient wisdom to navigate the complexities of modern life.

Rune Meanings

Fehu

Upright Meaning: Fehu symbolizes a strong sense of fulfilment and achievement. It heralds a time when your ambitions have been accomplished, and you find yourself experiencing love and relationships that feel deeply gratifying. The presence of this rune suggests that rewards are flowing in your direction, whether they manifest as monetary wealth, recognition, or a general sense of abundance in your life. It emphasizes good health and new beginnings that enrich your existence.

Reversed Meaning: In its reversed position, Fehu warns of potential frustration and setbacks. This could manifest as a variety of dispossessions or losses that can range from minor inconveniences to significant challenges. You may find yourself longing for what you had or struggling to gain what you desire.

Keywords: Wealth, Prosperity, Abundance, Reward, Good Health, New Beginnings.

Uruz

Upright Meaning: Uruz represents growth and transformation, often appearing when significant changes are on the horizon. This rune indicates that even losses can bring hidden opportunities and new beginnings. It calls for embracing the cycle of life and recognizing that every ending paves the way for a fresh start, thereby fostering strength and resilience.

Reversed Meaning: When reversed, Uruz warns of missed opportunities and the potential weakening of one's position. It may suggest a reluctance to adapt to changes or the consequences of avoiding necessary growth.

Keywords: Strength, Health, Power, Energy, Endurance, Creative Force.

Thurisaz

Upright Meaning: Thurisaz serves as a cautionary rune, urging you to be acutely aware of your circumstances and the implications of your actions. It signifies the importance of assessing risks carefully before proceeding, emphasizing thoughtful consideration and the value of patience during uncertain times.

Reversed Meaning: In reverse, Thurisaz indicates that hasty decisions made in a moment of impulsivity can lead to regret. It suggests a compelling need to reflect on your choices and to refrain from acting without thorough deliberation.

Keywords: Protection, Warning, Contemplation, Decisions, Luck.

Ansuz

Upright Meaning: Ansuz embodies the transfer of wisdom typically coming from an elder or a figure with profound knowledge. It highlights the significance of communication, especially when messages from enlightened sources guide you through complex decisions. This rune often brings great insight and illumination to the questioner, fostering a deeper understanding of both worldly matters and spiritual truths.

Reversed Meaning: When turned upside down, Ansuz points to failed communication or misunderstandings. There may be a lack of clarity in your interactions, leading to confusion or missed messages. It serves as a reminder to improve communication and seek clarity in relationships.

Keywords: Communication, Wisdom, Divine Power, A Message.

Raidho

Upright Meaning: Raidho heralds a journey that is likely to bring happiness and fulfilment. This journey may be physical, spiritual, or emotional, but it promises positive experiences and connections. It also signifies movement and change, indicating that new opportunities for reunion and growth are on the horizon.

Reversed Meaning: In reverse, Raidho reflects potential disruptions in your journey. You might face obstacles that derail your plans or lead to miscommunications during travels. This rune invites you to remain adaptable and open to adjustments along your path.

Keywords: Travel, A Journey, Movement, Reunion, Changes.

Kenaz

Upright Meaning: Kenaz is a beacon of light in the darkness, offering clarity and insight in challenging situations. It encourages you to reconsider your circumstances with fresh perspectives or new information that can illuminate the way forward. This rune symbolizes creativity and breakthrough, urging you to embrace the transformative power of illumination in your life.

Reversed Meaning: Kenaz does not have a reversed meaning, emphasizing its positive attributes of discovery and illumination regardless of orientation.

Keywords: Light, Heat, Illumination, Breakthrough, Creative Fire.

Gebo

Upright Meaning: Gebo signifies partnership and alignment, often embodying the concept of marriage or the strengthening of long-standing relationships. It is a rune of generosity and mutual support, indicating the importance of shared love and the gifts that stem from deep, meaningful connections.

Reversed Meaning: Gebo does not hold a reversed meaning, reinforcing the idea that its essence revolves around the positive aspects of love and giving.

Keywords: Gift, Generosity, Friendship, Harmony, Talents/Abilities.

Wunjo

Upright Meaning: Wunjo radiates happiness and joy, transforming life in profoundly positive ways. It's a symbol of emotional fulfilment and contentment, suggesting that bliss and well-being are paramount during this phase. When this rune appears, it encourages you to celebrate the joyful moments that enhance your relationships and overall success.

Reversed Meaning: When reversed, Wunjo cautions that things may not be proceeding as you'd wish, leading to a state of unrest. This rune advises against making significant decisions during times of emotional turmoil or dissatisfaction, urging patience until clarity returns.

Keywords: Joy, Happiness, Harmony, Bliss, Happy Relationships, Well-Being, Success.

Hagalaz

Upright Meaning: The appearance of Hagalaz signifies powerful forces of chaos that are beyond your control. This can manifest as sweeping disasters, debilitating illness, or unexpected problems that disrupt your path towards achieving your goals. When this rune appears, it serves as a reminder that certain interferences cannot be managed or fixed; attempting to resist these challenges may only lead to further frustration. It encourages you to adapt to the chaos around you instead of trying to fight against it.

Keywords: destruction, chaos, interference, misfortune, transformation.

Nauthiz

Upright Meaning: Nauthiz reflects a state in which your essential needs are not being met. This might encompass physical aspects like poverty and hunger, as well as emotional dimensions such as a lack of support or connection. It serves as a reminder to acknowledge your current limitations and the scarcity you may be facing. Understanding and addressing these areas are vital before you can move forward.

Reversed Meaning: Represents a caution against hasty decisions or rash actions. It encourages you to conserve your energy and focus on what is essential for the time being, rather than rushing into uncertain situations.

Keywords: need, necessity, scarcity, absence, restriction, patience.

Isa

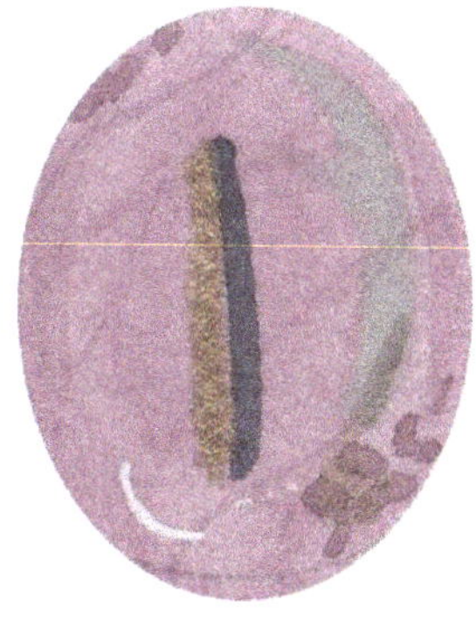

Upright Meaning: Isa suggests that accomplishments may not be attainable at this moment. It symbolizes pauses, obstacles, and delays that can create a standstill in your pursuits. While progress may feel stunted, this rune advises you to cultivate patience and resilience, understanding that sometimes the best action is inaction.

Keywords: obstacles, standstill, stagnation, delay, coldness.

Jera

Upright Meaning: Jera embodies the principle that the achievement of goals usually requires time and dedication. It emphasizes that your hard work and perseverance will eventually yield positive results. This rune symbolizes the natural cycles of effort and reward—reminding you that patience is key to reaping what you sow.

Keywords: harvest, reward, natural cycles, fruition, fertility, growth.

Eihwaz

Upright Meaning: Eihwaz prompts you to exercise caution and avoid being overly eager to push forward, especially at the start of new endeavours. This rune highlights the inherent difficulties that can arise with change and transformation. It encourages you to practice perseverance and thoughtful foresight as you navigate these transitions.

Keywords: death, regeneration, rebirth, changes, magic.

Perthro

Upright Meaning: Perthro signals that not everything is as it appears. It urges you to be aware of the subtle signs and signals your intuition provides, as they may unveil deeper truths. This rune points to the existence of mysteries and the need for reflection on the hidden aspects of your situation.

Reversed Meaning: Acts as a warning against having overly high expectations. It suggests that old ways may come to an abrupt end due to an unpleasant surprise or revelation, prompting you to adapt to new circumstances.

Keywords: mystery, secrets, revelation, chance.

Elhaz

Upright Meaning: Elhaz advises you to stay alert and maintain a clear mind, while remaining in touch with your intuitive senses. This awareness is crucial for achieving a favourable outcome in your endeavours. It highlights the importance of self-preservation and protective instincts in navigating external challenges.

Reversed Meaning: Indicates that someone in your vicinity may be attempting to take advantage of you. Exercise caution in both business and romantic relationships, especially with individuals whom you have only just met or do not know well.

Keywords: protection, defence, opportunity.

Sowilo

Upright Meaning: Sowilo embodies the spirit of illumination and energy, symbolizing the pursuit of your goals. It encourages you to draw on your creative strengths and inherent talents to bolster your efforts. This rune suggests that success is within your grasp if you harness your inner light and passion.

Keywords: light, energy, good health, success.

Tiwaz

Upright Meaning: The Tiwaz rune encourages you to stand firm and maintain your faith in yourself and your abilities. It signifies that you are well-equipped to face the challenges that lie ahead, provided you act with integrity and rely on your inner wisdom. This rune embodies the qualities of courage and victory, suggesting that you are in a strong position to achieve your goals if you approach situations with determination and a clear sense of purpose.

Reversed Meaning: When reversed, Tiwaz indicates that you may be moving too hastily, leading to impulsive decisions that could result in long-term repercussions. It serves as a warning against rushing into actions without careful consideration, urging you to pause and reflect before making choices that could affect your future.

Keywords: Courage, victory, strength, passion, masculine energy.

Berkana

Upright Meaning: Berkana represents new beginnings and is a powerful symbol of growth and development. It heralds the onset of exciting ventures such as launching a new project, entering a new relationship, embarking on a significant phase of spiritual growth, or nurturing a fresh idea that has the potential to yield positive outcomes. This rune signals a time of blossoming and renewal, encouraging you to embrace change and the opportunities it brings.

Reversed Meaning: In its reversed position, Berkana may suggest stagnation, indicating that you could be facing obstacles that hinder the start of something new. It serves as a reminder to reassess your current circumstances and identify the barriers that may be preventing progress.

Keywords: Birth, new beginnings, family, growth, regeneration.

Ehwaz

Upright Meaning: The Ehwaz rune emphasizes the importance of faithfulness and accountability in your relationships. It encourages you to nurture loyalty and trust with those around you, reinforcing the bonds that hold connections together. This rune signifies beneficial changes and possible movements or travels, underscoring the need for collaboration and support from others.

Reversed Meaning: When reversed, Ehwaz points to a potential lack of faith or trust that may be affecting your relationships or circumstances. It urges you to step back and consider the broader perspective, as this may be an opportune moment for introspection and realignment with your authentic self.

Keywords: Changes, faith, loyalty, trust, movement, travel.

Mannaz

Upright Meaning: Mannaz signifies significant personal growth and rectification in your life. It is a time for self-improvement and development, encouraging you to focus on your progress rather than seeking external validation or credit for your achievements. This rune represents the potential for deeper connections with humanity and emphasizes the importance of community and support in your journey.

Reversed Meaning: In its reversed state, Mannaz could indicate a period of self-isolation or emotional detachment from the world around you. During this time, it may be essential to nurture new ideas and perspectives that require solitude before they can flourish.

Keywords: Humanity, the self, support, assistance, intelligence, family.

Laguz

Upright Meaning: Laguz encourages you to release resistance and embrace the natural flow of life. It highlights the importance of adaptability, suggesting that fighting against your circumstances will only lead to further discord. When you embrace change and trust your intuition, you can find harmony and growth in your experiences.

Reversed Meaning: When Laguz appears reversed, it signifies a blockage in the flow of your life. This could manifest as feelings of stagnation or discomfort in your current job or relationships. It also suggests a neglect of your intuitive and spiritual needs, urging you to reconnect with your inner self for guidance.

Keywords: Water, flow, intuition, the unconscious, psychic ability, the feminine, growth.

Ingwaz

Upright Meaning: The Ingwaz rune denotes completion, signalling the end of a significant phase in your life. This closure allows for the release of energy, making way for new opportunities to enter your experience. It reassures you that any current difficulties are nearing resolution, resulting in relief and the chance to begin fresh.

Reversed Meaning: Ingwaz does not hold a reversed meaning, serving solely as a potent symbol of transition and fulfilment.

Keywords: Fertility, male procreative force, channelling energy, completion, safety.

Dagaz

Upright Meaning: Dagaz brings a message of optimism and enlightenment as new developments come to light. It encourages you to maintain a hopeful outlook, as unexpected successful outcomes may emerge as you remain focused on the positive aspects of your journey. This rune represents transformation and balance in your endeavours.

Reversed Meaning: Dagaz does not have a reversed interpretation; it stands firmly as a beacon of positivity and success.

Keywords: Daylight, success, hope, breakthrough, transformation, balance.

Othala

Upright Meaning: The Othala rune highlights the themes of heritage and tradition, particularly regarding the tension between your familial background and your current lifestyle choices. It calls attention to the influence of ancestral ties in your life and encourages you to reflect on how they shape your identity and decisions.

Reversed Meaning: In its reversed state, Othala may indicate conflict and disharmony within family dynamics. This could manifest as significant disputes, such as those surrounding inheritance or major differences in values. It serves as a warning to address these issues to avoid deeper rifts.

Keywords: Heritage, tradition, inheritance, ancestral property, family ties.

Blank Rune

Some rune sets include a blank rune, symbolizing the potential for self-change and personal evolution. When this blank rune appears in a reading, it encourages you to acknowledge the progress you're making in your journey toward self-discovery and transformation. Embrace the unknown and remain open to the possibilities it presents.

Reading the Runes

Before embarking on your journey to read or cast the runes, it is essential to prepare yourself both mentally and physically. Begin by finding a tranquil space that is free from distractions—this could be a quiet room, a serene outdoor setting, or any place where you feel at peace. Once you are settled, take a moment to relax your body and mind. Consider engaging in deep breathing exercises to help clear your mind and centre your thoughts. The objective here is to enter a meditative state in which you can focus entirely on your intention.

As you prepare for your reading, concentrate on a specific question or issue that you wish to explore. This could be a situation that is currently troubling you, a decision you need to make, or even a general inquiry about your life's direction. The clarity of your focus and intent is crucial; it will significantly enhance the accuracy and depth of your readings, allowing the runes to convey messages that resonate deeply with your inquiry.

Interpreting a rune cast can be likened to discovering and narrating a story. Your role as the reader is to identify the characters, themes, events, and wisdom that the runes present in response to your query. Allow yourself ample time to explore the meanings and connections among the runes. Sometimes, the runes will provide straightforward answers to your questions, while at other times, they may redirect your attention toward other aspects of your life—issues that you may have been reluctant to acknowledge previously.

One Rune Method

To perform a simple one-rune reading, start by calming your mind and concentrating on a specific question. Then, draw a single rune from your set. Once you have selected your rune, look up its meaning and reflect on how it applies to your current circumstances. This technique can be particularly valuable for daily guidance, giving you insight into what type of day to expect or providing clarity on a specific issue. It can also serve as a method for answering a "yes or no" question: if the rune is upright, the answer is affirmative; if it appears reversed, the answer is negative. Runes that do not have a reversed position suggest that it may not be the right time to pose your question.

Three Rune Spread

For a more detailed exploration of your situation, consider the three-rune spread. Pour your focus into your question, and draw three runes, placing them one at a time on your rune cloth or table.

1   2   3

Turn them over one by one and interpret the runes in the following manner:

1. The first rune represents the challenge, issue, or problem you are currently facing.

2. The second rune indicates the course of action you should take to address the challenge.

3. The third rune reflects the potential outcome of following the advice given by the second rune.

Five Rune Spread

If you seek even deeper insights, try the five-rune spread. Concentrate fiercely on your situation and select five runes. Arrange them face down in this specific order:

4

1   2   3

5

Then, turn them over one by one and read them according to the following interpretations:

1. The second rune symbolizes the Present, identifying your current problem, situation, or issue.

2. The first rune represents the Past; it reveals what has led to your current situation.

3. The fourth rune indicates Help, showing the assistance you may receive from friends, relatives, strangers, or even within yourself to navigate the current issue.

4. The fifth rune signifies Obstacles—elements of the situation that cannot be changed and must be accepted to facilitate your progress.

5. The third rune presents the Result, forecasting the outcome if you heed the guidance provided by the other runes.

Seven Rune Spread

For a comprehensive analysis, the seven-rune spread is a profound method to delve into various aspects of your inquiry. Focus intently on your issue and draw seven runes, placing them face down in this order.

When you're ready, interpret the runes as follows:

1. Turn over the first and second runes together. Their combined meanings illustrate the central issue or problem you are facing.

2. Turn over the third and fourth runes. This pair represents factors from your past that influence your present situation.

3. The fifth and sixth runes are the most significant in this reading; they offer crucial advice from the runes on how to proceed.

4. Finally, the seventh rune indicates the outcome that may result from following the advice offered in the spread.

By engaging deeply with this ancient practice, you will find that the runes serve as powerful tools for insight, guidance, and self-reflection. Embrace the journey of exploration with an open heart and mind, and you may discover profound truths about your path forward.

Sabbats

YULE
Dec 21 - Jan 1
Winter Solstice

SAMHAIN
Oct 31 - Nov 1

IMBOLC
Febr 1-2

MABON
Sep 21 - 23
Fall Solstice

OSTARA
March 20
Spring Equinox

LUGHNASADH
July 31 - Aug 1

LITHA
June 21 - 22
Summer Solstice

BELTANE
April 30 - May 1

<u>**The Wheel of the Year**</u>

The Wheel of the Year represents a rich and cyclical journey through the seasons, celebrated annually by many practitioners of modern witchcraft. This framework is deeply rooted in the interplay of natural solar events and represents a harmonious connection between humanity and the cycles of nature. The Wheel encompasses a series of seasonal festivals known as Sabbats, which are pivotal moments that encapsulate both the divine and earthly realms. These eight seasonal Sabbats correspond to key solar events—including the Solstices and Equinoxes—and the midpoints that bridge these significant moments. Each Sabbat unfolds with its own unique themes, rituals, and traditions that honour the changing landscapes and energies of the Earth.

The eight seasonal Sabbats which are celebrated around the year are:

Sabbat	Sabbat Type	Date
Yule	Winter Solstice	20th-23rd December
Imbolc	1st Fire Festival	1st February
Ostara	Spring Equinox	20th-23rd March
Beltane	2nd Fire Festival	1st May
Litha	Summer Solstice	20th-23rd June
Lammas	3rd Fire Festival	1st August
Mabon	Autumn Equinox	20th-23rd September
Samhain	4th Fire Festival	31st October

A simple yet meaningful way to celebrate each Sabbat is to decorate your altar in accordance with the themes and symbols of the season. This personal touch not only enhances the experience of each festival but also fosters a deeper connection to the sacred rhythms of the Wheel of the Year.

<u>**Yule**</u>

Yule is recognized as the first of the lesser sabbats within the Wheel of the Year, typically celebrated between the 20th and the 23rd of December. This festival aligns with the Winter Solstice, the darkest day and longest night of the year. As we gather to celebrate Yule, we acknowledge the diminishing daylight and the onset of winter's chill, knowing that the coldest days are still to come. Traditionally, Yule signifies both an end and a beginning—a time to reflect upon the past year while looking forward to the return of the sun.

During Yule, the energy is particularly potent for personal growth and magical workings. Individuals often find their spiritual vibrations heightened, making this an opportune time for deepening one's practice, setting intentions, and embarking on important personal transformations.

Yule Correspondences:

- Alter Decor: Decorate your space with natural elements such as holly berries, pinecones, a Yule log, sun symbols, and festive lights. Yellow candles can symbolize the returning light, while dark green and poinsettias evoke the resilience of nature in winter.

- Herbs: Use herbs like rosemary for remembrance, rue for cleansing, thyme for courage, bay leaves for purification, basil for protection, and lavender for peace.

- Crystals: Incorporate Snowflake Obsidian for balance, Ruby for vitality, and Snow Quartz for clarity.

- Incense: Light up cinnamon for warmth, clove for protection, mint for renewal, myrrh for healing, and pine for grounding.

- colours: Emphasize shades of green, yellow, blue, silver, and red to invoke life, joy, and the spirit of the season.

- Animals: Symbolic animals include reindeer, bears, owls, phoenixes, and stags, each representing various aspects of winter strength and renewal.

- Foods: Indulge in seasonal treats such as apple cider, gingerbread, eggnog, and an assortment of nuts, bringing warmth and joy to your gatherings.

Ways of Celebrating Yule:

- Watch the Sunrise: Embrace the return of light by enjoying the first light of the day.

- Make Potpourri: Create your own blend using seasonal herbs and spices to infuse your home with the scents of winter.

- Decorate a Tree: Adorn a tree with meaningful ornaments and natural elements that resonate with your intentions.

- Give Someone a Gift: Share your warmth and joy by giving thoughtful gifts to loved ones, reinforcing the bonds of community and love.

Imbolc

Imbolc is a significant greater sabbat marking the first fire festival of the year, celebrated on February 1st. This festival honours Brigid, the Irish goddess of poetry, wisdom, and protection. As Imbolc arrives, it heralds the gradual return of spring—a season known for healing, renewal, and the awakening of nature. This is a perfect moment to cleanse your space, both physically and energetically, and to set new intentions for the year ahead.

As winter gives way to spring, the energy of Imbolc inspires introspection and planning, particularly regarding your goals and aspirations. Whether you are a gardener contemplating what to plant or simply seeking personal growth, Imbolc offers a fresh start.

Imbolc Correspondences:

- Alter Decor: Utilize plants that signal the end of winter, green candles representing growth, chalices for the sacred, cauldrons for transformation, Celtic designs for cultural connection, and Brigid dolls as tokens of guidance and protection.

- Herbs: Incorporate blackberry for resilience, basil for purification, bay for success, and lavender for tranquillity.

- Crystals: Use Amethyst for spiritual insight, Garnet for strength, Onyx for protection, and Ruby for passion.

- Incense: Awaken your senses with the scents of cinnamon for energy, frankincense for spirituality, myrrh for healing, and pine for grounding.

- colours: Invoke renewal with green, red for passion, and white for purity.

- Animals: Bear, deer, lamb, phoenix, and sheep symbolize rebirth and new beginnings.

- Foods: Celebrate with bread, cakes, cookies, and milk to honour the nourishing aspects of Brigid.

Ways of Celebrating Imbolc:

- Spring Clean: Clear out the old to make way for the new, symbolically and physically.

- Make Offerings to Brigid: Create an altar space for Brigid and offer flowers, candles, or crafted items as a sign of respect and gratitude.

- Set Intentions for the Year: Take time to write down your aspirations and dreams for the coming year.

- Plan Your Garden: Research and decide what plants you wish to grow, making a detailed plan for implementations in the planting season.

Ostara

Ostara, celebrated between the 20th and 23rd of March, represents the second lesser sabbat of the Wheel of the Year. This festival coincides with the Spring Equinox, a time when daylight and darkness are perfectly balanced, symbolizing the renewal of life. Ostara not only celebrates the arrival of spring but also encourages us to reflect upon the duality of existence—light and dark, life and death.

With the invigorating energies of spring, Ostara serves as a perfect opportunity for self-reflection, balance, and rejuvenation. It is an ideal time to engage in chakra work, meditate, and consider how you can harmonize different aspects of your life.

Ostara Correspondences:

- Alter Decor: Use seeds and flowers as symbols of growth, black and white candles for balance, and pastel-coloured ribbons to celebrate the awakening of life.

- Herbs: Adorn your space with daffodils for rebirth, jasmine for love, irises for hope, lilacs for tranquillity, mint for renewal, and tulips for beauty.

- Crystals: Incorporate Rose Quartz for love, Moonstone for intuition, and Aquamarine for clarity.

- Incense: Light lemon for freshness, patchouli for grounding, ylang ylang for love, and rose for spiritual connection.

- colours: Embrace pastel hues, yellow for joy, gold for prosperity, blue for tranquillity, and pink for love.

- Animals: Celebrate with the elements of nature represented by butterflies, chicks, robins, and rabbits—symbols of fertility and growth.

- Foods: Delight in cheese, eggs, chocolate, fish, and cakes to symbolize abundance and festivity.

Ways of Celebrating Ostara:

- Meditate: Spend time in quiet reflection to connect with the energies of renewal and balance.

- Balance Your Chakras: Engage in practices that focus on aligning your energy centres.

- Practice Reiki: Share healing energy with yourself or others to promote well-being.

- Decorate Eggs: Create and adorn eggs as a manifestation of fertility and new beginnings, embracing the spirit of the season.

Beltane

Beltane is celebrated on May 1st as the second of the greater sabbats and is often known as a fire festival. This significant day honours the union of the Green Man and the May Queen, symbolizing the arrival of summer and the celebration of life in all its forms. As nature bursts forth in vibrant colours and fragrances, Beltane urges us to appreciate the beauty and abundance surrounding us.

This sabbat is particularly suited for feminine spell work, fertility rituals, and handfasting's. It is also a wonderful time for collective practices with fellow witches, fostering community and shared intention.

Beltane Correspondences:

- Alter Decor: Fill your space with flowers, seeds, acorns, antlers, and fairy symbols. Use wreaths and colourful ribbons in shades of green, blue, purple, and yellow to invigorate your environment.

- Herbs: Incorporate Lily of the Valley for love, clover for luck, and honeysuckle for happiness.

- Crystals: Use emerald for growth, amber for vitality, rose quartz for love, and carnelian for creativity.

- Incense: Engage the senses with lavender for peace, frankincense for spirituality, lilac for renewal, and rose for love.

- colours: Celebrate with vibrant yellow, green, blue, pink, and purple hues to reflect the joyful essence of the season.

- Animals: Symbolic wildlife includes doves, cats, bees, lynxes, cows, and swans, each representing the flourishing of life.

- Foods: Delight in seasonal fruits like cherries, strawberries, and honey alongside celebratory beverages like wine—a toast to the abundance of life.

Ways of Celebrating Beltane:

- Create Bonfires: Light bonfires to symbolize the sun's return and as a ritual of purification and affirmation.

- Dance Around the Maypole: Engage in dancing around a Maypole, intertwining ribbons that symbolize unity and the interconnectedness of life.

- Plant Flowers and Seeds: Honor the season by planting flowers and seeds, invigorating the earth and contributing to the cycle of life.

- Craft Wreaths: Create floral wreaths to adorn your home and connect with nature's beauty, celebrating its bounty.

Litha

Litha, known as the third lesser sabbat in the Wheel of the Year, is celebrated between June 20th and 23rd. This sabbat marks the Summer Solstice, the day when the sun reaches its highest point in the sky, resulting in the longest day of the year. As we bask in the energy of this vibrant season,

Litha signifies a time of abundance, joy, and the peak of summer's brightness. It is an opportunity to acknowledge the flourishing life around us and to harness the energy of the sun and fire for magical workings, as these elements are at their most potent during this time.

Correspondences for Litha:

- Altar Decor: To create a vibrant altar, consider using solar crosses, sun symbols, crystals imbued with solar energy, and colourful adornments in shades of yellow, red, and orange. Incorporating summer-themed artwork and an array of flowers or gemstones will enhance the atmosphere.

- Herbs: Key herbs associated with Litha include basil, chamomile, daisy, sunflower, and peony—each bringing its essence to rituals during this time.

- Crystals: Utilize crystals such as amber, citrine, diamond, jade, and tiger eye. These stones are perfect for magnifying the sun's energy and intentions of prosperity.

- Incense: Burning incense made from orange, rose, sage, lemon, mint, or clove can create an uplifting environment for your rituals.

- colours: The vibrant colours representing this sabbat are reds, yellows, golds, and oranges—impressions of the fiery sun and blooming summer.

- Animals: Encountering bees, butterflies, sea creatures, and snakes holds significance during Litha, symbols of transformation, fertility, and life.

- Foods: Seasonal delights include fresh summer fruits, colourful vegetables, honey, and refreshing ice cream—nourishing the spirit and body.

Ways to Celebrate Litha:

- Lay in the Sun: Reconnect with the solar energy by spending time outdoors, absorbing the sun's warmth and light.

- Practice Cloud Divination: Allow your imagination to roam as you watch cloud formations and interpret their shapes and movements for insight.

- Collect Herbs & Flowers: Gather herbs and flowers to craft your own magical potions, blessings, or create an herbal wreath.

- Practice Fire Magic: Engage in fire-related spells or rituals, perhaps lighting candles or a bonfire, channelling the powerful energy of flames.

Lammas

Lammas, the first of the greater sabbats and the third fire festival of the year, is celebrated on August 1st. This festival marks the beginning of the harvest season and embodies themes of gratitude and reflection on our achievements over the past months.

Lammas is a time to acknowledge the gifts of nature and to celebrate the hard work that brings food and sustenance to our tables. It invites us to embrace the transformation and nurturing energy of abundance in our lives.

Correspondences for Lammas:

- Altar Decor: Enhance your altar with straw braids, corn dolls, oils made with herbs and flowers, and items representative of the fall harvest such as cornucopias and gemstones.

- Herbs: Key herbs include ivy, yarrow, basil, goldenrod, and poppy, each contributing to ceremonies of gratitude and prosperity.

- Crystals: Crystals like golden topaz, citrine, and yellow aventurine align with the energy of abundance and growth.

- Incense: Burning sandalwood, frankincense, rosemary, and rose can deepen the spiritual connection during your Lammas rituals.

- colours: The colours of Lammas are warm and earthy—greens, browns, yellows, oranges, and reds reflect the harvest and the changing season.

- Animals: Common animals associated with Lammas include crows, pigs, roosters, salmon, and cows, each symbolizing various aspects of harvest and sustenance.

- Foods: Traditional foods feature breads, apples, grains, pears, and berries—symbols of the bountiful harvest.

Ways to Celebrate Lammas:

- Bake a Lammas Bread Loaf: Create bread using freshly harvested grains, honouring the gift of sustenance.

- Brew Beer: Celebrate the brewing tradition by crafting your own ale, symbolizing abundance and community.

- Make Corn Husk Dolls: Create dolls as a representation of the harvest and gratitude for nature's gifts.

- Practice Prosperity Spells: Focus on spells that draw in wealth and success as you prepare for the months ahead.

Mabon

Mabon, the final lesser sabbat of the year, takes place between September 20th and 23rd. This celebration aligns with the Autumn Equinox, a point of balance between light and dark as daylight dwindles.

Mabon signifies a shift as we prepare to welcome the darker months ahead. It is a time for reflection, gratitude, and the harvesting of what we have sown throughout the year.

Correspondences for Mabon:

- Altar Decor: Your altar may feature autumn garlands, apples, pumpkins, spices, skulls, besoms, and collected photos, invoking the spirit of the season.

- Herbs: Ingredients like rue, sage, thistle, oak leaves, and yarrow will enhance your rituals and offerings during this reflective time.

- Crystals: Choose crystals such as amber, citrine, cats eye, sapphire, and lapis lazuli for their grounding and balancing energies.

- Incense: Burn incense made from cinnamon, frankincense, myrrh, or sage to create a warm, inviting atmosphere that resonates with autumn.

- colours: Mabon is represented by rich colours—gold, browns, yellows, oranges, and reds—evoking the richness of the harvest.

- Animals: The energies of blackbirds, eagles, owls, and wild geese are predominant, each representing wisdom and guidance.

- Foods: Traditional Mabon foods include apple cider, root vegetables, corn, and grains, celebrating the abundance of the earth.

Ways to Celebrate Mabon:

- Collect Leaves & Make Leaf Rubbings: Engage with nature by collecting leaves and creating rubbings as a way to honour the changing season.

- Bake Apple or Pumpkin Pies: Infuse your kitchen with autumn flavours by baking seasonal pies, nourishing body and spirit.

- Make a Besom: Craft your own besom for sweeping away negativity and making space for newfound energies and clarity.

- Practice Protection Spells: Set wards around your home to maintain harmony and protect your space during the darker months.

Samhain

Samhain, celebrated on October 31st, is one of the most significant sabbats, marking the end of the old year and the start of the new. This greater sabbat represents the Feast of the Dead, a time for honouring those who have crossed over.

The veil between worlds is believed to be thinnest on Samhain, allowing for greater connection with the spirit realm, making it a profound time for divination and reflection.

Correspondences for Samhain:

- Altar Decor: Decorate your altar with pumpkins, harvest foods, nuts, berries, leaves, dark breads, skulls, skeletons, ghosts, and warm beverages like mulled cider, wine, or mead, invoking the essence of the season.

- Herbs: Incorporate fragrant herbs like cinnamon, garlic, rosemary, sage, and myrrh to enhance your rituals and offerings in remembrance.

- Crystals: Utilize protective and intuitive stones such as amethyst, jet, obsidian, and hematite to amplify your connection to the spirit world.

- Incense: Burning sandalwood, lavender, and patchouli will create a mystical atmosphere perfect for ritual work and invocation.

- colours: The colours of Samhain are deep and rich—black, orange, purple, and burgundy—reflecting the mystery and magic of the night.

- Animals: Symbolic creatures include bats, black cats, crows, spiders, and moths, each linked to the mysteries of death and transformation.

- Foods: Seasonal foods consist of apples, squash, root vegetables, and potatoes, grounding your connection to the earth.

Ways to Celebrate Samhain:

- Create An Ancestor Altar: Set up a special space to honour your ancestors with photographs, mementos, and offerings, inviting their guidance.

- Carve Pumpkins: Engaging in the tradition of pumpkin carving creates a festive yet sacred atmosphere while warding off negative energies.

- Practice Divination: Use scrying mirrors, black pendulums, or tarot cards to seek insights and guidance from the spirit realm.

- Share Stories of the Departed: Gather with loved ones to share stories and memories of those who have passed, honouring their legacy and spirit.

Each of these festivals reflects a deep connection to nature and the cycle of life, encouraging participants to engage actively with the changing seasons and embrace the potential for growth and transformation.

Sigils

Sigils represent a fascinating and accessible form of magic that anyone can explore. These intricate and unique symbols each carry a specific coded intention, allowing for direct and impactful results. Additionally, crafting sigils serves as a quick method of spell work, making it an attractive option for witches and practitioners alike.

Understanding How Sigils Work

The essence of a sigils power lies in the creative process itself. When you design a sigil, you are taking a clear intention and transforming it into a visual symbol. This transformation encodes the intention into your subconscious mind, where it can be most effective. The primary goal is to bypass any doubts or limiting beliefs that reside in the conscious mind. In doing so, you enable the symbolic representation to access the broader, unrestricted power of your subconscious, allowing the intention to manifest without interference.

The versatility of sigils ensures that there are countless ways to create and utilize them, making this form of magic both accessible and effective for those inclined to practice it.

Step-by-Step Guide to Creating a Sigil

1. Define Your Intention:

Begin by reflecting on what you wish to achieve with your sigil. This reflection will help clarify your intention and set a firm foundation for the symbol's purpose.

2. Craft Your Intention Statement:

Write out your intention in a concise sentence, phrased in the present tense as if you have already achieved the desired outcome. It's essential to avoid negative constructs, such as "I do not" or "I will not," as these can undermine the intention. A well-structured example might be:

"MY CLAIRE SENSES ARE ACTIVE"

3. Remove Vowels:

After you have your intention statement, eliminate all vowels. From the previous example, you would be left with:

"MY CLR SNSS R CTV"

4. Eliminate Duplicate Letters:

Next, take the consonants and remove any repeating letters. You should find yourself with a unique set of letters that will serve as the foundation of your sigil:

"MYCLRSNTV"

5. Decide on a Creation Method:

Choose how to design your sigil. You might opt for a personal artistic interpretation or employ established methods like the Witches Wheel or The Number Box.

Methods for Creating Your Own Sigil

Creative Expression:

There are no strict rules for designing your sigil. Let your creativity flow! You can rearrange, flip, or stylize the letters in any manner that resonates with you. Embrace both intricate and simplistic designs based on your aesthetic preference.

Using the Witches Wheel:

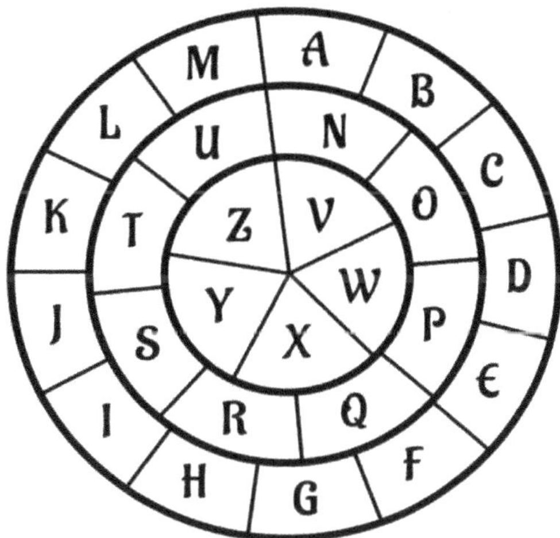

1. Take the letters derived from your intention and begin by marking the first letter with a dot.

2. Connect the remaining letters with straight or curved lines. Feel free to enhance your design with dots, arrows, or other small motifs to create a more visually striking symbol.

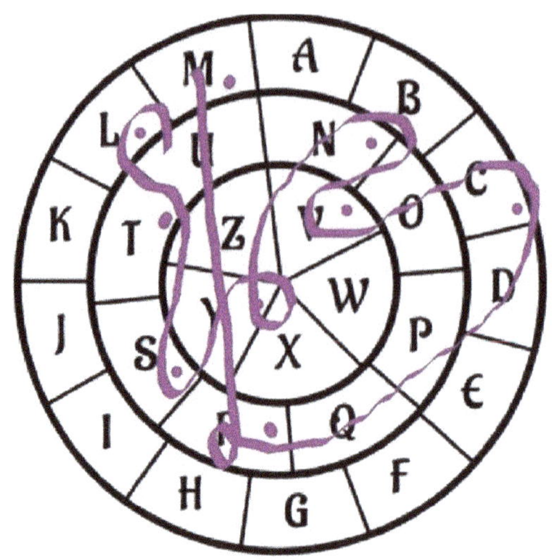

Applying the Number Box Method:

Each letter in your intention corresponds to a number based on a simple grid system. Translate the letters into their respective numbers.

1	2	3	4	5	6	7	8	9
A	B	C	D	E	F	G	H	I
J	K	L	M	N	O	P	Q	R
S	T	U	V	W	X	Y	Z	

MYCLRSNTV would become 4 7 3 3 9 1 5 2 4 for use in the number grid below.

1	4	7
9	2	5
6	3	8

Use the same approach as with the Witches Wheel to draw your sigil, connecting the numbers in a way that offers symbolism and personal significance.

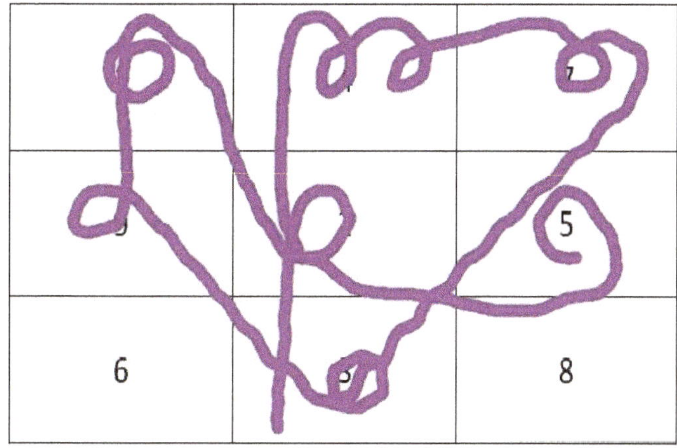

Activating Your Sigil

Before you can harness the power of your sigil, activation is a crucial step. There are multiple methods to activate your sigil, each tailored to enhance your intention:

- Using Crystals: Select a crystal that aligns energetically with your intention and place the sigil near it, charging the symbol with the crystal's energy.

- Elemental Activation:

  - Earth: Bury the sigil in the ground to connect with grounding energies.

  - Air: Tear the sigil into small pieces and allow it to scatter in the wind, symbolizing freedom and release.

  - Fire: Burn the sigil to transform its energy and release your intention into the universe.

  - Water: Immerse the sigil in water, symbolizing emotional connection and fluidity.

- Salt Infusion: Place the sigil in a jar filled with salt, which represents purification and protection, further amplifying your intention.

Sigils offer a unique and personalized approach to magic that invites you to connect deeply with your intentions. By crafting and activating your sigil, you not only engage in a powerful act of creation but also tap into the latent energies within you, allowing your desires to manifest more effectively. Whether through artistic expression or established methods, the practice of sigils is a fulfilling journey into the realm of the magical.

Tarot card reading is a captivating form of cartomancy that involves the use of tarot cards to gain insights into an individual's past, present, or future circumstances. Practitioners, often referred to as tarot readers, begin by encouraging the querent— the person seeking guidance— to formulate a specific question or focus on an area of their life where they seek clarity. Once the question is set, the reader shuffles the deck and draws a predetermined number of cards, each of which holds symbolic meanings and associations.

The cards drawn during the reading are then interpreted in the context of the question, allowing the reader to offer insights that tap into the querent's unconscious knowledge. This process can reveal hidden motives, opportunities that may not be immediately apparent, and potential paths the querent can take. The imagery and symbolism of the cards often resonate deeply with the individual, prompting reflection and self-discovery.

It's important to note that tarot readings do not predict unchangeable events destined to occur; rather, they serve as a guide to help individuals understand their circumstances and make informed choices. The insights gained during a tarot reading can foster personal growth and empower the querent to navigate their life with greater awareness and intention.

The Major Arcana

The Major Arcana consists of 22 cards, with 21 being numbered sequentially from 0 to 21, plus one unnumbered card known as the Fool. Each of these cards embodies profound life lessons, karmic influences, and overarching archetypal themes that play a significant role in shaping your existence and your soul's quest for enlightenment. These cards encapsulate the essence of human experiences and consciousness, serving as a bridge to timeless wisdom cultivated over generations.

At the heart of the Major Arcana lies the Fool, who symbolizes new beginnings, innocence, and the potential of a blank slate. As the Fool embarks on his journey through the different cards, he encounters numerous archetypal figures—each representing unique life lessons and challenges. This narrative, known as the Fool's Journey, creates a framework for understanding the interconnectedness of these cards and offers valuable insights into various stages of personal development.

In a Tarot reading, the emergence of a Major Arcana card signals a crucial moment—inviting you to reflect deeply on the fundamental life lessons and themes currently unfolding in your life. These cards often set the tone for the entire reading, with subsequent Minor Arcana cards providing context and elaboration on the core message that the Major Arcana card conveys. Because of their profound significance, Major Arcana cards can highlight pivotal shifts, karmic influences, or transformative events that shape your life path.

The Minor Arcana

Contrasting the Major Arcana, the Minor Arcana is comprised of 56 cards that capture the everyday experiences and challenges we face. While labelled as "minor," these cards hold significant importance and can profoundly affect our lives. They provide clarity and guidance regarding the specifics of our day-to-day interactions, situations, and emotions, illustrating how present circumstances impact our overall journey.

The Minor Arcana cards typically indicate temporary influences—energies that are currently present but are subject to change based on our choices and actions. In a Tarot reading, the appearance of a Minor Arcana card reflects the immediate challenges or events you are experiencing, guiding you on how to navigate these situations effectively. While Major Arcana cards denote the significant lessons of your life's journey, Minor Arcana cards illuminate the key situations and the practicalities of your current reality, emphasizing that these moments are fleeting and can evolve over time.

The Minor Arcana is divided into the following, four distinct suits:

The Suit of Cups –

This suit relates to your emotions, feelings, intuition, and creativity. Cards from the Suit of Cups frequently surface in readings focused on interpersonal relationships, emotional depth, and spiritual connections. They encourage you to explore your innermost thoughts and the dynamics at play between yourself and others.

The Suit of Pentacles –

These cards pertain to the material aspects of life, such as finances, career, and physical possessions. In Tarot readings, Pentacles cards often appear when discussing career advancement, financial stability, or the tangible resources you possess. They serve as a reminder to consider how your practical choices impact your overall sense of security and abundance in life.

The Suit of Swords –

Representing the realm of intellect, communication, and conflict, Swords cards delve into your thoughts, decisions, and the power of your words. They emerge in readings that explore decision-making processes, expressing ideas, or confronting challenges. The Swords remind you of the importance of clarity and assertiveness in your verbal and mental communications.

The Suit of Wands –

This suit embodies energy, passion, motivation, and inspiration. Wands cards often appear in readings about personal growth, life purpose, and creative endeavours. They inspire you to embrace your intrinsic passions and drive, highlighting opportunities for innovation and spiritual exploration.

Together, the Major and Minor Arcana provide a comprehensive framework for understanding both the profound journeys and the everyday experiences that shape your life, allowing for a rich exploration of personal development and spiritual insight.

<u>Card Meanings</u>

0 - The Fool

Description: The Fool is often illustrated as a carefree jester or a wandering vagabond, taking their first enthusiastic steps into the unpredictable world ahead. This figure is depicted standing at the edge of a cliff, symbolizing a blend of innocence and danger, joy and risk. The Fool represents a spirit of adventure and spontaneity, embodying the idea of embarking on a new journey without the burdens of fear or consequence.

Upright Meaning: When drawn upright, The Fool signifies the dawn of a new journey filled with optimism, wonder, and courageous enthusiasm. It often indicates that you may find yourself at a crossroads, contemplating various options and weighing the associated risks with a light heart. This card encourages embracing the unknown with a sense of excitement and trust in the unfolding path ahead. Key Words - New Beginnings, Innocence, Beginner's Luck, Improvisation, Adventure.

Reversed Meaning: In a reversed position, The Fool warns of missed opportunities due to misguided decisions or a disconnect from reality. This card suggests that you might be blinded by naivety or excess optimism, leading to potential exploitation by others. It serves as a cautionary message to step back, reflect, and reassess before diving into new endeavours, as situations may not be as favourable as they seem. Key Words - Naivety, Lack of Direction, Chaos, Carelessness, Misjudgement.

1 - The Magician

Description: The Magician stands as a central figure, confidently pointing skyward and downward, communicating the principle of "As Above, So Below." Surrounded by symbols representing the four elements (earth, air, fire, water) and cardinal directions, The Magician embodies the connection between the spiritual and physical realms. This card symbolizes mastery and the ability to harness a wealth of resources and skills for manifestation.

Upright Meaning: In an upright position, The Magician speaks to your potential and resourcefulness. It serves as a reminder that your thoughts and actions create your reality—encouraging you to leverage your skills and confidence to navigate your circumstances effectively. The card signifies determination and the power within you to initiate transformation and bring your dreams into fruition. Key Words - Determined, Resourceful, Potential, Transformation, Manifestation.

Reversed Meaning: When reversed, The Magician suggests a need for change, cautioning that not everyone around you may have your best interests at heart. You could be experiencing self-sabotaging behaviours driven by self-doubt or external manipulation. This card indicates a likelihood of confusion or deception—urging you to pause before making any rash or impulsive decisions. Key Words - Illusion, Deception, Lack of Energy, Confusion, Ill Intent.

2 - The High Priestess

Description: The High Priestess occupies a position of power and tranquillity, seated between the Pillar of Establishment (Jachin) and the Pillar of Strength (Boaz). This card symbolizes the balance of dualities—masculine and feminine, light and dark, known and unknown. The High Priestess embodies wisdom, intuition, and mystery, inviting you to explore the depths of your inner self.

Upright Meaning: When drawn upright, The High Priestess encourages you to trust your instincts and inner voice. It signals a potent period of introspection and growth, prompting you to meditate and reflect deeply on your feelings and thoughts. This card reinforces the idea that true knowledge lies within and emphasizes the importance of listening to your intuition, often leading to significant personal evolution. Key Words - Intuition, Unconscious, Inner Voice, Mystery, Reflection.

Reversed Meaning: In a reversed state, The High Priestess indicates a struggle with self-trust and intuition. You may be encountering uncertainty or feeling off-balance in your life. This card often represents hidden obstacles or repressed emotions that require attention. It acts as a reminder to seek clarity and confront any secrets that may be affecting your well-being. Key Words - Withheld Information, Secrets, Repressed Feelings, Inner Conflict.

3 - The Empress

Description: The Empress is depicted elegantly seated atop a throne amidst a lush, vibrant landscape that represents fertility, abundance, and the nurturing essence of Mother Earth. This card embodies femininity, creativity, and the manifestation of life in various forms, signalling the importance of self-love and care.

Upright Meaning: In an upright position, The Empress heralds new beginnings—be it the creation of new life, blossoming relationships, or flourishing projects. This card encourages you to embrace your nurturing qualities and invest in self-care, promoting personal growth and stability. It affirms that abundance and prosperity are close at hand, urging you to express your creativity and allow the flow of positive energy into your life. Key Words - Fertility, Expression, Motherhood, Stability, Abundance.

Reversed Meaning: When reversed, The Empress may indicate an overextension of care toward others at the expense of your own well-being. It can signify reliance on others for emotional support or the potential for stifling affection that leads to discomfort. The card urges you to address personal issues and work toward building self-confidence and independence. Key Words - Lack of Self-Reliance, Fertility Issues, Financial Strife, Overprotection.

4 - The Emperor

Description: The Emperor is portrayed with authority, seated on a ram-adorned throne positioned atop a rugged mountain, signifying the strength and sterility of regulation and control. This card symbolizes power, leadership, and the need for structure, reflecting the importance of discipline and perseverance in achieving one's goals.

Upright Meaning: In its upright position, The Emperor indicates a time of control and accomplishment. You may find yourself facing new responsibilities that lead to greater rewards thanks to your hard work and initiative. This card encourages the establishment of order and discipline in your endeavours, highlighting the significance of focused effort and leadership in your personal or professional life. Key Words - Leadership, Promotion, Structure, Law & Order, Authority.

Reversed Meaning: When reversed, The Emperor warns of potential misuses of power or authority. You may encounter manipulative forces that undermine your control, leading to feelings of powerlessness. This card signifies chaos and the breakdown of established rules, urging you to regain your footing and address imbalances in situations where you feel dominated. Key Words - Immaturity, Ego, Tyranny, Lack of Discipline, Rigidity.

5 – The Hierophant

Description: The Hierophant embodies a traditional figure associated with spiritual authority, often depicted as a representative or leader of a formal religious institution. In this imagery, the Hierophant raises their right hand in a gesture of blessing or benediction, signifying a connection to the divine. In their left hand, they carry a triple cross, a symbol closely linked with the Pope and the Catholic faith. This figure is accompanied by two acolytes at their feet, representing the transmission of sacred knowledge and the mentoring role of the Hierophant in guiding others on their spiritual paths.

Upright Meaning: When the Hierophant appears upright in a reading, it emphasizes the importance of adhering to established systems, traditions, and conventions. It may suggest that you should respect societal norms, follow guidelines, and pursue education or personal growth within a structured environment. The message is about finding comfort within routine and minimizing the desire for radical changes or innovative ideas. Key words - Religion, Ethics, Traditions, Marriage, and Education.

Reversed Meaning: In a reversed position, the Hierophant indicates a departure from conventional thinking and a desire to explore alternative paths. You may feel constrained by societal expectations or find yourself rebelling against established norms and traditions. The card serves as a warning that such defiance could lead to a sense of disorder or a loss of control in your life. Key words - Rebellion, Subversiveness, and Rejection of Values.

6 – The Lovers

Description: The Lovers card symbolizes not only romantic partnerships but also the deeper aspects of relationships that encompass balance, unity, and harmony. This card signifies the transformative power of love and the mutual support that gives individuals strength and confidence within a relationship. It highlights the significance of choices and the emotional dynamics that shape partnerships, emphasizing the importance of commitment and connection.

Upright Meaning: When drawn upright, The Lovers card signifies a pivotal moment in relationships where choices must be made. This could relate to the selection of a life partner or decisions involving emotional connections. The card prompts you to reflect deeply on what matters most to you and encourages you to make choices that align with your core values and beliefs. Trust your intuition while navigating the complexities of love and relationships. Key words - Partnership, Deep Love, Duality, Union, and Commitment.

Reversed Meaning: In reversal, The Lovers card suggests tension and conflict within relationships, whether with friends, family, colleagues, or internally within yourself. It may indicate a breakdown in communication, an imbalance, or avoidance of responsibilities. This state can lead to feelings of infidelity, separation, or disharmony. The card advises mending relationships and letting go of emotional baggage to restore harmony and balance. Key words - Infidelity, Separation, Disharmony, Loss of Balance.

7 – The Chariot

Description: The Chariot card portrays an individual seated confidently in a vehicle, typically a chariot, drawn by two powerful sphinxes. This imagery signifies determination and the ability to overcome challenges, symbolizing the right balance of control and direction necessary for moving forward in life. The Chariot emphasizes the journey and the triumph of willpower over adversity, encouraging you to steer your path with focus and confidence.

Upright Meaning: In an upright position, The Chariot speaks to your strength in overcoming obstacles and regaining dominance over your circumstances. It highlights the importance of focus, resilience, and confidence as you navigate the trials ahead. You must maintain concentration and stick to your strategic plan to achieve success and victory in your endeavours. Key words - Willpower, Drive, Confidence, Ambition, and A Journey.

Reversed Meaning: When reversed, The Chariot can signal a lack of direction or willpower. You might feel adrift or confused about your path, leading to impulsive decisions and a loss of self-control. It serves as a wake-up call to reassess your actions and regain your focus, as failure to do so could lead to further disarray. Key words - Travel Issues, Aggression, Self-Doubt, and Lack of Control.

8 – Strength

Description: The Strength card illustrates a serene figure gently holding the jaws of a powerful lion, symbolizing the balance of courage and control. This card embodies the idea that true power comes from inner strength and compassion rather than aggression. It emphasizes patience, resilience, and the ability to face challenges with grace and determination.

Upright Meaning: When the Strength card is drawn upright, it indicates that you are handling stress and challenges with a cool and composed demeanour. Your ability to stay calm under pressure reflects your compassion and patience, and this inner strength will lead to forthcoming rewards. You are encouraged to harness your determination to achieve great things and maintain composure in the face of adversity. Key words - Confidence, Virility, Focus, Compassion, and Valour.

Reversed Meaning: In a reversed position, the Strength card warns you of potential loss of control and rising tensions. You may be grappling with mood swings or feeling overwhelmed by situations that were once manageable. There is a suggestion to take a step back and reassess, as this card may indicate impending conflicts or a struggle with jealousy and insecurity. It emphasizes the need to regain your confidence and stability. Key words - Weakness, Aggression, Insecurity, and Indulgence.

9 – The Hermit

Description: The Hermit card features an individual standing alone at the peak of a high mountain, symbolizing solitude and introspection. They hold a lantern that illuminates the path ahead, containing a six-pointed star, known as the Seal of Solomon, which signifies wisdom and enlightenment. The Hermit encourages a journey inward to gain profound spiritual insights that can then be shared with others.

Upright Meaning: When upright, The Hermit suggests that you should heed your inner voice and take time for self-reflection. Stepping back from the hustle and bustle of daily life can provide essential clarity and insight. This is a period for soul-searching, meditation, and introspection, allowing you to connect with your deeper self and discover guiding truths. Key words - Solitude, Introspection, Meditation, and Self-Reflection.

Reversed Meaning: In the reversed position, The Hermit cautions against excessive isolation, indicating that solitude may lead to feelings of loneliness or disconnection from those around you. This card suggests the importance of reaching out and engaging with others, as seclusion could exacerbate feelings of sadness or being an outsider. It may also signal a need to investigate underlying issues that may be troubling you. Key words: Loneliness, Isolation, Exile, Sadness, and Misfit.

10 – The Wheel of Fortune

Description: The Wheel of Fortune is a powerful symbol representing the cyclical nature of life, illustrating the ups and downs that come with existence. This card features a large, rotating wheel, encircled by four distinct creatures that embody the four elements of the Minor Arcana: a lion for fire, an eagle for air, a bull for earth, and a serpent for water. Each of these creatures serves as a reminder of the natural forces that influence our lives and the perpetual motion of fortune.

Upright Meaning: When the Wheel of Fortune appears upright, it suggests that you are presently experiencing a blend of highs and lows, indicative of the unpredictable nature of fate. This card encourages you to embrace both the joyous moments and the challenging times, understanding that this ebb and flow is beyond your control. You are reminded that all situations are temporary, and with patience, you will find that no matter the current challenges, the wheel will eventually turn in your favour. Key Words - Change, Luck, Destiny, Chance, Opportunity, Fate.

Reversed Meaning: In the reversed position, the Wheel of Fortune often indicates a period of bad luck or misfortune. You may feel that circumstances are working against you, leaving you frustrated and powerless. It is crucial at this time to practice acceptance and let go of the urge to control every outcome. Holding on too tightly to a desired result will only lead to further disappointment. Instead, embrace flexibility and trust that this moment of difficulty is merely a phase that, like all things, will eventually pass. Key Words - Bad Luck, Misfortune, Disappointment, Mishap.

11 – Justice

Description: The Justice card embodies the principles of fairness, truth, and the balance between actions and outcomes. It depicts a figure sitting solemnly on a throne, holding a set of scales in their left hand, representing the delicate balance between intuition and rational thought. In their right hand, they wield a double-edged sword, signifying the impartiality and clarity needed when discerning right from wrong.

Upright Meaning: When Justice appears upright, it calls attention to the significance of your choices and the way they will resonate in your future. If you have faced injustice, this card brings a hopeful message of forthcoming relief and balance. Conversely, if you have contributed to someone else's pain, consider this a crucial moment for self-reflection and accountability. Justice encourages you to seek truth, whether about yourself or others, and to approach any major decisions with a solid moral foundation. Key Words - Clarity, Truth, Fairness, Balance, Responsibility.

Reversed Meaning: In its reversed state, the Justice card may indicate that you are confronting denial or evasion of accountability. You might need to come to terms with past actions that have led to imbalances in your life. This card reminds you to take responsibility with grace rather than self-judgment. It suggests that recognizing your mistakes and learning from them is essential for growth. Key Words: Dishonesty, Unfairness, Unaccountability, Imbalance.

Description: The Hanged Man represents a state of suspension and surrender, suggesting an invitation to pause and reflect. This card features a figure hanging upside down from the branches of a tree, illustrating a voluntary sacrifice for a greater understanding. The image serves as a metaphor for viewing life from a different perspective.

Upright Meaning: When drawn upright, The Hanged Man encourages you to embrace a time of solitude and introspection. This may feel like an ordeal of sacrifice, as those around you might not understand your need to step back. You are reminded to take this time of reflection seriously, considering your choices carefully before proceeding forward. This card speaks to the transformation that comes from patience and letting go of the need for immediate results. Key Words - Circumspection, Sacrifice, Metamorphosis, Suspension.

Reversed Meaning: In reverse, The Hanged Man often signifies feelings of stagnation and frustration. You might be struggling with a lack of progress, feeling as though you are trapped in indecision or are creatively blocked. This position warns against getting too caught up in your own perspective, as it can hinder your ability to adapt and move forward. Key Words - Egotism, Inability to Change, Fear of Sacrifice, Stalling.

13 – Death

Description: Contrary to its appearance, the Death card does not signify a literal end but rather transformative change and the conclusion of one phase to make way for another. Illustrated by a skeletal figure on a white horse carrying a black flag, this card symbolizes the universality of change and the new beginnings that follow an ending.

Upright Meaning: Death appearing upright signals the inevitability of change in your life. You may be on the brink of letting go of something that no longer serves you—be it an unhealthy relationship or a phase of life that has run its course. Embrace this transition, for every end births a new beginning. Allow yourself the space to grieve the past while welcoming the opportunities ahead. Key Words - Rebirth, Metamorphosis, New Beginnings, Change.

Reversed Meaning: When reversed, the Death card indicates resistance to change. You may find yourself clinging to the past, frightened of the uncertainty that change can bring. This card serves as a reminder that holding on too tightly slows down your progress and limits your potential for growth. Letting go is crucial for moving forward; confront your fears and embrace the natural flow of life. Key Words - Depression, Illness, Fear of Change, Stagnation.

14 – Temperance

Description: Temperance embodies the themes of balance, moderation, and harmony. This card features an angel gracefully manoeuvring between the fluid and the solid—one foot in water and the other on land—symbolizing the merger of different aspects of life, including the material and spiritual realms.

Upright Meaning: When the Temperance card is upright, it suggests a period of equilibrium and harmony. You are encouraged to find the middle ground in your decisions, approaching life with patience and mindfulness. This card reminds you not to rush into circumstances but rather to assess your priorities and strive for a balanced approach in all things. Key Words - Harmony, Moderation, Patience, Alchemy, Balance.

Reversed Meaning: In reverse, Temperance warns of potential chaos and extremes in your life. You may feel overwhelmed and unbalanced, prompting a moment of introspection regarding what is truly important to you. Take this opportunity to reevaluate your goals and aspirations, as well as the means by which you pursue them. This reflection is vital for restoring balance and harmony in your life. Key Words - Extremes, Disruption, Chaos, Excess, Lack of Balance.

15 – The Devil

Description: The Devil card often illustrates a satyr-like figure, widely recognized as Baphomet, prominently perched atop a pedestal. This powerful entity towers over two chained figures, one male and one female, symbolizing their subjugation and lack of agency. Their expressions convey a deep sense of shame and despair, as they gradually lose their essence as human beings, illustrating the dehumanizing effects of their bondage to the Devil's influence.

Upright Meaning: This card signifies feelings of entrapment and disillusionment. You might be grappling with unfulfilled desires, realizing that your life is dominated by the seductive pull of materialism or substances. Such attachments can render you powerless and lead to addictive behaviours. This card serves as a warning to reflect on what controls you and to seek liberation from these negative influences. Key words - Addiction, Excess, Materialism, Greed, Envy, Temptation, Fear.

Reversed Meaning: When appearing reversed, The Devil suggests a breaking of chains and a move toward self-awareness. You are on the brink of liberation, whether that means freeing yourself from detrimental habits, an unhealthy relationship, or toxic environments. This shift involves recognizing the illumination of a path to recovery, urging you to invest in personal reflection. Embrace this opportunity to reclaim your autonomy and heal. Key words - Freedom, Release, Recovery, Restoring Control.

16 – The Tower

Description: The Tower card depicts a formidable structure that has been violently struck by lightning, leading to its fiery destruction. Panicked figures are seen leaping from the windows, desperately seeking escape from the impending catastrophe. This vivid imagery serves as a reminder that such upheaval is essential for transformation; the old must crumble to pave the way for new beginnings.

Upright Meaning: In its upright position, The Tower heralds profound and often unsettling change that may be imminent or already unfolding. This kind of significant disruption can evoke fear, yet it is through facing and embracing these challenges that real growth occurs. The upheaval, while daunting, is a necessary precursor for the rebuilding of strength and resilience. Key words - Ruin, Disgrace, Disaster, Catastrophe, Destruction.

Reversed Meaning: The reversed Tower indicates that a crisis may be looming, one that you have been desperately trying to avert. The solid foundations you thought you had may actually be eroded and in dire need of deconstruction. Though what lies ahead may be tumultuous, enduring this painful process is crucial to emerging stronger on the other side. It's a call to face the impending change head-on rather than evade it. Key words - Loss, Illness, Fear of Suffering, Avoiding Disaster.

Description: The Star card typically portrays a serene, nude feminine figure kneeling by a tranquil pond, pouring water from a jug into its depths. Above her, a large golden star shines brightly, accompanied by seven smaller stars, symbolizing hope and guidance. This imagery embodies the benevolence of the universe and the abundance available to those who show kindness and generosity.

Upright Meaning: When drawn upright, The Star reveals a period of renewal and reawakening. You may find yourself in a state of heightened awareness and creativity, where optimism and spiritual growth flourish. It is a time to give generously of yourself and share your blessings with others. This card encourages you to embrace positive energy flowing into your life. It is an uplifting reminder that you are aligned with your higher self and your dreams. Key words - Good Health, Renewal, Faith, Spirituality, Inspiration, Hope.

Reversed Meaning: In the reversed position, The Star often points to a crisis of faith, revealing feelings of disconnection or a lack of inspiration. You might be experiencing doubts that smother your light. This card urges you to take proactive steps to regain your enthusiasm and seek activities that nurture your spirit. It is a prompt to get back on track and find the flicker of hope within. Key words - Despair, Disappointment, Illness, and Disconnection.

18 – The Moon

Description: The Moon card illustrates the contrast between wildness and civility through the depiction of a wolf and a dog standing sentinel on either side of a winding path. This imagery emphasizes the dualities inherent within us. Towering structures in the background suggest that choices lie ahead, each with its consequences, urging you to be mindful of the decisions you make.

Upright Meaning: The Moon indicates a time of confusion and illusion. It calls for trusting your intuition, as appearances can be misleading. You may be facing emotional turbulence, mood swings, or subconscious insecurities. If you seek clarity on a situation, patience is necessary as answers might take time to emerge. Embrace your instincts to navigate through the obscurities. Key words - Illusion, Unconscious, Risk, Intuition, Caution, Confusion.

Reversed Meaning: When reversed, The Moon suggests that negative fears and energies are beginning to dissipate, leading to the emergence of newfound self-confidence. Revelations you've been awaiting may soon come to light. However, this card can also indicate that secrets may surface, urging honesty with oneself and others. This is a time for clarity and truth to prevail. Key words - Confusion, Misinterpretation, Fear, Repressed Emotion.

19 – The Sun

Description: The Sun card radiates positivity, symbolizing joy and revitalization. With imagery of sunlight breaking through darkness, it embodies the essence of life and energy. The card reflects a time of abundance and warm feelings, highlighting the success and happiness that emerge from hard work and perseverance.

Upright Meaning: When The Sun appears upright, you are filled with optimism and gratitude for the blessings surrounding you. Expect a surge of joy, contentment, and success in your life. Your confidence and energy become magnetic, inspiring those around you to bask in your warmth. This card is a celebration of life's pleasures and the abundant gifts that circulate within your experience. Key words - Joy, Success, Enlightenment, Marriage, and Vitality.

Reversed Meaning: In its reversed form, The Sun might indicate struggles with maintaining a positive outlook. Obstacles may impede your growth, leaving you feeling uncertain and less confident. This could also be a warning against excessive optimism in dire situations, urging you to reevaluate your circumstances with a critical eye. Approach challenges with a grounded mindset to regain balance and clarity. Key words - Lack of Clarity, Sadness, Depression, and Negativity.

Description: The Judgement card depicts a powerful scene where individuals, both adults and children, rise from their graves in response to the clarion call of an angel's trumpet. This imagery symbolizes the awakening to a new phase in one's life, reflecting the deeper truths of existence and the inevitability of facing the consequences of past actions. The card underscores the idea of accountability and the universality of judgment, suggesting that all beings will ultimately confront their choices.

Upright Meaning: When Judgement appears in the upright position, it invites moments of deep self-reflection and introspection. You may find yourself at a pivotal point in your life's journey, one that has been fraught with challenges and obstacles. This is a time for honest evaluation of your past decisions, as you prepare to embrace a new chapter. It encourages you to confront your fears and insecurities rather than avoid them, fostering personal growth and renewal. Sharing your experiences with others can offer comfort and solidarity, creating bonds that help you navigate through tough times. Key Words - Reflection, Awakening, Transition, Decisions, Change.

Reversed Meaning: When Judgement is reversed, it often indicates a powerful reluctance to confront a necessary truth or an important decision. This avoidance may stem from self-doubt and critical inner dialogue, leading to feelings of inadequacy and stagnation. You could be repressing emotions or sidestepping accountability, which prevents you from progressing in your journey. This card serves as a cautionary reminder to allow yourself the time and space for introspection, as the lack of reflection may hinder your personal development. Key Words - Doubt, Self Loathing, Criticism, Stunted Growth.

Description: The World card stands as the culmination of the Major Arcana, illustrating the idea of completion and the intricate dance of life. The imagery often represents harmony and interconnectedness, highlighting the dynamic nature of existence and the endless cycles of beginnings and endings. This card signifies not just an ending, but also the sense of fulfilment that comes from successfully navigating through a journey, embodying balance and the evolutionary process of life.

Upright Meaning: In its upright position, The World card signifies a profound sense of unity and achievement. It heralds significant developments in your life—be it a marriage, the birth of a child, a new job, or another transformative experience. This is a time when your hard work and dedication are acknowledged, and the fruits of your labour are about to be reaped. It invites you to celebrate your accomplishments and embrace the wholeness you have created in your life. Key Words - Completion, Harmony, Accomplishment, Achievement.

Reversed Meaning: When The World appears reversed, it often signals the closing of a chapter that feels unresolved or incomplete. You may experience feelings of alienation or disconnection as you navigate the concluding stages of a significant event. There may be a sense of something lacking, leading to emotional emptiness. This card encourages you to take the time to reconnect, whether with yourself or with those around you, in order to realign with your path and intentions. Key Words - Delayed Success, Failed Plans, Stagnation, Emptiness.

Ace of Cups

Description: The Ace of Cups is a powerful and evocative card that typically depicts a hand emerging from the clouds, gracefully holding a cup that overflows with glimmering water. This imagery symbolizes the abundant potential for emotional and spiritual nourishment. The water cascades down in five distinct streams, each stream representing different aspects of intuition and emotional depth, suggesting a profound connection to both self and others.

Upright Meaning: In its upright position, the Ace of Cups invites you to release any emotional burdens that have been hindering your personal growth. This card signifies an opportunity for a fresh start, be it in the form of new relationships or rekindling old ones. It serves as a reminder that the choice to embrace this new chapter is ultimately in your hands. Pay attention to your intuition, as it may lead you toward meaningful connections and experiences. Key Words - Proposal, Marriage, Intuition, Spirituality, New Feelings.

Reversed Meaning: When drawn in reverse, the Ace of Cups indicates that you may be grappling with emotional instability, pain, or a lingering sense of loss. This card points to a creative blockage that may stem from unresolved emotional issues. Reflect on who or what has taken control of your emotional well-being and allowed your "cup" to be overturned. It's crucial to regain your grip and reorient yourself toward emotional stability. Key Words - Emotional Loss, Emptiness, Blocked Creativity.

2 of Cups

Description: The Two of Cups vividly illustrates a ceremonial exchange of chalices between two figures, embodying themes of negotiation, harmony, and mutual respect. This imagery underscores the significance of relationships, whether they be platonic friendships or romantic partnerships, and signifies a deep emotional connection.

Upright Meaning: When the Two of Cups appears upright, it indicates the presence of a strong partnership characterized by equality and shared aspirations. This card symbolizes a flow of positive energy in your relationships; it encourages you to nurture and share this energy with those around you. Emphasizing unity and support, the Two of Cups serves as a reminder to celebrate the connections that enrich your life. Key Words - Marriage, Romantic Love, Unity, Partnership, Connection.

Reversed Meaning: In its reversed form, the Two of Cups suggests that the once harmonious balance in your relationships may be faltering.

Disconnections have arisen, leading to misunderstandings and resentment. Small issues that might ordinarily be resolved easily are now magnified, creating cracks in your connections. It's essential to communicate openly and take the initiative to repair these fractures. Reflecting on how to be the bigger person can help mend relationships that are strained. Key Words - Imbalance, Broken Connections, Tension.

3 of Cups

Description: The Three of Cups captures a vibrant scene where three friends joyously celebrate life, their cups raised in acknowledgment of success, camaraderie, and celebration. Adorned with floral wreaths, these figures represent happiness, community, and the joy of shared moments.

Upright Meaning: When drawn upright, the Three of Cups heralds a period of joy and fulfilment. You may find yourself reconnecting with friends or family members after a significant time apart or celebrating an important milestone. This card encourages you to cherish these moments of connectivity and express gratitude for the support and love from those around you. Key Words - Friendship, Community, Support, Happiness, Celebration.

Reversed Meaning: The reverse of the Three of Cups can indicate a sense of isolation from the social circles that once brought you joy. Responsibilities or hectic schedules may have caused you to drift apart from friends and loved ones. It's crucial to invest time and effort into rekindling these connections. Additionally, be cautious of any gossip or negativity within your inner circle that could further disrupt your relationships. Key Words - Overindulgence, Isolation, Gossip, An Affair.

4 of Cups

Description: The Four of Cups portrays a figure seated under a tree, seemingly preoccupied with three cups positioned in front of them. A disembodied hand extends forth, offering another cup, yet the figure appears unimpressed, gazing at the existing cups and ignoring the new opportunity presented.

Upright Meaning: In its upright position, the Four of Cups suggests a sense of stagnation and discontent. You may find it challenging to focus on the joys and passions that once brought you happiness. The card serves as a cautionary reminder not to overlook opportunities that may lead to personal fulfilment. Reflect on your feelings of apathy; there may be vibrant opportunities waiting just outside your current perspective. Key Words - Apathy, Disillusion, Missed Opportunity, Remorse, Regret.

Reversed Meaning: When reversed, the Four of Cups signifies a shift toward openness and readiness for change. You might be starting to recognize and embrace new ideas, people, and opportunities that can reinvigorate your life. This is a time to release past patterns and relationships that no longer serve you, allowing for a fresh perspective and acceptance of new beginnings. Key Words -Sudden Awareness, Choosing Happiness, Acceptance.

5 Of Cups

Description: The imagery of the 5 of Cups depicts a figure cloaked in dark garments, standing in a forlorn posture with their head bowed low, suggesting deep sorrow and loss. Surrounding them are three cups lying on their sides, symbolizing missed opportunities and disappointment, while two cups remain upright, hinting at the potential for recovery and hope. A river flows between the figure and a distant castle, which may signify dreams, goals, or a sense of stability that feels out of reach.

Upright Meaning: When this card appears upright, it often points to experiencing profound heartbreak. This could stem from a variety of emotional upheavals, such as the pain of divorce, the sorrow of a breakup, the feeling of abandonment, or the heavy weight of bereavement. The card encapsulates a sense of mourning and can resonate with feelings of sadness and remorse for what has been lost. However, an essential silver lining reflects that even in the midst of these dark times, there's always a glimmer of hope. It encourages you to lift your gaze from the sorrow to recognize the positives that still exist in your life. Key Words - Sadness, Loss, Grief, Remorse, Trauma, Heartbreak, Anger.

Reversed Meaning: In contrast, when the 5 of Cups appears reversed, it signifies a period of acceptance and movement towards healing. Acknowledging and processing your grief provides a pathway to emotional recovery, indicating that you are beginning to let go of the burdens from the past. This transition allows for emotional release and encourages you to embrace the future with an open heart. Now is the time to take solace and strength from your journey toward acceptance and forgiveness. Key Words - Moving On, Forgiveness, Healing, Acceptance.

6 Of Cups

Description: The 6 of Cups showcases a nostalgic scene featuring six ornate cups filled with delicate white flowers, symbolizing purity and emotional connection. In the foreground, one child is depicted joyfully passing a cup to another, illustrating the warmth of innocence, generosity, and the continuation of traditions. This imagery evokes feelings tied to childhood and familial bonds, suggesting a strong sense of heritage and care present in one's life.

Upright Meaning: Upright, this card invites you to reconnect with your past memories, particularly those from your childhood that bring comfort and joy. It suggests a strong bond with family and friends, urging you to draw from the strength and support offered by your loved ones. This card often signifies a playful spirit and the importance of embracing innocence, kindness, and creativity in your current life. It encourages cherishing simple pleasures and nurturing your inner child. Key Words - Nostalgia, Innocence, Family, Kindness, Creativity, Protection.

Reversed Meaning: When reversed, the 6 of Cups portrays readiness to move beyond past experiences, indicating a pivotal moment of growth and transition into adulthood. Whether letting go of unhealthy relationships or outdated beliefs, this shift can represent a significant personal evolution. However, caution is advised, as you may be idealizing the past, which can obstruct your clarity of the present. It is essential to find balance and attain a full perspective on your journey forward. Key Words - Boredom, Child Abuse, Stagnation, Leaving Home.

Description: The 7 of Cups depicts a figure with their back turned to the viewer, standing at a crossroads with seven distinct cups before them. Each cup contains unique and vivid images representing dreams, choices, and the allure of possibilities. This card reflects a sense of wonder and contemplation, inviting self-exploration of desires and aspirations.

Upright Meaning: Upright, this card urges you to engage with your imagination and embrace the power of dreams in both your waking life and subconscious state. It emphasizes the importance of taking proactive steps to manifest your desires rather than passively waiting for them to materialize. You are encouraged to evaluate various options thoughtfully and carefully before making decisions, ensuring alignment with your true goals and aspirations. Key Words - New Possibilities, Fantasy, Illusion, Meditation, Decisions.

Reversed Meaning: When appearing reversed, the 7 of Cups serves as a warning against chasing elusive fantasies. It signifies a need to face reality and ground yourself in practical goals and intentions that will guide you forward effectively. This card might also indicate a cleansing of confusion, allowing you to gain clarity on what truly matters in your life. Pay attention to the clarity emerging from chaos and the importance of focused direction. Key Words - Lack of Purpose, Confusion, Overwhelmed by Choice.

8 Of Cups

Description: The 8 of Cups presents a cloaked figure walking determinedly away from eight golden cups, symbolizing treasured memories and accomplishments. The figure is moving towards a barren land, representing a search for deeper meaning and purpose in life beyond superficial satisfaction.

Upright Meaning: This card upright signifies a turning point, advocating for the release of the past to venture toward a more fulfilling future. It encourages embarking on a journey of exploration, whether that manifests as a major life change, such as pursuing a new career or relationship, or as subtle shifts like embracing new hobbies or perspectives. The message emphasizes that true recognition and satisfaction lie beyond your current circumstances. Key Words - Disillusionment, Abandonment, Withdrawal, Escapism.

Reversed Meaning: When reversed, the 8 of Cups reflects a fear of change that may be keeping you anchored in an unfulfilling situation. This fear can lead to aimless drifting and indecision regarding your path. It poses a reminder that while safety in stagnation might feel comfortable, it won't bring you the growth and fulfilment you desire. Eventually, a decision must be made to move forward, even if the choices are not ideal. Key Words - Avoidance, Fear of Change, Aimless Drifting, Stagnation.

9 Of Cups

Description: The 9 of Cups illustrates a content individual seated on a wooden bench, dressed elegantly, personifying achievement and satisfaction. Behind them stands a display of nine well-organized cups, symbolizing prosperity, abundance, and the fruition of desires.

Upright Meaning: Upright, this card signifies arrival at a place of emotional satisfaction following struggles and loss. It indicates that the journey has been long, yet you've reached a phase of joy and fulfilment. Now is a pivotal moment to pursue your dreams and aspirations with renewed confidence, as the universe aligns in your favour, promising profound happiness ahead. Key Words - Wish Fulfilment, Luxury, Satisfaction, Success, Gratitude.

Reversed Meaning: In a reversed position, the 9 of Cups warns that while you may have attained something you once deeply desired, the outcome may fall short of your expectations. You might find yourself grappling with feelings of dissatisfaction or a lack of progress. This card calls for introspection and emphasizes the need to realign your focus on what truly matters, prioritizing quality of experiences over mere material gain. Key Words - Smugness, Dissatisfaction, Materialism, Indulgence.

Description: This card depicts an idyllic scene where a joyful couple shares a warm embrace, symbolizing love and unity. In the foreground, children play happily, exuding innocence and joy, while a stunning home stands as a backdrop—representing stability and comfort. Above, the sky is adorned with a vibrant rainbow, accompanied by ten golden cups, each one shimmering with the promise of heavenly blessings and emotional fulfilment.

Upright Meaning: When the Ten of Cups appears upright, it signifies a time of profound happiness and contentment in your life. You are in a place where your deepest dreams, desires, and needs are being met. It's essential to take a step back, breathe, and fully appreciate the abundance that surrounds you. This card encourages you to remain present and to express gratitude for the blessings you've received. You are on the right path, harmoniously aligned with your values and loved ones. Key Words - Blessings, Divine Love, Family, Harmony, Alignment, Bliss

Reversed Meaning: In its reversed position, the Ten of Cups indicates that relationships with family or close friends may be strained and in need of attention. There may be unmet expectations, leading to feelings of disconnect or disappointment. It's crucial to take a moment to reflect on your actions and words; ensure that you remain mindful and considerate of those you cherish. Addressing these issues is vital to restoring harmony. Key Words - Domestic Strife, Broken Home, Shattered Dreams

Description: The Page of Cups showcases a youth dressed in bohemian attire, vibrant and expressive. In their hands, they hold a golden cup from which a playful fish emerges, signifying creativity and new emotional insights. The expansive sea in the background reflects the depths of intuition and the fluidity of emotions, inviting exploration of one's feelings.

Upright Meaning: When drawn upright, the Page of Cups invites you to tune into your heart's desires and embrace your sentimental side. This is a time to celebrate love, creativity, and all things romantic. Engaging fully with your emotions will allow you to express yourself freely and authentically; let go of inhibitions, and take delight in whimsical expressions of joy. Take time to enjoy life and connect with someone who inspires you. Key Words - Happy Surprise, Dreamer, Sensitivity, Intuitive Messages.

Reversed Meaning: Conversely, the reversed Page of Cups indicates that you may be feeling emotionally overwhelmed or disconnected from your true self. You may find yourself wrestling with deep feelings that are too heavy to handle. It's important to prioritize self-care and mental health during this time; don't hesitate to reach out for support if you find yourself struggling to cope. Key Words - Emotional Immaturity, Creative Blocks, Insecurity.

Knight Of Cups

Description: The Knight of Cups depicts a noble figure riding confidently on a white horse, exuding calm and grace. They hold aloft a golden cup, suggesting the delivery of emotional messages or invitations. This knight represents the quest for truth in matters of the heart, embodying idealism and romance.

Upright Meaning: When the Knight of Cups appears upright, it indicates a deep connection to your emotions and intuition. You are encouraged to listen to your heart and follow your passions, harnessing your imaginative side in your pursuits. Balance is key—while it's important to embrace your feelings, ensure you maintain perspective and not be swept away entirely. A message or an unexpected visitor may soon arrive to share good news or romantic gestures. Key Words - Idealist, Romantic, Emotional, Imaginative, Sensitive

Reversed Meaning: In its reversed position, this card warns of emotional turbulence and instability. You may find yourself feeling moody or overly sensitive, and those around you may notice your erratic behaviour. Untangling from the emotional chaos is crucial; strive to express your feelings constructively and seek a way to ground yourself before sadness or heartbreak takes hold. Key Words - Moodiness, Disappointment, Heartbreak, Sadness

Queen Of Cups

Description: The Queen of Cups sits gracefully on her throne, representing emotional depth and maturity. She holds a closed cup close to her heart, indicating the importance of the unconscious mind and the depth of her intuition. Her serene presence embodies a nurturing spirit, exuding calmness amidst the emotional chaos of the world around her.

Upright Meaning: This card heralds a time of heightened sensitivity and intuitive understanding. You are in tune with your own emotions and those of others, radiating kindness and empathy. The Queen encourages you to tap into your spiritual side and acknowledge the beauty and tragedies of life with compassion. Your loving nature fosters a sense of safety around you, making you a source of comfort for those in need. Key Words - Loving, Intuitive, Psychic, Calm, Spiritual, Tenderness.

Reversed Meaning - When the Queen of Cups appears reversed, it serves as a reminder to refocus on your spiritual and emotional well-being. You may find yourself feeling drained or overly dependent on others for validation and support. This card gently suggests that before you can nurture others, you must first nurture yourself. Pay attention to your emotional needs and don't shy away from seeking help if you're feeling overwhelmed. Key Words: Self-Care, Martyrdom, Insecurity, Dependence

King Of Cups

Description: The King of Cups portrays a wise and insightful ruler sitting on a majestic throne, holding a fish-shaped amulet that symbolizes creativity and emotional depth. His gaze is directed away from the cup, indicating a focus on broader concerns or possibly the emotions of others.

Upright Meaning: In its upright position, the King of Cups urges you to harness your emotions with wisdom and integrity. As a leader, balance your desires with those of others to create harmony. Approach challenges with maturity and sensitivity, asserting your emotional insights while remaining empathetic to the feelings of those around you. Your ability to stay composed, especially in turbulent times, earns the respect of others. Key Words - Wisdom, Understanding, Focus, Balance, Peacefulness.

Reversed Meaning: When reversed, the King of Cups cautions against emotional impulsivity and erratic behaviour. You may be feeling volatile or immature, leading to hasty decisions driven by your emotions. It's imperative to take a step back and regain your equilibrium. Additionally, be wary of manipulative individuals; take protective measures for your emotional well-being if you feel overwhelmed by external pressures. Key Words - Coldness, Volatile, Immature, Overreaction, Manipulative.

Description: The Ace of Pentacles features a mystical scene where a disembodied hand, emerging gracefully from fluffy white clouds, holds a shimmering gold coin emblazoned with a prominent pentacle symbol. Below this celestial offering lies a vibrant, lush garden that bursts with colours from a myriad of blooming flowers and rich green vegetation. The garden represents potential, growth, and nature's bounty.

Upright Meaning: The appearance of the Ace of Pentacles signals the initiation of a new cycle or beginning. Since this card is part of the suit of Pentacles, which is intrinsically linked to physical and material aspects of life, this shift could manifest as an exciting new career opportunity, significant improvements in health, or other aspects tied to material abundance. The promise of this card indicates that whatever is on the horizon will yield great prosperity and abundance. It's a reminder to stay ready and vigilant to reap the rewards of this new venture when it comes. Key Words - Manifestation, Abundance, Prosperity, New Venture.

Reversed Meaning: When reversed, the Ace of Pentacles carries a cautionary tone suggesting that challenging financial situations may lie ahead. There might be temptations to pursue illusive opportunities that seem too good to be true. This is a time to exercise caution and be wary of any financial risks. It's vital to think carefully before committing to new ventures, especially those promising quick monetary gains, as they may lead to downfall rather than success. Key Words - Bad Investment, Lost Opportunity, Lack of Foresight.

Description: The Two of Pentacles illustrates a dynamic scene where an individual skilfully juggles two large coins, seemingly dancing between them under the infinity symbol that represents the continuous flow of life. In the background, two ships brave rough seas, symbolizing the challenges and changes one must navigate while balancing responsibilities.

Upright Meaning: This card signifies adept management of multiple projects and time, showcasing your ability to navigate a busy schedule with grace. You are juggling your responsibilities effectively, but it's essential to ensure you take moments to breathe and maintain a well-organized routine. Balance is crucial to prevent feeling overwhelmed by your commitments. Key Words - Priorities, Time Management, Adapting to Change.

Reversed Meaning: When the Two of Pentacles appears reversed, it points to struggles in maintaining balance and control in various aspects of life. You may feel swamped by relentless responsibilities or financial pressures, creating a sense of overwhelm. It's important to prioritize effectively and say no to commitments that don't align with your main goals. Focus on what truly matters and avoid overcommitting to tasks or events that drain your energy. Key Words - Disorganization, Overwhelmed, Over-Committed.

Description: The Three of Pentacles captures an engaged stonemason diligently chiselling away at a grand cathedral. Alongside him, a priest and a nobleman study plans on a scroll, engaged in a collaborative discussion. Three pentacles are visible within the archway, symbolizing the importance of teamwork and the recognition of each other's skills.

Upright Meaning: This card represents success through collaboration and teamwork. As you work together with others, you'll witness the fruits of your labour coming together beautifully. It's a reminder not to overlook the talents and perspectives that those around you bring to the table. Continue fostering collaboration and communication to reach your collective goals. Key Words - Teamwork, Learning, Implementation, Collaboration.

Reversed Meaning: When reversed, the Three of Pentacles indicates a lack of synergy among team members. Discord and competition may hinder project progress. To remedy this, consider stepping into a mediation role to facilitate a more harmonious working environment and ensure that everyone feels valued for their contributions. The card may also indicate feelings of stagnation in a tedious job where you feel unrecognized or undervalued, suggesting that seeking a new opportunity may be beneficial. Key Words - Disharmony, Disorganization, Group Conflict, Working Alone.

4 of Pentacles

Description: The Four of Pentacles depicts a figure seated on a stool, tightly clutching four pentacles as if to guard them. One coin precariously balances on their head, while another is held firmly against their chest, with two more resting beneath their feet. This imagery conveys a sense of clinging to wealth and the fear of loss.

Upright Meaning: Representing the hard work that has led to the accumulation of material wealth, the Four of Pentacles also warns against the dangers of becoming overly rigid or greedy in the pursuit of financial security. It's essential to recognize that without taking risks, you may miss out on new opportunities for growth. Consider stepping out of your comfort zone and exploring new ventures or investments that have the potential to expand your horizons. Key Words - Security, Conservatism, Scarcity, Control, Restraint.

Reversed Meaning: In its reversed position, the Four of Pentacles suggests excessive materialism and reckless spending habits. It may indicate a need to regain control over financial matters before resources dwindle. Additionally, there may be challenges in trusting others, leading to possessiveness not only in finances but also in emotional relationships. Key Words - Overspending, Greed, Possessiveness, Stinginess.

5 of Pentacles

Description: The Five of Pentacles captures a poignant scene of two weary travelers trudging through a stark, wintry landscape. One person, struggling on crutches, leans heavily on their companion, while the other, barefoot and wrapped in a thin blanket, appears especially vulnerable. In the distance, a warm, illuminated church stands as a beacon of hope, yet the pair remain oblivious to its inviting presence, consumed by their own hardships.

Upright Meaning: This card resonates with feelings of financial struggle and significant hardship. You might be grappling with issues such as job loss, housing insecurity, or other financial crises, leading to a sense of isolation and despair. Nevertheless, it's crucial to seek help and support; there are resources available to assist you during these tough times. Avoid letting pride stand in the way of reaching out to those who can provide assistance. Key Words - Insecurity, Poverty, Financial Strife, Isolation, Worry.

Reversed Meaning: When reversed, the Five of Pentacles indicates that the difficult times are starting to lift. Although you might still feel as though something is amiss, there is a reassuring light at the end of the tunnel. It's important to focus on gratitude for what you have and not dwell excessively on the negative aspects. A shift in mindset could aid in your recovery from past financial losses. Key Words - Recovery from Financial Loss, Spiritual Poverty, Charity.

6 Of Pentacles

Description: The Six of Pentacles illustrates a well-dressed, affluent individual who symbolizes generosity and abundance. This figure stands confidently, holding a balanced scale in one hand while distributing coins to two kneeling figures, who represent those in need. The imagery captures a moment of charity, highlighting the dynamics of giving and receiving.

Upright Meaning: This card suggests that you are in a comfortable financial position, mirroring the wealthy person portrayed. You may find yourself in a role to extend help, support, or resources to others, experiencing the joy that comes with sharing your wealth. Alternatively, you might be on the receiving end of kindness, accepting support with a heart full of gratitude. The Six of Pentacles emphasizes the importance of charity, sharing wealth, and understanding the value of generosity in both directions. Key Words - Charity, Sharing, Giving, Generosity, Receiving.

Reversed Meaning: If this card appears reversed, it signals a need for introspection and self-care. You may have been so focused on giving that you've neglected your own needs, leading to feelings of exhaustion or being taken advantage of by others. This is a reminder to reclaim your boundaries; refrain from being overly generous to the point of detriment. It may also indicate financial strain or the risk of accumulating debt. When you do choose to be charitable, reflect on your motivations to ensure they stem from a genuine desire to help rather than a need for validation. Key Words - Power, Domination, Strings Attached, Stinginess, Self-Care.

7 Of Pentacles

Description: The Seven of Pentacles portrays a diligent individual resting against a hoe and contemplating a vibrant, well-tended field. This scene reflects the rewards of hard work and patience, encapsulating the satisfaction that comes from watching your efforts flourish.

Upright Meaning: This card reveals a deep understanding of the significance of dedication and long-term investment. You recognize that meaningful achievements often require time and perseverance rather than quick fixes. The Seven of Pentacles encourages you to take a step back and assess the progress you've made, reminding you that your hard work is building a strong foundation for future success. Although the results may not be immediate, patience will yield its own rewards. Key Words - Perseverance, Diligence, Investment, Hard Work.

Reversed Meaning: When reversed, this card indicates potential missteps in your investments—whether they be financial, emotional, or personal. You may be putting effort into areas that are not yielding the desired outcomes, leading to frustration or a feeling of wasted energy. This is a call for introspection: evaluate where you are investing your time and resources. It might be a signal to either persist with patience or to recognize when it's time to shift focus or abandon unfruitful projects. Key Words - Distractions, Lack of Rewards, Questioned Investments.

8 Of Pentacles

Description: The Eight of Pentacles shows a young apprentice who is fully absorbed in the meticulous work of carving out pentacles into a series of gleaming coins. This depiction emphasizes the dedication and attention to detail required in the pursuit of mastery.

Upright Meaning: This card suggests that you are at a point in your journey where honing your skills and pursuing education is paramount. Whether you're considering returning to school, learning a new trade, or refining an existing talent, the Eight of Pentacles signifies that hard work and diligence will lead to mastery and success. This is a positive reinforcement that dedication to your craft will ultimately result in personal and professional growth. Key Words - Mastery, Skill Development, Diligence, Passion, Standards.

Reversed Meaning: In its reversed position, the Eight of Pentacles warns against becoming overly fixated on perfectionism, which can lead to burnout and frustration. You may also be feeling uninspired, which can hinder your progress. This card serves as a reminder that while striving for improvement is important, it's equally vital to maintain a balanced approach. If you find yourself struggling with responsibilities or overwhelmed, don't hesitate to reach out for support when necessary. Key Words - Lack of Passion, Uninspired, No Motivation.

9 Of Pentacles

Description: The Nine of Pentacles features an elegantly dressed individual standing in the midst of a lush vineyard, symbolizing wealth and independence. A falcon rests on their left arm, representing mastery and the ability to enjoy the fruits of one's labour. The vineyard is abundant with pentacles, suggesting prosperity and achievement.

Upright Meaning: This card conveys a message of self-sufficiency and the enjoyment of life's luxuries. You are likely experiencing a phase of accomplishment, feeling proud of your achievements. The Nine of Pentacles encourages you to indulge in the rewards of your hard work—self-care and celebration are vital. It also serves as a reminder to cultivate your financial independence and not to rely too heavily on others for support. Key Words - Abundance, Luxury, Success, Independence, Prosperity.

Reversed Meaning: When reversed, this card may indicate a tendency to undervalue your own worth or take yourself for granted. It's crucial to practice self-care, prioritize your needs, and reassess your financial decisions to ensure stability in both your personal and professional life. The Nine of Pentacles reversed warns against taking on too much responsibility or sacrificing your well-being for the sake of others. Key Words - Dishonesty, Recklessness, Deceit, Termination, Cheap.

Description: The Ten of Pentacles depicts an elderly figure seated beneath an ornate archway leading to a grand estate, surrounded by two loyal dogs and a couple with a child. This imagery highlights themes of family, heritage, and the passing down of wealth and values through generations.

Upright Meaning: This card symbolizes generational wealth, stability, and a strong foundation for future generations. You are likely in a phase where you feel secure in your financial situation and appreciate the abundance around you. The Ten of Pentacles encourages you to embrace your accomplishments and consider ways to give back, whether through charity or by supporting your loved ones. You're establishing traditions and legacies that will endure. Key Words - Family, Wealth, Contribution, Financial Security, Legacy.

Reversed Meaning: In its reversed form, the Ten of Pentacles may indicate dissatisfaction with your current situation, suggesting a feeling of disconnection from friends or family or a sense of chasing material possessions without fulfilment. You may need to redefine what security means to you, focusing on aligning your investments and goals with your true desires rather than competing with others. This card invites reflection on the importance of emotional wealth over mere financial gain. Key Words - Fleeting Success, Financial Failure, Lack of Resources.

Page Of Pentacles

Description: The Page of Pentacles features a youthful figure standing alone in a vibrant field, adorned with a rich variety of flowers, each representing potential and growth. This youth is utterly captivated by a pentacle coin held delicately in their hands, symbolizing a new opportunity or venture. The imagery of the lush surroundings highlights the fertile ground for growth and the promise of abundance.

Upright Meaning: When drawn upright, the Page of Pentacles heralds the arrival of new beginnings and exciting prospects. This card often signifies the initiation of a new job, the launch of a business venture, or unexpected financial windfalls. It encourages you to harness your ambition and to cultivate a new skill or entrepreneurial project with diligence and focus. Those who approach their goals with determination and hard work will likely see their dreams materialize in rewarding ways. Key Words - Ambition, Desire, Manifestation, Financial Opportunity.

Reversed Meaning: In its reversed position, the Page of Pentacles serves as a gentle reminder to pause and reflect. You might be feeling overwhelmed or stuck in the drudgery of daily life, urging you to redirect your focus and perhaps narrow your pursuits. This card advises caution against impulsive decisions, particularly concerning relationships or financial commitments, which you might later regret. Key Words - Procrastination, Lack of Progress, Greediness, Laziness.

Knight Of Pentacles

Description: The Knight of Pentacles is depicted riding a sturdy, dark horse across a serene field. Unlike the more adventurous knights, this figure embodies diligence and steadfastness, emphasizing a grounded approach to life. With a coin in hand and a thoughtful expression, the knight gazes at the coin, contemplating the importance of preparation and patience as they work towards the next harvest.

Upright Meaning: The upright Knight of Pentacles symbolizes reliability and perseverance. It serves as an affirmation for maintaining trustworthiness in your actions and commitments. While the daily grind may seem monotonous and uninspiring, putting forth consistent effort will reward you in ways that are both meaningful and fulfilling. This card emphasizes the significance of routine and efficiency as foundations for success. Key Words - Efficiency, Responsibility, Hard Work, Positivity, Routine.

Reversed Meaning: When this card appears reversed, it calls for self-reflection and a push against the inertia of routine. It suggests you should strive for spontaneity and adventure; stepping outside your comfort zone can lead to personal growth and rejuvenation. Avoid getting trapped in perfectionism and resist the urge to constantly compare your path with that of others. Key Words - Boredom, Perfectionism, Laziness, Obsessiveness.

Queen Of Pentacles

Description: The Queen of Pentacles sits elegantly upon a beautifully decorated throne, encircled by blooming trees and rich greenery. Clutching a radiant golden coin, she embodies comfort and prosperity. Surrounded by various animals, she symbolizes nurturing energy and the importance of caring for both herself and those around her.

Upright Meaning: When upright, the Queen of Pentacles serves as a reminder to be mindful of your investments and financial decisions. This card embodies nurturing, stability, and practicality, reinforcing the importance of independence and wise decision-making. It encourages you to foster a sense of security and abundance in your life, both materially and emotionally. Key Words - Creature Comforts, Practicality, Financial Security.

Reversed Meaning: The reversed Queen of Pentacles indicates a need for self-care and introspection. You may find yourself expending significant time and energy on family or work obligations, leading to burnout. Now is the time to prioritize your own needs and recharge. Consider seeking external help to balance your responsibilities; don't hesitate to hire someone to assist with daily tasks if necessary. Key Words - Jealousy, Financial Independence, Self-Care.

King Of Pentacles

Description: The King of Pentacles exudes authority and sophistication as he sits on a grand throne, intricately carved with bullish motifs. Clad in a luxurious robe adorned with symbols of grapes and vines, he holds a sceptre in one hand and a golden coin in the other, both representing his mastery over wealth and resources.

Upright Meaning: Representing success and confidence, the upright King of Pentacles signifies your ability to attract and manage wealth effectively. This card often appears when you've reached a high point in your career or personal achievements, encouraging you to take a moment to bask in the rewards of your hard work. It highlights themes of abundance, security, and effective leadership, inviting you to enjoy the fruits of your labour while inspiring others around you. Key Words - Abundance, Prosperity, Security, Wealth, Leadership.

Reversed Meaning: In reverse, the King of Pentacles urges self-assessment regarding your relationship with money. It prompts you to question if your financial practices are sound; are you overspending or neglecting to save for unforeseen circumstances? This card advises exercising self-discipline in financial matters while still embracing life's pleasures. Ensure you maintain a healthy balance between work and personal life, as neglecting relationships and becoming overly entrenched in your pursuits can lead to dissatisfaction. Key Words - Financially Inept, Stubborn, Greed, Indulgence, Sensuality.

Description: The Ace of Swords features a powerful image of a hand emerging from a billowing mass of clouds, firmly grasping a gleaming double-edged sword. At the pinnacle of the sword rests a golden crown encircled by a laurel wreath, symbolizing victory and triumph. Below this striking imagery, the card showcases a dramatic landscape with towering mountains and a vast ocean, representing the challenges and opportunities that lie ahead.

Upright Meaning: When the Ace of Swords appears in an upright position, it serves as a strong indicator of encouragement and inspiration. This card suggests that you are ready to embark on a journey of new ideas and intellectual breakthroughs. Embrace the next opportunity that comes your way wholeheartedly and with open arms, as it has the potential to lead to significant growth. Surround yourself with individuals who uplift and inspire you, and focus your energy on pursuits that ignite your passion and joy. Key Words - Breakthroughs, New Ideas, Success, Sharp Mind, Clarity.

Reversed Meaning: In its reversed position, the Ace of Swords suggests that while you may have a potential breakthrough or innovative idea, you are hesitating to share it with others. This reluctance may stem from uncertainty about how to bring your vision to life or a fear of rejection and criticism. This card prompts you to reflect deeply on your desires, especially concerning a specific goal or project. Take the time to seek the truth within yourself, allowing clarity to emerge from the confusion. Key Words - Confusion, Brutality, Chaos, Clouded Judgment.

Description: The Two of Swords presents a scene of a blindfolded figure adorned in flowing white robes, holding two crossed swords in a poised manner. The blindfold symbolizes a state of confusion or denial regarding their circumstances, while the crossed swords indicate a delicate balance and the potential for resolution.

Upright Meaning: The upright Two of Swords often pertains to the themes of balance and the complexities of relationships. You might find yourself caught in the midst of conflicts or arguments, struggling to maintain your partnerships. This card serves as a cautionary reminder that, like the figure, you may be opting to keep your blindfold on, avoiding confronting issues that require attention. It urges you to confront your dilemmas rather than evade them. Key Words - Indecision, Stalemate, Impasse, Avoidance, Weighing Options.

Reversed Meaning: When reversed, the Two of Swords indicates that you are facing a tough decision that demands your attention. Procrastinating will only exacerbate the situation, potentially leading to further complications. You may be overwhelmed by conflicting opinions from others, making it challenging to determine the best course of action. Trust your intuition and let it guide you as you navigate this difficult choice, especially if you feel pulled into conflicting dynamics. Key Words - Confusion, Lesser of Two Evils, Information Overload.

3 of Swords

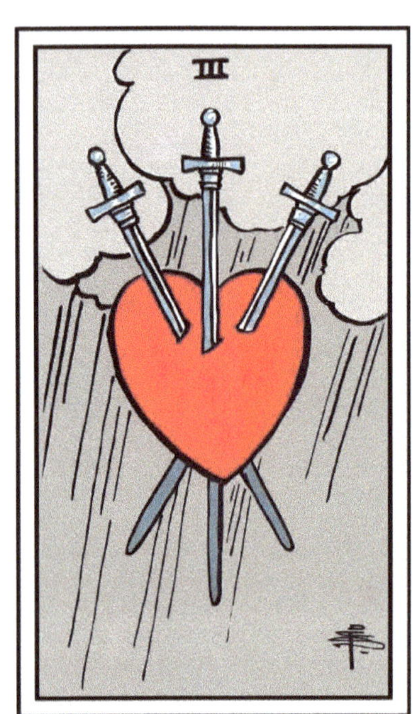

Description: The Three of Swords vividly illustrates a heart pierced by three sharp swords, an image that conveys intense grief and heartbreak. Above, dark, heavy clouds loom while rain pours down, symbolizing emotional turmoil and sorrow.

Upright Meaning: While the experience of grief and heartbreak is undeniably painful, the upright Three of Swords suggests that such moments can be transformative and character-building. This pain, while difficult to bear, is often a catalyst for personal growth and resilience. Rather than dwelling on past hurts, this card encourages you to look forward, gathering strength from your experiences. Dust yourself off, embrace new beginnings, and continue your journey with renewed determination. Key Words - Grief, Suffering, Heartbreak, Sorrow, Emotional Pain.

Reversed Meaning: In the reversed position, the Three of Swords indicates that you may still be grappling with the aftermath of a recent loss, struggling to find closure.

This card serves as a gentle nudge to begin the process of healing and to let go of the past that holds you back. Remember that all pain is temporary and that focusing on self-care and happiness can assist in your recovery. Engage in activities that lift your spirit and help you move forward. Key Words - Recovery, Forgiveness, Optimism, Letting Go of Pain.

4 of Swords

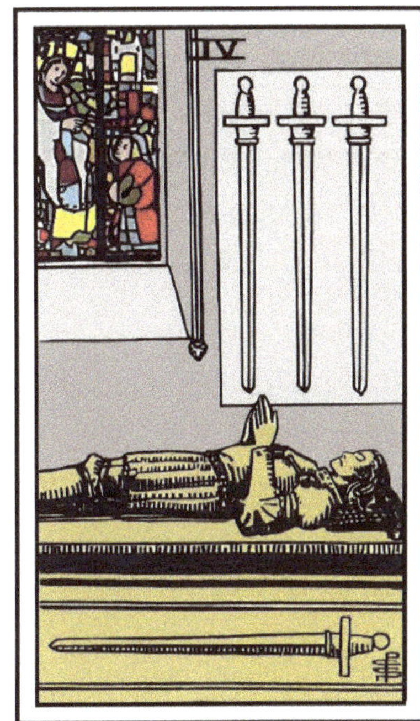

Description: The Four of Swords portrays a knight resting peacefully in a tomb, clad in full armour. Three swords hang above him, while a fourth sword lies beneath him, symbolizing the culmination of battles fought and a well-deserved respite.

Upright Meaning: The upright Four of Swords encourages you to pause and take a well-earned break. Whether you've just emerged from a difficult situation or have been labouring excessively at work, this card emphasizes the importance of rest. Allowing yourself time to recharge will enable you to return with renewed vigour and a sharper focus. This period of contemplation and meditation is vital for your overall well-being. Key Words - Relaxation, Meditation, Rest, Contemplation, Restoration.

Reversed Meaning: When the Four of Swords appears reversed, it carries a strong warning that you are approaching burnout and need to take a break immediately. Pushing yourself too hard may feel necessary, but it can lead to serious damage to your physical and mental health. This card urges you to quiet the chaos within and prioritize self-care to avoid exhaustion and stagnation. Key Words - Restlessness, Burnout, Stress, Exhaustion, Stagnation.

5 of Swords

Description: The Five of Swords depicts a cunning figure who has claimed five swords from other warriors in an arena. The defeated combatants appear solemn, while the victorious individual enjoys a sense of satisfaction, highlighting themes of conflict and discord.

Upright Meaning: The upright Five of Swords suggests that you may be stirring trouble and creating significant tension in your environment. Although you may believe you have emerged victorious, your actions have likely created a hostile atmosphere and damaged relationships. This card encourages you to focus on mending the rifts you've caused before it's too late, prompting reflection on what truly matters: being right or maintaining your connections. Key Words - Sneakiness, Conflict, Defeat, Competition, Ego.

Reversed Meaning: In its reversed position, the Five of Swords indicates lingering resentment from past conflicts. You may be struggling to find common ground with others or feeling a deep-seated sense of discord. This card advises you to seek forgiveness and healing, recognizing that holding onto grudges serves no one. The best path forward is reconciliation; strive to make amends and rebuild bridges where possible. Key Words - Past Resentment, Reconciliation, Making Amends.

6 Of Swords

Description: The Six of Swords presents a poignant scene featuring a figure with a veil obscuring their face, accompanying a young child. They are being rowed across a vast, still body of water, heading towards an unseen shore that signifies new beginnings. Within the boat, six swords stand upright, symbolizing the mental challenges and decisions that accompany their journey. The water represents a transition, a passage between the known and the unknown.

Upright Meaning: This card signifies a period of significant transition. You may find yourself in a situation that forces you to leave behind your comfort zone or escape from a difficult past—this journey is essential for your personal growth, even if it feels unwelcome. It's an opportunity to reflect on and release emotional baggage, allowing you to move on towards a more positive future. Take this time to evaluate what burdens you can leave behind, as you navigate through this pivotal phase of your life. Key Words - Transition, Moving On, Change, Rite of Passage, Release.

Reversed Meaning: In its reversed position, the Six of Swords suggests a hesitance to embrace necessary changes due to obstacles in your path. Though you might recognize the need for transformation, you may feel stuck or resistant. This card encourages you to confront these inhibitions and continue forging ahead, pushing through discomfort to seek out growth and renewal. Key Words - Resistance to Change, Unfinished Business, Resisting.

7 Of Swords

Description: The Seven of Swords depicts a figure sneaking away from a military base, clutching five swords while leaving two behind. The individual's cautious glance over their shoulder reveals a mix of pride and apprehension about having escaped unnoticed. This imagery conveys themes of stealth and resourcefulness, yet also hints at the precariousness inherent in such actions.

Upright Meaning: This card often indicates cunning behaviour or deceit, suggesting that you may be attempting to sidestep responsibilities or consequences. While you might feel clever for manoeuvring around difficulties, it's essential to weigh whether the potential risk of being caught is worth your actions. Alternatively, the upright Seven of Swords can signify the need to focus on prioritizing your goals, finding efficient shortcuts to manage your time and responsibilities better. Key Words - Trickery, Deception, Betrayal, Sneaking Around.

Reversed Meaning: When reversed, the Seven of Swords hints at feelings of inadequacy and imposter syndrome, where you believe you don't deserve your accomplishments. Alternatively, it may indicate that self-deception is causing inner turmoil, where burdens of secrecy weigh heavily. This card urges you to confront these feelings, to be honest with yourself, and to embrace vulnerability and self-forgiveness. Key Words - Imposter Syndrome, Deceit, Extra-Marital Affair.

Description: The Eight of Swords illustrates a stark scene featuring a blindfolded and bound figure surrounded by eight swords planted in the ground, evoking a sense of entrapment. The barren and damp landscape signifies feelings of desolation and restriction, reflecting the struggle of perceiving oneself as a victim of life's circumstances.

Upright Meaning: This card suggests that your previous thought patterns are limiting your potential. Acknowledging that there is a shift in thought needed is crucial. You might be falling into a victim mentality—feeling trapped and hopeless—when in reality, you have the power to reclaim your agency. By recognizing your choices and trusting your intuition, you can begin to dismantle these mental barriers. Key Words - Entrapment, Imprisonment, Victim, Negative Thoughts.

Reversed Meaning: In reverse, the Eight of Swords indicates that you may be overly critical of yourself, functioning as your own worst enemy. It serves as a reminder that everyone has flaws, and personal growth is possible if you allow yourself the grace to change. This card invites you to release those negative thought patterns and embrace a more empowering perspective that will help you regain your freedom and confidence. Key Words - Inner Critic, Open to New Perspectives, Freedom.

9 Of Swords

Description: The Nine of Swords captures an intense moment, showcasing a figure sitting upright in bed, buried in their hands in a posture of distress. The visual suggests they have been abruptly awakened from a nightmare, mirroring deep emotional turmoil. Nine swords hang ominously on the wall, symbolizing fears, worries, and mental anguish.

Upright Meaning: This card speaks to the pervasive nature of anxiety and fear, highlighting the difficulty many face in seeking help during times of distress. There's an encouragement to share your experiences and trauma, as doing so can facilitate healing and help regain control over your emotional landscape. Don't shy away from vulnerability; reaching out can alleviate some of that heaviness. Key Words - Hopelessness, Anxiety, Trauma, Worry, Fear, Nightmares.

Reversed Meaning: The reversed Nine of Swords suggests that past trauma is resurging, affecting your mental landscape once more. However, it also brings a sense of hope; with willingness to confront and address these feelings, there's a potential for healing. Caring for your mental health becomes paramount, as understanding that others might share similar struggles can foster a sense of connection and support. Key Words - Secrets, Deep-Seated Concern, Inner Turmoil, Releasing Worry.

10 Of Swords

Description: The Ten of Swords is striking and difficult to ignore, portraying a figure lying face down, draped in a red cloth, with ten swords protruding from their back. This vivid imagery symbolizes betrayal and deep wounds, marking a moment of profound loss and the inevitability of endings.

Upright Meaning: This card represents the culmination of a painful ordeal, suggesting that while you have endured much suffering, a new chapter is upon you. Although the scars may linger, the Ten of Swords emphasizes that healing is essential. The past cannot be rewritten, but how you decide to move forward is pivotal; utilize this acknowledgment to cast aside what has been and embrace the possibilities of tomorrow—light will emerge from darkness. Key Words - Failure, Defeat, Deep Wounds, Loss, Crisis, Betrayal.

Reversed Meaning: In its reversed form, the Ten of Swords signifies that change is imminent, and you may not feel prepared for it. This transition could be challenging, but it often heralds a period of recovery and renewal. Reflect upon the burdens of the past you've been dwelling on, as this card encourages you to let go and accept that transformation can lead to a healthier, more positive future. Key Words - Recovery, Regeneration, Mending, Moving Upwards.

Page of Swords

Description: The Page of Swords features a young individual standing confidently with their sword raised high, pointing skyward, symbolizing clarity of thought and determination. Their body language exudes an eagerness to take on challenges, reflecting a mindset overflowing with energy and curiosity. The background hints at a landscape filled with potential, a reminder that they are on the brink of discovery.

Upright Meaning: When the Page of Swords appears upright, it signals that you are standing at the threshold of new ideas and creative endeavours. The vibrant energy surrounding this card suggests that you have the resources and motivation needed to tackle a project head-on. This is an excellent period for innovation—whether you're considering writing a blog, authoring a book, or starting a podcast, this energy can be harnessed to express your thoughts and ideas. Moreover, the card encourages open communication; now is the ideal time to discuss your feelings and thoughts with colleagues or those close to you. Key Words - Curiosity, Mental Energy, Innovation, Thirst for Knowledge.

Reversed Meaning: In its reversed position, the Page of Swords indicates a retreat into introversion. You might be grappling with a fear of public speaking or uncertain about how to present your thoughts. This card urges you to confront those fears and assert yourself. Additionally, it's essential to think carefully before speaking or making decisions, as impulsive actions could lead to misunderstandings. Be cautious about making promises that you may not be able to keep; it's vital to follow through to maintain your reputation. Key Words - Manipulation, Deception, Haste, Haphazard Action.

Knight of Swords

Description: The Knight of Swords illustrates a valiant knight, clad in armour and charging forward on a fierce white horse. Their sword is raised defiantly, symbolizing readiness to conquer obstacles. The backdrop is filled with ominous storm clouds, emphasizing the intensity of their mission and the potential for conflict or challenges on the horizon.

Upright Meaning: The Knight of Swords, when upright, conveys a powerful message of commitment and relentless ambition. You are driven by a sense of purpose and feel an urgent need to act decisively. However, this intensity may lead you to rush into situations without adequate planning. While your enthusiasm is commendable, consider tempering it with strategic thinking to avoid unnecessary conflicts. Remember to be mindful of those around you; in your quest for achievement, don't disregard the feelings of others. Key Words - Action, Impulse, Defence of Beliefs, Ambitious.

Reversed Meaning: When reversed, the Knight of Swords highlights a surge of unchanneled energy and confusion. You may feel a mounting restlessness because you lack direction or a clear objective. This internal chaos can lead you to flit from task to task without completing anything. The knight's cautionary message is to find a singular focus before moving on to new pursuits. Mistakes are inevitable, so don't allow fear of failure to hinder your growth; use them as stepping stones to develop your life experience. Key Words - Lack of Direction, Restless, Unpredictability, Impulsive.

Queen of Swords

Description: The Queen of Swords is depicted sitting regally upon an ornate throne adorned with cherubs and butterflies, representing a juxtaposition between nurturing and intellectual strength. Her stern expression indicates a deep wisdom and clarity of thought, as she holds a double-edged sword—a tool for both protection and discernment.

Upright Meaning: This card's upright position encourages you to engage in fair and logical decision-making, free from emotional bias. Now is the time to analyse the facts and draw conclusions based on intellect rather than feelings. The Queen's wisdom urges you to embrace your independence and rely on your insights rather than seeking excessive validation from others. This level-headedness will serve you well in complex situations, enabling you to navigate challenges with grace and authority. Key Words - Perceptive, Clear Mind, Complexity, Independent.

Reversed Meaning: When the Queen of Swords appears reversed, your emotions may be clouding your judgment, leading you to make hasty or ungrounded decisions. This card serves as a reminder to step back and reassess the situation from a more objective perspective. While it's crucial to follow your heart, this time calls for careful consideration and perhaps a reassessment of priorities. Don't be afraid to assert your needs; those who truly care will understand. Key Words - Cold-Hearted, Cruel, Bitter, Resentful, Isolation.

King of Swords

Description: The King of Swords exudes authority, sitting confidently on a throne while adorned in a blue tunic that symbolizes spiritual wisdom. He holds a double-edged sword, a representation of intellect and moral clarity, reflecting a mastery over thought and communication.

Upright Meaning: In its upright position, the King of Swords embodies the qualities of leadership and mental strength. You are likely in a phase where your truth is crystal clear, empowering you to communicate effectively and command respect from others. This card may also signal the need to seek wise counsel from mentors or professionals, such as financial advisors or legal representatives, to help you navigate complex decisions. Your ability to articulate ideas and stand firm in your beliefs will be crucial during this time. Key Words - Discipline, Truth, Mental Clarity, Authority, Intellect.

Reversed Meaning: When reversed, the King of Swords serves as a cautionary tale about the misuse of power and intellect. This card indicates a risk of coming off as overbearing or arrogant—be mindful that the loudest voices are not necessarily the strongest. Reflect on whether you're allowing your intellect to diminish others' self-worth. Additionally, you may feel uncertain about your path or options, which can lead to stagnation; progress requires action, not mere contemplation. Key Words - Manipulative, Cruel, Weak, Abuse of Power.

Ace of Wands

Description: The Ace of Wands features a disembodied hand emerging from a cloud, extending a vibrant, sprouting wand. This wand, adorned with new growth, symbolizes potential and advancement, urging you to embrace fresh beginnings. In the backdrop, a majestic castle rises, representing the myriad of possibilities that lay ahead, beckoning you to explore the unknown.

Upright Meaning: This card serves as a powerful motivational boost, encouraging you to stop doubting yourself and dive headfirst into the creative project that has captured your imagination. The Ace of Wands is a clear signal that now is the time to act, even if you feel unprepared. It emphasizes that action is essential for growth and that opportunities are ripe for the taking if you seize them. Trust in your creativity and let it guide you toward your goals. Key words - Creation, Willpower, Desire, Inspiration, Enterprise.

Reversed Meaning: When reversed, the Ace of Wands indicates a moment of uncertainty and hesitation. You might find yourself teetering on the edge of a daunting journey, unsure of your desires or bogged down by current obligations. The inspiration you once felt may seem elusive, making it challenging to muster the motivation to move forward. It's crucial to grant yourself the time needed for that creative spark to reignite. Instead of forcing it, allow inspiration to return at its own pace. Key words - A Lack Of Energy, Distraction, Delays, Resistance To Change.

2 of Wands

Description: The Two of Wands depicts a figure elegantly dressed in a long robe and hat, standing confidently with the world literally cradled in their hands. This imagery suggests that although vast opportunities lie ahead, the figure is currently anchored to their home, symbolized by the castle that represents security and tradition.

Upright Meaning: The appearance of this card signifies a newfound spark of inspiration that propels you to contemplate how to transform your creative energy into actionable steps. It's essential to lay a solid foundation as you chart your path forward, ensuring that you do not trip over your own ambitions. Trust your instincts and let them direct you as you strategize and make decisions. Key words - Discovery, Future Planning, Decision-Making, Progress.

Reversed Meaning: In its reversed position, the Two of Wands signals a moment of indecision and confusion. You may find yourself at a crossroads, grappling with what truly suits your desires. Fear of venturing into the unknown can hinder your progress, leading to a sense of stagnation. It's a call to refocus and ground yourself, reconnecting to your true intentions and moving forth with clarity instead of uncertainty. Key words - Personal Goals, Fear Of The Unknown, A Lack Of Planning.

3 of Wands

Description: The Three of Wands illustrates a figure standing at the precipice of a cliff, gazing out across a vast ocean towards distant mountain ranges. Surrounding them are three firmly planted wands in the earth, while they hold one firmly in their right hand, suggesting readiness for action and exploration.

Upright Meaning: This card signifies that your plans are in motion and new opportunities are emerging, enabling you to realize your potential. The energy is ripe for expansion, encouraging you to explore avenues such as travel, education, or business. It serves as a reminder to transcend your comfort zones, signalling that growth opportunities will present themselves if you stop imposing limits on yourself. Key words - Expansion, Foresight, Progress, Rapid Growth.

Reversed Meaning: When reversed, the Three of Wands may indicate that you are playing it too safe and reluctance may be holding you back. You may have faced setbacks in your personal goals, leading to fear or hesitation in taking further steps. This card encourages you to shake off any disappointment and persist, as setbacks are a natural part of growth and evolution. However, be cautious not to overcommit yourself as you seek opportunities. Key words - Obstacles, Lack Of Foresight, Unexpected Delays.

4 of Wands

Description: The Four of Wands presents a scene of joyous celebration, featuring two figures dancing merrily beneath a large, beautifully adorned wreath, which is affixed to four elegantly crystal-tipped wands staked into the ground. This imagery evokes feelings of comfort, security, and community.

Upright Meaning: The card conveys a profound sense of welcome energy associated with returning home or being around familiar places and people. It suggests a time for relaxation and appreciating the little joys in life. Consider this an opportune moment for home projects likc rcdccorating or personal renovations, fostering harmony in your living space. Key words: Harmony, Relaxation, Celebration, Home, Community.

Reversed Meaning: In its reversed aspect, the Four of Wands might point to a celebration of personal achievements or an enhanced sense of inner peace. However, it can also reflect underlying tensions, possibly indicating unsettling communication or uncertainty within family or relationships. This is a critical time to address conflicts and mend relationships, letting go of any that do not serve your well-being. Key words: Transience, Conflicts With Others, Seeking Inner Harmony.

5 of Wands

Description: The Five of Wands depicts a vivid scene of disagreement, showcasing five figures engaged in a lively struggle, brandishing their wands as they attempt to assert themselves amidst the chaos.

Upright Meaning: This card signifies heightened tensions, where conflicts or competitions arise that hinder your progression. The environment is rife with a sense of competition, and amid the struggle, meaningful communication is lost. Everyone involved in the conflict is fighting for their voice to be heard, yet dialogue remains unproductive. The card encourages you to calm the storm within and to actively listen to others' perspectives, fostering an atmosphere that promotes productive communication. Key words - Conflict, Competition, Tension, Rivalry, Disagreement.

Reversed Meaning: When the Five of Wands appears reversed, it suggests feelings of internal conflict and uncertainty about where you stand in a particular situation. This may follow a stressful episode, leaving you with relief and the need for introspection. It's essential to align your emotions with your thoughts, enabling you to select the path that resonates best with you. You may be emerging from a challenging time, and it's okay to release lingering anger or hostility. Key Words - Avoiding Conflict, Tension Release, Respecting Differences.

6 Of Wands

Description: The 6 of Wands portrays a triumphant figure riding a magnificent white horse, symbolizing purity and victory, as they traverse through a jubilant crowd. The crowd is filled with enthusiastic onlookers who cheer and celebrate the rider's achievements. A lush wreath of triumph adorns the rider's head, signifying recognition for their accomplishments. In this scene, six wands are prominently displayed, with one held high by the rider, further emphasizing their leadership and success. The adorned wand held by the rider mirrors the wreath, creating a harmonious symbol of victory and acknowledgment.

Upright Meaning: In the upright position, this card signifies that you have reached a significant milestone on your journey and are embracing a sense of confidence and assurance in your abilities. Not only have you successfully accomplished your goals, but your hard work has not gone unnoticed; you are basking in the admiration and validation from those around you. This card encourages you to celebrate your success and revel in the achievement without letting guilt overshadow your joy. Key Words - Progress, Confidence, Victory, Public Acknowledgment.

Reversed Meaning: When reversed, the 6 of Wands suggests that you may be grappling with self-doubt or experiencing feelings of imposter syndrome, questioning whether you truly deserve your accolades. You might be seeking validation from others but struggling to receive it, leading to feelings of inadequacy. It serves as a reminder to define your own version of success instead of chasing external approval. Additionally, if you're feeling overly proud or egotistical, this card invites you to take a step back and reflect on humility before circumstances force you to confront it. Key Words - Fall from Grace, Egotism, Punishment, Excess Pride.

Description: The 7 of Wands illustrates an individual standing resolutely atop a steep hill, symbolizing their elevated position amidst a challenging situation. Below, several opponents wield six wands, exhibiting aggression and intent to undermine the figure's achievements. The person on the hill defiantly raises their own wand in an act of defence, highlighting their determination to stand firm against adversity.

Upright Meaning: In its upright position, this card represents the struggles you are currently facing in your journey. Despite having recently reached an important milestone, you find yourself contending with naysayers or competitors who challenge your progress and validity. However, the 7 of Wands encourages you to hold your ground and remain steadfast in your beliefs and capabilities. You possess the strength and resilience needed to overcome these challenges, and it is crucial not to let others deter you from your path. Key Words - Challenge, Protection, Competition, Perseverance.

Reversed Meaning: When reversed, the 7 of Wands suggests that the competitive nature of those around you may have left you feeling vulnerable and inadequate. The pressures of external judgments might cause you to question your decisions and choices, leading to feelings of overwhelm. You may find yourself contemplating retreat or giving in, yet deep down, you know that you possess a strength far greater than any opposition you face. The card encourages you to recognize your hard-fought achievements and maintain your resolve despite these external pressures. Key Words - Exhaustion, Overwhelmed, Lack of Confidence.

8 Of Wands

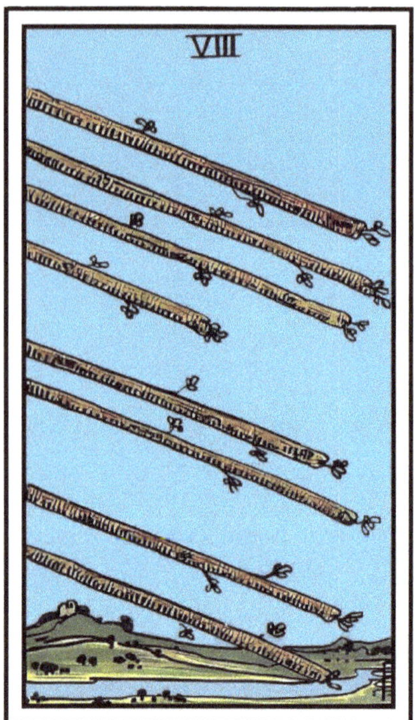

Description: The 8 of Wands depicts eight vibrant, blossoming wands soaring through a clear, azure sky at a rapid pace, conveying dynamism and forward momentum. The image evokes a sense of urgency and excitement, suggesting that the energy surrounding you is propelling you toward your aspirations.

Upright Meaning: When upright, the 8 of Wands signifies a period of rapid activity and positive progress. You are busy in the best way possible, making significant strides toward your goals. This card urges you to seize opportunities while they are ripe and to focus your energy on productive activities, stripping away distractions to fully devote yourself to the tasks at hand. Your alignment with your goals will lead to remarkable advancements. Key Words - Alignment, Air Travel, Action, Movement, Quick Decisions.

Reversed Meaning: In its reversed state, the 8 of Wands warns against hastiness. You may feel the urge to rush into new endeavours or ideas, leaving many loose ends untied from previous projects. This card advises you to slow down and ensure that you complete current initiatives before diving into new ones. It may also indicate unexpected delays that, despite your eagerness and enthusiasm, might hinder your progress. Take a moment to breathe and strategize around these challenges rather than succumbing to frustration. Key Words: Panic, Slowing Down, Waiting, Frustration, Resisting Change.

9 Of Wands

Description: The 9 of Wands features a weary figure clutching a wand, glancing over their shoulder with a guarded expression. Behind them, eight wands loom ominously, symbolizing the challenges and obstacles they have faced. This imagery conveys a deep sense of battle fatigue yet also hints at the strength derived from perseverance.

Upright Meaning: In its upright position, this card embodies resilience in the face of adversity. Even when the journey weighs heavily upon you, the 9 of Wands emphasizes your determination and grit. You have demonstrated the courage to push through difficult times and are encouraged to keep going, as you are closer to your goals than you realize. Lean on your support system for help, and trust in yourself and your ability to weather the storm. Key Words - Resilience, Persistence, Courage, Boundaries, Grit.

Reversed Meaning: When reversed, the 9 of Wands reflects a sense of exhaustion and overwhelming pressure. Continuous struggles may have left you questioning your capacity to endure. This card serves as a reminder to dig deep into your reserves of strength and resilience, even when the odds seem stacked against you. If you find yourself feeling overly defensive or paranoid, remember that these fears often stem from internal doubts rather than external threats. Have faith in yourself, as this card encourages you to acknowledge the endurance you possess. Key Words - Exhaustion, Fatigue, Struggle, Defensive, Paranoia.

10 Of Wands

Description: The 10 of Wands illustrates an exhausted figure laboriously carrying a substantial bundle of wands, symbolizing the burdens they have taken on. The character's weary expression indicates the weight of their responsibilities, yet they are close to reaching a nearby village, hinting at the nearing completion of their arduous journey.

Upright Meaning: In its upright position, this card conveys that you are on the cusp of completion, having worked diligently to achieve your goals. While you may have taken on additional responsibilities, whether intentionally or inadvertently, the hard work and effort you have invested are about to yield rewarding results. The message here is to recognize your accomplishments and the nearing end of your struggles. Key Words - Accomplishment, Responsibility, Burden, Completion, Hard Work.

Reversed Meaning: When reversed, the 10 of Wands advises you to relinquish some of the burdens you carry and delegate responsibilities to avoid burnout. You may be feeling the early signs of mental and emotional fatigue; thus, it is essential to invest in your well-being and prioritize self-care. Additionally, this card suggests that this might be an ideal time to declutter and simplify your life, leading to a greater sense of organization and peace. Key Words - Burnout, Over Stressed, Delegation, Release.

Page of Wands

Description: The Page of Wands portrays a youthful figure, elegantly dressed in vibrant attire that reflects their adventurous spirit. They stand confidently on a barren landscape, a setting that signifies the potential for growth and exploration. In their hand, they hold a wand, an emblem of creativity and inspiration. As they gaze inquisitively at the tip of the wand, which surprisingly displays budding leaves, it symbolizes the youthful energy and fresh ideas waiting to sprout.

Upright Meaning: The arrival of the Page of Wands indicates that you're at the threshold of a new adventure. This phase may feel exhilarating, but it also comes with uncertainty about your destination. You're brimming with creative energy, yearning to initiate something meaningful. However, it's crucial to channel this enthusiasm thoughtfully; consider devising a plan or mapping out your path before diving headfirst. Seeking guidance from a mentor or someone with experience can provide invaluable insights as you navigate this journey. Key Words - Inspiration, Freedom, Limitless Potential, Exploration.

Reversed Meaning: In its reversed position, the Page of Wands suggests an internal struggle with the manifestation of your creative impulses. While you sense a powerful urge to create, you might feel lost or unsure how to translate these feelings into tangible actions. This is a vital moment for reflection rather than hasty movements—taking time to contemplate your thoughts can lay a stronger foundation for your ideas. Explore alternative expressions for your creativity, as this may lead to a richer, more developed vision. Avoid letting anxieties or indecisiveness trip you up. Key Words - Lack of Direction, Procrastination, Spiritual Path.

Knight of Wands

Description: The Knight of Wands is depicted as a bold and fearless figure, clad in full armour, symbolizing readiness and protection. Sitting atop a rearing horse, their powerful stance conveys a sense of urgency and excitement, as if at the brink of a thrilling adventure. With a wand held confidently in their right hand, the Knight embodies the spirit of determination and enthusiasm for the challenges ahead.

Upright Meaning: This card encourages you to embrace your ambitions with passion and resolve. The Knight of Wands signifies a time to pursue your goals relentlessly, igniting your vision into reality with your boundless energy. While enthusiasm fuels your journey, it's essential to balance this vigour with thoughtful decision-making to avoid reckless missteps. Now is the moment for action—trust your instincts and be daring, but remain mindful of the steps you take to ensure steady progress. Key Words - Passion, Energy, Adventure, Impulsiveness, Action.

Reversed Meaning: When the Knight of Wands appears in reverse, it signals a potential internal conflict. Although there's a surge of passion simmering within, you might feel disoriented about where to channel that energy. You may find yourself overwhelmed, juggling too many projects or distractions instead of honing in on a singular, sustainable endeavour. It's a time to recalibrate and re-centre your focus; excessive impulsiveness can lead to regrettable outcomes. Embrace patience and prioritize your objectives effectively. Key Words - Anger, Impulsiveness, Recklessness, Haste, Delays.

Queen of Wands

Description: The Queen of Wands radiates confidence and warmth as she sits gracefully on her ornate throne, signifying her mastery of life's complexities. Surrounding her are vibrant sunflower motifs, representing vitality, joy, and prosperity. At her feet rests a sleek black cat, a symbol of independence and intuition, emphasizing her powerful connection to her inner self.

Upright Meaning: This card reveals a period of self-discovery and empowerment. The Queen of Wands embodies a deep sense of self-awareness and assurance, as you confidently navigate towards your life's purpose. You possess a clear vision of your desires and are strategically poised to achieve them. Maintaining a focused mindset and a positive, friendly demeanour will enhance your journey, attracting opportunities and support from others. Key Words - Confidence, Determination, Independence, Cheer.

Reversed Meaning: In its reversed state, the Queen of Wands may point to a struggle with self-esteem and confidence. You might feel overwhelmed by the weight of your responsibilities or become moody, distracting you from your goals. This is a moment for introspection; take time to assess your feelings and listen to your instincts. Stand firm in what you believe, even if you face scepticism from those around you. Strengthening your inner resolve is vital during this time of uncertainty. Key Words - Frustration, Introversion, Insecurity, Moodiness.

King of Wands

Description: The King of Wands embodies the archetype of a visionary leader, seated regally on his lavish throne decorated with lions and salamanders—symbols of strength and transformative power. He grasps a blossoming wand that represents both creativity and the vitality of life, affirming his role as a catalyst for action and inspiration.

Upright Meaning: The King of Wands signifies leadership and assertiveness as you embark on significant pursuits. His presence encourages you to inspire and rally others around your vision, as your natural charisma and capabilities are unmatched. It's essential to define your objectives clearly and communicate them to your team, ensuring that everyone is aligned with your ambitions. Embrace your role as a motivator, as your influence can help turn innovative ideas into reality. Key Words: Motivation, Leadership, Entrepreneurship.

Reversed Meaning: Reversed, the King of Wands serves as a warning against excessive assertiveness or dominance. While ambition is commendable, brashness can lead to tension and conflict. It's a reminder to moderate your impulses; being overly controlling or demanding may drive people away or foster resentment. Take a step back to reassess your approach and ensure that your leadership style remains inclusive and supportive rather than abrasive. Key Words: Possessiveness, Controlling, Impulsiveness.

Card Spreads

One Card Spread -

The One Card Spread is a simple yet profound method for quick insights into your thoughts, feelings, or specific situations. To effectively use this technique, find a serene environment where you can centre your thoughts free from distractions. Take a few moments to practice mindfulness: close your eyes, breathe deeply, and clear your mind.

Once you feel focused, think deeply about a particular question or area of your life where you seek guidance. This could pertain to your emotional state, a relationship issue, career decisions, or any life dilemma. After formulating your question, shuffle your tarot deck while keeping it in mind. When you feel ready—perhaps after shuffling for a while or when you feel a pull towards a certain card—draw a single card from the deck.

Upon revealing the card, take time to interpret its meaning. Reflect on the card's symbolism and how it relates to your question. Each card has nuanced interpretations depending on its suit and number, so consider both the traditional meanings and any personal connections you may have to that imagery. This card can serve as a daily oracle, giving you guidance on the energies that may influence your day or specific advice for a challenge at hand.

Additionally, this method can effectively provide a quick "yes or no" answer. An upright card typically suggests a positive affirmation (yes) regarding your inquiry, while a reversed card generally indicates a negative response (no). After interpreting your card, consider journaling your thoughts and feelings to deepen your understanding, helping you track your personal growth over time.

Three Card Spread -

The Three Card Spread offers a structured way to gain insight into your current situation and potential paths forward. Begin by taking a moment to gather your thoughts on the specific issue or question at hand. Find a comfortable space where you can concentrate, and as you shuffle the deck, keep your focus on the question.

Once you feel ready, draw three cards from the deck and arrange them in front of you from left to right as follows:

1   2   3

1. First Card (Challenge):

This card represents the challenge, issue, or problem you are currently facing. It reveals obstacles that may be affecting your life, whether they are internal struggles, external circumstances, or relational dynamics. Reflect on how this challenge manifests in your daily experience.

2. Second Card (Advice):

The second card signifies the course of action you should consider to navigate or resolve the challenges highlighted by the first card. Analyse what steps or mindset shifts this card suggests. It may provide practical guidance, emotional support, or a shift in perspective that could lead to a breakthrough.

3. Third Card (Outcome):

This card presents the outcome or resolution based on the course of action you take as advised by the second card. It gives insight into what might unfold if you follow this guidance, providing a glimpse into successful resolution or growth stemming from your efforts.

As you interpret this spread, contemplate how the cards interact. Look for connections between them and consider how the challenge and advice might shape your potential outcome. This spread can offer clarity and direction as you navigate your questions.

Weekly Spread -

The Weekly Spread is a wonderful tool for preparing yourself for the week ahead, highlighting areas of focus and potential challenges. Take a moment to centre yourself with a few deep breaths, releasing any anxiety or stress as you think about the upcoming week. Visualize the days ahead and the energy you wish to invite into your life.

After you've grounded yourself, shuffle the cards while holding the intention of gaining insight into the week to come. Draw six cards and place them in a vertical column from top to bottom, interpreting them as follows:

1

2   3   4

5   6

1. First Card (Theme):

This card signifies the dominant theme or energy of the upcoming week. It sets the tone for the days ahead, hinting at what major focuses or lessons will be present.

2. Second Card (Challenges):

This card reflects the challenges you may encounter during the week. It highlights obstacles, unexpected events, or emotional struggles you should prepare for, prompting you to plan proactively.

3. Third Card (Blessings):

This card showcases the blessings or positive aspects you will experience in the coming week. It illuminates what you can be grateful for and the supportive influences around you, allowing you to cultivate an attitude of appreciation.

4. Fourth Card (Support):

The fourth card guides you on the considerations you need to make for self-support during the week. It may suggest practices or actions you can adopt to nurture your well-being.

5. Fifth Card (Let Go):

This card indicates what you should release to have a productive week. It pinpoints old patterns, beliefs, or circumstances no longer serving you, encouraging you to create space for new growth.

6. Sixth Card (Focus):

The final card indicates where you need to direct your attention during the week. It can help prioritize your energy and efforts, ensuring you stay aligned with your goals and intentions.

While interpreting your cards, take time to journal about your reflections. This will enhance your personal insights and help you track your progress through the week.

Celtic Cross Spread -

The Celtic Cross Spread is a comprehensive method that provides a deep and nuanced understanding of your current situation, guiding your decisions and reflecting on past influences. Begin by meditating on your question or situation, focusing your intention deeply as you shuffle the deck. When you feel energetically moved, draw ten cards from the deck and lay them out in the traditional Celtic Cross pattern as follows:

```
                    5                    10

        3           1           4         9

                    2                     8

                    6                     7
```

1. First Card (Present Situation):

Represents your present situation. It reflects where you currently stand regarding your question, indicating the main energies influencing you right now.

2. Second Card (Challenges):

This card illustrates the challenges you are currently facing. Analyse the obstacles and struggles that may stand in your way.

3. Third Card (Past Actions):

This card tells about the past actions or influences that have contributed to your current situation. Understanding your past behaviours helps provide context to your present challenges.

4. Fourth Card (The Future):

Represents the future outlook. This card reveals the potential developments and changes that may arise if your current trajectory continues, indicating what you can expect moving forward.

5. Fifth Card (Foundation)

This card signifies the foundation or the core beliefs, values, or support systems you need to strengthen to face your challenges successfully. It may identify resources or inner strengths to draw upon.

6. Sixth Card (New Situation):

Indicates the immediate future. This card offers insights into what is likely to happen soon and what decisions may need to be made in the near term.

7. Seventh Card (Feelings):

This card explores your feelings regarding what lies ahead. Reflect on your emotional state as it relates to future possibilities, as this can affect your actions and decisions.

8. Eighth Card (External Influences):

Represents external influences that may affect the outcome of your question. It encompasses outside factors, people, or situations that could sway the direction of your situation.

9. Ninth Card (Hopes & Fears):

This card encapsulates your hopes and fears moving forward. Consider what you aspire to achieve contrasted with any underlying anxieties that may hold you back.

10. Tenth Card (The Outcome):

The final card serves as a potential outcome based on your current path. It provides insight into the resolution of your question if you follow the guidance of the previous cards.

As you analyse the entire spread, pay particular attention to how the cards interrelate and what overall narrative they convey. The Celtic Cross Spread can facilitate a rich discussion with your intuition, helping you understand complex situations and make informed decisions as you navigate your life journey.

Tasseography

Tasseography is an ancient practice that involves the art of interpreting symbols and messages found in the shapes and configurations formed by tea leaves at the bottom of a teacup after drinking. This intriguing form of divination, although less popular than tarot cards, crystals, or other mystical arts, holds a significant place in the history of fortune-telling. The patterns left by tea leaves can reveal insights into one's life, offering a glimpse into the past, present, and future through the unique shapes they create.

At its core, tasseography is about harnessing and directing energy while focusing one's intentions on the tea. As you drink, the tea leaves serve as conduits, mirroring your past experiences and projecting potential future outcomes. By posing questions, you invite the tea leaves to communicate with you, conveying messages, advice, and predictions.

Reading the tea leaves involves examining their shape, density, and placement within the cup. The tea leaves' positioning conveys different meanings: the bottom of the cup suggests the distant future, the sides refer to the near future, the rim indicates the present moment, the handle represents the drinker, and the saucer reflects the past. This layered interpretation allows for a deeper understanding of what the shapes may signify in the context of your life.

To perform a tasseography reading, you'll need a few essential items:

1. A Teacup:

Opt for a cup that is wide at both the top and bottom for clear visibility of the interior. A plain white interior is ideal, as decorative designs can obscure the shapes made by the leaves.

2. Loose Tea Leaves:

Avoid using tea bags or cheap powdered tea, as they may not produce the distinct shapes necessary for effective readings. Loose tea leaves are preferable, as they allow for greater variability in shape and density.

3. Hot Water:

This is needed to steep the tea leaves. For an advanced twist, you might consider using moon water or water infused with crystals, which some practitioners believe can enhance the reading's depth.

4. A Saucer:

This will be used to hold the teacup upside down after the reading, allowing excess liquid to drain properly.

Preparing for a Reading

Follow these detailed steps to prepare for and conduct your tasseography reading:

1. Place the Loose Tea:

Start by adding a tablespoon of your chosen loose tea leaves into the teacup.

2. Add Hot Water:

Pour 4 to 6 ounces of steaming hot water over the leaves, ensuring they are well submerged to release their flavours.

3. Brewing Time:

Allow the tea to brew until it reaches a temperature that is comfortable for you to drink. This might vary based on personal preference.

4. Focus on Your Intentions:

As you enjoy your tea, take time to reflect on your questions and intentions, creating a mental space for clarity.

5. Stop Before Completion:

When approximately one tablespoon of tea remains in the cup, cease drinking. This will allow for a clearer reading of the tea leaves.

6. Handle the Infuser:

If you have used an infuser, empty it into the cup, and remove it carefully, ensuring the leaves are ready for reading.

7. Swirl the Tea:

Grasp the cup with your left hand and gently swirl the remaining liquid three times from left to right. This act helps to energize the leaves and direct your intentions.

8. Flip the Cup:

Using your left hand, carefully turn the cup upside down over the saucer, allowing it to sit for about 30 seconds to a minute. This waiting period lets the excess liquid drain while the leaves settle into intriguing configurations.

9. Rotate Again:

Once the cup has drained, rotate it three times on the saucer to further mix the leaves.

10. Return to Upright Position:

Position the cup upright again, ensuring that the handle faces south.

11. Observe the Shapes:

At this point, the tea leaves should be affixed to the cup in various shapes, clusters, and arrangements, each of which can be interpreted to yield insights and guidance.

Each reading can be a personal journey, uniquely reflective of your energy and intentions, making tasseography a captivating practice for those interested in exploring the depths of their intuition and destiny.

Tea Leaf Symbol Directory

Acorn –

Signifies that prosperity is on the horizon for you, suggesting that autumn will bring noteworthy changes and opportunities into your life. It represents potential and growth, indicating a time when you might reap the rewards of your hard work.

Airplane –

When the airplane symbol appears, it points to long-distance travel. If the aircraft is oriented toward you, it suggests that a visitor is likely to arrive from afar, bringing new energies and potentially significant news.

Anchor –

In its upright position, the anchor symbolizes a period of safety and stability, indicating that you are grounded and secure. When reversed, however, it warns of feeling weighed down by responsibilities or circumstances outside of your control.

Apple –

Represents the possession of great wisdom and knowledge. It suggests that growth and new opportunities are on the way, possibly encouraging you to share your insights or seize new ventures that can be beneficial.

Arrow –

 Indicates that news is traveling quickly, and you may soon find yourself at the centre of discussions or gossip. It serves as a reminder to be prepared for both positive and negative attention.

Axe –

Symbolizes your ability to overcome obstacles through determination and effort. It implies that while challenges may arise, you have the strength and capability to tackle them head-on.

Baby –

The appearance of a baby signifies new beginnings or the arrival of a child. It carries connotations of innocence, fresh starts, and the potential for new life paths.

Balloon –

Symbolize celebration and joy. Their presence indicates that a festive occasion, such as a party or gathering, is being celebrated, marking a time of happiness with friends and family.

Bell –

The bell has multiple meanings; it can signify an awakening or a significant announcement. It may also relate to the remembrance of those who have passed, suggesting a funeral or a moment of reflection.

Birds –

A symbol of good luck, particularly when in flight together. Their appearance can signal that positive developments are on the way and that ventures undertaken with others will bring joy.

Boat –

Symbolizes a visit or connection with a friend or loved one. It indicates a journey to meaningful relationships and the importance of companionship.

Bones –

Suggests a spirit visitor, where the essence of someone who has passed might be nearby. Crossbones serve as a warning, highlighting the presence of danger or an unsavoury situation.

Book -

Represents wisdom and the thirst for knowledge. Its appearance suggests that you may be starting a new class or hobby that will enrich your understanding and skills.

Broom –

A broom calls for change, indicating that it may be time to clean your physical or mental space. It encourages you to clear away negativity and make room for new energies or perspectives.

Butterfly –

Symbolizes transformation, rebirth, and positive beginnings. Its presence brings a message of hope and renewal, marking a time when you may experience significant personal growth.

Candle –

Signifies enlightenment and hope. They suggest that illumination in a situation is approaching, and you may soon find clarity or a path forward in a challenging circumstance.

Cat –

Symbolizes both luck and cherished companionship. It reminds you that while relationships can bring joy, they may also have their challenges.

Chain –

Indicates feelings of being trapped or constrained by circumstances out of your control. It serves as a reminder to evaluate your situation and seek ways to break free.

Circle –

Represents the cycle of life and encourages you to go with the flow. It emphasizes the importance of balance and the interconnectedness of experiences.

Clock –

Symbolizes the passage of time and may highlight feelings of being rushed or overwhelmed. It serves as a reminder to manage your time wisely to avoid stress.

Clouds –

Indicate potential trouble on the horizon, suggesting that a storm may be brewing in your life. This symbol serves as a caution to prepare for possible challenges in the near future.

Coin –

The coin is a sign that financial stability is on its way. It can indicate good fortune with money and the potential for a prosperous period ahead.

Cross –

Serves as a warning of impending trouble. It may suggest delays, setbacks, or obstacles that require attention and navigation.

Cup –

Symbolizes joy, celebration, and the fulfilment of all your needs. It indicates a time when you might experience abundance and happiness in your personal life.

Dagger –

Warns of betrayal or danger in your surroundings. It represents hidden threats or conflicts that require caution and vigilance.

Dog –

Symbolizes loyalty and deep companionship, representing a close friend or beloved pet. It highlights the importance of trust and support in your relationships.

Dots –

Signify success in business ventures or endeavours. They represent innovative ideas and unexpected gains, indicating that good fortune may be on the way.

Duck –

Indicates that work is occurring beneath the surface, suggesting that events are unfolding quietly. It reminds you to be patient as things develop.

Eagle –

Symbolizes facing challenges with strength and the promise of success. It reinforces that perseverance will lead you to triumph over difficulties.

Egg –

Represents a nurturing phase, particularly regarding creative projects. If the egg is broken, it serves as a warning of potential disappointment in an endeavour you may be undertaking.

Envelope –

Heralds unexpected news or communiqués, possibly hinting at financial matters or bills arriving that require your attention.

Feather –

Signifies spiritual fulfilment and messages from the divine. It serves as a reminder of the support of a higher power in your life.

Fire –

Signifies the arrival of prosperity, security, and warmth. It represents passionate pursuits and the energetic forces that will benefit you.

Fish –

Symbolize the depths of the subconscious mind, encouraging you to tap into your creativity and explore your inner thoughts and emotions.

Flag –

Indicates travel, particularly to foreign lands. It may allude to governmental or political developments that could affect your circumstances.

Flowers –

Represent eternal love and beauty, suggesting a blossoming partnership or romance. They celebrate new beginnings and indicate that spring will hold significant opportunities for growth.

Goat –

Symbolizes the need for discretion; it advises you to keep your plans secret and avoid gossip or temptation that could derail your aspirations.

Grapes –

Suggest a period of abundance and prosperity is approaching, often signifying happiness and celebration coupled with its bounty.

Gun –

Serves as a sign of distress or discomfort, suggesting that you may feel threatened or face challenging situations that require caution.

Hammer –

Represents overcoming obstacles and repairing relationships. It encourages you to take constructive actions to mend what may be broken in your life.

Headstone –

Indicates the presence of an ancestor or deceased loved one, reminding you of their influence or guidance in your life.

Heart –

Represents a happy and secure relationship, suggesting new romantic opportunities or advancements in existing partnerships. It is a positive omen indicating love and connection.

Horseshoe –

Symbolizes a lucky period, encouraging you to keep a good luck charm close as you move through this phase.

Hourglass –

Warns you to be cautious as danger may be lurking. It suggests that an important decision lies ahead, advising you to discern any hidden threats.

House –

Represents planning for the future and a strong desire for stability. It encourages you to consider how you can secure your domestic life.

Initials –

Initials signify important people, places, or things in your life, reminding you of their significance and the connections they bring.

Insect –

Indicates the need to pay attention to the finer details of a project you are undertaking. It suggests careful observation to avoid any oversights.

Kettle –

Symbolizes a search for healing, whether physical or emotional. It encourages you to reconnect with your community for support and recovery.

Key –

Represents unlocking your potential and taking control of a situation. It symbolizes empowerment and the ability to access new opportunities.

Kite –

Symbolizes a period of growth and excitement, encouraging you to embrace the enthusiasm surrounding your life's possibilities.

Knife –

Indicates potential quarrels or disputes that may arise, signalling the possibility of betrayal or injuries that take time to recover from.

Ladder –

Symbolizes professional advancement, suggesting that you are moving upwards in your career and achieving your aspirations.

Lamp –

Suggests illuminating hidden secrets and navigating difficult situations. It encourages you to uncover the truth that may not be immediately visible.

Letter –

Expect important news soon; the letter symbolizes communications arriving that could hold significant meaning for your plans or finances.

Line –

A straight line represents the beginning of an important journey, indicating that life-changing events are approaching. A wavy line suggests an emotional journey filled with insights, while a broken line indicates that a relationship or journey may end prematurely.

Lion –

Encourages you to exhibit courage and take pride in your accomplishments. It suggests that influential friends or supporters are present to help you in your endeavours.

Lock –

Symbolizes the need to proceed with caution, signifying that obstacles are present and careful navigation is necessary to overcome them.

Log –

Signifies that your hard work will yield substantial rewards. It encourages perseverance and dedication to your efforts.

Moon –

Symbolizes the presence of spirits and divine guidance as you are led towards success. It evokes intuition and the need for reflection.

Mountain –

Signify formidable challenges ahead, but they also represent accomplishments achieved through hard work and the presence of supportive, powerful individuals around you.

Mouse –

Warns of potential theft or betrayal, reminding you to remain vigilant against deception, particularly from those you consider friends.

Mushroom –

Symbolizes leadership and the assertion of your rightful respect. It encourages you to step forward and claim your position among peers.

Necklace –

 Represents something truly precious and significant in your life. It often signifies that you may have many admirers or suitors, highlighting feelings of being cherished or desirable.

Numbers –

Symbolize the passage of time, marking important milestones such as days, months, or weeks. They may refer specifically to a birthday or anniversary, or even a house number that holds special meaning.

Owl –

A powerful symbol of wisdom and insight. It suggests a quest for deeper understanding and foreknowledge, encouraging the development of your intuitive or psychic abilities.

Palm Tree –

Signifies material acquisition and prosperity, often linked to receiving an inheritance. The summer season will be a particularly significant time for you, bringing about change or growth.

Parrot –

Represents an inner struggle with imposter syndrome; a feeling that others may be taking credit for your ideas or efforts. It serves as a reminder to acknowledge and assert your own contributions.

Pine Tree –

A symbol of gathering, often pointing to a family reunion or get-together. Winter will play an important role during this time, suggesting warmth and togetherness amidst the cold.

Question Mark –

Indicates a search for answers that you may not be ready or meant to find. It suggests patience and urges you to seek clarity later, rather than forcing immediate understanding.

Rabbit –

Embodies themes of fertility and growth, symbolizing the hard work you've invested in a project or personal endeavor. It may also reflect feelings of shyness or nervousness in social situations.

Rainbow –

Symbolizes the presence of a beloved pet's spirit and a promise that all your wishes and dreams will come true. It evokes a sense of hope and joy amidst challenges.

Rake –

A call to action to tie up loose ends in your life; it encourages you to create space for new opportunities and experiences to take root and flourish.

Raven –

Represents the gift of prophecy and healing; it may serve as a warning about an impending loss or the necessity of being cautious regarding health issues.

Ring –

A symbol of romantic engagement, commitment, or a significant offer that you cannot refuse. It denotes feelings of security and a deepening relationship.

Rose –

Represents good luck and everlasting love, urging you to take a moment to appreciate the blessings and relationships in your life.

Scales –

Symbolize the need to address legal issues and indicate that balance and harmony are on the horizon, promoting a sense of fairness and justice.

Scissors –

Indicate the need to break free from toxic situations or relationships. They signify an impending separation or the necessity to cut ties with what no longer serves you.

Shark –

A warning of hidden danger; it suggests that an enemy may be lurking among friends, which can evoke feelings of anxiety or worry regarding trust.

Shell –

Symbolizes a spiritual offering and protection from your ancestors. It signifies that you are being watched over as you navigate through your life's journey.

Ship –

Represents the beginning of a long and significant journey, one that will bring about important experiences over a considerable period.

Shoe –

Indicates that you are on the right path, encouraging you to embrace simplicity and adapt to changes gracefully.

Sickle –

Signifies a need to let go of anger or pain; it warns of a potential lack of self-control or willpower, and may suggest that a period of illness or grief could be approaching.

Skull –

A foreboding symbol that warns of danger, potential power struggles, or disputes that may arise in various aspects of your life.

Snake –

Represents untrustworthiness or deceit coming from someone close to you. A reminder that small misfortunes and setbacks may also be occurring.

Spider –

Symbolizes recognition for your efforts and the rewards that come with your hard work. It's a time for creativity and embracing your achievements.

Squirrel –

A symbol of preparation for the future. It suggests you are blessed in love and friendship as you make thoughtful plans for what lies ahead.

Stairs –

Suggest a time of spirit communication, inviting you to consider situations from new perspectives, particularly in family matters or home-related issues.

Star –

A highly positive omen indicating an important victory on the horizon. It serves to encourage you to maintain hope and optimism in your endeavors.

Sun –

Symbolizes a newfound peace of mind concerning a difficult situation. It brings a message of brighter days ahead and positivity surrounding your life.

Table –

Represents stability and support in your life, fostering feelings of being grounded and secure as you navigate through your commitments and relationships.

Teardrops –

Indicate a time of mourning or grief; they forecast that tears may soon be shed as you process emotional experiences.

Tower –

A symbol of new beginnings, suggesting a transition, such as starting a new job or embarking on a new phase of life.

Triangle –

Represents good luck and fortunate events or meetings that could lead to beneficial changes in your life.

Turtle –

Incorporates qualities of dedication and persistence. It encourages you to take your time and be cautious in your actions as you navigate your path.

Umbrella –

A protective symbol, signifying that you are shielded from harm with the loving watch of those close to you, both living and departed.

Volcano –

Represents intense emotions that are reaching a boiling point. It suggests addressing conflicts and settling disputes quickly to avoid eruptions.

Wasp –

A negative omen, serving as a serious warning about potential betrayal by someone close to you, advising vigilance in your relationships.

Wheel –

Encourages continuous movement forward in your life, urging you to maintain a positive attitude despite any obstacles you may face.

Wolf –

A symbol of loyalty towards family and friends, highlighting the importance of finding your place in the world and staying true to your connections.

Zebra –

Represents the appearance of new opportunities and suggests a change in direction, encouraging you to embrace flexibility and adaptability in your life.

This directory serves as a guide to understanding the meanings behind various tea leaf symbols, encouraging reflection on how they may relate to your personal experiences and circumstances.

Book of Shadows

<u>**New Moon Spell to Ward Off Evil & Negativity**</u>

Empower yourself to banish negative energies and harmful influences from your home and your being with this protective ritual. This spell is designed to help you ward off enemies and remove malevolent spirits effortlessly.

Ingredients Needed:

- 1 red apple (symbolizes temptation and purification)

- 1 bay leaf (fresh or dried, known for protection and warding off negativity)

- A knife (or your boline, if you have one)

Step-by-Step Instructions:

1. Create Your Space:

- Find a quiet place where you won't be disturbed. Set up your altar or a clean table by placing a cloth or a special surface to create a sacred space.

2. Prepare the Apple:

- Place the red apple directly in front of you on your altar. Take a moment to observe its vibrant colour and remember its symbolism.

3. Focus Your Intent:

- Begin to concentrate deeply on your goal: the removal of negativity from your life. Close your eyes and visualize a protective barrier surrounding you, something strong that repels all negative energies. Imagine these energies bouncing away from your aura.

4. Cut the Apple:

- Using the knife, cut the apple in half carefully. Make sure to do this with intention, focusing on the removal of negativity. Place each half on the table with the cut side facing upwards, allowing the apple's inner essence to be exposed.

5. Invoke the Protection:

- Take the bay leaf and place it on top of one of the apple halves. As you do this, say the following incantation with confidence and clarity:

"Red and Green, Banishing Grace. Cast all Evil out this place."

- Repeat this phrase three times loudly, letting the power of your voice amplify your intention.

6. Manifest Your Belief:

- As you complete this step, hold strong faith that your spell is manifesting. It is essential to believe wholeheartedly that this protective energy will envelop you.

7. Concluding the Ritual:

- After reciting the incantation, place the two halves of the apple back together and bury them in fresh soil. This could be in your garden, a nearby park, or a serene forest setting. As you bury it, envision the negativity being trapped within the earth, away from you.

<u>**Waxing Crescent Spell for Money**</u>

Harness the power of this Waxing Crescent moon with a money spell designed to create a spiritual contract with your higher self, letting prosperity flow into your life as you share the energy today for a fruitful return later.

Ingredients Needed:

- 1 green candle (symbolizes abundance and growth)

- Peppermint incense (known for its invigorating properties)

- Cinnamon powder (to attract prosperity)

- 5 coins and 5 bills of any denomination (representing wealth)

Step-by-Step Instructions:

1. Prepare Your Space:

- Find a comfortable space on the floor or on cushions where you can sit in a circle.

2. Create a Prosperity Circle:

- Arrange your 5 coins and 5 bills in a circle around your seated position. This circle acts as a boundary to contain your intention.

3. Light the Candle and Incense:

- Inside the circle, light the peppermint incense and the green candle. Allow the fragrant smoke to envelop you, helping to elevate your energy.

4. Visualize Your Goals:

- Take a few deep breaths to center yourself. Close your eyes and envision your money problems dissolving away. Picture yourself surrounded by the exact amount of wealth you desire; this vision will serve as your focal point.

5. Sprinkle the Cinnamon:

- While deeply immersed in this visualization, take a pinch of cinnamon and sprinkle it over each bill and coin, infusing the money with your prosperous intentions.

6. Chant for Abundance:

- As you sprinkle, chant the incantation confidently:

"I have all the money I could need. I am truly prosperous indeed!"

- Repeat this phrase five times, allowing the energy to build with each repetition.

7. Complete the Ritual:

- Gather all the money, moving clockwise around the circle. Place it into your wallet or purse. Let the candle and incense burn completely, allowing the energies you've generated to flow freely.

8. Flow of Energy:

- In the following days, spend a little of the money you've used in this spell. This action encourages the energy of abundance to circulate further, ensuring prosperity continues to flow.

<u>**Waxing Gibbous Spell for Peace of Mind**</u>

If you find yourself in times of fear or uncertainty, this Waxing Gibbous spell is a perfect remedy, offering a momentary escape into peace and tranquillity. Remember that you are a being filled with potential, peace, love, and power. The light within you is indomitable.

Ingredients Needed:

- 9 white tea light candles (symbolizing purity and tranquillity)

- Matches or a lighter

- Ambient music (to create a soothing atmosphere)

Step-by-Step Instructions:

1. Set the Mood:

- Begin by playing some calming ambient music to help you relax and immerse yourself in the moment.

2. Create a Sacred Circle:

- Find a comfortable spot either sitting on the floor or in a chair. Arrange the 9 tea light candles in a circular formation around you, ensuring they are spaced evenly.

3. Relaxation Techniques:

- Assume a comfortable position and take three deep, cleansing breaths. With each exhale, feel the tension of the day releasing from your body.

4. Tension Release:

- To further relax, tense your muscles and then release them, letting go of any residual worry. Focus on your breath as you do this.

5. Light the Candles:

- Starting with the first candle, light it while moving in a clockwise direction, continuing until all nine candles are illuminated. As each candle lights, envision it adding light and warmth to your aura.

6. Visualization of Inner Light:

- Now, turn your attention inward, imagining a white light emerging from your abdomen and spreading throughout your entire body. Concentrate on each area: first your core, then moving to your shoulders, arms, hands, legs, feet, and finally the crown of your head.

7. Finding Peace:

- As you visualize this light, feel the warmth and serenity filling you. Allow that feeling to permeate every part of your being, washing over you and bringing a profound sense of peace.

8. Closing the Ritual:

- When you feel ready, either gently extinguish the candles or leave them on your altar until they burn completely. Know that you can return to this place of peace whenever you need it.

<u>**Full Moon Spell for Love**</u>

If you're seeking a touch of magic to enhance your love life, consider invoking the energy of the Full Moon. Find a serene outdoor space or a window that offers a clear view of the sky. Even if the night sky is filled with clouds, remember that the Moon's energy is powerful enough to transcend those veils, so focus on visualizing her presence through the clouds.

Ingredients:

- A night when the Full Moon is visible

- A peaceful outdoor spot or window that faces the Moon

Step-by-Step Instructions:

1. Find Your Spot: Locate a comfortable place outside or by a window where you can see the Moon. Sit quietly and centre yourself.

2. Connect with the Moon: Gaze at the Moon as you sit in silence. Imagine her luminous energy enveloping you, washing over you in waves of light and warmth.

3. Focus on Your Love: Take a moment to think about the person you love deeply. Picture their face and recall the feelings you share.

4. Raise Your Hands: With this love in your heart, raise your arms toward the sky. Inhale deeply, filling your lungs completely.

5. Release and Centre: As you exhale, slowly bring your hands down to rest on your lap, one on top of the other. This symbolizes grounding and accepting the energy around you.

6. Invoke the Moon's Magic: Speak the following incantation aloud, allowing the words to resonate with your intent:

"Dear Moon, Mother, and Sister, by your feminine powers I summon the forces. Use your light tonight so that we can be closer."

7. Deepen Your Connection: Continue to breathe deeply as you maintain your focus on your beloved. Visualize the Moon's energy strengthening the bond between you.

8. Meditate and Absorb: Relax and enter a meditative state, fully absorbing the Moon's soothing energies. Trust that her power is here to help you achieve your desires.

9. Empowered Conclusion: Once you feel a sense of empowerment and clarity, gradually return to your surroundings. Allow yourself to feel grateful for this connection with the Moon.

10. Consistent Practice: Repeat this ritual for three consecutive nights, allowing the energies to build and strengthen over time.

<u>**Waning Gibbous Spell to Remove Bad Luck**</u>

If you're feeling overwhelmed by persistent bad luck, fret not! This simple yet powerful spell is designed to clear negativity and invite positive energies.

Ingredients:

- 1 green candle (symbolizing prosperity and good fortune)

- A sprinkle of cinnamon powder (for its properties of attracting success)

- A pinch of salt (to cleanse and provide protection)

Step-by-Step Instructions:

1. Prepare Your Space: Begin by placing the green candle on your altar or another sacred space that feels comfortable.

2. Create a Protective Circle: Take the salt and sprinkle it in a circle around the candle. This serves as a protective barrier against negative energies.

3. Set Your Intention: Stand quietly for a moment and focus your mind. Then assertively command, "Bad Luck, I command you to leave me right now!" as you visualize the bad luck dissipating.

4. Ignite the Candle: Light the green candle, watching the flame flicker to life, representing the emergence of positive energy.

5. Visualize Release: With your eyes closed, envision all the bad luck you've encountered. See it as a dark mist that surrounds you, ready to fade away.

6. Dissolve Adversity: Say aloud, "All adversity now dissolves," empowering your belief in the transformation taking place.

7. Meditate on Positivity: Spend about five minutes in meditation, maintaining focus on your intention. Imagine any challenges in your life melting away, replaced by waves of good fortune.

8. Complete the Ritual: After your meditation, sprinkle the cinnamon powder atop the salt circle with intention. Say: "Only good luck and positive energy flow to me now," feeling the shift in your energy.

<u>**Waning Crescent Spell for Anti-Stress Tea**</u>

In times of stress and anxiety, a simple calming spell can provide the release needed for peace of mind and body. This spell harnesses the soothing properties of Hyssop, combined with visualization, to foster tranquillity.

Ingredients:

- Freshwater (for brewing)

- Hyssop tea (either 1 tea bag or 1 tablespoon of loose leaves)

- 1 mug or teacup

- 1 blue candle (symbolizing calmness and serenity)

- Calming music (to set the atmosphere)

Step-by-Step Instructions:

1. Prepare for Brewing: Start by heating fresh water until it reaches a rolling boil, then remove it from the heat.

2. Eliminate Distractions: To create a serene environment, turn off your phone and silence any notifications. This moment is just for you.

3. Breath and Gather Yourself: Take a few moments to breathe deeply and allow your body to relax.

4. Brew Your Tea: Add the hyssop tea to your mug, then carefully pour the hot water over it. As you do this, visualize the steam carrying away your worries.

5. Set the Mood: Light the blue candle, focusing on the soft glow as it casts a calming light in your space.

6. Enjoy Your Tea Mindfully: Sit back, listen to the calming music, and slowly sip your tea. Allow each sip to envelop you in warmth and relaxation.

7. Release the Tension: Once you finish your tea, take a deep breath. As you exhale, visualize all tension and stress leaving your body, dissipating into the air around you.

8. Reinforce Calmness: Repeat the last step six more times, letting go of any lingering stress and embracing a state of inner peace.

<u>**Yule Spell for Manifestation**</u>

You will need:

- A red candle

- A circle of paper (minimum 5 cm in diameter)

- Fresh mistletoe berries

- A red pen

- A cauldron

Method:

1. Begin by finding a quiet space where you can reflect without interruptions on Yule. Take a moment to center yourself, considering your intentions and hopes for the year ahead.

2. Choose a single word that encapsulates your most profound hope or desire. This could be "abundance," "growth," "love," or any other word that resonates deeply with you.

3. Using the red pen, carefully write this word in the center of your circle of paper. Infuse your intention into each stroke as you write.

4. Surround the written word with the mistletoe berries, imagining them as powerful tokens of your hope. You may also sprinkle in some herbs associated with your hope, like basil for prosperity or rosemary for remembrance.

5. Gently twist the edges of the paper to create a pouch that encloses the berries and herbs, sealing in your intention.

6. Place this paper pouch in the cauldron, serving as a vessel for transformation.

7. Light the red candle, and as the flame flickers, focus intently on the word you wrote. Visualize the energy of the flame igniting your hopes.

8. Carefully light the paper and its contents, allowing it to burn while you envision your hope growing and expanding with the flames.

9. Once the paper has completely burned to ashes, let the cauldron cool. When it is safe, take the ashes and release them into the wind, symbolizing the release of your spell into the universe to manifest your hope.

Imbolc Spell for Cleansing Negative Energy

You will need:

- A besom

Method:

1. On Imbolc, begin your ritual at your front door. Stand with your besom in hand, feeling the threshold between your indoor space and the outside world.

2. Sweep the air above your head with the besom, making broad strokes. As you sweep, chant: "I am sweeping away the bad to make room for the good to come in and fill this space."

3. Move from room to room, repeating this action. Envision negative energy dissipating and being replaced by fresh, positive energy that flows into your home.

4. As you complete this ritual in each space, take a moment to appreciate the cleansing process, allowing gratitude to fill your heart.

<u>**Ostara Spell for Growth**</u>

You will need:

- An altar space adorned for Ostara

- A bowl of fresh soil

- A large seed, such as a broad bean

Method:

1. Begin by casting a circle around your space, creating a sacred area to perform your spell.

2. Once your circle is cast, raise your voice in a chant: "It is time to greet the Spring. Light and dark are equals. Earth is awakening from its slumber. Welcome beautiful spring! As the sky fills with light and the sun warms the earth, let us cast the darkness of winter behind us. Now is a time for rebirth and growth."

3. Holding the bowl of soil, lift it up and declare, "This is a joyful time for growth." Place the bowl onto your altar, creating a focal point for your intentions.

4. Take the seed and ceremoniously place it into the bowl, covering it gently with soil. As you do, say: "Let me grow and flourish as this seed grows and flourishes. I am thankful that Spring has come and will walk with me on my journey of growth."

5. Close the circle, thanking any deities or spirits you may have invited, and release your intentions into the universe.

Beltane Charm Bag for Love

You will need:

- Dried Mallowsweet

- Dried Ginger

- Dragons Blood Resin

- Apple Blossom

- Jasmine Flowers

- Lavender

- Rose Petals

- Patchouli Oil

- Sandalwood Oil

- A red or pink cloth bag

Method:

1. On Beltane, take the red or pink bag and begin adding the dried ingredients one by one, focusing your thoughts on love and attraction.

Once the dried ingredients are added, take both patchouli oil and sandalwood oil and add 6 drops of each into the bag, infusing love and grounding energy.

3. Include the Rose Quartz crystal, a powerful stone for love and healing, ensuring it rests among the other items.

4. Seal the bag tightly, visualizing your intentions for love sealing within.

5. Place the charm bag on your altar on Beltane night, allowing it to soak in the energy of the festivities for three days.

6. Carry the bag with you in your pocket or purse until your new love arrives, keeping your heart open to the possibilities.

<u>**Litha Spell for Prosperity**</u>

You will need:

- A green candle

- Dried sage leaves

- A cauldron

- An athame

Method:

1. On Litha, start by using your athame to carefully carve your name into the green candle. Next, carve a symbol of money, such as a pound sign (£), to deepen your intention.

2. Light the candle and place it securely in your cauldron, creating an area for energy to flow freely.

3. Gently sprinkle the dried sage leaves onto the burning candle, watching them smoke and infuse your space with their cleansing properties.

4. As the candle burns down, visualize all the ways you could receive abundance and how you would use this wealth for good, benefiting yourself and others.

5. Chant with conviction: "By the power of the sun, bring now to me wealth and prosperity. Bring it to me with harm to none. So mote it be."

6. Allow the candle to burn down completely, sealing your spell and your intentions.

<u>**Lammas Spell for Gratitude**</u>

You will need:

- A large jar

- Paper and a pen

Method:

1. As Lammas begins, take a moment each day to reflect on what you are grateful for, starting a positive habit of recognizing daily blessings.

2. Write down one thing you are thankful for on a piece of paper every day. This can range from simple joys to significant accomplishments.

3. Fold the paper and place it into the jar, all the while thanking the gods and goddesses for the blessings in your life.

4. As the jar fills with gratitude, allow it to transform into a powerful well of appreciation that will inspire positivity.

5. During difficult times, revisit the jar, reading through the notes to remind yourself of the abundance of love and joy you have experienced.

<u>**Mabon Ritual for Healing**</u>

You will need:

- An apple tree

- A piece of blue fabric

- Scissors

Method:

1. On Mabon, cut a strip of blue fabric measuring approximately 20 cm long and 5 cm wide. This colour is often associated with healing and tranquillity.

2. Hold the strip in your hands for a moment, closing your eyes and concentrating. Channel your healing energy into the fabric, either for yourself or someone else in need.

3. After charging the fabric, carefully tie the strip to a branch of an apple tree, ensuring it is secure and won't be disturbed.

4. As the piece of fabric disintegrates over time, envision the healing energy being absorbed by the person it was intended for.

<u>**Samhain Ritual to Connect with Spirits**</u>

You will need:

- Photos or mementos of departed loved ones

- Sandalwood incense

- Obsidian crystal chips

- Sage and myrrh herbs

- Silver candles

Method:

1. On Samhain, carefully place the photograph or memento on your altar or designated workspace. This will serve as a focal point for your connection.

2. Arrange the obsidian chips, herbs, and silver candles around the photograph or memento, creating a circle that fosters a sacred space.

3. Light the sandalwood incense and allow its smoke to rise, focusing on the thinning veil between realms as you do so.

4. As you light the silver candles, speak the names of your departed loved ones, expressing gratitude for their presence in your life and the gifts they imparted.

5. Sit quietly, allowing space for communication. Pay attention to any messages, feelings, or signs you receive during this sacred time. Take note of them, whether mentally or in a journal.

<u>**Spell Jars**</u>

The information gathered in this Grimoire is designed to guide you through the process of creating your very own spell jars. To assist you in getting started on your spell jar journey, I have included ten of my personal recipes at the end of this section. Each recipe is crafted to complement the following method, ensuring that you have a solid foundation for your magical endeavours. With this combination of guidance and inspiration, you can confidently embark on your spell jar creation.

Before you begin:

Clearly define your intention or goal for the spell jar. This could be anything from attracting love, manifesting abundance, or bringing protection into your life. Write this intention down to anchor your focus.

You will need:

- Incense: Select an incense that resonates with your intention.

- Four Types of Herbs: Choose herbs that align with your intention.

- Salt: to absorb negative energy.

- Two Types of Crystal Chips: Select crystals that align with your intention.

- Two Types of Oil: Choose oils that correspond to your intention. For example:

- Sealing Wax: This will be used to seal the jar and secure your intention within. Choose a colour that aligns with your intention.

Method:

1. Write Your Intention: On a small piece of paper, clearly write down your intention. Be specific and concise, as this will serve as the foundation of your spell jar.

2. Cleanse the Jar: Before you begin, cleanse your jar to remove any lingering energies. Use your selected incense, allowing the smoke to envelop the jar while concentrating on clearing it of negative vibes.

3. Add Incense Ash: Once you have burned the incense, place a small amount of the ash into the bottom of the jar. This adds the energy of your intention and purification to the mixture.

4. Burn Your Intention: Take the paper on which you wrote your intention and carefully burn it in a fire-proof dish. Allow it to burn completely, then add the ashes to the jar. This symbolizes releasing your intention into the universe.

5. Layer Your Ingredients:

Begin by adding the first two herbs (the ones that correspond to your intention) into the jar.

- Next, add the first crystal chips. These crystals will amplify the energy of your intention.

- Drip in the first essential oil to infuse the jar with its fragrance and energy.

- Add a pinch of salt to the mixture. This helps to purify and protect the energy within the jar.

- Follow with the third and fourth herbs, adding them into the jar to further strengthen your intention.

- Now, add the second crystal chip, enhancing the jar's energy with another powerful stone.

- Drip in the second essential oil for additional potency.

- If you have a second type of salt, add it now for an extra layer of protection and purification.

6. Seal the Jar: Finally, seal the jar with your chosen sealing wax. As you do this, visualize your intention being locked in, safe and secure. You may wish to focus on your intention one final time before the wax sets.

Your spell jar is now complete! Place it in a special location where it can continue to work on your behalf, and remember to revisit your intention regularly.

Spell Jar Recipes

Abundance	
Bag & Wax Colour	Orange
Crystal Chips	Green Aventurine
	Orange Calcite
Salt	Orange
Herbs	Basil
	Holy Thistle
	Orange Peel
	Red Sandalwood
Oils	Ginger
	Cajeput
Incense	Mint
	Patchouli

Courage	
Bag & Wax Colour	Red
Crystal Chips	Labradorite
	Tigers Eye
Salt	Red
Herbs	Chicory
	Horsetail
	Thyme
	Yarrow
Oils	Fennel
	Geranium
Incense	Cinnamon
	Honeysuckle

Happiness	
Bag & Wax Colour	Yellow
Crystal Chips	Red Coral
	Sunstone
Salt	Yellow
Herbs	Hibiscus
	Lemon Peel
	Mallowsweet
	Marjoram
Oils	Bregamont
	Ylang Ylang
Incense	Apple
	Dandelion

Healing	
Bag & Wax Colour	Blue
Crystal Chips	Aquamarine
	Rhodonite
Salt	Blue
Herbs	Ashwagandha
	Chives
	Comfrey
	Valerian Root
Oils	Citronella
	Peppermint
Incense	Jasmine
	Rose

Meditation	
Bag & Wax Colour	Grey
Crystal Chips	Lapis Lazuli
	Moonstone
Salt	Grey
Herbs	Cramp Bark
	Dandelion
	Peppermint
	Tansy
Oils	Eucalyptus
	Frankincense
Incense	Gardenia

Peace	
Bag & Wax Colour	White
Crystal Chips	Amazonite
	Unakite
Salt	White
Herbs	Chamomile
	Lavender
	Motherwort
	Passion Flower
Oils	Chamomile
	Myrrh
Incense	Lemongrass
	Grapefruit

Prosperity	
Bag & Wax Colour	Green
Crystal Chips	Jade
	Rutilated Quartz
Salt	Green
Herbs	Bladderwrack
	Coltsfoot
	Goldenrod
	Oak Bark
Oils	Patchouli
	Vetivert
Incense	Patchouli
	Orange

Protection	
Bag & Wax Colour	
Crystal Chips	Tourmaline
	Clear Quartz
Salts	Black
Herbs	Clove
	Cumin
	Juniper Berries
	Sage
Oils	Juniper
	Rosemary
Incense	Violet
	Sandalwood

Self-Love	
Bag & Wax Colour	Pink
Crystal Chips	Red Agate
	Strawberry Quartz
Salt	Pink
Herbs	Lemon Balm
	Raspberry Leaf
	Rose Petal
	St Johns Wort
Oils	Rose
	Sweet Orange
Incense	Lemon Balm
	Rose

Spiritual Development	
Bag & Wax Colour	Purple
Crystal Chips	Amethyst
	Blue Apatite
Salt	Purple
Herbs	Bay Leaf
	Cinnamon
	Eyebright
	Mint
Oils	Cinnamon
	Lemongrass
Incense	Lemongrass
	Rose